The
WEDDING
Game

OTHER TITLES BY MEGHAN QUINN

All her books can be read on Kindle Unlimited

GETTING LUCKY SERIES

That Second Chance

That Forever Girl

That Secret Crush

BRENTWOOD BASEBALL BOYS

The Locker Room

The Dugout

The Lineup

The Trade

The Change Up

The Setup

MANHATTAN MILLIONAIRES

The Secret to Dating Your Best Friend's Sister

Diary of a Bad Boy

Boss Man Bridegroom

THE DATING BY NUMBERS SERIES

Three Blind Dates

Two Wedding Crashers

One Baby Daddy

Back in the Game (Novella)

THE BLUE LINE DUET

The Upside of Falling

The Downside of Love

THE PERFECT DUET

The Left Side of Perfect

The Right Side of Forever

THE BINGHAMTON BOYS SERIES

Co-Wrecker

My Best Friend's Ex

Twisted Twosome

The Other Brother

STAND-ALONE TITLES

The Modern Gentleman

Dear Life

The Virgin Romance Novelist Chronicles

Newly Exposed

The Mother Road

BOX SET SERIES

The Bourbon Series

Love and Sports Series

Hot-Lanta Series

The
WEDDING
Game

MEGHAN QUINN

Montlake

Text copyright © 2021 by Meghan Quinn
All rights reserved.

Published by Montlake, Seattle

www.apub.com

Amazon, the Amazon logo, and Montlake are trademarks of Amazon.com, Inc., or its affiliates.

ISBN-13: 9781542025195
ISBN-10: 1542025192

Cover design by Caroline Teagle Johnson

Printed in the United States of America

To my wife, for putting up with our very own DIY wedding, and to our bridesmaids, for being warriors with glue guns

PROLOGUE
THADDEUS

First things first: this story isn't about me.

Well . . . technically, it is about me, but it isn't about *me*.

It's about my brother, Alec Baxter. Ever hear of the gorgeous bastard? He's the top divorce lawyer in New York City.

Cunning, devilishly handsome—just like me—has big hands, and scowls at almost any mention of a hot dog. Not a fan—he doesn't get it, never will.

He's my best friend, my partner in crime, the guy I look up to, and my one and only hero . . . despite talking to him maybe every three months, barely seeing him on holidays, and waiting weeks just for a simple response to a text message.

Sounds like a one-sided brother-ship, right? Kind of is, but hey, that's okay. The man is busy. And he spent most of our childhood making sure I wasn't completely scarred by our parents and their inability to shield their children from their awful marriage. They really had a habit of airing out their grievances like dirty panties on laundry day.

I can still remember Alec charging into my room whenever our parents started going at it, then leading me down the fire escape of our Park Avenue apartment and taking me to the bakery down the street. We would share a cannoli and just stare at each other, both knowing what was happening a mere block away but never talking about it.

But enough with the sob fest—that's not what this story is about. No, it's about the complete and utter betrayal I've suffered at the hands of the aforementioned brother. My own kin, my own blood, my hero . . .

He may be my best friend, but he's betrayed me in every way possible.

Hefty words, right?

Fighting words.

Well, I speak the truth.

What happened? Let me give you a little prelude to the disaster that my life has turned into.

It all started when I found out my beautiful fiancée, Naomi, is pregnant. I had to make some hard decisions, and the wedding of my dreams—yes, *my* dreams—had to be swapped out for a wedding on a budget. I needed to save for a home, not the event of the century.

It was a tough pill to swallow. I may have hyperventilated into the drawer of my office desk a few times as I tried to come to terms with it all.

But then one day, after a good breathing session into beautifully stained mahogany, I thought of something: freebies.

I'm a corporate-event planner for Golf Galaxy, Manhattan's premier golf range and party center for executives. For all your corporate-event needs, please contact Thaddeus Baxter.

I rub elbows with the wealthy on a daily basis, and I figured, why not take advantage of that. Ask around, see if I can find any perks from my job.

Unfortunately, all the asses I've been kissing for the past few years want nothing to do with me. Can't possibly see why. I'm charming—slightly dramatic, perhaps—but I can make the best margarita when pressed to, and I'll even shake my maracas when handing it over. And when I say *maracas*, I mean my burly balls. Ahem, my nutsac.

An absolute delight of a gentleman. That's me.

So, once again reduced to a deeply depressed state, I found myself hunched over my computer—leftover margarita from an event in hand, scanning through wedding websites—when I saw it.

The answer to all my prayers.

It was as if God had parted the clouds and, with his lightning-striking finger, booped me on the nose and pointed me in the right direction.

The Wedding Game *was casting.*

TV's favorite wedding reality show was looking for couples to take on the challenge of creating a wedding on a budget. Tulle, roses, bunting, tea lights, tuxes—all there, ready to be pulled together into the best wedding ever.

Sign me up.

But being in the spotlight of every bridezilla's dream wasn't my main reason for filling out the application.

You can bet your belly button–caressing tits there was a prize.

You'll never guess what it was. I'm not even going to give you a chance to figure it out.

It wasn't your typical Sandals destination honeymoon with all-you-can-eat buffets.

Nope. It was a GD penthouse in New York City.

Penthouse!

The dream of all dreams.

Before I even read the fine print, I had the application filled out and ready to send.

So what does this have to do with the kind of betrayal that would make the *Game of Thrones* cast blush?

The number one rule of *The Wedding Game*: you have to have at least one family member on your team. Given my childhood's emotional baggage, there was only one person I could rely on.

Alec.

And that, my friends, is where the betrayal comes in.

Don't believe my brother could be so coldhearted as to deceitfully ensnare his own flesh and blood?

Guess again.

He did.

Just see for yourself . . .

Chapter One
LUNA

"Look out, she's coming in hot . . . with the glue." I chuckle as I squeeze my glue gun, releasing the smallest dollop of glue before applying a bead to a vest I've been working on for the past twenty-four hours.

I'm not normally one to glue-gun beads. I like to sew them in like the proper crafter I am, but when your favorite waiter down at the singing diner begs you to jazz up his vest on short notice for his first solo performance, you break the rules.

"Ouch!" I yelp when the glue singes my already-calloused fingertips. You would think at this point in my life I would have no nerves left in the tips of my fingers, but apparently there are still some in there. "You little beaded bastard," I whisper to the vest as I sit back to evaluate my work.

Not too shabby for a quick glue job. I still have some gold beads to add around the collar, which I'll need my special glasses for, but before I snap those on, I need a tiny break.

I lean back in my chair and grin when I see what time it is. Six thirty means only one thing: *The Crafty Duo* is on.

Eeep!

After locating the remote in record time, I flip the TV on and change the channel from Bravo (my roommate Farrah's favorite) to the DIY Network. Farrah and I have been best friends since high school. We have one giant thing in common—a passion for expressing our creativity, Farrah being in fashion—but that's pretty much it. In every other way, we're polar opposites. I tend to try to bring joy to every aspect of life, while she can be rather aggressive but also outgoing. The great thing about our relationship is we can take my "glass half-full" attitude and mix it with her "glass half-empty" one and offer a full glass of life to the world when we're together. So when we both decided to move to New York City, we couldn't think of better room-mates than each other.

The show comes on, and the theme song rings through the living room. I shimmy along while I prepare myself for the next round of beads.

I love crafting.

Actually, that's a lie: I don't just love it. I live for it.

You know the saying "jack of all trades, master of none"? Well, that's me, except I'm the jack of all trades, queen of every one.

Need me to crochet, knit, needlepoint, sew? I'm your girl.

Looking for someone to bead, bedazzle, jewel, mold? Call me up.

In search of a seamstress, an embosser, a lettering expert? Hey, right here! *Waves*

I am multifaceted, talented in every way, and I have creativity spilling out of my pores, begging to be used every day. It's why I own one of the top Etsy shops in the world, why I'm the first crafter under thirty to win a Webby for my outstanding YouTube channel, why I can afford an apartment in Manhattan, and why I'm highly sought after to bedazzle showtime vests in a matter of twenty-four hours.

I slip on my glasses and, like a grandma, flip over the magnifier that's attached so I can get a much closer look at the work I'm doing.

This is a typical Friday night for me: hunched over my craft desk, glasses strung around my head, TV on in the background, tea at my side. I don't get out much, I definitely don't date much, and I sure as hell can't remember the last time I saw a naked man, but that's okay, because I'm thirty, not really flirty, but I'm glittery and thriving.

"Are you getting married in the next few months? Are you crafty? Do you have what it takes to plan a wedding on a ten-thousand-dollar budget in New York City?"

I know that voice.

I crave that voice.

My head pops up from the vest, and I lift my glasses to focus on the TV.

It's her. The goddess of all crafts.

Heart eyes pour from me as I take in the one and only beautifully talented Mary DIY.

You know how Martha Stewart took the world by storm in the nineties? And then Chip and Joanna Gaines came along and enthralled us with shiplap and barn doors before conquering every Target in the country? Well, Mary DIY is the next trend. She rose from her humble beginnings as a Michaels employee, where she used her employee discount to try out every form of crafting there is. Since then, she has built an empire around her YouTube channel, *Mary DIY*.

She's creative and talented, and I like to think—late at night, when my fingers are numb from needlepoint—that we're best friends and frolic together in meadows of twine and lace. I know if we ever meet that we'd get along so swimmingly that we would exchange phone numbers and text each other funny crafting memes.

(I might have some saved in my phone . . . can never be too prepared.)

Despite Mary DIY being my soul sister—though she doesn't know it—that's not what has me turning up the TV. It's *The Wedding Game*.

"We're looking for fun, unique couples willing to put their relationship to the test while we put you through a slew of challenges to see if you and your family can create a beautiful wedding, under budget. America will vote for the winner, and the grand prize is a penthouse in the heart of Manhattan, the perfect place to start a family after the 'I dos.'"

"Holy . . . hell," I mutter, my heart racing, my mind swirling with ideas. "Cohen needs to apply."

◆ ◆ ◆

I pace the compact distance of my apartment, waiting for my brother and his fiancé to arrive, repeating my talking points over and over in my head.

This is the opportunity of a lifetime.

You can skip the courthouse wedding and actually have the wedding you've always dreamed of.

With my help, you can win.

You can get out of Queens, live near me, cut the commute.

You can start that family you've always wanted . . .

I can feel it in my bones: I was meant to see that commercial. And all the hand lettering I've been practicing has to have been for a reason.

I just have to convince Cohen first.

Yes, *convince.* Let's just say my big brother keeps his feelings to himself, and he definitely doesn't like attention.

But I also know his deepest desires when it comes to being a family man, getting married, and having that magical wedding that people talk about for years to come.

But because he's in construction and his fiancé is a public school teacher here in the city, they decided to cut out the cost of a wedding and just get married in a courthouse.

Ugh, a travesty. Especially since I know that when my brother gets a shot of tequila in him, he unhinges his perpetually stiff shoulders and actually lets loose.

Knock. Knock.

My head whips to the door and anxiety washes over me like a tidal wave, drowning me in shaky breaths.

Steel yourself, woman. This is just your brother.

My brother, who deserves this more than anyone, who'd win with my help. I have no doubt that I could create a wedding that not only America would love, but one that would reflect the strong, loving relationship that my brother shares with his fiancé, Declan.

With a deep breath, I open the door to find the two most important men in my life standing on the other side.

"Hey, sis," Cohen says, stepping up and giving me a hug and a kiss to the top of my head. "How are you?"

I squeeze him back, loving how the top of my head just reaches the bottom of his chin, which makes for the perfect hug. "Great." I step out of his embrace and quickly wrap my arms around Declan, squeezing him just as tightly.

I can still remember the day Cohen came out to me. It was a windy, rainy day in Connecticut, on the coast where our parents would take us to vacation. The wind was so harsh that it felt like the house was going to blow away. Lightning flashed and thunder roared like a war in the sky just outside our window, and in the midst of it all, while playing two-person Uno, Cohen paused, looked up at me, and said, "Luna, I'm gay."

I was twelve; he was sixteen.

I blinked. His eyes welled up with tears.

I set my cards down. He set his down.

I pulled him into a hug. He cried on my shoulder.

I rubbed his back. He held on to me like a lifeline.

I don't remember most of what I rambled in response, but I do remember saying "I love you so much" over and over again until he stopped crying and pulled away, eyes puffy and red.

He told me he was too afraid to tell Mom and Dad. I told him that no matter what, I would stick by his side—I would be his rock.

Cohen was gay. I never expected it. I never envisioned having that conversation with him, but in that moment, I knew I would do whatever it took to make sure the worry etched on his brow would never stop him from having the life he deserved.

When he told our parents, I held his hand.

When they blinked a few times, I squeezed his hand tighter.

When they wrapped him up in their arms, I held on to him as he cried into my shoulder.

When they told him they would love him no matter what, I gave him a tiny "I told you so" nudge.

When he decided to move to New York City, I followed closely behind, with Farrah on my heels.

And when he introduced me to Declan, I pushed my brother to the side and welcomed the handsome Chinese American schoolteacher with a heart of pure gold right into my arms.

"How's my favorite fifth-grade teacher?" I ask now, my mind returning to the present as I pull away from Declan.

"Good. I only had to break up one fight today during recess, so I call it a win."

I usher them inside and shut the door. I watch as Cohen—like always—takes in my apartment, shaking his head.

"When are you going to hang pictures instead of ribbons on your wall?"

As everyone knows, Manhattan apartments aren't very spacious, at least not the affordable ones. So when Farrah and I were looking for a place to live, all we cared about was scoring two bedrooms in a decent area. The rest we could figure out.

Which we have, but we've had to be creative.

Every inch of our walls is covered in shelves, dowels, and organizational storage, holding all my supplies in a decorative and stylish way. I've actually gained thousands of followers on Instagram for my creative storage techniques alone. Organizational hashtags are very popular.

But it drives Cohen crazy; he's very neat and . . . plain when it comes to decorating. He and Declan are minimalists, to say the least.

"Leave my ribbons alone, unless you want me to go all the way to Queens and put glitter handprints all over your walls."

"No crafts allowed," Declan says, walking around me with a smile and going straight to a bouquet I've been working on for a bride. She sent me about a hundred acrylic flower brooches and asked me to make bouquets and boutonnieres for her vintage wedding. It's been painstakingly hard—especially since I'm so particular about where each and every one of them is placed—but I'm almost done, thankfully. "This looks interesting." Declan holds up the bouquet. "Still have fingers left?"

I lift my hands and wiggle my fingers at him.

"Barely."

Cohen heads to the kitchen, where I've prepared our favorite goulash dish. It's his one request whenever he comes over.

He doesn't turn to me to defend him when people take a second look at him and Declan. He doesn't ask me to protest his rights with him, nor does he ever look for my help when I know he needs it. But when he makes the trek from Astoria to the Upper West Side to sit in the middle of a craft explosion for the whole night, he asks for our family's special Italian version of hearty goulash.

He doesn't even have to ask at this point. It's my favorite too. Farrah is ravenous for it and usually has to fight Cohen for rights to leftovers. Farrah claims roommate privileges. Cohen slams down the sibling card.

It's an epic battle that I look forward to watching every time I hover over the pot as it cooks.

Declan glances in the pot and says, "Shocking . . . goulash again."

"Hey." I playfully push his shoulder. "Are you knocking an age-old recipe?"

"Age old?" Declan asks, a lift to his brow. He walks over to my sink and lifts up an empty jar of Prego. "When did jarred spaghetti sauce become age old?"

"Prego is age old, since 1981."

"Holy crap—1981? That's unheard of," Declan says full of sarcasm, making us all laugh. "If you want an age-old recipe, try my grandma's recipe for egg drop soup." He leans down and kisses the top of my head. "But I do love your goulash, even if you don't slave over homemade sauce."

He winks at me, and I smile back. "One day, Declan. Also, grab that egg drop soup recipe for me."

"It's sacred. I don't think Grandma will hand it over too kindly."

"Tell her it's for your future sister-in-law who wants to honor your side of the family as well."

"Well, in that case, consider it done." He gives me a side hug while Cohen walks over to the pot on the stove and takes in a deep breath.

"Smells good, Luna. Almost ready?"

"The big boy is hungry," Declan says. "Was bitching the entire train ride over here that he only had a ham sandwich at work today."

I glance over at my brawny brother and chuckle. He's always had an appetite.

"Let me guess; it was a measly sandwich that barely sated your ravenous hunger?"

I head to the tiny kitchen, where I lay out a few Campagna Sea Blue bowls—a gift from our nonna before she passed—and ladle heaping servings into each of them, topping them with some freshly grated parmesan that I picked up at the delicatessen this morning.

Cohen takes two bowls from the counter and hands one to Declan. We all take a seat at the bar top, me on one side, the boys on the other, and we dig in.

Cohen closes his eyes and quietly moans to himself. "This is so much better than a ham sandwich."

"Maybe you should try bringing more than just a sandwich to work. You do realize you burn a lot of calories with all the physical labor you put in."

"We don't have much time to take a break, so a hearty lunch isn't easy to take down in the middle of the day." Cohen scoops his goulash so fast into his mouth, and I have to chuckle as the broth drips down his chiseled chin. When you think of Cohen, think of the Italian version of the Brawny man—flannel and all—with a hint of that heavy New York accent.

In a matter of minutes, Cohen is hopping off his chair and heading for seconds while Declan and I stare at each other in horror, both of our bowls still mostly full.

"Uh, slow down there, buddy," I say as Cohen hops back up on his stool, bowl full.

Instead of responding, he starts in on his second bowl. "So, bouquets, huh?" he asks between gulps of elbow noodles.

Oh, Cohen. Goulash gets him every time.

"Yeah. Thousand-dollar commission. It's taken me about two days so far. Put me a bit behind on my other projects and stock in the shop, but I really wanted the challenge. So, I'm okay with the minor setback. I'll catch up."

"A thousand dollars for two days of work, which you do from home, where you can watch TV all day." Declan shakes his head. "Boy, did I go into the wrong profession."

"What are you talking about?" I ask. "Sure, you get paid shit, come home with a head cold at least once a month, and have been kicked in the shin at least a few dozen times. But you get to shape the minds of future generations. How is that not rewarding?"

He laughs. "When you put it like that . . ."

"Did Declan tell you about the parent who's raising a shitstorm with the principal?"

"Cohen," Declan warns.

"What?"

They have one of those silent conversations, using only their eyes—the kind of conversation only a couple that's been together for years can have.

Leaning in, I break up the eye contact. "He hasn't, but please, do enlighten me."

"It's nothing," Declan says, going back to his spoon.

I sigh. "Declan, you can either tell me now, or Cohen can tell me when you're not around. You know how things are with us. We share every last detail." I raise an eyebrow. "Every detail."

"Not every detail," Cohen quickly says, placing his hand on Declan's thigh, under the counter. "Trust me . . . not every detail."

"Better not be. Some things need to stay between a man and a man, you know."

I rest my chin on my hand and take in my favorite couple of all time. God, I love them so much. The give-and-take between them. The teasing, the little knowing looks, the silent exchanges. The comforting, loving touches here and there that I only get to see when we're out of the public eye. They're not in your face, but you can see it in their eyes, in the way they care for each other: they're deeply in love—another reason I really want to make this wedding competition happen for them.

"This doesn't need to stay between a man and a man, though." Cohen turns toward me. "A parent in Declan's class found out about the engagement party the faculty threw for Declan and me and flipped his lid." Cohen's jaw grows tight as he stares down at his bowl. "He doesn't want his child being educated by a gay man."

"Oh Jesus." I roll my eyes, annoyed with the ignorance that still runs rampant in the world. Just absurd. I'm about to brush off my soapbox and go off, and then I realize that the last thing Declan and Cohen need is a tirade. They need someone to comfort them—and in the best way we know how. "That douche parent must have read that one article."

Declan's brow creases. "What article?"

"You know, the one about catching 'the gay.' Didn't you read it? It was all about how if you're touched by a gay man while he's drinking a cup of tea, pinkie up, you can transform into one yourself. Devastating read. Looks like there was an outbreak of 'the gay' down in SoHo, at a poetry reading. Pinkie-up gays were attacking hipsters one at a time. Downright travesty. They had to shut down the snapping, hemp-loving tea shop, fumigate it with testosterone, and then reopen it as an exclusive biker bar slash fight club that no one is supposed to know about, but everyone knows about." I take a bite as Declan and Cohen both fold their arms across their chests, grinning despite themselves. "You really didn't catch that article . . . on your gaydar? Man, you guys must be getting old if you're missing breaking news like that."

Cohen frowns. "That's not how gaydar works."

"In my head it does." I wink, and they both shake their heads at me as they go back to their dinner. "Don't even worry about it, Declan," I say, getting serious. "That parent is an idiot. At some point, he'll realize his ignorance and then regret not only taking away an opportunity for his child to learn about the differences in humanity, but also not getting to know what a true gem you are."

Declan softly smiles. "Thanks, Luna."

I wink. "Anything for my future brother-in-law. Which brings me to the main event." I rub my hands together, and Cohen's eyes narrow.

"I don't like it when you rub your hands together. Rubbing hands means trouble for me."

"Not trouble, brother. Opportunity."

"Opportunity equals trouble."

"Just hear me out."

His shoulders visibly tense. "Whenever you start a sentence with 'Just hear me out,' I know it's going to involve working with a glue gun."

He may have helped me on occasion when I've been behind on orders. That's neither here nor there right now.

"This *might* involve a glue gun—"

"Count me out." Cohen dismisses me with a shake of his head. "Not going to happen, whatever it is. Nope. Sorry, sis."

"Just hear her out," Declan says, nudging Cohen with his shoulder. And this is one of the many reasons I love the man so much. When Cohen gets salty or closed off, Declan has a way of easing him out of his shell.

Cohen picks up his napkin and wipes his mouth, then sits up, arms crossed. He gives me that look, the one that I grew up watching, the thoughtful but guarded expression as he waits for my next "madcap" idea—at least that's what he calls it. "Okay, why am I firing up the glue gun?"

"Well." I place my hands on the counter and lean forward. "You know how you guys have always wanted to live in Manhattan, in a large apartment, and start a family?"

"Yes . . . ?" Cohen drags out skeptically.

"What if I told you that you could win a penthouse in Manhattan, just by getting married?"

"I'd say, 'Not interested.'" Cohen goes back to his bowl, not even giving me a second thought. Declan, the kind soul that he is, elbows Cohen, making my brother roll his eyes and say, "Spit it out, Luna."

I guess it's now or never. I prepare for one hell of an epic letdown and spill the beans.

"So. *The Wedding Game* . . . you know, the show on the DIY Network? It's looking for contestants in New York City. You must be getting married in the next few months, you must live in New York City, and you must be willing to plan a wedding under ten thousand dollars. Winners are chosen by America—and just from the ruggedly handsome lumber-gay vibe you've got going on, the win is in the bag—then you go home with keys to a fantastic apartment to start your life in."

Cohen stares at me.

Blinks.

Chews another spoonful of noodles and says, "No."

"Ugh, why not?" I whine. "This could be your chance, Cohen. You could get the wedding you always dreamed of. Remember? You *told* me you don't want a court—"

"Luna," Cohen firmly says. "No."

"You don't want what?" Declan asks, turning in his chair.

Uh-oh . . .

Did Declan not know?

Crap.

I shrink into my seat, trying to become one with my stool. Getting caught between my brother and Declan is never good. It never ends well, and I usually earn a good lecture afterward. From the way Cohen's staring daggers at me, I should probably pencil in a ten p.m. bedtime lecture now.

"Nothing," Cohen says through clenched teeth.

Maybe I should make it for nine thirty.

"You don't want a courthouse wedding?" Declan asks, and Cohen looks over at me again, his eyebrows almost touching in the middle of his forehead.

Gulp.

Nine. Yup, it's going to be a nine o'clock tongue-lashing.

With a deep sigh, he turns to Declan. "It's nothing you need to worry about, and nothing Luna should be sticking her nose in. I said no, and that's final."

CHAPTER TWO

ALEC

"I can*not* believe you scored the Hamptons house," Lucas, my coworker and friend, says as he leans back on the couch in my office, awestruck eyes directed at the ceiling. "How the fuck did you get the asshole to cave?"

Pleased with my showing in arbitration today, I kick my feet up on my desk and smile. "Threw down a file of photographic evidence."

"Oh shit." Lucas chuckles. "Who was it this time? The assistant?"

"Maid. In the solarium. With a vibrator up the ass."

"His ass or her ass?"

"His."

Lucas sits up and folds his hands in front of him.

"You're telling me you caught the president of Markman and Wire, the most prestigious advertising company in New York City, with a vibrator up his ass in a sunroom?"

I nod.

Lucas lets out a low whistle and leans back again. "You need to pay your private investigator more."

"I think that every goddamn day. Then again, if I were Elijah Markman, I wouldn't be cheating on my wife in a sunroom, where anyone could take pictures from surrounding bushes." Then again, I would never cheat on my wife either . . . or even have a wife, for that matter.

Marriage is not for blackhearted, realistic assholes like me. Marriage is for naive, love-blinded fools who believe another soul can make them happy. Fact: the only person who can make you happy is yourself.

Being the top divorce attorney in New York City will enlighten you: men are pigs. Granted, there are some great men out there, and women screw them over, but in my profession, it's usually the man. He's usually cheating, and he wants to fuck over the wife as much as possible when it comes to the divorce proceedings. Not on my watch.

To sum it up: I'm never getting married.

"I'm getting married!"

The door to my office busts open, startling both Lucas and me. Our eyes zero in on the door as Thaddeus floats—yes, floats—in, arms spread, before taking a huge, idiotic bow.

"Thad, what are you doing here?" I ask, standing from my desk, hands on the cool glass surface.

"Came to delight my big brother with the news of my engagement."

"I know you're engaged. You called me two months ago with the news."

"Yes, well, I'm still waiting on that engagement gift. Thought you forgot."

How could I possibly forget about Thad's engagement? He bawled on the phone, recounting every last detail. And the only reason I picked up the phone was because he texted me at least a dozen times beforehand, telling me he was going to call me at 8:00 p.m. sharp, and I'd better answer.

For a brief second, I considered letting the call go to voice mail, just to make his blood pressure skyrocket—the brotherly thing to do—but I thought better of it and answered.

In all honesty, I question Naomi's sanity. Thad is an interesting character. A man's man when he wants to be, a ladies' man in college, and a whiny baby for the majority of his day-to-day life. Maybe some of it's my fault. I did baby him when we were kids, but someone had to make sure he didn't become as jaded as me. I still saw the hope in his eyes that we could have the perfect family, despite our parents' constant screaming matches.

Dad was a workaholic on Wall Street; Mom was an emotionless trophy wife. They were picture perfect on the outside, a tragedy of a marriage on the inside. It was rare that we saw them happy together. It was rare that they were in the same room and not arguing.

Always about money.

It's what everyone fights about. Money.

It's why I despise it.

I hate that I need it to uphold a certain image for my job, and I hate that it's what makes the world go round.

I sit back down in my chair and cross my ankle over my knee while picking up a pen to fiddle around with. "Didn't forget. Didn't think it was necessary."

"Not necess—" Thad stops abruptly when he spots Lucas, finally. My friend looks like he has whiplash from our conversation. "Hey, man." He holds his hand out. "Thaddeus."

Lucas stands and takes Thad's hand, giving it a good shake. "Lucas. Nice to meet you."

"Likewise." Thad adjusts his suit jacket. "Ever buy an engagement present for a sibling?"

"Don't have any. Sorry, man," Lucas answers, a slight hitch in his voice.

"Would you?" Thad asks, clearly trying to prove a point.

A smirk crosses Lucas's face, and I know he's about to make things exponentially worse for me. "I would throw a party."

Slowly, Thad swivels on his heel, hands on his hips, nostrils flared. Speaking through his clenched teeth, he says, "Did you hear that, Alec? A GD party."

I stare down at my ankle. "Yeah, I heard the asshole." I lift my head just enough so I can see the giant smirk on Lucas's face. "You can leave now."

He salutes me with two fingers. "My work here is done. Let me know if you're still on for lunch."

"You're buying!" I call out right before he exits.

Thad stares after him and then turns back to me. "He seems like a stand-up guy." Not waiting for an invite, Thad rounds one of the chairs in front of my desk and plops down. "I have a favor to ask."

Hell . . . this can't be a favor that I'm going to like. Just from the excitement in his eyes and the fact that he came to my office, I can tell that this isn't only a big favor but one that's most likely going to make my life a billion times harder.

"No 'Hey, brother, how are you?'" I ask, forcing my voice steady. "Just getting down to business?"

"As if you even enjoy small talk."

"I might be in the mood for it," I say, just torturing him at this point.

"You want small talk? Fine." Thad crosses his arms over his chest. "Hi, brother, how are you? Oh, is that so? Busy? Great. Yeah, I've been busy too, but still find time to text. Did you know it was Mom's birthday the other day? I did, because I went to the brunch she held. I was the only child she birthed who was there, which was sad since she only birthed two. It was a boring-as-shit brunch with a bunch of old ladies in hats talking about Candace Howe's latest face-lift, which, according to them, has wreaked havoc on her eyebrows. Oh and hey, did you know vaginas get dry when they're old, making it harder to have sex? I do now, thanks to Mom describing the best lube—"

"No more small talk." I hold up my hand as bile starts to rise in the back of my throat.

"Oh, you *don't* want to talk about Mom's dry vagina?"

"Get to the favor."

"That's what I thought." Thad smirks. "Now, to business. As you know, I'm getting married to my beautiful Naomi. Weddings are expensive—"

"So you need money? How much?" I reach into my drawer for my checkbook, irritated that once again, money is taking hold of one more thing in my life.

"I don't need money." Guilt stabs through me at the insulted look on Thad's face. I should know better at this point. Thad never asks for money. Just my attention. And the thought of him asking for my attention makes me wish he wanted just a check.

"Sorry." I grip the back of my neck. "What do you need?"

He looks off to the side, and his demeanor morphs from annoying little brother to concerned fiancé. "I want to give Naomi a great life, the one that she deserves." He chuckles. "For putting up with me and loving me. We want to move to Manhattan, make the leap, finally. But I can't do that and put on a wedding at the same time. That's when I came across an opportunity to compete on a wedding show, where contestants plan a New York City wedding on a budget." He glances up at me.

Ohhh.

Shit.

I think I know where this is going.

"*The Wedding Game*. Have you heard of it?"

"No."

"Didn't think so. Well they're looking for couples. Naomi and I would be perfect. The wedding would be paid for, and the grand prize is a penthouse in Manhattan. I definitely have the charisma for television. America votes, and there's no way they won't choose this handsome face." He vogues a frame around his face, and I repress the deep, passionate urge to smack his hands away. "I can feel it in my bones. We can totally win, but there's one catch."

"There always is."

Ignoring me, he says, "Every couple needs at least one member from their family to participate. Since Naomi's family lives in Oregon . . ."

"No."

Don't even have to think about it. That's a big fat no from me.

Television.

Wedding planning.

Dealing with what I can only imagine will be a groomzilla of a brother . . .

Not to mention the fact that I specialize in gut-wrenching divorces, not happily ever afters, and wouldn't know what family bonding is if it was a wedding bouquet that slapped me in the face.

No fucking thank you.

"You can't just say *no* like that."

"I can and I did." I move the mouse of my computer and light up my screen. "I have work to do, Thad. If that's it, you should go."

I turn to my computer, but I can feel his deep-green gaze on me as the tension starts to rise between us.

He's about to explode.

From the corner of my eye, I can see his chest rise and fall rapidly. I can see the clenching of his jaw, the narrowing of his eyes, the anger on the tip of his tongue.

"No is not an acceptable answer." His voice is so low, so menacing, that if I didn't actually know my brother was all talk, I might have been a little frightened.

Keeping my eyes focused on the screen in front of me, I say, "You're going to have to find it within yourself to accept no as an answer, because I'm not changing my mind."

Instead of storming off like I thought he would, he leans forward, picks up a pen off my desk, and chucks it at my head, hitting me right in the temple. When I whip around to face him, he doesn't even flinch.

"Naomi's pregnant."

Okay, was not expecting that. I spin in my chair and face him straight on. "Seriously?"

"No, I would joke about that." He rolls his eyes, and I realize it was a stupid question.

"Wow, I mean . . . wow," I repeat. "Are you . . . excited?"

"Of course I'm excited. I'm going to be a father, for fuck's sake. It's a total dream. A little out of order, but still, it's amazing."

"Well, congrats, Thad. That's really great."

"It's the biggest reason why I want this, why I need this opportunity." He pauses. "It would be a giant head start for my family."

"You can have a simple wedding, Thad. Save up for an apartment in Manhattan."

"Saving up isn't really easy when you're a single-income household. You know Naomi got laid off a few months ago, and now that she's pregnant, she won't be getting a new job for a while. I'm not a divorce attorney. I'm an event coordinator."

"There are other ways—"

"There aren't, Alec. You're it, the only option, and even if you weren't, I would still want you by my side."

"Because I'm so well versed on the light and joy of a beautiful marriage," I answer with a sarcastic lilt.

"Noooo," Thad drags out in an irritated tone. "Because you know how to make everything better." I pause, the hairs on my arm standing up with apprehension. He continues. "Growing up, you knew exactly how to make me laugh, how to help me forget the environment we were living in, and how to turn a shitty situation into a lifelong memory. You've always come through, and I know you would come through on this and help us win. You're scrappy like that."

"I'm not scrappy," I say, pulling my hand over my face. "I'm not the same guy, Thad. I'm—"

"You're a shitty brother." He looks me dead in the eyes, and despite myself, I'm offended. Sure, I've been a little absent lately, but to be called out like that? I don't fucking think so.

"Because I won't parade around with you, draping tulle over chairs on national television?"

He shakes his head. "No, because the minute you went off to college, you basically forgot about me. Getting you to hang out is like trying to herd cats into a room. You barely give me any of your time, and when I do get to see you, you're not really there. Your mind's always on work. I don't want us to be brothers who drift apart, who never talk until something traumatic happens in the family. I miss you, Alec. And I'll be damned if my child is raised in a world where he or she doesn't know you."

He stares at me, his eyes growing larger with every second that passes. How is that even possible?

"I want them to play with Uncle Alec, to experience the guy I grew up with. The fun, protective, intelligent guy who helped me become the man I am today. Please, Alec. If not for me, for my unborn child . . ."

Mother.

Fucker.

CHAPTER THREE

ALEC

"So that was your brother, huh?" Lucas asks.

"Yeah," I say, leaning against the bar top, beer clutched in my hands. I'm not much of a day drinker, even on the weekend, but after everything Thad just put me through, I needed a beer.

"You're nothing alike."

Which is weird since I'm the one who apparently "raised him." But it's true: we're nothing alike. Thad's sensitivity level is frighteningly high, whereas I feel pretty much dead inside.

I'm not just walking through life with no purpose, though. After I graduated high school and was accepted into Columbia, I knew one thing: I was going to become a lawyer so when assholes like my father cheated on their wives, I could help deliver exactly what they deserved . . . giant settlements in favor of their soon-to-be exes. I represent only women, I seek revenge for them, and I go home to my moderately sized, minimally decorated apartment, sip on my whiskey, and then call it a night. Then I repeat the entire thing the next day. There's an occasional one-night stand or an outing with friends, but both are rare when you're a workaholic.

Thad, though . . . he's not a workaholic. He puts in his hours, does a decent job at work, then goes home and watches every new show on Netflix with Naomi. They're always going out—the reason I know this is that Thad continuously asks if I want to join them—and they're in the business of experiencing new things, mostly free things. Art galleries, movie screenings in Central Park, comedy shows—you name it; they've done it.

Thad has fun.

Whereas I think I've forgotten the meaning of fun.

But what's scaring me most right now is Thad's closing statement, which he delivered over his shoulder on his way out the door.

Don't turn into Dad. Don't become a workaholic who only cares about himself.

That fucking cut deep. The last person I ever want to be is my father. I make sure every day that the apple has fallen as far away from the tree as possible.

But Thad made me think. He made me assess my life, and hell, he made me consider his proposal.

It's why I'm sitting at a bar with Lucas, waiting on a huge burger and the biggest-possible order of fries.

"Whatever he said must have rocked you, man. You look pale."

I sip my beer. "He wants me to be on a TV show with him."

"What?" Lucas laughs. "What TV show?"

"The Wedding Game."

"Oh shit, with Mary DIY? Dude, she's hot. I would totally let her sew me something. I catch the show occasionally just to watch her."

I rotate my head to eye my friend. "You're into a DIY lady?"

Lucas is already typing away in his phone, and he holds it up a moment later. Damn, okay, I see why he's watching *The Wedding Game*. Sleek blonde hair, bright-blue eyes, gorgeous body. Yeah, I get it. "She's hot. And she's clever, dude; she comes up with some crazy shit." He pauses, and then his eyes light up. "Holy shit, if you do the show, you could introduce me to her."

I shake my head and turn back to my beer. "It's not a guarantee Thad and Naomi would even be picked. I also didn't commit to doing the show."

"You didn't?" Lucas actually looks perplexed, like saying yes was a no-brainer. "Why the hell not?"

"Why the hell would I?"

Lucas shrugs. "I don't really know your family dynamics, but from the tension in the office, I could tell there's some resentment between you guys."

"Not as close as we used to be" is all I say while downing a large gulp of my beer.

"Alec . . ." Lucas is quiet for a minute before he exhales loudly. "I lost my brother from alcohol poisoning." *Oh shit.* "He was pledging my fraternity, drank too much, and passed out. No one noticed." He looks down into his drink. "If I were you, I would do just about anything to make sure there's nothing standing between you two. You never know when you won't have the chance to see him again."

"Fuck, Lucas, I had no idea," I say, feeling like a complete ass.

"I don't talk about it much, and I really don't want to focus on it now. I just want to give you some perspective. Whatever you two went through can't be so bad you can't fix it, right?"

I scratch the side of my jaw, knowing exactly what's holding me back.

Whenever I see Thad, I see the scared little boy he used to be. I see the fear in his eyes, the uncertainty of what was going to happen to our family. It makes me sick, and it makes me angry. Angry that two adults couldn't pull it together for their kids, that they left us, alone, without anyone to talk to but ourselves, a ten-year-old and a fourteen-year-old. We were drowning in their problems, with no life raft. And that anger takes over—it builds and builds inside me until I can't even take a breath.

"It's complicated," I finally answer. "And just got a whole lot more complicated." I roll my head to the side, trying to ease the stress headache that's creeping up on me. "Thad's fiancée, Naomi, is pregnant. Thad wants me to be a part of the baby's life."

"Ah." Lucas nods. "Thad thinks participating in *The Wedding Game* could help you mend things, start a new chapter in your relationship."

"That and other reasons as well." Reasons I don't need to get into with Lucas.

"Seems like enough of a reason to say yes."

"I know." I drag my hand over my face. "I really don't think I have a choice in the matter."

Lucas shakes his head just as our plates arrive. The burger I ordered isn't looking at all appetizing anymore.

I tap my foot, hands in my pants pockets, waiting for the door in front of me to open. After a long lunch with Lucas, I tried to convince myself I didn't have to say yes to Thad, that I could figure out another way to repair our relationship, but I just kept picturing Thad's desperate face. He wants this so much, and at the end of the day, I've always tried to make my brother happy.

Which has led me here.

The door opens, and I see Naomi's bright-red hair on the other side, followed by her shocked eyes, a lighter shade of green than Thad's and mine. More beautiful.

"Alec." She opens the door wider. "I wasn't expecting to see you. Come in."

I step into their one-bedroom Bronx apartment, and Naomi gives me a brief hug. I remember when Thad and Naomi moved in. I brought them a housewarming gift—a new smart TV—but wasn't considering their limited space when I purchased the seventy-inch screen. It takes up almost an entire wall.

I can see why Thad wants a bigger place. I know they already pay over $2,000 for rent, and for what, really? The kitchen, dining area, and family room are squeezed into one long room. Off to the right is their bedroom and bathroom, with an additional coat closet near the front door—that's about it. Far cry from the Park Avenue apartment we grew up in, the one my dad took in the divorce, despite my mom taking custody of the kids.

"It's so great to see you." Turning toward their bedroom, Naomi calls out, "Thad, it's your brother!"

Instantaneously, Thad's head pops past the doorframe. "What?" When he sees me, his mouth falls open for a second before he snaps it shut and walks out into the living room, wearing sweats and my old high school baseball shirt that I gave him before I left for college. How does it even still fit him? Granted, we wore them big back then, but still . . .

"Hey, Thad," I say, rocking back on my heels, feeling really fucking weird and wishing I'd just done this over the phone.

But in usual Thad fashion, he pulls me into a warm hug and says, "I got some carrot cake from the bakery around the corner. We were just about to have some. Want a piece?"

"I'd like that."

Naomi retrieves an extra plate while Thad gives me another hug. His arms feel familiar . . . like home.

I return the embrace with a quick pat to the back and then pull away, done with the lovefest.

"Too much too soon?" Thad asks, clearly sensing my need to flee the scene of the crime, where I hugged my brother twice in a row just for showing up at his apartment.

"Uh, yeah."

"Fair enough. Baby steps."

Naomi brings over cake, and we all sit down on the sofa in their living/dining/kitchen area. While they pick up their forks, I just stare down at my piece. They're acting so normal, as if we do this every Sunday night. This might be a lot harder than I thought.

Wanting to get to the point and then get the hell out of here, I say, "Uh, I'll do the thing."

Thad picks up my fork and forces me to take it. "Eat up, bro."

I glance between the two of them and then repeat myself. "Did you hear me? I said I'll do the thing."

"I know," Thad responds, mouth full of cake. "I knew you would. You always come through when I need you." He smiles and continues to dig into his cake.

Well . . . hell.

Mr. Reliable: apparently that's me.

CHAPTER FOUR

LUNA

"What's wrong? You love my biscuits and gravy. Just like I can't get enough of your hearty goulash, and—I'm going to be frank—I'm peeved you only saved me one bowl," Farrah says as we sit at the counter in our dim apartment, *Grey's Anatomy* playing in the background.

"You weren't home." I sigh, poking one of the biscuits with my fork. "Cohen claimed the sibling card and took the rest home with him. Sorry. He was irritated with me, so I didn't put up a fight. I'll make you some this weekend."

"Cohen? Irritated at you? I don't believe it. Cohen is never irritated at you."

"Well, he is right now. He's been texting me one-worded answers. I know he's busy and all with some new renovations his company took on, but one-worded answers aren't like him."

Farrah takes a big bite of a biscuit. "Okay, tell me what happened. Clearly it took place when he was here the other night."

I nod as I lean back in my chair and then just stare at my food. "Have you ever seen *The Wedding Game*?"

"That budget wedding show? It's like a crossover of *Top Chef* and *America's Got Talent*, but with crafts?"

"That's it."

"I've caught a few episodes here and there. The Nashville season, I believe."

"Well, they're coming to New York, and I suggested Cohen and Declan fill out an application. They would be perfect for it."

"Uh, yeah, they would be. New Yorker lumberjack and sexy Asian schoolteacher? The show was made for them. America would vote for them in a heartbeat."

"That's what I said. And I'd be helping them put together everything, so they would win. I just know it. I can feel it. And the prize is a penthouse in Manhattan. They could finally be close."

"And let me guess—Cohen wants nothing to do with it," Farrah says.

"You could not be more right." I wad up my napkin and toss it on the counter. "I hate how . . . uptight he is sometimes. Loosen up, man. This could be a fun opportunity, but it was an immediate no."

"I can't believe you even expected him to think about it. This is Cohen. He hates the spotlight. He's not the type of guy who wants to parade his life around on a reality show."

"He could be. I've seen him loosen up."

"When he's drunk," Farrah counters. "Which is rare. Face it, Luna, there's no chance you could ever get him to fill out that application."

"Maybe Declan?" I ask, knowing the answer already.

"Declan is almost too honorable." Farrah shakes her head. "Cohen said no, then no it is."

I hate that she's right.

"God, why do they have to be so annoyingly perfect?" I rest my head on the edge of the table and flail my arms above me. "Don't they understand how amazing this could be? A free wedding—a beautiful, free wedding. I could make it their dream. They don't have to settle. And when they win, because we know they would win, they could live so much closer to us, which would mean more goulash." I lift my head just enough that Farrah can see me wiggle my eyebrows.

"I'm not the one who needs convincing." She takes another big bite of biscuit.

"He wants more," I say quietly, looking away.

"What do you mean?" Farrah asks.

Gnawing on the side of my lip, I take a deep breath and push at my biscuit again. "As you know, Cohen doesn't flaunt his love. He keeps it quiet because he doesn't want to make other people uncomfortable." I roll my eyes. "Ridiculous, I know. But before Declan came along, when gay marriage was just legalized in New York State, Cohen and I were watching it all unfold live on CNN, holding hands the whole time. When the law passed, Cohen let out this heavy exhale, as if a weight had been lifted off his shoulders. I can still hear it in my head, how utterly relieved he was. Relieved over a basic human right."

"I remember all the rainbow flags we texted each other that day." Farrah smiles thoughtfully.

"Once I'd stopped humping the air in victory, Cohen pulled me back down on the couch and told me he was done suppressing his love, and when he met the right guy, he wanted to make it a day to remember. It didn't have to be costly or fancy, but he wanted a celebration, a moment to bask in the love he knew he would share with someone one day." I swallow the lump in my throat. "I want him to have that day. This show could be *it* for them, but he shot it down before even giving it any thought."

Farrah pops the rest of her biscuit in her mouth and says, "You know, if it was my brother, I would just fill out the application without him knowing. What's that saying? 'Act now, beg for forgiveness later'? That's what I would do."

Fill out the application myself?

Why didn't I think about that?

As if her suggestion has given me life again, I stand up from the counter and raise my fist, declaring, "I shall fill out the application myself."

Farrah freezes, fork midway to her mouth. "Wait, I didn't mean for *you* to do that."

"It's so simple. I'll just fill it out, and then when they're accepted, they can't be mad because, hello, free wedding."

"Luna, I was just talking—I didn't mean what I said."

"I have all those pictures from their engagement," I say, mentally flipping through the many, many candid photos I took of Cohen proposing on the Brooklyn Bridge, which was where they first met during a gay men's running club that neither of them participate in anymore. "I could use one of those for the application picture. We know they're handsome as ever in all of them."

"This is a bad idea."

"I can fill it out right now. I know their information."

"Luna!" Farrah calls out as I walk like a deranged but happy zombie toward the coffee table, where my computer innocently sits.

"Imagine the relief in their faces when I tell them they've been selected and they didn't have to do anything."

"I think they would kill you, and I'm not paying this rent by myself."

In a daze, I type in my password. "They'll for sure buy me something pretty. Oh, maybe that new set of watercolor markers I've had my eye on."

"Luna, think about what you're doing. Cohen is going to be—"

"I bet they'll buy me one of those giant cannolis they always talk about. The pistachio one. My mouth is watering just thinking about it."

"They'll murder you."

"Murder me with praise." I search for *The Wedding Game* application and then click on the first link I see. When the application comes up for New York City, excitement blooms in the pit of my stomach. This is going to be great.

Amazing.

They are going to wonder what they ever did without me.

Cohen is so lucky to have me as a sister.

The Wedding Game is ours to win.

Evil laugh

Lightning flying from fingers

Veins popping hideously from neck

Computer dying; forgot to plug it in

I've never really understood the point of hyperventilating into a paper bag. What does a bag really do? You're just breathing in the same air, over and over again, while the bag puffs in and out. I'm sure if I did some internet searching, it would tell me something about CO_2 levels or some crap like that, which is why I'm currently grateful for the paper bag I'm holding up to my mouth as I stand outside Cohen and Declan's apartment.

Courtesy of the bagels I bought for our Sunday brunch, I hold half a dozen everything bagels in one hand, sans bag, while I lean against the wall of the hallway leading to their apartment, breathing garlic and sesame seeds into my mouth, over and over again.

I can still see the email in my head, practically imprinted on my brain.

> Congratulations, Cohen and Declan! You've been chosen to compete on *The Wedding Game*.

Have you ever seen Whitney Houston perform on stage? She gave it her all, and you could tell because tiny beads of sweat were always above her finely lined and painted lips. When I was young, I'd watch recordings of her performances and wonder why people sweat on their upper lip. It had never happened to me before.

That is, until today.

The instant I opened the email, a sheen of sweat coated my upper lip. It was the oddest sensation: nerves, excitement, and impending doom all hit me at once, like an atomic bomb, bursting over my face.

I don't know why I was so surprised. They were a shoo-in, but the reality of the show has set me into a tailspin of dread. Hence the hyperventilating just outside their apartment.

I considered just not telling Cohen and Declan about the application and replying to the email with a kind, "No thank you." No harm, no foul, right?

But then I kept thinking about how they could win. How this could change their lives for the better. And because of that thought, I sent back a reply accepting the spot on *The Wedding Game* with the plan of begging for forgiveness today.

I glance at their door, at the pristinely polished brass 6B, and wonder if this is the last time I'll get the chance to run my finger over it and leave a smudge that will drive Cohen crazy when he comes home tomorrow. Will this be the last time I get to imagine him using the sleeve of his flannel to furiously buff out the smudge? Will I ever get another text from him simply stating: *I know it was you*? Will I never again be able to send him my favorite GIF of *Star Wars* stormtroopers humping the air?

I really didn't think this thing through.

Before I can think of a way to get myself out of this, the door to their apartment whips open and Cohen steps out, bag of trash in his hand.

He startles when he sees me, but then his brow furrows in confusion.

I don't blame him—his sister is balancing six bagels on top of each other and leaning against his apartment wall, all while breathing in and out of a paper bag.

I chuckle awkwardly but keep the bag over my mouth, and my voice booms weirdly against the paper. "Hey, Cohen." I wiggle my fingers at him. "Love the smell of bagels, don't you?"

His eyes narrow. "What did you do?"

He's annoyingly observant—not that I'm being very coy.

"Nothing at all," I say. Standing up straight and still balancing the bagels, I walk past him. "Just submitted an application for you for *The Wedding Game*." I step over the threshold of his apartment. "And they picked you, so you're going to be on TV, and wow, I need to set these bagels down."

"You what?" Cohen booms, but before I can answer, I slip away and walk straight to their kitchen, where Declan is finishing up one of the most miraculous fruit salads I've ever seen.

"Hey, Luna." He glances at the bagels in my hand and chuckles. "You're always bringing the party tricks. Let me help you."

Feeling the storm that's building and circling in the hallway, I desperately look up at Declan and say, "I love you so much and think you're perfect for my brother. Thank you for loving him, and if I don't make it out of here alive, just know that you are wickedly intelligent, so you should use it to your advantage. Fuck with him. Get him out of his comfort zone. Move things around. Play with his mind. It will keep him alive." I glance behind me and whisper, "I smudge the 6B."

Looking confused, Declan takes the bagels and sets them down. I bring the bag back up to my mouth and breathe in and out, my heart hammering in my chest.

The thing with Cohen is he's not a yeller. When he's mad, he doesn't lash out irrationally and stomp around, flinging his arms about, making a true show of his anger.

No, he's the scary type of angry.

The kind that bottles it up and slowly, ever so slowly, lets it out, like the steam trying to fit through the tiny spout of a kettle. His chest puffs—which I think comes from him consuming the anger—his eyes turn pure black and widen, like some freaky character in *The Witcher*, and there's this tiny vein that runs parallel to his left eyebrow that all of a sudden makes itself known and starts throbbing with impending death.

Throb.

Throb.

Throb.

It's horrifying when the vein comes to life. It adds a certain petrifying vibe to the entire experience.

But it's the slow and deliberate way he speaks that really cuts to your soul. I almost wish he would make a scene. I wish he would be overtly dramatic, snap his fingers in my face, and then cry while screaming at me. I wish he'd put on more of a show than the stern, thought-out lecture that's waiting instead.

Still looking confused, Declan asks, "What's going on—?"

Slam.

Declan and I both startle. Together, me with the bag over my mouth, we spin to see Cohen standing in front of the door, arms tense at his sides, jaw clenched, looking just about ready to murder. I can hear the knife-wielding *reet reet* noise sounding off in his head as his eyes connect with mine. And just as I suspected, his eyes are black, his nostrils flared so wide that for a brief second, I wonder if I could stick a marble up them—only brief, since terror is taking over, after all—and heavenly lord, hold my breasts, because there it is . . .

The Vein.

Throbbing, pulsating, sending out a message in Morse code that he's coming for me.

"Luna," Cohen says, his voice so menacing that I can feel my toenails shrivel up in my shoes.

I gulp and, without even thinking about it—this is my actual initial reaction—I open the paper bag wide and plop it over my head before casually leaning against the counter. "Only Paper Baggie here. Luna couldn't make it. But please refrain from relaying information through me. I hate being the middleman."

His steps draw closer.

That Whitney Houston sweat hits me again.

And before I can take my next breath, the bag is torn off my head, and my six-foot-two lumberjack brother towers over me. "You're about to die."

There's only one thing I can do at this point as we face off in the kitchen, Declan observing the entire interaction with bagels clutched to his chest . . .

Ramble.

It's my only saving grace.

"I'm so sorry. I didn't think you were going to get picked—well, that's a lie, I knew you would get picked but I just thought you were missing out on an amazing opportunity if you didn't fill out the application, and I know you don't want me talking about it, but you even said yourself you wish you could have an actual wedding with a party because you worked so hard at finding love and the whole gay rights movement, you know, celebrating love that you weren't really allowed to celebrate until the law was passed, but now that you can have a party to truly show off your beautiful relationship and you were settling, and I didn't want you to settle so I filled out the application, submitted your pictures, and you two were obviously picked and it's going to be great. I know it sounds scary right now, being on TV and all and you being shy and reserved, but I promise we will create a beautiful wedding that celebrates your relationship, and then you'll win and move to Manhattan, which will make everyone's commute that much easier, and oh my God, you can show off your carpentry skills and maybe get hired by someone who sees you, or maybe *Playgirl* sees you and thinks, 'Wow, we would like him to be a centerfold because look at that beefcake, but the shoot would be modest, no penis shots, maybe a side butt, or even butt crack, but we would make sure we show off your physique, not the goods, keep it tasteful,' and trust me, when the invitations for gay porn start rolling in, that's where we put our foot down, because my brother will not be subjected to all the freaky crap that's out there, not when he has a sweet Declan at home, though I'm sure they'll want him involved because just look at him, what a Greek god, I can see why you fell for him in the first place, real hubba-hubba kinda guy—"

"Luna."

I stick my finger in the air. "To close this out, I'm sorry. Your wedding will be spectacular. Tasteful nude shoot. No porn." I smile, or at least attempt a smile.

I stare at my brother, and I just know he's about to unleash a verbal barrage that will put me very firmly in my place.

"I think it's a great opportunity," Declan says, breaking the most epic of staredowns ever to happen on this side of the Mississippi. I knew I loved Declan, that somewhere, deep inside, we've always been soul mates.

"What?" Cohen asks.

After setting the bagels on the counter, Declan places his hand on Cohen's chest and speaks softly, calming the plaid-wearing beast in front of me. "It could be a wonderful opportunity, not just to show off your carpentry skills, like Luna said, but to show off *her* skills as well—"

"No, that's not why—"

Declan holds his hand up, and I quickly snap my mouth closed.

"There are a lot of positives here. A wedding that you apparently want, one that I kind of want too. And even better, a *free* wedding, a chance at a penthouse, an opportunity to grow closer as a couple as we work to create a wedding on a budget, not to mention the exposure for your sister and her many talents. The kind of exposure that could help her get to Mary DIY's level."

"This has nothing to do with me," I interject, and I truly mean it. "I don't have to be a part of it. I'm sure we can find another family member to help out. I want this for you guys."

"Of course we'd use you," Cohen says with an irritated sigh as he pinches his brow. "We'd be stupid not to."

"Wait." Hope blooms inside of me. "Does that mean you want to do it? You want to be on the show?"

"I don't *want* to be on the show," he says, looking at me again, though this time the menacing, throbbing vein has subsided, leaving just a clenched, exasperated jaw behind.

"But . . . ," I add for him.

Cohen's gaze bounces between Declan and me. "You really want to do this?"

Declan shrugs. "You didn't seem too thrilled about the courthouse wedding." He takes Cohen's hand. "Did you really dream of a bigger wedding?"

"Don't lie to him," I whisper, and Cohen shoots me a death glare. I hold up my hands and try to become one with the kitchen cabinets.

Focusing on Declan, Cohen scratches the back of his neck. "Well, you know that coming out wasn't easy for me, especially since I don't fit the stereotypical gay-man type. I'm not this flamboyant, fun, *Will & Grace* character. I'm just a regular guy who never really felt like he fit anywhere. But now that I finally feel comfortable in my own skin—thanks to you—I want to celebrate our journey with our closest friends and family."

"Why didn't you say anything?"

"He doesn't like confrontation," I say, leaning forward.

"Luna," Cohen snaps, and once again, I melt into the background. "I wanted to make you happy, and because it was the first thing you suggested, I thought that's what you really wanted."

Declan shakes his head. "I only said 'courthouse' because we're trying to save up to move. I want what you want, Cohen." With a finger, Declan tips up Cohen's chin. "Let's do the show."

I hold my breath, awaiting Cohen's response, and I swear he takes extra long, just to make me pass out. Finally, he says, "Okay."

I spring forward excitedly and wrap my arms around both of them. "Group hug."

Cohen peels my arm away and bends down so we're eye to eye. "Are you listening to me, Luna? As Declan would say to his students, 'Do you have your listening ears on?'"

I give him a crazed smile and nod. "Listening."

"Good, because I'm only going to say this once. Never go behind my back again. The only reason I'm not revoking your sister privileges is because Declan is okay with this, but it's going to take me a while to forgive you. What you did was out of line, deceitful, and out of character. We don't hide shit from each other, and we don't go behind each other's backs. Don't. Do. It. Again. Got it?"

Yeesh.

"Got it," I whisper, the guilt now consuming me. Cohen's right: we don't go behind each other's backs. We've always been honest about everything. I may have had good intentions, but Cohen has every right to be angry. "I'm sorry I tampered with your trust. It won't happen again."

"Better not." He straightens up and sighs. With a roll of his eyes, he pulls me into a hug, and I revel in the feel of his protective arms around me. "The only other reason I'm doing this is because I truly want to see you shine. You've worked so hard to get to where you are—it's about time you get a little acclaim."

"That's not why—"

"I know." He kisses the top of my head. "I know, Luna. It's just an added bonus."

After a few more seconds of hugging, Declan says, "So, are we doing this?"

We both turn to Cohen. Despite his scowl, I think I can detect a shimmer of excitement in his eyes. "We're doing this."

I pump my fist in the air. "Those other couples can eat my glitter dust!"

Chapter Five
ALEC

What the hell have I gotten myself into?

Three seconds after walking on set, I immediately realized I'd made a colossal mistake.

Centered in the large space are three workstations, decked out in crafting supplies, all organized and displayed like a kitschy version of the most elaborate workbench ever created. Each station contains two industrial-size packing tables with smooth wooden surfaces, three stools, what I can only assume is a vision board—kill me now—and multiple crates, stashing away God knows what.

Along the outer edge of the three-walled set are designated sections for what seem like the important aspects of a wedding: invitations, venues, and centerpieces. Every section contains a variety of tools, supplies, and products. My stomach drops, and I get the feeling that this is going to be more cutthroat than I imagined.

And of course, the colors are kick-you-in-the-dick bright, with white tables, parquet floors in teal, pink, and purple, and aqua walls. Who let a teenager design this set?

Easy to say that this is not my scene. Nothing about it screams I belong here, and definitely not in my dark-wash jeans and black T-shirt.

Thad, on the other hand, is wearing a goddamn linen shirt because in his words, he won't "sweat as much with a breezy fabric."

He looks like a jackass.

In a matter of seconds, I've come up with at least five excuses that could get me out of this, all very viable.

Client just called, arbitration has been moved to a Saturday. Got to go.

Forgot to pay my taxi driver, and the meter's still running.

Ate some funky shrimp last night, need a bathroom, stat.

Cough *Cough* Picked up malaria at the bar last night, don't think I'll make it.

Made a mistake, really don't want to be here, peace.

The last one is the truth, but malaria is looking like a viable option right about now.

The idea of losing what little freedom I have left in my life to making bouquets and helping my brother prance around with tulle really doesn't feel appealing in the slightest. Not to mention feeling completely out of my element and having to be recorded while creating an event I don't necessarily believe in.

Typical divorce lawyer, hates marriage; I get it. I'm a walking cliché, but I have yet to be exposed to a positive, healthy relationship to prove my thoughts otherwise.

I'm sure Thad and Naomi have a wonderful relationship, but I guess we'll find out once it's put through the wringer for the next two months.

"You're so tense—relax," Thad says, walking up next to me, a sandwich in hand. Is that . . . bologna? Talking with his mouth full, he continues, "Go hit up the craft services table. They have fucking gummy worms, man. I know where I'll be when we're taking five." He taps my arm and points to his pocket. "Already stuffed some in my jeans. They're free, bro."

Jesus Christ.

Naomi walks up holding a sandwich as well and smiles. "Can't have deli meat because of the baby, but I stacked this guy with cheese and mustard, and it's truly wonderful. Their bread is so crunchy on the outside."

"But heaven on the inside," Thad finishes for her. "Never had anything like it."

"I might ask them where they get it." Naomi examines her sandwich—it's overflowing with so much cheese that it actually makes me want to throw up in my mouth.

So much cheese . . .

"I should ask about this bologna."

"And this cheese."

Thad wiggles his brows. "And the gummy worms."

"Probably all from Costco," I say, rolling my eyes.

"I sure as hell hope so," Thad says. "With the baby coming along, Daddy Dearest is going to roll in with a membership and buy his weight in diapers." Thad nudges me. "Did you hear me call myself Daddy Dearest? That was funny."

"It wasn't."

Thad studies me. "Your blood sugar must be low. You're quite irritated right now. Why don't you ask a PA for some coffee or something? Liven yourself up. We have a long day of filming."

Don't I fucking know it.

The schedule was delivered via email this past week, and I nearly called Thad up and told him I wasn't coming. We'll be subjected to filming on every weekend over the course of two months. The weekdays are for us—how kind—Saturdays are for challenges, and Sundays are for confessionals. We are required to show up for both days. Weddings are the last weekend, all in a row—Friday, Saturday, and Sunday—and the results of the winner will be filmed a few weeks later, since there's a delay in filming when the show airs.

Every weekend we will be presented with a challenge that will either give us opportunities to earn more money for the weddings or decide what kind of decor or design will be incorporated into them. Honestly, I skimmed over that section, not the slightest bit interested. All I could focus on was the fact that my weekends had just been snatched away from me for the summer.

I rub my eyes and let out a long sigh. "Yeah, coffee." With that, I leave them to their sandwiches and pocket-lint gummy worms, looking for a PA to help me.

The set is bustling with people, everyone walking around, a job to do. Contestants were told to mill about until called upon. Well, I haven't seen any other contestants, nor have I seen any of the judges or the host Lucas was drooling over.

There is zero direction. There is no schedule for the day. Not one single person is controlling the chaos or communicating the agenda, and I'm the only one who seems to care.

Irritation boiling up inside me, I decide to visit the craft table for some coffee. And, I would like to add, it's incredibly strange that Naomi and Thad are eating sandwiches at eight in the morning, especially since when I walk up to the table, it's full of breakfast items.

Spotting the coffee carafe, I snag a paper cup, place it under the faucet, and pull down on the lever. Nothing comes out.

You've got to be fucking kidding me. No coffee? Not that I really need it to survive, but there's no reason it should be empty, not with this many people walking around. I scan the room and spot a coffee station across from me. Thank God.

I go to that carafe, place my cup underneath, and pull down on the handle. Empty again.

Seriously?

"Jesus," I mutter, whipping around to the first person who passes me. "Hey, are you going to refill the coffee?"

The girl stumbles back, her long black hair floating over her shoulders as her dark eyes widen at me.

"I . . ."

I thrust the cup at her. "Coffee, please. If you're going to make me get here at seven and then wait around for an hour and a half, the least you can do is get me coffee."

"That's not my job," she says, trying to hand the cup back to me.

"Don't care. Coffee . . . please." When she doesn't move, I grow angrier and lean in so our faces are only a foot apart. "I'm not above reporting you. I said please, so find me some coffee. Thank you."

Her lips twist to the side as her eyes search mine, fear and anger lacing them before she turns away. "Right away . . . ," she says before mumbling something under her breath that I can't quite hear and speeding away. I drag my hand over my face—I just took out my irritation on an innocent PA. Ten bucks says when she returns, there's something foreign in my coffee.

I'm not in a good frame of mind for this. Crafting, being creative, using my hands to make things . . . yeah, not in my wheelhouse.

Need someone for a debate? I'm your guy.

Need someone to stick up for you, research the facts, and make a valid argument? Look no further.

But wedding invites? Tiered cakes? Wedding playlists? Hell . . . I should have walked away when I had the chance.

Fucking Thad and his guilt trip.

Fingers pressed into my brow, I make my way back to where Thad and Naomi are finishing off their sandwiches and talking to two men. When Thad spots me, he says, "Alec, get over here—I want you to meet Declan and Cohen." Then his eyes narrow as I approach. "What happened to taming the beast with some coffee?"

"Don't get me started," I mutter as I turn to the two men. Both tall, both fit, both looking just as terrified as me.

"Cohen, Declan, this is my brother, Alec. Alec, this is Cohen and Declan, one of the couples we're competing against."

Couple? Ahh hell. Hate to admit it, but there is no way we're going to stand a chance against what I can only describe as a dark, short-haired Thor and an Asian Clark Kent. I love my brother, but he has nothing on these two, especially when his fiancée is chowing down on a triple-decker cheese sandwich and has mustard on her chin.

"Nice to meet you," I say, giving them both a handshake. I stick my hands in my pockets. "Either of you creative?"

Declan adjusts his glasses. "Cohen is a carpenter, and his sister is our secret weapon. What about you?"

"Well . . . we know how to tie our shoes, so at least we have that going for us," I say, dread spreading through me at the thought of two months of weekends washed away . . . for nothing.

Thad knocks me in the stomach, buckling me over slightly. "We can do more than just tie our shoes—we are multitalented."

At bullshitting.

"Naomi has quite the eye for design."

"Love bright colors," Naomi chimes in, mustard still on her chin.

So the set must be quite appealing to her.

"And I am an excellent baker," Thad says. "Just the other day I made a batch of scones that would have had Queen Elizabeth herself kissing my knuckles in appreciation."

What is he talking about? I've had his scones before—they could crack a tooth if you're not careful.

"And Alec here . . . well, he's our ringer. A lawyer by day, but a regular old Martha Stewart, minus Snoop Dogg, at night."

Wow, where the hell is that coming from? Sure, I can make a pot roast in the slow cooker and fold a fitted sheet properly, but that's the extent of my Martha Stewart abilities.

"We are quite the team to worry about," Thad adds.

"That's so great. I'm excited to see what you guys come up with," Declan says as Cohen stares at the ground. The quiet type, it seems. "I'm here to help, but Luna and Cohen are the ones who are going to lead the team."

"Luna, that's a pretty name," Naomi says, finally wiping the mustard off her chin. At least we have that going for us now—all three with clean chins.

"Speaking of which, there you are," Declan says as a cup of coffee is thrust toward me, spilling over the side and onto my shoe.

"Luna," Cohen lightly scolds, but the boldness in her eyes doesn't waver as she looks up at me.

Fuuuuuck . . . not a PA.

Nope, the girl with the raven-black hair and dark eyes is my competition.

"Here you go, Master. Added some cream and sugar and something extra special." She winks, and I inwardly cringe, wondering what that "extra-special" thing could be. "Is there anything else you would like me to get you, Your Majesty?" Wow, she doesn't hold back at all, which only makes the situation worse as four pairs of eyes stare at me, the most intimidating being her brother's.

"Uhh . . . ," I say, at a loss for words.

"Because if you need something else, you'll need to make your demands now before we start filming. I can't possibly do two things at once, despite what you might think. So, any more requests?" Hands on her hips, she taps her foot.

At the challenge in her gaze, I attempt to laugh it off with a joke that falls completely flat. "Homemade doughnuts tomorrow morning, delivered straight to me, hot and fresh from the fryer. Thanks." Her eyes narrow, and with a whip of her head, she grabs Cohen's and Declan's hands and drags them away.

Yeah, probably not the best thing to say to an already-angry girl, someone I'll be seeing every weekend for the next two months. Apparently she doesn't quite get my humor.

"Why the hell did you piss her off?" Thad asks, smacking my arm again once they're out of earshot. "She doesn't seem like someone you should piss off. She actually looks like she could see straight through your soul and use it to take you down." He looks off toward the group, clustered around a workbench and clearly talking about me—they keep glancing over their shoulders in my direction. "And I don't know about you, but I would rather be friends with the competition, not enemies. Did you see the muscles on Cohen? What if we need him to lift something? And Declan, he looked like he knew his numbers. He tried to be modest, but I bet you anything that dude knows how to budget, down to the last penny. That was really stupid of you, Alec. Really fucking stupid. You put us at a disadvantage already. And why ask her for coffee? Clearly she's not a PA."

I drag my hand down my face. "Shut the fuck up, Thad."

"I think this is it," a female voice says from behind us. "Are you one of the families competing in *The Wedding Game*?" I turn to find three women standing side by side: two girls in their late twenties, one blonde with deep-blue eyes, one brunette with deep-brown eyes, and an older woman who looks just like the taller blonde.

Oh hell.

A lesbian couple.

We're toast.

◆　◆　◆

Team Hernandez

Contestants: *Luciana, Amanda, and Helen—the overbearing mother with an unbelievably loud opinion on pretty much everything (shoes, workstations, lighting, the nose on the cameraman). You name it, she has an opinion.*

Experience: *Amanda is a personal trainer. Luciana owns and operates her own doggy day spa. Helen is skilled in telling everyone how things should be.*

Notes: *Nauseatingly kind, always smiling, and have admitted more than once to wearing matching pajamas to bed . . . because they can.*

Team Rossi

Contestants: *Cohen, Declan, and Luna—the scowling sister who has a hard time laughing off an awkward encounter.*

Experience: *Declan is a public schoolteacher with secret budgeting skills (hearsay), Cohen is a carpenter with a well-honed death glare, and Luna is a jack of all trades, master of everything (at least that's what she said in her intro).*

Notes: *There is no doubt in anyone's mind who's going to win. Not just from experience but from the terrifying look of determination and competitiveness in Luna Rossi's midnight eyes.*

Team Baxter

Contestants: *Thad, Naomi, and Alec—the saddest-looking trio.*

Experience: *Zero. (Unless bullshitting about being the next Martha Stewart and having a "keen sense" of what's trending counts.)*

Notes: *What kind of lies were transcribed on the application in order to be picked to participate? Team has a penchant for mistaking fellow contestants as coffee runners and hides gummy worms in pockets.*

"And cut. Great intros, everyone. Thank you. Take five, and then we'll get started with the first challenge," the director, Diane DeBoss, says. I look up from my notes on the competition as Diane removes her headphones and grabs Mary DIY, the host who is also one of the judges. The teams are at their respective workbenches, and four sets of cameras move around, setting up for the next take while Diane and Mary DIY make their way to their respective chairs to go over the script.

Mary DIY made quite the entrance when she arrived on set: dropping her robe to the floor, fluffing her blonde locks, and cinching her hands at her waist while adjusting the belt of her dress.

I have to admit, she's gorgeous, but not very welcoming. In my opinion, a good host would have come up to each team, introduced herself, and then gotten to know us—or at least our names. But Mary walked on set right before we began, plastered on a smile, and introduced each team to the cameras. Now she's wearing the aforementioned robe that she haphazardly tossed to the ground, and she's getting her hands rubbed down while Diane talks to her about her perfect angle.

Christ, it's not like she's a movie star. It's a crafty wedding show, for fuck's sake.

"Stare longer. Maybe you won't look as creepy," Thad says next to me.

"She's a diva," I say, pulling my gaze away.

"A diva with beautiful hair," Naomi cuts in. "Do you think she has extensions?"

"Easily," Thad says. "I spend enough time with executives' wives to know what extensions look like, and she has them."

"Wow, a talent you should have listed in our intro—might have boosted our self-esteem a little more," I say sarcastically.

"What's that supposed to mean?" Thad asks.

I lower my voice. "Look around. We're clearly the underdogs, with no chance of winning."

"What?" Thad actually looks shocked. "That's not true. We have a strong team. A very strong team. If you'd accepted my invite to dinner last night, you would have marveled at the talents we were able to write down on paper, *and* you would have taken part in our wedding action plan. But you missed out, and now you're questioning me?" He points to his chest and shakes his head. "Participation in all activities is key, Alec. But if I must reiterate, we are quick, we're fierce, and we have a fourth member." Thad rubs Naomi's belly. "Baby Baxter is on duty."

"Ah yes, I heard fetuses are experts at wielding a glue gun." I drag my hand over my face in exasperation.

Thad's face falls. "You're in a bad mood." Wow, he's a regular old Sherlock Holmes. "Is this because of the coffee miscommunication? Are you uncomfortable because she keeps staring daggers at you?"

I glance toward Luna, whose head is down as she draws something on a piece of paper. "No."

"I don't believe you." Thad nudges me toward the middle of the floor. "Go apologize."

I hold my ground. "I'm not apologizing."

"You really should apologize. We don't want bad blood with the other contestants." He nudges me again.

"I'm not fucking apologizing."

Nudge.

Nudge.

"Go on."

"Stop pushing me."

Nudge.

"Don't be scared." Nudge. "She's a little thing—she won't bite."

"The little things are usually what bite."

Thad glances over my shoulder. "She doesn't look like she has sharp teeth. She won't break skin. Now go."

Nudge.

"Stop, Thad. I'm not—"

"Hey, Luna," Thad calls out, pushing me to the other side of the aisle, where I stumble against Team Rossi's workbench. "Alec wants to apologize."

Repair your relationship with your brother.

It will be great.

It will bring you closer together.

Family is everything.

Do it for the baby . . . the baby you want a relationship with.

Bullshit . . . it's all bullshit. My feelings for my brother are shifting from annoyed to hateful.

"He's very sensitive. Likes his hair stroked for reassurance," Thad adds with a smile.

Scratch that, I'm not *starting* to have hateful feelings. I have them. Hateful, hateful feelings.

Because I have no other option, I turn toward Luna, who quickly sweeps the paper she was drawing on behind her back and scowls at me—a look I'm becoming very familiar with.

"Hiding secrets behind your back?" I ask, straightening up. Cohen and Declan both take off toward the bathroom, leaving me alone with Luna and the heaping pile of disdain sitting between us.

"Mind your own business," she shoots back.

"You're friendly," I say sarcastically.

Her brows raise. "Are you kidding right now? Kind of the pot calling the kettle black, don't you think?"

"No. I'm a nice guy." A nice guy who's living in his own personal hell surrounded by crafts and mushy love.

"Is that your opinion? Or do other people actually think that, because I can say I'm a unicorn until I'm blue in the face, but it isn't true until someone else validates it."

"That's not accurate at all. I don't need another human's validation to characterize myself."

Her face reddens in anger. "You're not a nice person. Now go away so I can finish my idea. I don't want you stealing it."

Back away, Alec. Back away.

But I can't seem to listen to the voice of reason. I'm irritated, Thad has pushed all the right buttons to heighten that irritation level, and frankly . . . I'm embarrassed.

Embarrassed that everyone on set seems to have a connection with their loved ones while I'm struggling to find common ground with my brother. I knew going into this that it wasn't going to be easy, but this hard, this soon? There doesn't seem to be any reasoning with Thad, and we haven't even started to compete; we've only done the intros.

And for some reason, the anger that's building up inside me has to be spilled out somewhere. Luna seems to be the lucky one to receive the wrath.

I place my hand on the workbench and lean forward. "I am a nice person," I say through clenched teeth, like if I say it any harder, I can Jedi mind trick her into thinking it. "And I don't want to steal your ideas because I'm sure they're not as good as the ones I have up here." I tap my temple. I know full well there are zero wedding ideas up top, but a guy's got to save face, you know?

"Oh yeah, I'm sure a divorce attorney has a lot of ideas. If anyone knows anything about weddings and marriage, it's the person who helps rich assholes get out of them."

Well, she's fucking rude. She has no idea what I actually do and whom I represent.

"Told you he was a great guy," Thad calls out. "Real stand-up fella. Great at apologies too, huh, Luna?"

We both ignore him as we start the most epic staredown of the century.

Gloves on. Ding, ding, ding . . . time to duke it out.

"Judging a book by its cover, huh?"

She tilts her head to the side, lips pursed. "I don't have to flip open the cover to know what's inside."

"Oh yeah?" I fold my arms over my chest. "Please, enlighten me about myself."

She doesn't even blink. "You're an entitled asshole who believes everyone works for him. You spend your career dissolving marriages rather than creating them. You're rude and have acquired no manners in the"—she looks me up and down—"thirty years you've been alive."

"Thirty-two."

She rolls her eyes. "In the thirty-two years you've been alive, and frankly, Helen was right. Your shoes are hideous."

I glance down at my black loafers. "What's wrong with my shoes?"

"Entirely too fancy for a show like this."

"Well, I'm not about to wear work boots."

"And a snob as well," she huffs, bringing her paper back out and examining it but not showing me anything.

"You think you have me all figured out, don't you?"

"Doesn't take a genius to spot a rotten tomato."

Wow . . . just . . . wow.

"Well, it doesn't take a genius to spot a self-absorbed egomaniac either," I say, forgetting that the whole point of getting pushed over here was to apologize.

Her eyes whip up to mine. "Egomaniac? How do you figure? Because the way I see it, an egomaniac would never have gotten a self-righteous boob some coffee."

"Jack of all trades, master of every one," I repeat, ignoring her comeback, because frankly it's a little true, and I'm trying to make a damn point here.

"Uh . . . okay." Her confused look is almost cute . . . almost.

"That's what egomaniacs say." It's an incredibly weak argument, especially for an attorney, but with very limited research, it's all I've got.

She doesn't answer right away. Instead, she studies me . . . hard.

It's unfortunate that she's gorgeous. Smooth skin, dark lashes, silky hair, and lips that look entirely too tempting. But the scorn in this girl's eyes ruins any chance at actually getting to know her.

Her tongue runs over her teeth, and then she gives me the slowest once-over I've ever experienced. Starting at my shoes, which she raises a brow at—*seriously, what's wrong with them?*—up to my torso, and then stopping at my eyes. She crosses her arms over her chest and very calmly says, mind you, with a smile, "You're reaching."

What a wench.

She's a goddamn wench.

"You're obnoxious," I shoot back, reverting to an admittedly juvenile comeback.

But . . . she joins me.

"You're pompous."

"You're repugnant."

Her mouth falls open for a second before she says, "You're terribly unpleasant."

"You're . . . you're short." *Good one, Alec.*

"You have horrendous taste in shoes."

"There's nothing—" I take a deep breath. "There is nothing wrong with my shoes. But there is something wrong with your personality." I give her a once-over too. "And taste in clothing. 1990 called—they want their bedazzler back."

Luna gives me a look that could tear any man in half.

"I suggest you walk away," she practically spits at me.

"Already on it. Hope your glue gun burns your finger off."

Before she can respond, I stride back to our workstation, where Thad has his hands clasped, waiting impatiently for my return.

"How did it go?"

"Swimmingly," I mutter.

Thad grips my shoulder. "I knew you could do it. See? A little apology goes a long way."

In this case, I'm sure name-calling is going to go a long way too . . . but in the wrong direction.

Chapter Six

LUNA

His shoes really aren't ugly, but ugh . . . he made me so mad I had to do something about it.

"Are you breathing heavily for a reason?" Cohen asks me.

"What were you doing in the bathroom for so long?" I snap, my irritation at an all-time high.

The nerve of that man.

Alec Baxter.

Divorce attorney, as we learned in the intros. No special talents but apparently knows how to make a wicked pot roast.

Ha, doubtful.

Pot roast is only wickedly delicious when caressed every hour while in the Crock-Pot. Everyone knows this. Alec doesn't seem like a caresser: he's more of a dump it, leave it, and eat it kind of Crock-Pot human. Just because it steams and cooks the food on its own doesn't mean it should be left unattended. Crock-Pot meals need friends too!

Bet the guy doesn't have any friends, not with his surly, ostentatious attitude.

"Get me coffee . . ."

Honestly, who talks to other humans like that? We all have to unzip our flies when we pee, which means we should all be treated equally. That's how I see it. Apparently, Alec's pants magically vanish when he has to pee and then reappear when he's done. Must be fun in public restrooms, his two butt cheeks just hanging out in the open. Talk about an awkward encounter.

And yes, I spat in his coffee, multiple times. Three to be exact, and I'm not even sorry about it. I know he didn't drink it. I watched him toss it in the trash can and mumble something to himself, but the sheer fact that he had the coffee he'd demanded but couldn't drink it was all I needed to feel justified.

I felt like I got what I needed, and yes, I might have been scowling from time to time during intros, but it was because I couldn't believe the man's audacity. And then having to watch him so effortlessly talk to the camera with that handsome, stupid face of his . . . it irritated me more than I care to admit.

Yes, handsome; the man is handsome. I want to say his face looks like a garbage can and call it a day, but we all know that would be a lie, and do you know why? Because, I swear on my Cricut Maker—my most prized tool—Alec Baxter is Chris Evans's long-lost twin brother, but I think we know who ended up with the winning personality . . . and who didn't.

Don't want to take my word for it? Well, Declan even leaned in and whispered, "He looks just like Chris Evans without the shaggy beard." Yup, just annoyingly smooth man skin.

Man skin and pretty eyes. Not Chris Evans blue, but this pretty green that seems to darken when he throws insults. I would refer to it as "meadow green." Not that it matters, because it doesn't. He's rude and abhorrent.

And that apology was laughable. It wasn't even an apology. And I felt myself sinking down to his level, tossing insults right back at him. That's not something I do. I actually never get this wound up over anyone. Maybe I'm overreacting a little because I still haven't had a chance to introduce myself to Mary DIY. Or any of the judges, for that matter, though they're all standing at the other end of the set, clustered around what they're calling a "craft services table." Marco Vitally, the king of wedding invitations, is present, looking handsome as ever with his signature black hat and wedding-themed tattoos that cascade up his forearms and disappear under his shirtsleeves. Standing beside him is Henrietta Hornet, a staple in the wedding-planning community who started out her career throwing parties for children but is now world renowned for her lavish celebrity weddings. The type of weddings we peasants could only dream of. I ignore a stab of jealousy as she turns and murmurs something to our third judge, Katherine Barber, cake master with a perpetually sour face. She's the reason there was an epidemic of lavender in cakes in New York City. She made it popular.

But Mary DIY, *sigh*, she's a goddess with a pair of scissors, a goddess I have yet to say hi to. Not that meeting her is the reason I'm here, but *hello*, we're breathing the same air—it would be nice if I could grab her attention for two seconds.

"Did you hear me?" Cohen asks, poking me in the side.

"What?"

"What's going on with you? You're acting weird."

Giving Cohen my full attention, I turn my back on Team Baxter. "What were you doing in the bathroom for so long?"

"I peed and then grabbed a quick bite of a muffin. Thad was raving about them, so I wanted to try one. That okay with you, Mother?"

"Don't call me that."

Declan looks at his watch. "It's been longer than five minutes. Think I can grab a muffin too?"

"Not if you're going to take as long as Cohen."

"Hey." Cohen pokes me in the arm. "You're the one who dragged us here, so lighten up."

Guilt instantly hits me, and I press my hand to my forehead. "Sorry," I say. "I'm just . . . irritated. That Alec guy really presses my buttons."

"Which buttons?" Declan asks, raising his brows suggestively.

"Not those buttons." *Yes, those buttons.* "While you guys were gone, Thad sent him over here to apologize, and all he did was pick a fight with me."

"He's scared," Cohen says casually, as if he can see right into Alec's soul. "Knows they don't stand a chance against us." Smiling for the first time since we've been here, he adds, "He knows the gays always win when it comes to weddings."

"Facts." Declan offers Cohen a fist bump, and just like that my mood brightens. I can see the excitement in their eyes, the confidence, and Cohen actually looks like he's ready to tackle this competition.

I shake off the presence of Alec Baxter and set my drawing on the workbench. "Look at what I came up with for a chuppah."

"We're not Jewish," Declan points out. "Not even close to it. Catholic and Chinese American, care to forget that?"

"Noooo," I drag out. "You don't have to be Jewish to be married under a chuppah. If we were sticking to Chinese tradition for Declan, then you guys would have multiple 'costume' changes, or at least the one who wants to act as the bride would."

Both Declan and Cohen stare at each other for a second. "And who might the bride be?" Declan asks.

I smile. "Isn't it obvious?"

"No," they say at the same time.

"Cohen. He's more moody." I wink and go back to my drawing as Declan laughs.

"I'm not moody," Cohen grumbles but then hunkers down next to me as I lay out my chuppah idea.

"Okay, bro." I pat his hand and turn to Declan. "This reminds me—are there any cultural traditions you would like included in the wedding?"

He nods. "The tea ceremony, but we can do that the night before the wedding. I spoke with my parents, and since it's more of an intimate ceremony, they would like to keep it out of the spotlight. They would also like to be in charge, so you don't have to worry about it."

"Got it." I smile. "Does Cohen need to wear a dress for that?"

Declan laughs out loud. "It will be required."

"What's a wedding without a theme?" Mary DIY says as she spreads her arms, shining brightly at the camera.

She's so magical.

"The families are going to have thirty minutes to devise a wedding theme from the mystery objects behind me, which are meant to serve as inspiration. They are to create a vision board that incorporates an overall theme, colors, and a catchy phrase that describes their wedding. Once a family takes an object, that object is off the table, so think fast, families. Your dream wedding might be swiped away by another contestant before you can say 'wedding bells.' And remember, whatever you put on your vision board must be incorporated into your wedding, so be careful with what you choose." Mary moves to the button that will flip down the curtain and reveal the vision-board materials. "Contestants ready?"

Clad in our team-color aprons—Rossi is pink, Hernandez is blue, and Baxter is purple—we all stand behind the competition line and get in position.

Before today, I sat down with Cohen and Declan and, knowing the show's format, went over the challenges I knew we would face. We drew up plans for each one so we'd know what we'd be looking for going into each challenge. Preparation is key.

Prepared, I nod and get into a runner's position, with reclaimed wood and tree trunks on my mind. Cohen is in charge of eucalyptus and greens. Declan must find all the lace and burlap.

"On your marks, get set . . . plan." Mary hits the button. The curtain falls, revealing the giant display, and for a brief moment, I'm overwhelmed.

I've seen supply reveals many times, and I always shout at the contestants on TV to use their heads. I've never realized why they flail about until this very minute.

A large countdown clock is right above the display, there are what feels like a million options, and everyone is rushing to the table at the same time, causing such a commotion that you have no time to think.

Tulle and flowers, birdcages and vases, pearls and . . . gah! The insanity!

"Remember, whatever you grab and put on your workbench must be used!" Mary shouts as I finally snap out of it and hurry to the table where Team Hernandez is already digging in. They've grabbed a lace tablecloth. Damn it.

"Burlap, find the burlap!" I shout to Declan, who is furiously looking through a pile of tablecloths.

"Luna, mason jar," Cohen says, tossing me a glass mason jar that I miraculously catch.

"Don't throw things!" I yell, but I run it back to our workbench because it's a great find.

"I don't see any burlap!" Declan calls out.

"Keep searching!" I scream, my voice sounding more shrill than normal. At the very end of the table, I see wooden objects, and I quickly take off to grab them all—and run straight into Alec's chest. Like I've run into a brick wall, I smash my face against his pecs and stumble backward. On my way down, I reach for anything to grab on to, which turns out to be Helen's apron strings. She spins away from the table and lands on top of me.

"Sabotage!" she shouts as her arms flail around my head. "Judges, she is sabotaging me."

"I am not!" I reply, trying to push her off me, desperate to get to the wood. "I accidentally grabbed on to you." I glance up to find Alec staring down at me. For a brief second I can sense him wanting to reach out to help me up, but it's fleeting, and he instead takes off, clutching a bundle of palm fronds. *Jerk!*

"She was headed for the wood. Luciana, grab the wood while I have her down!" Helen calls out, clearly not understanding the word *accident*.

"What? No! Get off me." I try to shove the old woman now, but the broad holds her ground, pinning me to the floor. "Judges, judges, is this legal?" I look back toward the cameras and the crew, who are all just standing there, laughing. Great, I know what they're thinking: *perfect television.*

Looks like it's every man for himself.

"Cohen, the wood, for the love of God, the wood!"

Before I can locate Cohen, Alec steps over me to go back to the display, where Thad is running in place, hands on his head, yelling, "I can't decide, I can't decide! What? Naomi, put that down. We are not having a circus wedding! Are you out of your beautiful mind? You're pregnant—go sit down."

"Hey!" she replies, clutching the colorful glass figurine. "I'm carrying a child—I'm not an invalid."

Thad gestures to me, still struggling to push away a fifty-year-old. "Do you see the mess of limbs on the ground? That could be you. Now put the clown down and step away from the table."

"It's not a clown, it's a . . . a . . ."

"It's a clown!" Thad shouts.

"This isn't a clown."

"It's a clown," Alec says, being the relay person for Thad, who is now picking up random objects.

"Got the wood!" Cohen shouts.

"Still no burlap," Declan announces.

"Ooo, feathers," Thad gleefully cheers.

"Do we want the clown?" Luciana asks.

"Let me see the clown!" Helen calls out, now straddling my stomach.

"How dare you!" Thad snatches the clown away. "That's our clown."

"No stealing!" Mary DIY calls out. *Oh, now she intervenes.*

"We saw it first," Thad says.

"And you set it down. Your loss!" Helen calls out.

Luciana snatches the clown and shows it to Amanda, who shakes her head, and the poor clown is tossed back on the table . . . where Declan picks it up.

"Do we want the clown?"

"Put the clown down, for the love of God!" I scream. "Burlap, Declan, find the freaking burlap!"

"Two more minutes at the table, then return to your workstations!" Mary calls out.

"Ugh, get . . . off . . . me." I shove Helen with all my might, but she doesn't budge.

So . . . I pinch her.

"You nasty rat," she yelps, and she jumps just enough for me to roll away, right into Alec's shoes. He topples over me from the force of my roll. Our bellies touch, our bodies forming a cross.

"Watch it!" he says, just as something crashes down to the floor.

We all pause, and silence falls as we stare at the shattered glass on the ground.

The clown.

Naomi stands over it, tears welling up in her eyes. "Oh no . . ."

Looks like no one will be using the clown.

No time for a memorial. I push Alec away, finally stand, and scour the tables.

Skeletons, no.

Disney princesses, no.

Shrek. What? No.

Camo, no.

Playing cards, no.

"Thirty seconds."

"Crap." I sift through the items, tossing boas and scarves to the side.

"Look, a boa," Thad says, snaking one away from me. He wraps it around his neck. "Alec, want a boa?"

"I'd rather stick my dick in a pickle jar."

"What?" I whip my head around just as Amanda swoops in next to me.

"Found the burlap, Mom."

The rough texture of the fabric slides under my hand, and before it disappears, I clutch it in my palm.

"Drop it," I say through clenched teeth.

"You don't have to be—"

"I said, drop it, Amanda. I have no problem driving my elbow into your breast."

Her eyes widen, and she drops the burlap just as the timer goes off. "To your workstations!" Mary calls out as guilt floods me.

"I'm sorry," I quickly say to Amanda, who looks terrified to even be within a ten-foot radius of me. I can feel the crazy in my eyes, the snarl of my lips, the tension in my neck that's likely making every vein pop out. Cohen's not the only one with a throbbing vein. Lucky for me, it runs in the family.

She dodges my gaze and hurries back to her workbench.

Damn it.

"Luna, come on!" Cohen calls out, waving me over to our bench.

It's the first time I'm getting a chance to take in everything we collected and, to be honest, I could not be more proud of Cohen and Declan, especially because I was trapped under Helen's ass for the majority of the challenge.

"You may purge one item!" Mary calls out. "Only one, so if you just so happened to collect something that won't work, put it in your purge box, but beware: another team is allowed to steal."

Knowing how it works, I lay everything out and assess. Greens, creams, and natural wood. Textures, soft and hard. And rustic all around. I look up at Declan and Cohen and give them a giant smile. "I think we have a winner here, boys."

"America picks the wedding winners, but our judges pick the challenge winners, and the judges have spoken."

Standing between Declan and Cohen, I hold their hands and can't stop looking at what we've put together for a vision board. Stunningly beautiful, it's romantic and natural with earth tones—everything the boys wanted.

I glance over at Team Hernandez and wince just slightly. Even though I love our board, I can't help but fall in love with theirs too. Filled with pastel pinks, cream, and gold, their vision board is decked out in dream catchers, macramé, flourishes of green, and succulents.

Obsessed.

Then . . . there's Team Baxter. All I can say is . . . wow.

Just wow.

Pink, green, and yellow, their board is overflowing with feathers, palm leaves, and flamingos kissing. There's no rhyme or reason to the board, no cohesion, just an array of items taped and pinned.

I almost feel bad for them. How on earth are they going to work with that?

Key word being *almost*.

To top it off too, Thad made the team dress up in boas, so the snob himself, Alec Baxter, is sporting a yellow boa—looking like he'd prefer to use it as a noose.

Now we wait quietly as the judges take in our vision boards and make a decision. This is how it is after every challenge: they clean up, and then we're judged. I've seen the show more than a dozen times, and this is the most nerve-racking part, when the judges silently walk around, taking everything in, before deliberating off to the side, never in front of the contestants.

Each vision board is labeled with a theme to give the judges an idea of what we have planned.

Team Rossi's Modern Rustic.

Team Hernandez's Boho Romance.

And . . . Flamingo Dancer. Team Baxter's unfortunate mess of a board. It's practically stapled together and has no cohesion—not to mention they wrote and said *flamingo* dancer, when in actuality it's *flamenco* . . . not the pink bird.

The judges confer for a few more minutes before Mary DIY nods. They separate, and she turns to the camera. "The first-place winner of today's theme challenge will get an extra five hundred dollars to add to their budget. Second place will receive an extra one hundred dollars, and third place will receive nothing."

The extra money would be great, but I know we can deliver a great wedding for under $10,000. If anything, I'm scrappy, and if you give me a spork and an avocado, I can make a beautiful centerpiece.

Based on the vision boards and the judges' reactions, I would say Boho Romance is first, just because they spent the most time marveling at what Luciana, Amanda, and Helen put together. We're surely in second, and the unfortunate Flamingo Dancers will be in third, which makes me feel a little bad for Naomi, who can't seem to stop tearing up about the broken clown. She keeps muttering something about it not being able to live out its destiny. Her pregnancy psychosis is making me rethink ever having children.

"The judges have deliberated, and it was a close competition," Mary continues. "In third place, receiving no extra money, is . . ."

She pauses, the dramatics of it all a little too much.

Flamingo Dancer—just get it over with. We all know who's last.

"Team Rossi."

"What?" I shout before I can even stop myself. "How is that—?" Cohen claps his hand over my mouth before I can say anything rude, and believe me, a rant is simmering on my tongue. There is no way in hell Flamingo Dancer is better than our theme.

"In second place . . ."

"This is an outrage," I mutter as Cohen shushes me and squeezes my hand.

"Team Hernandez, which means Team Baxter adds five hundred dollars to their overall budget."

A shrill scream fills the set. You'd think it came from Naomi, but nope, she's frozen in silent shock along with Alec as Thad puts his hands on his hips and starts doing an Irish jig.

"Hell yeah! I knew the feathers would tickle the judges' fancy." Thad winks, and it's right then and there that I decide Alec is paying off the judges.

It's the only explanation.

How on earth would they even consider feather boas and palm leaves a number one wedding theme? It screams tacky. They might as well have stuck the clown in there.

While Mary talks about next week's episode and challenge, I stew between Declan and Cohen, staring down Alec and watching his every move. Is he nodding at the judges? Winking? Making any kind of gesture that would represent being in cahoots?

He swipes his finger under his nose, and I shout, "Ah ha!"

All eyes focus on me as Diane yells, "Cut!" She sighs. "Please, no outbursts while Mary is talking."

"Sorry." I wave my hand in apology and melt behind Declan and Cohen. While Mary jumps back into her closing statements, I glance back at Alec, who's looking at me, a smirk on his face. A knowing smile. The kind of smile that says . . . "Gotcha."

To which I silently respond . . . *No chance in hell, you pretentious, snobby, loafer-wearing, flamingo-themed-wedding Chris Evans look-alike.*

Think he could read all that in my eyes?

Chapter Seven

Luna

"Hey, you're home . . . uh-oh. Why are the fudge-striped cookies out and dangling off your fingers?" Farrah asks as she shuts the door to our apartment and sets her purse on the side table in the entryway.

I hold up my bag of booze with my cookie-free hand. "I'm drinking this too."

"You brought out Parrot Bay?" Farrah winces. "I'm guessing today didn't go well?"

"An understatement." I take a giant sip from my straw. "Grab one, join me. There's a strawberry daiquiri with your name on it."

Farrah, being the loyal friend she is, doesn't even ask questions. Nope, she strips out of her pants—just like I did—leaves them in the entryway, and then goes to the freezer, where she collects her sugar-laden alcoholic beverage of choice and joins me.

We clink the plastic bags together, and Farrah starts decorating her fingers with cookies as well.

I nibble on one of mine but don't break it off. Frankly, these decorative cookie rings are the only thing I have going for me at the moment.

"Lay it on me. Was the competition tough?"

"Lesbians," I mutter, leaning back, my booze bag clutched to my chest.

"Lesbians are on the show?"

I nod. "The lesbians—"

"Names, Luna, names. I know you're upset, but lesbians have names too."

I give her a look. "Luciana and Amanda, along with Amanda's overbearing mother, named Helen, who sat on my stomach while we had to collect items for the theme of our wedding."

"Luciana and Amanda," Farrah says dreamily. "Short or long hair?"

"What? Long—blonde and brunette. Does it matter?"

"Long-haired lesbians—oh, I see you, *Wedding Game*, trying to get the male demographic involved." She shakes her head. "Perverts."

"Are you even listening? Get over the lesbians. A middle-aged woman sat on my stomach today."

"I heard you. I thought the lesbians were more important than your demise. It's not very often you get to see lesbians in the wild, especially on television."

"That's not true. There's plenty of lesbian representation."

"Name some. Name some major network TV series that have lesbians."

"Well . . . *Ellen*—"

"Got canceled shortly after the gay episode. Next."

"*Will & Grace*—"

"Main characters are stereotypical gay men that the media portrays as fun and exciting. What about the fun and exciting lesbians? They're always tool-belt wearing, short haired, and hot tempered."

I think on it, truly think on it, and yes, she has a point, but there has to be some lesbian representation . . .

"*Glee* . . . oh, and duh, *Grey's Anatomy*."

She mulls it over, sips her pouch, and says, "I'll give you *Grey's Anatomy*."

"Oh, and *The Fosters*."

"Ehh, not major network TV."

"This is getting off topic."

"Just trying to give the lesbians some love."

"Which I appreciate because lesbians need love too . . . but can we focus on how the elderly sat on me today?"

"Yes, sorry." She clears her throat. "So a crazy mom sat on you."

"She did, but if I'm honest, that's not the worst thing that happened to me."

"A lady sitting on you is tame? In comparison to what?" She bites down on a cookie and eats it whole. "What the hell happened?"

Staring off, I mutter, "Alec Baxter."

"Ohhh, I'm intrigued. Who is this Alec Baxter you speak of?"

"Brother to one of the contestants. Divorce attorney. Rude. Thought I was a production assistant."

"How so?"

We both take long sips of our drinks, and the bitter cold of the frozen alcohol hits me directly in the brain, freezing it over for a few torturous moments. Once the pain subsides, I say, "He stopped me on set and demanded I bring him coffee."

"He didn't," Farrah gasps.

"He did." I chew on a cookie, narrowing it down to just a ring that I easily pop in my mouth. "Yelled at me, actually, for not refilling the carafe, blamed me for having to get to set early, and sure, he said 'please' and 'thank you,' but he didn't mean it. You can't say 'please' and 'thank you' with malice dripping off the tip of your tongue."

"God, I hate when malice drips," Farrah says sarcastically.

"Dripping malice is hot garbage."

"Total hot garbage." We clink our drinks again and down them until the bags are sucked dry. "Want another?" Farrah asks.

"Do you even have to ask?"

She gets up from the couch and heads to the freezer, where she pokes holes in the bags with our reusable straws. "So, he asked you for coffee—the nerve. Then what?"

"His brother told him to apologize to me for being rude."

"So manners do run in the family, even if some of them drip with malice." Farrah hands me my drink and starts stacking her fingers with cookies again.

"Very few manners, but they're there."

"Did he apologize?"

Cheeks puckered, I suck hard, swallow, and then say, "No. Instead, he came over to my workbench in between takes and started insulting me." Granted, I might have started the name-calling, but Farrah doesn't need to know that.

"What did he say?"

"Called me 'repugnant.'" Farrah's eyes widen. "And then he said 1990 wanted their bedazzler back." With my cookie-heavy fingers, I drag them carefully over my beautiful sequin shirt.

Farrah sits up, brows sharpening in pure anger. "He did not."

I nod. "He so did."

Looking away, she whispers, "The motherfucker."

"And to top it all off, we had to put together the themes for the wedding today, and Cohen, Declan, and I built a beautiful vision board for a modern rustic wedding."

"That's so Cohen and Declan."

"Right?" I groan and lean my head back against the couch. "The les—"

"Luciana and Amanda."

"Right, sorry, you would think I'd be more sensitive. Blame the stress of it all." I slurp some more booze, starting to feel the effects of all the sugar and alcohol combined. "Luciana and Amanda put together a boho-chic wedding that made my soul clench with jealousy. God, it was gorgeous, so dreamy." I roll my head to the side and look Farrah in the eye. "And then there was Team Baxter."

"Pretentious?"

"If only." I shake my head. "No, it was themed 'Flamingo Dancer.' Which makes no sense whatsoever. There *were* flamingos on their vision board, but the dance is actually pronounced *flamenco*, and the dancer traditionally wears red with ruffles. It was a hot mess on all fronts."

"What did they have?"

"Pink, yellow, and green with feathers."

"Oh God, that seems hideous."

"It was . . . and yet, the judges picked it for first place and put Team Rossi in last place."

"No way. You can't be serious."

I fiddle with my straw. "Wish I was joking. The judges picked it as their favorite theme, which I'm still racking my brain over. They had palm leaves, for fuck's sake. Palm leaves." I sigh heavily and shake my head. "How am I supposed to help Cohen and Declan win when I'm faced with a theme board that would have been more aptly named 'A Night in 1980s Miami'?"

"Oh, I like that title. I totally would have picked it, based on the title."

"Farrah."

"Oh right, yeah. Boo, Team Baxter. Kick them in the crotch, right in the dingles."

"Maybe no kicks to crotches. Naomi, the soon-to-be wife, is pregnant. The baby doesn't need to know they're going to be birthed into a world where people get kicked in the crotch over a wedding competition."

"You're right. Better let the kid figure that out on their own. But I'm ready to throw some punches."

"I could punch." I pop a cookie in my mouth and lick the melted chocolate off my finger. "I would punch Alec Baxter right in his stupid handsome face."

"Uhhhh, hold on a second." Farrah perks up. "You said handsome."

"Yeah, so?"

"Umm, you didn't mention that he's handsome in your rant."

"What does it matter?" I ask.

"It changes the whole dynamic. You could be hate-crushing on him."

"Have you lost your mind?" I tuck my legs under my butt and curl into my drink, clutching it tightly to my chest while I sip. "I am not hate-crushing on the man. I don't even know him."

"You don't need to know him to crush on him. Looks alone can get the heart pitter-pattering."

"Trust me. There was no pitter-pattering around him."

"Okay, then, tell me this: What does he look like?"

Not giving it a second thought, I say, "Chris Evans, freshly shaven, straight from the gym."

Oh crap.

Farrah throws her head back and laughs. "Oh my God, you are so hate-crushing on him."

"I am not." I bite off my last cookie and chew. "Okay, so yeah, he's attractive, in this Hollywood-hunk type of way, but who really likes Hollywood hunks?"

"Everybody, even your brother."

"He's gay—he doesn't count."

"Oh, he counts. His opinion counts the most." Farrah snags my phone from my hand and starts typing away.

"What are you doing?"

"Asking Cohen if he thinks Chris Evans is attractive."

"No." I fling my body over hers and take the phone away. "He'll know I'm talking about Alec. Even Declan said he looks like Chris

Evans." I set my phone to the side, as far away from Farrah as possible. "Fine, Chris Evans is gorgeous and Alec Baxter has the face of an angel, all chiseled and perfect with smoldering green eyes."

Farrah snorts. "You said smolder. Oh, you are so crushing on him. Bet you wish he was the one sitting on you rather than the demon lady."

Maybe a little.

What am I thinking? No. I want nothing to do with Alec Baxter.

"This conversation is getting out of control. We're losing track of the problem."

"And what's the problem?" Farrah smiles at me.

"Well, you see . . . the problem is . . ."

She laughs some more. "Oh you sooooo like him."

I sooooo don't.

"Mother effer, I'm hurting."

"You're hurting?" Farrah asks. "I'm the one up at six on a Sunday morning because my friend dragged me out of bed so she didn't have to eat greasy food alone."

"I needed a hangover buddy, and I have to report to set by ten today for confessionals."

"I'm going to remember this the next time I need a hangover buddy."

We both plop into our booth, not even needing a menu. Dining Hall, the diner a block away from our apartment, is our second home. We know everyone. I can tell you exactly what the person in the booth before us ate, just from one whiff. The red leather seats are worn, and the subway tiles covering the wall remind me of old-school New York City, which adds to the nostalgia of the diner. The chalkboard up front, listing the specials, hasn't changed since 2016, despite not having the specials anymore.

Meghan Quinn

With one look at us, our favorite waitress, Fay, gives us a brief nod. Two hangover cures coming right up.

"You could have at least let me change into something a little more presentable."

"You look wonderful," I say, leaning my face against the cold, sticky surface of our table. A shower is in my near future, but bacon first.

"I'm wearing a chicken onesie."

I snort. "And you look fantastic in it." Fay sets down two waters and a shot of what she refers to as her cure-all in front of us. We don't ask what's in it.

"Booze bags?" Fay lifts a brow.

"How did you know?" Farrah asks, plugging her nose and throwing back the shot.

"There are two types of hangovers when you girls come in. The first is just a regular hangover, where you look like death but still have your wits about you. Then there's booze-bag drunk, where you both look like you slept in a dumpster and sucked on sugarcane the whole night."

"Yup." I nod and hold up two fingers. "It was number two." I quickly down the shot and start coughing when its heat hits me. "Holy hell, Fay."

She smiles. "Put some extra Tabasco in there to get your legs moving."

"And bowels," Farrah says, gripping her stomach. "Dear heaven, please don't let me do something nasty in this chicken onesie."

Fay gives her a pat on the back. "You know where the bathroom is. Food will be out shortly."

When Fay leaves, I say, "Do you really have to go to the bathroom?"

"Can't be sure. Will let you know."

"Really, I'm good." I hold up my hand and then again rest my pounding head on the cool table. "Four booze bags each was not a good idea."

80

"Should have stopped at two." Farrah flips her hood over her head, revealing the red sewn-in chicken comb on top.

"Agreed." The scent of day-old syrup fills my nose, and to avoid losing my shot on the table, I sit up and press my hands to my forehead. "Did I dance last night?"

"With your sewing bag on your head."

I nod. "That's what I thought. Why the bag?"

"You didn't want to fall and bang your head on a table because, and I quote, you're 'famous now, and Mama needs to protect her face.'"

I chuckle. "Oh yeah. That's right."

"And then you muttered something about not wanting Baxter to have one more thing to pick on."

"Ugh, Alec Baxter." I drop my hands. "I hope his brother accidentally uses his ass as a pincushion."

"From what you told me, he very much might."

I chuckle. "I can hear his girlish cry now."

"Whose? Alec's or the brother's?"

"Thad, the brother's. He has one hell of a shrill cry. When they won, I thought it was Naomi who screamed. Nope, it was Thad." I shake my head, still in disbelief. "Their whole theme screams tacky in every way possible, the title had nothing to do with what was on their board, and everything was haphazardly stuck everywhere. No cohesion, no mix of textures and colors. Truly, one of the biggest pieces of garbage I've ever seen."

"Dumpster fire?"

"Epitome of dumpster fire. If you looked up *dumpster fire* in the Urban Dictionary, you would find a picture of their vision board."

"And yet we still won," a very familiar male voice says as the booth behind me squeaks with someone's movement.

My heart sinks.

Embarrassment screams up the back of my neck, and that familiar Whitney sweat breaks out over my lip.

Farrah's eyes widen, and she points behind me, mouthing, "Chris Evans."

Squeezing my eyes tight, I suck in a deep breath and turn around in my booth, my head screaming with pain from the quick movement. My vision blurs, but when it begins to focus, the first thing I see is a pair of green eyes, followed by a smarmy smile and a chiseled jawline.

Yup, it's "Chris Evans" all right.

"Good morning." He smiles so wide that I instantly want to wipe the grin off his face with the back of my hand. "Looks like last night treated you well. Is that five-dollar booze I smell on you?"

"Technically, two ninety-nine," Farrah chimes in with a lift of her finger.

"Oh, even better."

I narrow my eyes. "What are you doing here? Following me?"

"Yup. That's what I like to do on the weekends—follow irritable egomaniacs around just to annoy them."

"Sounds about right." I cross my arms over my chest and turn to Farrah. "A real creep, this one." I jerk a thumb toward Alec. "Watch out, total pervert."

"You can tell he's a pervert just from his shoes," she responds with a grin.

"You can't even see my shoes," he snaps.

"Heard they were hideous, and that's all I need to know to label you a pervert."

"Ah, I see." He twists so he's now kneeling on the bench and leaning over the top. "Just like your friend, judging a book by its cover."

"So, you're admitting to looking like a pervert?" Farrah asks. Always the best at comebacks, that girl.

"No."

"Then tell me why you're not a pervert."

"Why?" He gives her a good look. "I don't owe you anything, and honestly, I don't think you should be throwing stones in a glass house when it comes to looks."

"Excuse me?"

"*Ba-gawk!*" Alec says in the best impersonation of a chicken I've ever heard. I don't ever want to give this man credit for anything, but that was good, and it takes everything in me not to crack a smile.

Farrah flips her hood down, revealing her mess of hair, sticking up on all ends thanks to the static electricity formed from the fleece lining of her onesie. Yikes, she looks insane.

"I'll have you know, I'm not wearing anything under this besides a ten-year-old bra and a pair of underwear that snaps over my belly button, and even though it's a fashion disaster and I could ruin my budding fashion career by being seen in this, I've never felt so breezy and comfortable in my entire life. So judge all you want, ya chump, but I'm way more comfortable than you."

"I see your friend's just as feisty as you," Alec says to me, his eyes quickly traveling up to my hair and then back to my eyes.

"Why are you here?" I ask, exasperated. "It's bad enough I have to breathe the same air as you in a few hours. Can't you leave me in peace to cure this hangover the right way, by shoving piles of greasy food into my mouth?"

"I'm here because this is my favorite diner and I wanted some proper coffee this morning."

"This is not your favorite diner. This is *my* favorite diner. I've been coming here for two years."

He holds up his hand, fingers spread. "Five years for me—ask Fay. Which means I get squatter's rights. Pick a different place, Martha, this is my diner."

"It's Luna," I say with such venom that Farrah leans over and taps me on the arm.

"I think he was calling you Martha as in Martha Stewart. Is that correct?"

He nods. "Can't slip anything past the chicken."

"I prefer 'hen' if you're going to go the name-calling route."

"My apologies."

Farrah smiles, and for a brief second, I question her loyalty—until she points at him and says, "You're an asshole."

"Okay, that came out of nowhere."

"You can't call my friend 'repugnant.' She is the opposite of that. She's . . . she's . . ." Turning toward me, Farrah whispers, "What's the opposite of repugnant?"

"Uhh . . . if he weren't here, I would totally look it up in my phone—"

"Pleasant," he groans, dragging his hand over his face.

"Thank you," Farrah says, but then turns her stern face back on. "She's 'pleasant.'"

"Is that so? Do pleasant people usually talk about others behind their backs in such an abhorrent manner?"

"She wasn't being abhorrent. That was the leftover booze talking. It has to seep out of you like the devil, slowly bringing you back to life. Anything you overheard is clearly just Satan himself exiting the body."

"Interesting." He scratches the side of his jaw. "So, what explains her behavior yesterday?"

"Simple," Farrah says. "Your shoes were offensive."

"Jesus fuck," he mutters, shaking his head. "Just for that, I'm wearing them again." He turns toward me. "And I would appreciate it if you didn't talk about my brother the way you just did. You don't even know him."

Guilt floods me. I don't want to admit it, but . . . he's right.

CHAPTER EIGHT
ALEC

What are the chances that I would run into Luna Rossi, the diabolical jack of all trades, somewhere other than *The Wedding Game* set?

She must live close to me if she goes to Dining Hall and shows up in her pajamas. No matter how good the grease tastes here, no self-respecting New Yorker is going to travel farther than a few blocks in their red heart pajama pants.

So the question is, Have we seen each other before? Have we sat back to back at the diner before? Passed each other on the street? Flagged down the same taxi? It's a weird sensation, wondering if the person you just met might be someone you've been crossing paths with for years.

I saw the train wreck walk in. The "hen" caught my eye first because it's not every day you see a grown-ass woman in a chicken onesie. I didn't even know Luna was sitting behind me until she said my name. Her rendition of the day before was fun, but hearing her unguarded opinion was even more entertaining—she's got me all wrong.

Thad, on the other hand. Could not have been more accurate, at least in the dramatics department, but that doesn't mean she has the right to talk about him like that behind his back. I can say he screams like a girl because he's my brother, but when someone else says it, they're crossing a line.

Which, from the look on Luna's face, she realizes she just did.

Despite the attitude she seems to sport whenever I'm around—and yes, I'll own up to the coffee mistake that launched this battle—I will say, it doesn't seem like she's usually so vindictive.

From the way she was interacting with her brother and soon-to-be brother-in-law yesterday, I could tell she's compassionate, empathetic—despite all the yelling for burlap—and she listens intently. And the way she nods in agreement; it's not just a regular nod. You feel she actually believes in what you're saying.

I know what you're probably thinking . . . staring at her, teasing her to the point of irritation, calling her names. I'm crushing, right?

Just to clear the air, no. No, I'm not.

Yes, she's extremely gorgeous, and I may have thought about what her hair would feel like wrapped around my fist, and I really like her fucking name, but that doesn't mean I have a crush. It means I'm a man who finds a girl attractive. That's it.

Nothing more.

From the other side of the booth, Luna winces. "I'm . . . uh . . . I'm sorry."

"What?" The friend, Farrah, who really looks like a good time, frowns. "Don't apologize to him. You owe him nothing. He should apologize to you for listening in on a private conversation."

"It's not very private when you're talking loud enough for the entire diner to hear."

"We weren't that loud," Luna says, still looking guilty.

"I thought the Satan was oozing out of you. How could you tell?"

"God," Farrah huffs out, "do you have a comeback for everything? How infuriating—I can see how you lost it on him, Luna."

"He's a lawyer," Luna says casually, as if she knows me. "Of course he's going to have a comeback for everything."

"Not true."

Farrah points at me. "See, right there. Comeback."

"That's not a comeback. That's me engaging in conversation."

"Well, we don't want your engagement." She dismisses me with a wave of her fingers. "Begone with you."

I ignore her and turn to Luna. "Just because you're scared we're going to beat you, that doesn't give you the right to be rude about my brother."

"I wasn't . . . I didn't mean . . ."

"Your brother is tacky," Farrah butts in.

"Hey, chicken, stay out of this."

"Hen," she mutters.

"I wasn't trying to be rude," Luna says, looking up at me with apology in her eyes, and hell, it makes me lighten up for a second.

That is, until she says, "But your vision board was atrocious, and there is no way you could have won unless you were paying the judges off."

Poof.

Just like that, I'm back to wanting to make her life a living hell.

"Keep thinking that, Rossi." I throw some bills down on my table and stand from the booth. "Helpful hint: take a shower before you show up today. You have an unappealing stench wafting about you."

I give her a smile and then take off as Farrah shouts a string of obscenities in my direction. Today should be interesting.

"I have never eaten more buffalo wings in my life than I did last night," Thad says, holding his stomach. "Dude, I could not stop. When they say endless, they mean it. I was burping hot sauce all night long. Naomi made me sleep on the couch."

"Why are you telling me this?" I ask, revolted by my very own brother. Mind you, I'm not a snob. I can take down a platter of wings, but why does he have to hold his stomach and burp while talking about it?

"Because, that's what brothers do: they talk about burping and shit like that."

"Or they don't talk at all." I look across the set at the confessional room, wishing I could hear what Team Rossi is saying.

We just finished up our interview, during which Thad went on and on about the goddamn feathers he can't seem to stop touching. He talked for five minutes about how they feel against his fingers and how they make him feel young again. The producer finally cut him off and asked us to talk about the other teams and what we thought of them. Naomi took the lead on that question, complimenting everyone. When they looked to me for an answer, I kept my mouth shut. I may have some opinions about Team Rossi and the distaste for my shoes on set, but I wasn't about to say anything that could be taken the wrong way, especially since I have a job that requires me to be professional.

But that doesn't mean Luna isn't saying something nasty about me this very minute.

I sigh loudly, resenting the producers, who insist we stay even after our interviews are over, just in case they want to ask us another question about what the opposing team might have said. So it's another long day, to say the least.

"Why are you staring at the confessional room?" Thad asks. "Do you want to go back in there?"

"What?" I shake my head. "No. Just wondering how much longer we're going to have to wait. They should be booking us in time slots rather than making us all come at the same time and wait around. We have lives."

Just as I say that, the door to the confessional opens and out walk Cohen, Declan, and Luna. They're all laughing, and it sends a bolt of insecurity through me.

Are they laughing about me?

What does it matter? It shouldn't.

But for some reason, it does.

Cohen and Declan go to the workstation as Luna takes off for the food table.

Before I can stop myself, I stand from my chair and head in her direction. When she arrived this morning, I did a double take—she looked nothing like the girl I saw this morning. Her hair was smoothed out, straight and silky. Her face was devoid of any leftover mascara from the night before, and instead of smelling like death, I caught a whiff of her as she passed me and she smelled like brown sugar and vanilla. It was incredibly appealing. Almost too appealing.

She's making a sandwich as I walk up next to her. "Did you have an exorcist come to your place this morning and remove the rest of the devil from you?"

She doesn't even look at me. "No, you did a good job of that at the diner. You seem to pull the worst out of me."

Not a pleasant compliment.

Not something I've ever heard anyone say to me before.

Not something I'm proud of.

And yet, I can't quite stop poking the bear.

"Maybe you're just starting to discover yourself."

She lifts a brow and glances at me. "Are you saying I'm coming into my womanhood? Because I did that when I was twelve, at my brother's basketball game. Want to hear the whole story?"

I stuff some pretzels into a cup. "I'm good, thanks." Turning toward her, I pop a pretzel in my mouth and ask, "Talk about me in there?"

"Who's the egomaniac now?"

"Seriously." I nudge her with my foot. "What did you say?"

"Looks like you're going to have to watch it on TV."

"So you *did* talk about me." I smile.

Placing her sandwich on her plate, she faces me. Her dark eyes are framed by black, catlike eyeliner and mascara. Captivating—it's the only way I can describe her eyes: completely captivating. "I didn't talk about you, but I did mention Team Baxter and how I can't wait to see you incorporate feathers into everything you do. I also think I mentioned wanting a pink tux for each groomsman, especially the best man."

"Cheeky." She's turning to walk away when I say, "You're scared."

She freezes and slowly faces me, a hand on her hip. "I'm not scared."

I cross my arms over my chest. "You are. You don't want to fail your brother." Her lips purse to the side and her jaw clenches. "You don't want to fail him, so you're deflecting and focusing on everything we're doing." I take a step forward. "Do you know why we won yesterday?"

"Because you're paying the judges. I told you that already."

"No. Because we're not focused on anyone but ourselves. We're not overthinking it. We're just putting together what we like. We're not screaming about wood and burlap and trying to be the best."

Her eyes search mine, her nostrils flair, and I can tell she's not even close to happy about my little moment of advice.

"You lucked out yesterday, Baxter. Enjoy your rare win, because it will be your last."

"Wow." I rock back on my heels. "That confident, huh?"

"I know men like you, the ones who don't care about love or marriage, who think it's all a joke." *Accurate.* "Well, I care." She points to her chest. "My parents have a beautiful marriage, the kind of love you read about, and they set the perfect example of what my brother deserves. Cohen found his forever in Declan. He struggled getting there, but he found him, and I'll be damned if I don't help kick-start his marriage with one hell of a wedding . . . and an equally amazing penthouse." She gives me another searing once-over. "Stay out of my way, Baxter."

"Are you declaring war?"

"It's been war ever since you demanded coffee."

Dismissing me with her back, she walks away, leaving me to wonder: *What did I just start?* Or, I guess, *What did I start yesterday?*

"There's the craft queen himself." Lucas pops into my office, a smirk on his face. "How was it?"

"Annoying." I lean back in my chair and fold my hands over my stomach. "More annoying than I thought it was going to be."

"A show about love and marriage doesn't necessarily read Alec Baxter."

"You could say that."

I recount how yesterday was a giant waste of time, and that I asked the director if they could schedule out time slots for confessionals so I wouldn't have to wait around all day for nothing. Diane told me it was a great way to get to know the other contestants. I told her it was a great way to fall behind on my cases. Thankfully, she granted my request, and all confessionals will be specifically scheduled from now on.

"And how was my girl Mary?" Lucas asks.

"No idea." I shrug. "She wants nothing to do with the contestants. I don't think she's talked to one of us without the camera rolling."

"Damn, a stone-cold bitch?"

"You could say that. Bit of a diva." Then again, guess I was a bit of a diva with the whole coffee incident, but we don't need to get into that.

"She just needs me to warm her up. So, you're going to take me to the set next week?"

"No."

"Alec, come on. Be a good friend. Introduce me to Mary DIY and make all my dreams come true."

"Dude, she's pretty, but there's no spark in her eyes. She's like a robot. Zero personality."

"Doesn't mean she doesn't have great tits I can bury my face in."

Jesus Christ.

I sit up and open an email from one of my clients, who's been a nervous wreck ever since she decided to leave her husband. She's shown me pictures of the bruises he's given her and recounted multiple accounts of assault, but it took months to convince her to actually send the pictures to me, or to even file for divorce. But after some persuading from her friend and getting a safe place to stay—courtesy of me, free of charge—we're finally pressing charges and divorcing the bastard. And boy am I going to bleed him dry and send his ass to jail.

"Did you hear me?"

"Huh?" I look up from my computer.

"Did you win the challenge?"

"Oh, yeah. We did. Thad put together some feather-boa wedding. I don't know—I was just there to hand him things."

"Feather boa? I fear for you." We both laugh, and then he asks, "I'm guessing you're not catching the spirit of the show?"

"Not even a little. I'm counting down the minutes until it's all over."

"How does Thad feel about that? He doesn't seem like he's going to let you skate by."

I shrug. "I'm there, aren't I? I'm doing what I'm supposed to be doing." But even as I say that out loud, I know it's probably not going to be enough for Thad. Hell, he invited me over again this week to review the next challenge and prepare by watching clips of previous episodes. I feigned work and took off before he could start begging or lecturing me about my participation, or lack thereof.

Here's the problem: Thad and I are on different wavelengths when it comes to love.

He wants the fairy tale Luna was talking about.

The marriage her parents have.

He wants everlasting love and happiness with Naomi.

And that's not something I understand. I've seen pictures of my parents before everything started going downhill. Hell, I've seen videos of them. They were in love. I could see it in their eyes, the way they touched each other, or held hands. But that was in the videos, in the past. In reality, I never witnessed that type of adoration, or any adoration. Dad was always working; Mom was always trying to be the perfect Park Avenue wife. They argued every night about pretty much anything they could argue about: money—always money—engagements, working late, Dad staying at hotels when he should have been home. You name it, they argued about it.

Why is that the life Thad wants?

Naomi is great, and yes, I can see how perfect she is for him. But they're having a baby. Babies bring stress, stress brings fights, fights bring hatred, hatred brings you right back to where you were—single. Why go through all the pain and heartache for nothing?

"Just remember what I said," Lucas says, growing serious. "You only have one brother, man. Don't waste the time you have with him."

"I know." I pull on the back of my head and look out my office window. I was so out of my element on Saturday, so uncomfortable in front of the camera.

Showing up is the best I can do right now, because honestly, how am I supposed to help when I don't believe in what we're creating?

CHAPTER NINE
LUNA

"Are you ready?" Farrah says, coming from behind me and massaging my shoulders. I move my head side to side while we both hop up and down. "Did you do those finger exercises I told you about?"

I flex my fingers and nod. "Yup, all warmed up."

"Do you have your game face on?" Farrah spins me around and grips my shoulders as I mean mug it at her. "Ooo, you've been practicing in the mirror. I can tell."

"When I brush my teeth. I really feel like I've mastered the scowl."

"Honey, you mastered the scowl years ago. Now you're just coming into your own with it." She holds up her hands, and I start boxing into them as we leap around the apartment. "Quick on your feet, quick on your feet." Farrah swings her hand at me, and I duck. "Focus, hone your attention."

"Focused."

"Tell me, who's going to kill it today?"

"I am." I bob back and forth and then give Farrah a one-two punch to her hands.

"Who's going to do anything necessary, even sit on someone's face if you need to, in order to win today's challenge?"

"I am. Show no mercy. My ass is coming for your face."

Farrah pauses, winces. "I'm not sure I like that."

"Just go with it."

"Okay, Luna's ass is coming for your face." She shrugs. "Next week let's work on your trash talk."

"Might be necessary."

Circling again, I box at Farrah's hands, feeling light on my feet and ready for anything that comes my way. "You're going to ignore all conversations from Mr. Snobby Shoes."

"I don't even know he exists."

"Your eyes are on the prize. And what is that prize?"

"Giving Cohen and Declan the best wedding possible."

"Exactly." She lowers her palms. "Quick, flash me your hands."

I lift my hands, and she inspects them carefully.

"You lotioned—good. Nails are clipped to a perfect length, and those fingers are stretched and strong. Rotate your wrists for me." She lowers her ear to my wrists as I circle them around. "Perfect, no cracking, no tension." She points to the ground. "Fast feet."

My feet start bouncing up and down, like in those football movies, and I hold my hands at my hips, ready for the call . . .

"Draw!" Farrah shouts.

I pull my glue gun from my hip and point it at her. "You've been glued."

Farrah claps her hands. "Reaction time was spot on. You're ready."

"Yeah?"

She nods. "You got this, girl. This competition is yours for the taking. And remember what we talked about: don't focus on what you think will win . . ."

"Focus on what will bring Cohen and Declan joy."

"Precisely," Farrah says with an endearing smile.

After some deep thought about the first challenge, I realized that unfortunately Alec Baxter was right: they won that competition because they were playing from the heart. They picked what they wanted and created something that spoke to them, not something they thought was going to win.

Blame it on the lights, the cameras, the plethora of craft supplies, but I was momentarily blinded, and from here on out, I plan on making sure I focus on Cohen and Declan and what would be great for them, not great for the win.

"Don't worry about anyone else. Just focus on what you're trying to accomplish. And if Alec Baxter starts talking to you, what do you do?"

"Start barking like a rabid dog."

"Exactly. That shit freaks people out." She pulls me into a hug. "You got this."

"Thank you."

She hands me my bag and cups my cheeks. "Make Mama Farrah proud."

"I will."

Hoisting my bag over my shoulder, I give her a parting wave and stride out of our apartment to grab a cab to Midtown and the studio where the show is filming.

After last week and everything that went down—the loss, the miscommunication, the outbursts on my end, and the unfortunate conversations with a certain Chris Evans look-alike—I realized one thing: I'd lost all sense of why I was there and what I was doing.

This is about Cohen and Declan and giving them a great wedding, one I know we can do within budget, one that will wow America and highlight the beautiful love they share.

So, that's what I'm setting out to do.

Focusing on Cohen and Declan and barking at any distractions.

I smile to myself as I hail a cab. Even though this is about Cohen and Declan, I secretly can't wait to see the look on Alec's face when he tries to talk to me and I let out a big woof.

Let's just hope they don't catch it on camera.

Now . . . cue the wedding-competition montage in five, four, three . . . two . . . one . . .

◆ ◆ ◆

Week Two—Venues

"Have you looked at what's left on the board?" Cohen asks, looking nervous. "I haven't heard of any of these places."

"I have," I say. "I've done tons of decorations for people in the city, *and* I've made deliveries and hung things as well." I talk quietly as we prepare for our turn to pick. To our dismay, we drew the short end of the crochet hook, and we have to choose our venue last. From a list of five.

Only five. Of course Team Baxter got first pick, and they went with a warehouse down in Meatpacking. Team Hernandez went with an old flour factory turned event space in Brooklyn, which I know offers cheap food and beverage—it's where I was looking for Cohen and Declan before they opted for a courthouse marriage. That leaves us with the Harbor House, the Rooftop Restaurant—which is so not them—and the Shed.

"One minute, Team Rossi!" Mary calls out while the other teams wait for us to choose. I can feel Alec's gaze on me, his smirk from picking the best venue. Thankfully, though, I'm not letting it bother me.

"Harbor House is out," I say.

"They might have good seafood," Declan says.

All we have is one picture of each venue, a few dimensions, and their best food option, along with the budget. So unless you know the venues, you're going to have to just base your decision on what's handed to you. Lucky for me, I know the venues.

"They have a good crab cake, and that's it. They've also been flagged for food poisoning a few times, and their decor is 1980s-sailboat themed. Captain's chair in a horrible orange. Trust me, it's a bad choice."

"The Rooftop won't go with our theme," Cohen says, looking worried, "and the Shed sounds like a place we'd take wedding guests to chop up."

"Rooftop is a no go. It won't go with our theme, like you said, and that will hurt us. But I've heard the Shed is actually nice. I believe there's reclaimed wood throughout the rooms, which are small and sectioned off. The space isn't open, but it can be cute if we do it right."

"Then let's go with that," Declan says.

"The Shed!" I call out.

Mary picks up an envelope with *The Shed* written in perfect calligraphy on the back and hands it to me. "Each envelope contains two food-and-beverage plans. Choose wisely. You're going to have twenty minutes to decide, which includes making your selections for alcohol, appetizers, setup, and where you're going to have the actual ceremony. All decisions are final. The challenge: make the best use of your space. Go."

We tear open the envelope, and I zero in on the floor plans. "You guys take the food. I've got the space."

And just like that, we get to work. The rules state that we're not allowed to have over one hundred guests, so with that in mind, I scan through the maximum occupancy for each room and start dividing up the party. Not only do I develop a seamless space to walk through, but I also come up with a brilliant idea for the ceremony's layout, where guests sit in a circle around the couple in the loft, forming a ring of love and trust. As I look through the pictures and the floor plan, I manage to select only three rooms total, saving us money and creating a warm environment for everyone—as well as a pretty awesome dance space.

"Hey, I can save a few hundred with limiting our rental space," I say, doing the math.

"Really?" Cohen asks with excitement. "We can up the food-and-beverage package then."

"Macaroni bites, here we come," Declan says just as the timer goes off.

I finally lift my head and take a deep breath. As the judges walk around, inspecting our work, I scan the other workstations. Helen and the girls look frazzled, while Thad and Naomi nervously chew their lips. But the guy who thinks he's going to win it all barely looks like he's broken a sweat.

After the judges deliberate, they relay their choices to Mary, and she nods.

Cameras on.

She smiles.

And . . .

"In third place, Team Hernandez. You'll be receiving no extra money. In second place . . ." I hold my breath. "Team Baxter. Which means Team Rossi takes first. The judges were very impressed with your ability to maximize the space and save money while doing it."

I can't help it—I yelp and jump into Cohen's arms. He chuckles and whispers, "There's my girl."

◆ ◆ ◆

Week Three—Invitations

"Luna, where did you learn such great penmanship?" Luciana asks as the crew wraps up around us. PAs are bustling about, cleaning up and setting up for next week, while Mary DIY and Diane walk off the set, studying something on a clipboard. Another missed opportunity to speak with Mary, another week gone by without getting to share my crafty memes with her.

"I've been doing hand lettering for a while now. I've actually created a few fonts that I sell on Creative Market." I swivel on my stool and plaster on a smile. I like Luciana and Amanda. Helen . . . well, she's a different story.

"Wow, well, it shows. Congrats on the win." She gives me a short wave and then takes off with Amanda, hand in hand.

"Yeah, really wonderful invitation," Naomi says as she walks by me, a soft smile on her face. Thad trails behind her, head down. And I know why: this is the second week in a row they haven't won, and they actually came in last this time.

We had to create our invitations on a computer and were provided all the tools, from a drawing pad, to Photoshop, to Word for the people who don't know the systems.

Well, I got to work right away, creating a flawless rustic design on the drawing pad that transferred onto the computer. I kept it simple, using hand lettering to showcase Declan's and Cohen's names, and then used a sans serif font for the rest. I was honestly a little shocked at how great they came out. Luciana and Amanda used a template and put their names on it. It looked nice, but it wasn't original. And then poor Thad and Naomi . . . they tried to do something in Word and wound up with just a black-and-white invitation written out in Times New Roman.

At least they used all caps for their names.

I tried to block them out, but there was a lot of irritation coming from their end of the set, and when I peeked up just once, I caught Alec sitting back, arms crossed, not helping at all. In his defense, Thad kept saying, "Let me do this, let me do this."

Maybe he should have let someone else do it.

"Breakfast for dinner tonight?" Declan asks as he kisses me on the cheek.

"I'll be there. We can strategize next week's challenge . . . wedding attire."

"Can't wait." He winks, and Cohen gives me a hug before walking away as well.

I'm gathering up my things when, out of the corner of my eye, I spot a tall figure walking up next to me. I don't have to look to know who it is. We're the only two left on set, we haven't spoken in the last two weeks, and we're the only two contestants who seem to hate each other. Well, besides Helen, but I think Helen hates everyone.

"Who's paying the judges now?" Alec says, and instead of acknowledging him, I finish taking pictures of the invitations we worked on today and then gather up my samples of cardstock, envelopes, and embellishments to take home so I can look them over. "What, not going to talk to me, now?"

Nope.

I carefully slip the invitation paper and envelope we chose into a stiff file folder so they won't bend. While the other teams chose online invitations because they spent extra on their venues, we were able to spring for paper invites. Cheap paper—but at least we have something tangible to offer.

"I see. Because you won two challenges, you're too good to talk to me."

Ignore, ignore, ignore.

"I would like it to be known, after we won our first challenge, right out of the gate, I still spoke with you. It wasn't beneath me to have a conversation with you."

Conversation or argument?

"Fine, you don't want to talk? That's your choice. But just so you know, I actually was going to pay you a compliment."

"Ha!" I exclaim before I can stop myself. "That's why you started off by insinuating I was paying the judges." After the words have fallen past my lips, I remember what Farrah told me to do. "I mean . . . woof."

"Woof?" Alec's brow furrows.

I clutch the folder to my chest and face him now. Trying to look as snarly as possible, I go at him. "Woof, woof, woof." I use my best baritone impression of a Saint Bernard. "Bark, ra-ra-ra-ra-roof. Bark. Woof."

"Uhhhh . . ." He scratches the top of his head.

"Woof." I take a step forward. "Woof." One more step. "Woof." He stumbles backward.

"Are you barking at me out of choice, or are you experiencing some kind of psychosis and need me to call someone?"

"Bark. Woof. Woof."

"Psychosis for sure."

I move past him and am starting to walk away when he calls out, "Hey, as long as you don't lift a leg and pee on me, you can keep barking all you want."

I smile to myself, not wanting him to see that I actually found him funny . . . for a second.

◆ ◆ ◆

Week Four—Wedding Attire

"For the love of God, where is the pincushion?" Thad shouts, his voice echoing through the set.

I glance over at their workstation and cringe.

Of all the weeks on *The Wedding Game*, week four is by far the fans' favorite. Just like how the technical challenge is clearly the best challenge on *The Great British Baking Show*, because it can easily turn into a hot mess—well, that's what week four, wedding-attire week, is.

Each team has to design and construct the entire wedding party's outfits.

Yup, design and construct. Which means we're provided four mannequins. Each mannequin has to have a corresponding sketch that goes along with the ensemble it's dressed in. Some of the items have already been constructed, like button-down shirts and pants, but everything else needs to be cut and pinned together. Luckily, we don't have to sew in a certain time limit. The pieces are brought to a tailor, who then replicates the look.

Tables at the back of the set are covered in fabrics, accessories, embellishments . . . yes, even *feathers*, and once again, whatever we choose has to be used in our designs, though we have the option of dumping one item.

Can you imagine why this might be the best episode? Some of the creations that have come out of it are Hall of Fame worthy, and I mean, "Ugliest Dress of All Time" worthy.

Because of the mix of couples, there is no budget for wedding attire. It's first come, first served, since wedding dresses cost more than a suit.

"You don't think we need more than this?" Declan asks, staring at the mannequins draped in button-up shirts and tasteful vests.

"No, keep it simple. Trust me on this, okay?" I say, tongue sticking out as I carefully pin my "best man" dress together.

"I'm sorry to pull a groomzilla moment for a second," Cohen says, "but don't you think you're spending a little too much time on your dress?"

"If you'd allowed me the honor, I would be spending just as much time on *your* dress. But you chose a suit, which was easy—I just cut out a nice vest for the both of you. A bow tie for Declan, a tie for you. Done and done. You need to remember: we're competing against a lesbian couple with *two* dresses, and if you haven't peeked, they are flowy and gorgeous, so we need to make this dress pretty."

"She has a point," Declan says. "Maybe add a layer of tulle?"

I shoot him a look. "Stick to your bow tie."

He throws his hands up in defense just as Thad's familiar scream rattles the set. "That was my ball sack, you dick nozzle!"

Thunk.

Everyone lifts their heads and glances over to the slowly self-destructing Team Baxter; Thad is curled up on the ground, and Alec is standing over him with a pin in his hand and a smile on his face.

"I think we should have designed on the mannequins," Naomi says. The poor girl is wrapped up like a sausage in white as she stares down at her fiancé.

"Yeah, but then Thad wouldn't have gotten a 'feel for the attire,'" Alec says with air quotes. He nudges Thad with his foot. "Are you getting the feel for it now?"

◆　◆　◆

Week Five—Bouquets and Boutonnieres

"Pass me the twine!" I shout, sweat dripping down my forehead. Declan tosses me the twine as Cohen sits in front of me, telling me what to do.

Remember when I said wedding-attire week is a fan favorite? Well, bouquets and boutonnieres is where the drama really ramps up. It's not as simple as decorating and putting something together.

Nope, you have to play the game of "trust your family." Which means the person in charge of distributing tools and supplies must stay silent. That would be Declan. Then there are the eyes and the hands. One "eyes" member of the team has to stand in front of the "hands" member and tell them exactly what to create. And "hands" just has to trust them. Basically, my chest is plastered to Cohen's back, my arms looped under his as he tells me what to do, and I try to blindly replicate what he says.

This was the week I was dreading the most—I may be good with my hands, but I'm nothing without my eyes.

"Is everything centered?"

"Looks like it," Cohen says.

"*Looks* like it? Cohen, I need a solid yes or no."

Cohen shifts against me. "Cool it with the attitude. We practiced this—just repeat what we did this past week."

"Repeat? How can I repeat when I don't know what I'm seeing? Stop being so casual. This needs to be perfect."

Knowing we would be creating boutonnieres and bouquets blindly, Cohen and Declan had me over this past week, two nights in a row, to practice. It was rather cute, actually. Cohen had it all planned out: he'd bought the supplies and told me exactly what he and Declan wanted. We practiced, over and over, and going into today, we felt like we knew what we were doing . . . until Helen took the twine I wanted, and the time started ticking down. The pressure of it all is getting to me, and it's showing.

"One minute!" Mary calls out.

"Shit," I mutter, knowing production will have to bleep that out. "Cohen, is it straight?"

"Yes. Just tie it."

"But I can't see where I'm tying—you have to tell me where to tie it."

"Right there."

"Right where?" I yell.

"Right where your hands are. Christ."

Fortunately, we're not the only ones yelling at each other, which makes bouquets and boutonnieres a great week to watch on TV, though not a great week to actually create in. Luciana and Amanda, the quiet ones, have been at it, yelling back and forth about the silk peonies they picked and how the lace they chose to wrap around the bouquets isn't secure enough and they should have grabbed floral tape, but they forgot.

Rookie mistake.

And then there's Team Baxter, who for some odd reason has put Naomi in charge of supplies, Alec in charge of overseeing everything, and Thad in charge of creating. You can imagine how well that's been going.

Thad has yelped at least three times and, I think, cried, because at one point, Alec yelled, "Are you wiping your snot on my back?" To which Thad replied, "You created the snot with your sarcasm, so deal with it!"

"Thirty seconds."

"Hurry, Luna!" Cohen stresses.

"It's not that easy," I reply, upper lip sweating.

I twist the twine around, form a knot, and hope for the best just as the time runs out. I unlatch myself from Cohen and quickly step around him so I can see what we've created.

Twigs and wheat are askew, the fake baby's breath—fake because all items made today need to last, plus they're cheaper—is off center, and the bow I tied is vertical rather than horizontal.

Christ on a cracker!

"Cohen, what the . . ."

"Don't blame me." He steps away, hands held up.

"You were the eyes. You should have told me the wheat was clumped weird."

"Looks fine to me."

"And cut!" Diane says. "Take a ten-minute break."

"It does not look fine." I push up from the table and walk away, needing some distance from Cohen and the worst challenge ever created.

As I leave the set, my head down, I bump into someone. I look up and straight into the blue eyes of Mary DIY—and I nearly jump out of my skin.

"Oh my gosh, I'm so sorry. I didn't see you there. Guess we're both ready to get off the set, huh?" She gives me a quick once-over but says nothing, so I continue: "Now that I have a moment with you, I thought I would officially introduce myself. I'm Lun—"

"Harper, where are my sandals? Now!" she yells, bumping my shoulder as she steams past me, robe flapping in the breeze.

Well . . . that was rude and not exactly what I needed.

I head toward the food table, scoop up a giant cupful of unwrapped Rolos, and start plopping them in my mouth two at a time.

I'm standing to the side of craft services, staring at the ground and trying to control my frustration, when I feel someone sidle up beside me. At first, he just leans against the wall as I keep shoving Rolos into my mouth. But after a few short seconds, he finally says, "That was torture." I glance over at Alec. He looks a little crazed. He must have run his hand through his hair after they yelled cut, because it's wild. "I have snot on my back, my knees are aching from not being able to move for twenty minutes, and I'm pretty sure Thad's plotting my death right now." His gaze falls on me. "If you're going to bark, just don't respond."

So I don't.

I was able to peek over at their creations, and I really didn't think they were that bad. I wouldn't be surprised if they actually place today—Team Hernandez's bouquets looked like they were ready to fall apart from the lack of floral tape.

When I don't answer him, he nods and pushes off the wall. "Still trying to be a dog—got it." He moves to walk away but then stops and turns back to me. "For what it's worth, trying to describe how to create is a lot harder than you think."

As I watch his retreating back, I can't help the way my eyes fall to his backside, or the way I want to say something back to him. We really haven't said much to each other since the first week. I've caught him looking at me here and there, but that's about it. No other exchanges.

And sure, I've observed him from afar too. He's the same infuriatingly confident guy every week. But just now, he seemed a little bit . . . off.

Is it because I'm not talking to him?

Is it the challenge itself?

This is the week when teams start to fall apart, and I can see why. It all looks so fun when you're watching the show, but when you're in the thick of it, the stress is so palpable you can actually taste it on your tongue.

107

The anger, the yelling, the miscommunications: it's a real testament to your relationships. Mine was certainly tested with Cohen today.

And as for Team Baxter, it's easy to see that their relationships were tested. Then again, they've never seemed like they were fully united. More like they're being held together by cheap tape. Is this their breaking point?

Team Rossi in the lead. Team Hernandez trailing close behind. And Team Baxter—well, let's just say they might have lucked out with one win.

CHAPTER TEN

ALEC

Stewing in pure irritation, I ask Thad, "Why are you crying?"

This last month has been miserable. Not only have I lost my weekends, but I've also had to put in extra hours during the week to make sure I can get all my casework done. I have to wake up early on Saturday and Sunday to come to this godforsaken studio, which is basically a torture chamber of crafts and challenges, each and every one of which we lose.

If this were a show that eliminates contestants, we likely would have been gone after the second week, and for sure after the wedding-attire week.

"Why am I crying?" Thad asks, wiping under his eye. Naomi went to the bathroom, which is where she spends most of her time when not filming. Morning sickness is rearing its ugly head. We even had to stop filming for a while today after she sprinted off toward the bathroom, hand over her mouth. "Maybe because we're sucking so hard it's embarrassing."

"What did you expect?" I stare down at the pitiful boutonniere and bouquet we've put together. "We have zero experience in any of this shit."

"I expected you to try," Thad shoots back. "If only you'd come over this week, we could have practiced, or at least talked about it. Naomi is no help right now—the pregnancy is really taking hold of her. She's tired, sick, or buried in the fridge, eating all of our food. I need you to be present, Alec."

"I'm here now, aren't I?" I take a seat on one of the stools at our workbench, really not in the mood for an argument.

"You're physically here, but you're not mentally here. You realize everything we create will be a part of the wedding, don't you? Naomi is going to have to walk this pathetic bouquet down the aisle." He tosses the bouquet made of feathers to the side. "She deserves better. I deserve better, more . . . more from you."

"I'm doing the best I can."

"Are you?" Thad asks, tears gone now. "Because this project was also supposed to bring us closer together, make us a family again, but any chance you get, you flee. Your heart isn't in this competition. It's like you're here to check a box, to say you did your brotherly duty. But what happens after the show, Alec?" Naomi walks up behind him and places her hand on his back. "What happens when the cameras turn off and we no longer have to mandatorily see each other on the weekend? Do we go back to seeing each other once every six months?"

"Come on, Thad."

"Come on, what, Alec? It's the truth. Ever since you left for college, it's like you've forgotten I even exist."

I glance around, at the PAs listening in on our conversation. "Now is not the time."

"It's never the time." He turns on his heel and stalks off toward the green room, leaving me alone with Naomi.

Silence fills the air between us, and I can feel her disappointed gaze settle on me.

"He loves you so much, Alec. Do you realize that?"

"I love him too," I say, pushing my hand through my hair, feeling the need to go for a run, hit the gym, expel this pent-up energy inside me.

"No, I don't think you understand. He idolizes you." With a finger on my cheek, she turns my head to meet her gaze. "Idolizes. On our very first date, he told me about his brother, the top-notch attorney. He told me about how you always looked out for him, how you were always there for him. On our third date, he told me about your childhood, how your parents fought constantly, but you always made their fights into something fun and took him as far away from them as possible. On our tenth date, he showed me pictures of you two at his high school graduation, how you gave him a notebook and told him to use it for his dreams in life. To write them down and figure out how to accomplish them. Do you know the first dream he wrote down?"

Hell, I don't think I want to know.

She takes my silence as permission to continue. "Be a protector, like his brother, Alec."

Fuck.

"Do you know what his second dream was?"

I scratch behind my ear as my heart hammers and my head fills with visions of fourteen-year-old Thad saying goodbye to me as I moved out, his shaggy brown hair rumpled, his eyes rimmed with red, silently begging me not to leave him alone. That was the first moment I ever let my brother down, when I walked away from him so I could finally be free of the anger suffocating our house.

"No," I answer, unable to look Naomi in the eyes now.

"To find unconditional love, the kind you gave him."

Fucking hell.

"And do you know what the third thing was?"

Have future wife torture older brother to point of a mental breakdown?

I shake my head, knowing that what she says next will probably be the final nail in the coffin.

111

"To have a loving marriage and never follow in his parents' footsteps." She pauses, letting that sink in. "This might be a joke to you. You might not believe in love or the sanctity of marriage, but Thad does, and at what point in your life did you stop caring about what he found important? From the stories he's told me about his hero, his older brother, it seemed like never." Naomi gives me a slow once-over and shakes her head. "But honestly, I'm unimpressed. You're nothing like the Alec Thad talked about. I'm sad that my future husband holds you in such high regard and probably always will. Maybe take a second to think about that, instead of counting down the seconds until you're done with this show."

Without another word, she heads off toward the green room after Thad, leaving my heart in a lurch and putting a period on the brutal verbal smackdown she just delivered.

Naomi could give me a run for my money in the courtroom.

"Dude, week five is where it all falls apart—don't you know that?" Lucas asks as he brings his beer up to his lips.

"No. I never watched the goddamn show." Not wanting to face the outside world, I had Lucas come over to my apartment for beer and wings. I provided the beer; he brought the wings. By the time he showed up, I was already four bottles in and cracking my fifth, which has made me, let's say . . . a little loopy.

"The producers put bouquets and boutonnieres in week five on purpose, because at this point, you've either felt the pressure of consistently losing and you need a win, or you've been on top and a failure would be devastating. The challenge is brutal, not being able to see, being timed, and having to communicate by describing what to do." He chuckles. "Fuck, I can't wait to see this air."

"Glad you think it's so fucking funny."

"It really is." He picks up a wing and bites into it. "But from the way your eyes are glassed over, I'm going to assume it's not the challenge that ate you alive today."

"Nope," I say, slouching in my chair. "It was my soon-to-be sister-in-law."

"Ahh, Naomi, right?" I nod. "Did she yell at you for not making a bouquet that's worthy of her hands?"

I shake my head. "No, she told me what a shitty brother I am and how Thad idolizes me, but she doesn't get it. Direct quote: she's 'unimpressed' with me."

"Ouch, really?"

"Yup." I take a long pull from my beer, and I mean long, letting the cold liquid soothe my throat.

"Is she right?"

I sigh and stare down at the brown bottle in my hand, as if I've never seen a beer bottle before. Is she right? Well, do I want to admit to being a shitty person?

I chug the rest of my beer and set down drink number five on the coffee table before I reach for drink number six.

I pop the top off. "She's unfortunately very accurate about how I treat my brother."

Lucas nods. "Which says something about your current level of alcohol consumption."

I tip the bottle toward him. "Truth."

"So you're feeling like shit."

"Pretty . . . much." I down half the bottle, staring up at the modern light fixture that hangs over my living room. There's nothing personal about it, just plain black with lights attached to it. Sleek lines, no character . . . probably a direct reflection of the person I've become. "Have you changed?" I ask Lucas, suddenly.

"Changed? In what regard?"

"Since you became a lawyer. Do you feel like your character has changed?"

"Not really. I'd say I'm the same—maybe bigger balls than when I was in college, even though back then I was a know-it-all punk. At least I have facts to back up my statements now. Why? Do you feel like you've changed?"

"I know I have." I press my palm to my eye. "I wasn't always this . . . emotionless, unattached. But the minute I exited that apartment and left Thad behind, I felt so free, like I could finally breathe. And I clung to that feeling. I'd carried the burden of my parents for so long that the minute I didn't have to carry it anymore, I ran."

"Leaving Thad behind."

"Precisely."

"Brutal, man. And now you're feeling the consequence of running."

"Not only feeling it, living it." I shake my head. "He wants this so bad. Really fucking bad, but we're so far behind, easily the underdogs, with no chance of coming back. And with every loss, I can see Thad's spirit fall further and further. Today was . . . fuck, it was rough, seeing him like that—not just emotional, but truly beside himself. I know he's more sensitive than other men, but he was in tears today. Not dramatic tears, but tears that basically said he was giving up on a dream."

"Hell, man." Lucas takes a sip of his beer. "I wasn't expecting to get all the feels tonight."

"Tell me about it. I have no idea what to fucking do."

Lucas passes me the tray of wings, but I push them away. He pushes them toward me again. "Eat, dude. You need food in your stomach."

He's right. I put down the beer and place a few wings on my plate.

"Now, did you bring me over here to help you, or to just listen?"

I pause for a moment, chewing on a wing. "At first listen, but now I feel like I need some advice."

"I don't think you're going to like what I have to say."

"I've already been dragged through the mud—might as well put the cherry on top of the cake."

He chuckles and clinks the neck of his beer bottle against mine. "Then let me ask you this: Do you miss your brother?"

"What?" I ask, feeling a little too drunk to be having this conversation now.

"The boy you grew up with, the friend you could rely on. Do you miss him?"

"I mean . . . yeah." I set my wing down and stare at it. "But I don't think I know the man he's become, and that . . . fuck, that's shameful."

"Do you want to know him?"

I've spent my adult years avoiding my family, ignoring invitations to birthdays, casual hangouts, even holidays. I've sent texts here and there, but the majority of the correspondence from them has gone unanswered. I kept telling myself I would catch the next call or the next text. I would answer later, until I just never answered. I never called back.

Now Thad is getting married, to a woman I barely know.

Thad is a grown-ass man, about to become a dad, and I don't even know the man he's become. I don't know the kind of dad he wants to be.

I know practically nothing about his life, the boy I raised, the boy who would cry on my shoulder whenever Dad slammed the door and we wouldn't see him for days.

All I know is what we used to have. I have no idea what kind of relationship we could have now, and hell, that pains me, especially when I see how close Luna and Cohen are.

I notice the way she looks up to her brother, the love in her eyes, the same kind of love Thad has for me. The kind of love I don't deserve.

But it's the kind of love I *want* to deserve.

And even though the last five weeks have been hell on earth, this is the most excitement I've ever had in my cold, sterile adult life.

"Christ," I mutter. "I do. I want to know him. I want to know Naomi. I want to know their child. I want to be a part of their lives, but I have no idea how to do it. I've been so goddamn neglectful."

"Well, what matters to Thad?"

"The wedding, and giving his family a great life."

"Then it's time to start taking this competition seriously. You have three weeks left before the weddings. There's still time to change everything. And mind you, if you've saved up enough money, the last challenge of the competition before the weddings is what you're going to spend the rest of your budget on."

"What do you mean?"

"I mean . . . the shitty bouquet and boutonnieres you made can be switched out. Those aren't final—just what you're stuck with if you can't afford anything else. Use your money wisely, bro. This is *The Wedding Game*. Anything goes."

"Really?" I sit up taller.

"Yeah, dude. You still have a chance at winning."

"So . . . I could actually help Thad?"

"Yup." Lucas smiles over his beer. "If I were you, I'd start looking up YouTube videos on DIY weddings. Next week is cakes. Know your shit."

Know my shit . . . I can do that, right?

"What the actual fuck?" I say the next morning as I squint at my computer screen, pen in hand and notepad next to me. Thank God we have the day off from filming. A PA called this morning, saying Mary DIY had come down with food poisoning last night and we're rescheduling for a double shoot next Sunday.

Which is why I'm hunkered over my computer, nursing more beers—because why not at this point?—and taking notes as I watch DIY wedding cake videos.

And when I say taking notes, I mean writing swear words over and over in my notebook as I listen to one YouTuber after another talk about different types of flour, letting the cakes cool, decorating with a flat knife, and the difference between each frosting and the look it can give you.

All I can say is . . . *holy fuck.*

I've become overwhelmed in the half hour since I started searching simple wedding cakes, thinking, *Hey, that is a great place to start.*

Wrong.

There are a million different types of "simple" wedding cakes.

"Simple, right?" the current YouTube star says after flipping a cake on top of another with a knife and just her hand, not a crumb out of place.

"Yeah, okay, lady." I lean back in my chair, sip my beer, and jot down my first actual sentence in my notepad.

Flip cake with knife, simple, right?

This morning, after spending two ruthless hours in the gym, I sat down with my lunch—steak salad with gorgonzola sauce—and watched clip after clip of cake week on *The Wedding Game.* I was really confused at first, wondering why we were going to make a cake for a wedding that's not going to happen for a few weeks, but I quickly realized the cakes we're making would be judged for prizes. First place doesn't just get to work with a top baker in the winner's respective city, but they also get a dessert bar at their reception and an unlimited budget for their real wedding cake. The second-place team is given a modest three-tier cake and has the option of a dessert bar if it's within budget. Third place . . . hell, third place is a death sentence. Third place is given a box of ingredients and a Hail Mary. They need to replicate their cake two days before the wedding, which only adds to the stress leading up to the nuptials.

For the love of God, we can't get third place.

I can't even imagine the kind of nightmare Thad would be if we were making a wedding cake two days before the wedding.

I hate to admit it, but Luna has been dominating the competition, with Team Hernandez coming in a solid second every time. After the first week, it's like something lit a fire under her—probably my brilliant insults—good job, Alec—and she's been crushing all of us. And when I say it's Luna, I mean it's Luna. Cohen and Declan are decent supporting characters, but her skills have been on full display this last month.

I even heard some PAs talking about Luna's YouTube channel and how—

Hold on a GD second.

Luna's YouTube channel.

I set my beer down and feverishly type "Luna Rossi" into the search bar.

The screen fills with videos of her face, her branding of a blue and yellow stitching lighting up the page along with her smile.

Holy hell, why didn't I think of this earlier?

I click on her YouTube channel and quickly scroll through all her videos.

How to knit your first blanket.

Hand letter a card from scratch.

Homemade glitter bombs.

Nonna Rossi's almond drop cookies.

Bedazzling isn't just for the nineties.

That last one makes me smile as I think of the shirt she wore on the first day of filming and how insulted she was when I dropped my nineties comment.

But holy shit, this girl knows so much. No wonder she's been leading the competition with such ease, especially since she's up against such an incompetent moron like me.

Curious, I scroll through her videos, wondering if there's one on how to master a wedding cake, but the only baking videos I see are for cookies.

Hmm, does that mean she might not *be the master she claims to be?*

Off to the side, under her profile, there's a link to her Instagram. I don't think twice before clicking it.

Instagram is always weird on a computer, but it still allows me to creep on her.

And of course, her Instagram is one of those accounts where everything is color coordinated and aesthetically pleasing. There are pictures of her claiming to "fail" at a craft, where she's holding up the failed piece of macramé or pottery or sewing. There are pictures of her laughing, smiling, just enjoying life, and as I stare at them, desire jolts through me.

Desire to smile like that. To laugh, feel joy, have fun.

Hell, when was the last time I actually had fun?

I can't even remember at this point. I've had my head down for so damn long, caught up in my job and obsessed with seeking justice . . . for what? For my mom, who's a pretty shitty mom to begin with?

For fourteen-year-old Thad with his shaggy hair?

For the kid I used to be? Who only wanted his parents to hug him, not turn him away?

Probably all three at this point.

A lit-up rainbow ring encircles her profile picture, which I click on, revealing her Instagram stories. Watching her stories feels oddly more personal than just scrolling through her Instagram page. It feels wrong, but there's no way I can turn it off, not when I see her smiling face, a swath of colorful pillows behind her.

Is that her bed?

It has to be.

I turn up my computer so I can hear her.

"Thank you for all the recipe suggestions. I really appreciate it. You baking warriors are amazing."

Recipes? Is she researching for next week too?

Hell, of course she is. It's what she probably spends every waking moment doing, especially after I foolishly threw down the gauntlet.

"I think I'm going to go for a naked cake, topped with berries." Oh hell, why does that cake remind me of Thad's birthday five years ago? He had a cake just like it and gushed about how much he loved it. "It really fits with what I have planned. Which means, Hot-Lanta Baking, you win the recipe competition. I'm tagging you here. Send me a DM and I'll send you a surprise box of goodies."

Clever marketing. All right, I can see why she has over five hundred thousand followers.

"Tomorrow, I'm going to hit up Cakes and Bakes downtown to pick up some ingredients and supplies to practice. Don't worry—I'll keep you guys updated on the process. That's it for tonight. I hope you had a wonderful weekend, and, as always, keep it crafty." She waves to the camera and the video ends.

Huh.

I lean back in my office chair and rock back and forth for a few seconds, my fingers drumming on the desk, a million terrible thoughts coursing through my head.

Terrible thoughts that could be helpful.

Very helpful.

Helpful enough to possibly keep us out of last place.

Before I can stop myself, I log out of Instagram and quickly create a fake account. I connect the account to my work email, ready to cancel it the minute I get what I need, and I create a username. Uh . . .

Hmm . . .

Something that doesn't give me away. Something that won't connect me to the account at all. Something that keeps me completely anonymous . . .

Ah ha, I got it.

Smiling to myself, I type out the username, ChrisEcrafts, and hit enter.

I've been told a few times that I look like Chris Evans, and Chris can be a male or female name, so it's perfect. Fucking clever, right there. She'll never guess.

Once I'm signed in, I go straight to Luna's profile and follow her. I consider liking a few of her posts, but that might be weird. Is it? Maybe not. A new fan likes things, right? I don't want to draw too much attention to my fakeness, especially since I don't have a profile picture.

Shit, I should have a profile picture, make myself seem more legit.

I spend the next few moments searching for a picture of a bird, because honestly, that's the only thing that comes to mind, and people trust birds, right? ChrisE could be an old lady bird lover.

Hell, ChrisE *is* an old lady bird lover, and she wears knee-high stockings because she fucking can.

A photo of a cardinal catches my eye with its vibrant colors and proudly puffed chest. I quickly make that the profile shot, and then I sign in on my phone before downloading and posting a few more pictures of random crafts with comments like "Check out this bunting" and "Crochet hooks on fire, am I right?" I add some flavorful hashtags that make me chuckle. A half hour later, I'm completely absorbed in ChrisEcrafts and knee deep in posting other people's pics.

Hell, I can easily see how catfishing is a thing.

Once I feel confident about my posts, I go back to Luna's profile and click on the blue message icon.

When the text box pops up, I start typing, hoping she'll message me back . . . sooner rather than later.

Hey Luna,

Uhh . . .

I sit back, sip my beer, and think about what I want to say. *Cake, ask about the cake.* Compliment her profile and thank her for her help.

Clears throat, cracks fingers

I don't mean to gush, but I absolutely adore your profile. I came across it a few months ago and finally had the courage to like it.

Is that weird? I mean, I don't want to be a flyby fan. She'll know I just liked the profile.

I've kept coming back to your profile, typing your name in the search bar.

Huh . . . is that stalker level?

I think I need to start over.

Backspace, backspace, backspace

~~I don't mean to gush, but I absolutely adore your profile. I came across it a few months ago and finally had the courage to like it.~~

~~I've kept coming back to your profile, typing your name in the search bar.~~

Cracks fingers, blows on them

Here we go.

Long time crafter, first time follower.

Ha, clever.

I chuckle and roll my shoulders back.

I came across your profile from one of your delightful hashtags. It was #Procraftinating. Should be doing laundry but can't put down that decoupage. Am I right?

I chuckle even more, down the rest of my beer, flex my fingers.

Anyway, I just saw your story about a cake you're making and I'm dying to know the recipe. Care to share with a new fan? Tipping my sewing needle at you—your friend, ChrisEcrafts.

There.

I hit send and get up from my office chair. I go to the kitchen for another beer. When I pop the cap off, my phone dings.

Did she . . . did she already message me back?

In a hurry to get to my phone, I trip over the leg of my dining room table, stumble forward, and crash straight into my couch. By some miracle, I manage to keep the beer held high and avoid any spillage.

Christ.

Straightening up, I laugh and thank the good lord himself that no one else saw that. When I reach for my phone, the screen lights up, announcing a new message on Instagram from LunaMoonCrafts.

And like I'm a damn idiot, my heart skips in my chest.

"Keep it in your pants," I mutter, flopping on the couch and taking a pull of beer—as my brain starts to inform my sweat glands that I'm about to cross into dangerous territory.

But the sweat that starts to tickle the back of my neck can't stop me from opening up her message and reading it.

Hey ChrisEcrafts,

Thank you so much for your message and the follow. I love when I get to bring a new friend into my little world of crafts.

Huh, cute and nice. Unlike anything I've seen from her.

#Procraftinating all day, every day. I have a mountain of laundry that needs to be done, can't tell you the last time I cleaned my shower, and my roommate is one half-full mug of tea on the coffee table away from kicking me out of the apartment. But it's all worth it when I hold up a finished product.

Damn, she really is nice, relatable. Not sure many people fess up to keeping their place less than suitable for company.

And of course you can have the recipe. I'll link it below. Maybe we can practice together. I'm making mine tomorrow. Send me a pic when you make yours and we can compare and contrast. Happy baking and keep crafting. Lots of love—Luna.

Right below is the recipe for the cake. I feel a bit bad that she's given it up so easily, but then again, sometimes you have to catfish a little to get what you want, right?

Okay, okay, what I did wasn't entirely kosher, but I'm telling you, between Thad's dramatics and Naomi's vomiting, baking the cake on our own a few days before the wedding is not an option.

A desperate man must resort to desperate things.

I click on the recipe and take a screenshot before messaging her back.

My inner girl comes out.

OMG, you're the best. Thank you so much. I can't wait to try it. I'll send you pictures but there's no doubt in my mind yours will be so much better than mine.

Send.

She must be perusing Instagram because she starts typing back immediately.

*LunaMoonCrafts: A secret between crafters . . . *whispers* cakes are my kryptonite. I always seem to mess them up somehow, whether it's forgetting to add the sugar, leaving it on the windowsill for an NYC rat to eat, or dropping my tea on it while dancing to a Bruno Mars song that I couldn't help but shake my booty to. So, I'm a little nervous about this cake.*

Hell, now all I can envision is her shaking her "booty." And I know it's a pretty cute ass because I may have looked at it a time or two. You know, researching the competition.

ChrisEcrafts: I'm not much of a baker either. Been known to burn anything I put in an oven, even when I set a timer.

LunaMoonCrafts: That's really impressive, even with a timer? Burning with a timer takes true talent.

ChrisEcrafts: My talents extend beyond just a kitty cat needlepoint.

No idea what I'm talking about, but it feels right.

LunaMoonCrafts: Are you a needlepointer too? I was sent a kit from a company a week ago, and I'd never heard of them so I was excited to try it. You'll never guess what it was. I didn't post it on my IG for obvious reasons.

ChrisEcrafts: From the way you describe it, I'm going to say maybe it was inappropriate?

LunaMoonCrafts: It was a penis. Not just one penis, but a basket of penises with lettering that said "Eat a basket of dicks."

Beer dribbles out of my mouth as I try to keep it from projecting all over my apartment. I swallow hard and then cough out a laugh. Hell,

I would have loved to see Luna's face when she opened that package. She's still typing, so I wait before responding.

LunaMoonCrafts: I mean, I like a good penis, but I was not expecting that from a needlepoint company.

Beer shoots out of my nose this time, and I set the bottle down. Drinking while messaging Luna might not be the best idea. I wipe at my nose and chuckle. Damn, she's funny when she's relaxed—and not hating me.

ChrisEcrafts: I have to know, did you make the kit?

LunaMoonCrafts: Hell yeah! It's in our entryway, hanging proudly. No better way to welcome people into the apartment than by telling them to eat a basket of dicks.

I laugh out loud and wish that I had the same greeting in my apartment. Or anything personal. It's an insane asylum in here. But what am I going to hang? Pictures of my family? Yeah, don't need to be reminded of that.

A thought crosses my mind: a baby picture I could possibly hang soon, one of my niece or nephew. Warmth spreads through my veins as I stare up at the built-in shelves next to my fireplace. I can see frames lining the shelves, me with the baby, Thad and Naomi with the baby, all of us together . . .

Smiling, I message Luna back.

ChrisEcrafts: I might need you to send me the company name so I can get one. My apartment needs a little basket of dicks too.

LunaMoonCrafts: On it. I got you covered, boo. Keep me updated on the cake. I'll be shopping tomorrow so keep an eye out for my stories. Keep crafting (or procraftinating)—Love, Luna

Hell, everything about that last message has my stomach turning in anticipation. I need to see her again, to see if I can bring out the sweet, charming person who sent me these messages, to see if she might call me "boo" in person . . .

Christ.

I drag my hand down my face and toss my phone to the side. Reminder, Alec: *Luna is the competition, she hates you with more passion than she has for her basket of dicks, and the last time you tried to have a conversation with her, she* barked *at you.*

I lean over to the table, grab my beer, and drain it. Then, impulsively, I pick my phone back up and read over her last message one more time.

Keep an eye out for my stories . . .

Why do I feel like I'm going to graduate from catfisher to full-on stalker?

CHAPTER ELEVEN
ALEC

"Do you have a fake mustache?"

"What?" Lucas says, looking up from his computer. Through the wide picture window behind him, the Manhattan skyline acts as his backdrop. Gloomy skies blanket the city, but I feel invigorated, excited. "A fake mustache? Are you drunk?"

I step into his office and shut the door. My sleeves are rolled up, my tie is loosened, and I know my hair is crazed. I just spent most of the morning going through a bunch of pictures a private investigator sent me that barely prove infidelity in a case I just took on.

But everything came to a halt when I picked up my phone and watched Luna's stories.

"I know you don't have a mustache right now, you moron. I can see your face."

"Can you? You look insane right now."

"Because I don't have much time. Do you have a mustache or not?"

Lucas leans back in his chair and crosses his arms over his chest. "In what universe do you think I would have a fake mustache in my office?"

"Fuck," I mutter, hands on my hips. I knew it was a long shot, but I thought I would ask. "Do you have a hat and sunglasses?"

"What the fuck are you up to, Baxter? And if it's illegal, I want nothing to do with it."

"Just . . . stalking someone. Don't worry about it. I need a disguise, though."

"*Stalking?* What happened to the private investigator? Going into fieldwork now?" Lucas stands and goes to the small closet in his office.

"No, not for work."

He pauses and raises a brow at me. "Does this have to do with Luna and the show?"

"Maybe," I say, feeling my face flame.

"Christ, don't tell me. I don't want to know." He flings a gray felt fedora with a black stripe around the base, and then a pair of sunglasses. I manage to catch them both. "If you're arrested, I'm not an accomplice."

I stare at the hat, turning it in my hands. "Why the hell do you have this? I've never seen you wear it in my life."

"There's a reason you haven't."

"Where did you get it?"

"My mom got it for me the last time she was in New York. She thought it was a very old-school city and wanted me to give it a shot, since it's what they wore in the old days. It's been hanging in my closet ever since."

Not going to be picky, I plop it on my head and slide the aviators onto my face. "What do you think?" I ask, holding my hands out to the side. "Do I look different?"

"Sure do." Lucas holds back a laugh.

"Is it bad?"

"I'll admit, I feel intimidated by your good looks whenever we're out together, but I really think you should start wearing this ensemble more often. Really levels you down."

"Thanks," I say sarcastically before taking off toward his door. "I'm calling you if I get arrested."

"I'm not bailing you out!" he calls after me.

When I make it outside my office building, I run smack into a line of tourists waiting outside of Papaya Dog, needing their touristy fix. My office building is right next to the Empire State Building, which means I'm constantly fighting through throngs of humans with cameras and wandering eyes. I hurriedly push through the line and make quick work of flagging down a taxi and giving the driver the address of Cakes and Bakes, where I know Luna is headed to right now. Starting in Midtown gives me a head start, and I know I can still beat her, assuming she's coming from the Upper West Side. I'll have just enough time to stalk her when she walks through the door of the shop.

Recipe for disaster, right? I know that's what you're thinking. Stalking someone in a small shop is never a good idea, but I have to see what she's getting. And the shop isn't that small. It's a supply store for bakers. I checked the website last night and realized exactly why she's going there: for the best products and tools you'll need to make a cake. Which is just what I need too, since I don't even have a cake pan.

And yes, I might not be entirely incognito, but I'm pretty stealthy. I can hide behind pillars and endcaps. I mean, I haven't done it before, but it can't possibly be that hard.

I pull up Luna's Instagram profile and click on the lit-up stories. Shit, I hope she's not there yet.

There's a picture of a stray cat on the subway platform. The cat is sitting next to a bowl, and the bowl has a few dollars in it. Her comment is: "I hope she buys a fancy hat for herself. Imagine how perfect this picture would be if she had pearls and a hat. Also, why is this cat so bold?"

Hell, I'm wondering the same damn thing. Now that I know she lives in my neighborhood, based on our diner run-in, she has to be on the 1 train, heading toward Battery Park, where the shop is. We very well might arrive at the same time. Which means one thing: I need to be on my A game the minute I leave the taxi.

Phone in hand, I keep refreshing Instagram over and over again, waiting to see where she is. I'm standing in the shop, off to the side of the entrance, wheelie basket in hand, looking like the creeper who wears sunglasses indoors. I scanned the shop—quickly—and didn't see her. My eye has been on the door ever since. I checked the subways app for delayed trains, and it's no worse than usual—yes, I've taken my stalking to the next level.

But still, nothing.

Ready to give up and leave, I stuff my phone in my pocket just as Luna walks through the door. Her hair is in a tight bun on the top of her head, showing off the beautiful curve of her neck. She's wearing one of those one-piece romper things, in navy blue, paired with simple sandals. She lifts her sunglasses on top of her head and takes in a deep breath before smiling, as if she's just stepped into her happy place.

Relaxed—it's the only way to describe her as she grabs a wheelie basket of her own and pulls out a piece of paper from her purse. She glances at it, looks up at the signs in the store, and then starts heading back toward the flour.

Stealth, Alec. You can do this.

Keeping my distance, I move along with her, trying to be as casual as possible. I pick up a few things, all the while keeping my eyes on her. I even put some birthday candles in my wheelie basket. I have no intention of buying them, but it gives off the vibe that, *yeah*, I'm wearing sunglasses inside, but I'm trying to make a birthday cake, so leave me alone.

She stops in front of the flour. I park my basket across the aisle from her and pull a box of molasses cookies off the endcap and make a show of taking in the ingredients. In my back pocket, I have a list of my own, knowing exactly which basics I need when I practice making the cake every night this week. But the question here is: Which ingredients is she buying? Which brands? Because you can bake the recipe all you want, but there's always something special about the actual ingredients you pick up. It's kind of like getting that special recipe from your grandma, and it says to add some sugar but doesn't give you the measurement. *Well, how much fucking sugar, Grandma?*

This is like that, but with the ingredients themselves, and there are, in reality, a million different flours to choose from. It makes my head feel like it's about to explode.

I watch her do an IG story about being in the shop and how excited she is; then she reaches up and grabs a bag of flour with blue color squares on it. She returns to her list and goes around the corner. Like a bull out of his block, I toss the cookies away, take off down the flour aisle, and grab the blue flour, which is actually bread flour . . . interesting. See, this is exactly what I'm talking about. The secrets. The fucking secrets.

Pleased already with my idea of ditching work to stalk Luna, I pull out my list and check off flour.

Evil laugh

Smiling to myself, I pocket my list and continue on.

I spend the next few minutes following Luna around, going undetected thanks to her intense concentration on picking the right ingredients—for the both of us.

Item for item, I stack my basket, practically giddy from my brilliant idea. Not only am I going to show up on Saturday with my game face on and perfect ingredients in tow, but I'm also going to make one hell of a cake. A cake that's going to blow Thad's mind—show him how serious I am—and shock the judges, the contestants, the entire crew. They'll see that I'm not just a lawyer but a master baker too.

The *Ace of Cakes* guy with the goatee will want my number.

Buddy Valastro, Mr. *Cake Boss* himself, is going to wonder where I've been all his life.

Paul Hollywood will fly to America personally to give me the coveted Hollywood Handshake without even taste testing, just on appearance alone.

I'm going to be so damn prepared by Saturday that—

SMACK.

I run straight into Luna and stumble backward, my basket colliding with hers, and careen right into a display of macadamia nuts, knocking them to the ground and creating a giant commotion in the middle of the vanilla extracts.

"Shit," I say under my breath as the nuts continue to fall. "Shh," I whisper to the falling cans, trying to capture them before they tumble to the concrete floor. "You're going to—"

"Didn't see you there. Sorry about that."

Luna.

Shit. Shit. Shit.

Lowering my voice to a deep tone I don't think I've ever tapped into before, I say, "Uh, no problem."

"Why are the nuts even here with the extracts? Poor planning, if you ask me," she says, bending down to help with the display.

"Yeah, fine. I got it." I keep my head down and my back to her as much as possible. *Please don't recognize my back, please don't recognize my back.*

Why can't she be the evil wench who's been barking at me for the last few weeks, rather than the nice girl in the store helping me pick up my nuts?

The *store's* nuts, not my nuts. She's not picking up my nuts. My nuts are secure in their briefs, not on display.

The store's nuts.

"Store's nuts," I whisper for God knows what reason.

"What's that?"

Fuck. *Get it together, man.*

"Nothing, I got this. You can keep shopping."

"Well, we both made the mess. Here, let me help you." She moves to grab the cans from my arms, but I twist away, slamming right into the shelf of extracts. Boxes teeter and totter on the edge, and I watch, horrified, as they domino down to the ground.

Fucking hell.

Glass crunches and brown liquid flows over the floor like blood, representing the death of my stealth-like abilities.

"Oh goodness. Uh, let me go get—"

"Everything okay?" a clerk asks, joining us in the extract aisle.

"Think we need a cleanup in the extracts," Luna says, a note of barely suppressed laughter in her voice. "If you can find me a mop, I don't mind cleaning it up."

"That's okay, we'll get someone on it. Just don't touch anything. We'll clean it up."

"Thank you," Luna says so kindly that I actually wonder if she's the same person I've been spending my weekends with. She turns back toward me. "If you let me help you, we might be able to put the display back."

"Uhh, they don't want us touching anything. I'll, uhh, I want these nuts. They're mine," I declare, clutching at least five cans to my chest.

"Oh . . . okay." Luna sounds a little unsure, but then she slowly backs away. Thank God.

She glances back down at her list, then reaches up, grabs some almond extract, and puts it in her basket. Without even thinking, I revert back to my original plan, copying the grab and putting a bottle of extract in my basket.

She pauses, turns, and looks at my cart.

Fuck.

Then she looks at hers.

Back and forth until she glances back at me, still clutching my nuts in one hand. I keep my head tilted down and my body stiff as her gaze sears through me.

She takes a step forward. Sweat breaks out on the nape of my neck. Another step. Unease flips in my stomach.

One more step. She's so close that I actually stop breathing. Maybe, just maybe, if I don't make a move, I'll disappear.

But it doesn't work. Before I can even consider turning to flee, she tears the hat off my head and removes my glasses.

"Alec." She practically spits out my name.

"Chris, actually. My name is Chris," I say, still using the preposterous fake voice, only to realize that that probably wasn't a smart move, given my fake IG handle.

"What the hell are you—?" She sucks in a sharp breath. "Are you copying me? Are you—" Her hand flies to her forehead, and her eyes widen. "Oh my God, are you ChrisEcrafts? Chris *Evans* crafts?"

Pretty sure I can't be beamed up by Scotty at this point, so instead, I act . . . ignorant. "Luna, is that you? Wow, wasn't expecting to see you here. Yeah, just picking up my weekly allotment of macadamia nuts. Can't get enough of these guys." I toss the cans into my basket and grip the handle. "What a coincidence seeing you here! Well, I'll let you get back to whatever you're doing, and I'll be on my way."

I move to push away, but she grips my cart and holds me in place. For such a small lady, she's pretty damn strong. Through clenched teeth, she asks, "Are you ChrisEcrafts?"

"What? *Psshh*, I don't even know what you're talking about. I'm just trying to get my ingredients, lady." I have one thing left on my list; I decide to push my luck. "Just wondering, if you were to get a certain kind of powdered sugar, what would you get?"

She tosses her hands in the air. "Unbelievable. You're copying me."

"You know, that's a pretty heavy accusation to make without any evidence."

She shoves the nuts to the side and points from my cart to hers.

"Your point?" I ask.

"Hand me your list."

"No, that's private." I back away.

But she does some crazy spin move I feel like I've only seen on the football field, and before I can figure out what the hell she's doing, my list is out of my back pocket and in her hand. Her eyes fly over the paper. I try to grab it back, but she's too quick for me.

When she's done reading it, her eyes bore a hole in me. "You're copying me."

"You don't have proof."

She points to the paper. "Right here it says, with an asterisk next to it, *Don't stray from the list, get what Luna gets.*"

Huh, I forgot I wrote that.

"I had a few drinks last night. I can't be held accountable for what I write."

She holds her hand out. "Give me your phone."

"Yeah, not going to happen." And before she can pull another spin move on me, I back up to the shelf behind me, careful not to knock anything over this time. "None of that tricky spinning shit."

"Let me see your phone."

"No."

"Alec, let me see it."

"Luna . . . no."

"Because I'm right—you're ChrisEcrafts."

"Or you're insane and—"

"Fine," she says, pulling her phone from her bag and quickly typing away on it.

"What are you doing? Calling the police? Just so you know, I know people at the precinct. I'm a friend of the men and women in blue, and I've done nothing—"

Bling.

Smirking, Luna lifts her phone, showing me the message she just sent ChrisEcrafts. The message that just sounded off on my phone.

Fuck.

"Coincidence."

She rolls her eyes and starts lighting up my phone with *blings* as she sends message after message.

"Okay, fine. Stop." I push her hands down. "It's me."

"I knew it," she says, as if she just solved New York's most infamous crime. "I freaking knew it. Last night when I saw the name come across, it seemed too coincidental. But then you sounded so girly in the message that it threw me for a loop." *Ha, maybe I still have a little bit of stealth left in me.* "But I was right," she continues. "You're trying to steal my ideas. Wow, Alec, I knew you were desperate, but not desperate enough to troll me on—" She pauses, as if she remembers something. "Oh my God, your profile . . . were you catfishing me?"

"Don't flatter yourself." I roll my eyes. "I am not a catfisher."

Deny, deny, deny.

"So you're telling me all those things you posted, you created?"

"You looked through my profile?" I ask with a smile. "I'm flattered."

Her eyes narrow. "You seriously have a screw loose. I can't believe you would stoop this low. Well, actually, I probably should believe it, given your losing record. It's pathetic, Alec, really pathetic."

As I stare at her contemptuous face, I don't think I've ever felt worse. It *is* pathetic. It's pathetic that I'm creating a fake profile to stalk a competitor on a wedding show, all so I can feel like I'm repairing my relationship with my brother.

It's pathetic that I've taken so long to realize our relationship even needs repairing.

And it's pathetic that the only way I know how to fix it is by stalking a competitor.

She starts to walk away.

"I am reaching," I blurt out, honestly, bringing our conversation full circle. She pauses and looks over her shoulder. "I'm reaching because my relationship with Thad is practically extinct. I barely know him, I barely know his wife, and if I don't fix the broken communication

136

between us, I know I won't have a relationship with my soon-to-be niece or nephew." Since she hasn't left, I keep talking, one hand gripping the back of my neck. "This is important to him, and I'm failing him. He came to me because I'm his hero, the guy he's depended on to protect him his entire life, and weekend after weekend, I've failed him." Gripping even tighter, I look Luna dead in the eyes. "I don't want to fail him anymore."

I watch the indecisiveness in her eyes—the war between staying and going. Her body is telling her to flee, with one foot in the right direction, while her mind or maybe her heart—who knows?—is keeping her firmly in place.

"I know this isn't your problem and I'm sorry for coming here, for setting up that fake profile. I know it wasn't right, but like you pointed out, I'm pathetic, and when you're this desperate, you'll do pretty much anything."

She still doesn't respond, just continues to stare at me, as if she can't quite understand what's going on. Hell, I don't understand what's going on either, Luna.

But as the store's employees come to clean up the vanilla, the silence between us stretches and awkwardness takes over, until I sigh, grip my basket, and start to walk away.

I'm about to turn the corner when she calls out, "Wait."

I look over my shoulder. "Any type of powdered sugar should be fine," she says. "Just be sure to sift it so there are no chunks when you whip it into icing."

As if she's shot an arrow at me full of fresh air, I feel my lungs expand in relief. I look over my shoulder and smile. "Thank you."

Then I turn the corner, grab some powdered sugar, and wheel my basket to the checkout counter, macadamia nuts and all.

Chapter Twelve
Luna

The door slams shut and Farrah's voice rings through the apartment. "God, I swear choosing to live with you was one of the best decisions I ever made, despite the glitter I find on my Q-tips after cleaning my ears." She sets her bag down. "What is that heavenly smell?"

"Cake," I say in a monotone voice, staring off at the basket of dicks needlepoint in the entryway.

"Oh, Mama likes herself some cake. What kind?" Farrah steps into the kitchen and picks up a fork.

"Vanilla bean with a berry and buttercream filling." I don't mention that I had to make the cake batter twice because I messed up the first round. I blame it on being distracted, not the fact that I never seem to make a cake right the first time. Hence the practicing.

"Smack my ass, that sounds delish. Where is it?"

"Cooling." I'm still staring at the needlepoint when Farrah pokes me in the shoulder with her fork.

"Hey, what's with you? Were you shot by a tranquilizer? If you were, tell me where, because I could use some tranquilizer after the kind of day I had."

I keep staring, the look in Alec's eyes burned in my memory.

Embarrassment.

Desperation.

Regret.

Hope.

They all collided and reached out to me when he admitted to his and Thad's less-than-great relationship. I had an inkling that was the case, given the bickering I kept hearing from their workbench, and the way his apathy clashed with Thad's general drama and intensity.

But to see the pure sorrow in Alec's eyes over admitting to it . . . hell, it cut through me. I couldn't imagine feeling estranged from Cohen— the thought of it just about knocks the wind out of me. My relationship with my brother, and with my whole family, really, is everything. I rely on them for moral support, for good times, for encouragement, and to be my cheerleaders. And it seems like Alec doesn't have any of that.

I always wondered what he was hiding behind those green eyes, and now I know what it is: fear of losing his brother.

The look on his face, his sullen voice, it's all been on repeat ever since the shop, putting me in this weird funk where I can't quite feel anything. Instead, I've just gone through the motions of baking, not thinking, just dumping. I haven't paid attention, I haven't put thought into how I plan on decorating, and I sure as hell haven't been tracking my progress like I said I would on Instagram. If I really think about it, I'm not even sure how I have two cakes cooling in the fridge. Have you ever driven somewhere but can't quite remember how you got there? That's how I feel right now.

"Hey, you there?" Farrah snaps her fingers in front of my face, pulling my attention away from the needlepoint.

"Yeah, sorry," I shake my head and take a deep breath. "Just an odd day, that's all." I stretch my hands above my head. "I think I'm going to go lie down for a second. Probably too much taste testing, you know?"

"Okay . . . ," Farrah answers cautiously. "Do you want me to do something with this frosting?"

I made frosting? I glance over at the bowl of white frosting that's resting beside a mound of cut-up berries. Good lord, I really did zone out. "Uh, just leave it there. I'll be back out to ice everything, and then we can dig in."

"Sure, yeah." Farrah studies me a little longer. "Are you sure there's nothing you want to talk about?"

Oh, there's so much I would love to talk to her about. But after our last conversation about Alec, I'm pretty sure she would show zero sympathy toward the man.

"I'm good. Just a little loopy." I give her a quick peck on the cheek and head toward my room. I quietly shut the door, flop on my bed, and reach for my phone, which has been charging on my nightstand. I unplug it, open up Instagram, and click on my messages, secretly hoping there's one from ChrisEcrafts.

But I'm let down.

I don't know what I was expecting—another apology? An update on the cake he was going to make? Maybe a jab or an insult like we used to exchange? But nothing is somehow even worse.

I nibble on my bottom lip, wondering if I should message him, see how the cake is, but the thought makes my stomach flutter with nerves. So instead, I click on his profile and review the obvious stock images he's turned into his own. As I look at it more closely, I notice all of them were posted yesterday. If I'd been more suspicious, I would have picked up on that immediately. But how was I supposed to know Alec Baxter was going to make a fake profile to try to weasel some information out of me?

Weasel information . . . a small smile creeps up my lips.

The man created a fake profile.

Chatted with me about procraftinating—which required research.

Was astute enough with social media—despite his snobby attitude—to watch my IG stories to figure out where I was going to be.

Dressed up in some weird hat and sunglasses.

Followed me around the store, making sure to grab everything I grabbed . . .

I chuckle.

Fumbled massively with cans and cans of nuts.

A huge smile cracks over my face.

Made up a lie about loving macadamia nuts to save face.

I snort and cover my mouth.

The more I think about the entire situation, the funnier it becomes.

So out of the realm of what I would ever expect from the man who seems like he carries wet bread in the crotch of his pants.

The man with the nuts.

Alec Baxter of the fancy shoes.

Mr. Stodgy Bread Pants.

I snort again, and tears squeeze out of my eyes from the laughter that's bubbling up inside me. If Farrah knew I was laughing hysterically in here by myself, she would think I'd officially lost my mind.

Maybe I have, because before I can stop myself, I'm typing a message out to Alec in Instagram.

LunaMoonCrafts: Enjoying all those nuts?

Still lying on my bed, I cover my mouth again as I try to hold back more laughter. I don't have to wait too long to see a response from him.

ChrisEcrafts: Didn't realize macadamia nuts are an acquired taste.

I laugh quietly, turn on my bed so I'm lying on my side, and type him back.

LunaMoonCrafts: And here you were so convincing that they were your favorite.

ChrisEcrafts: Oh yeah . . . they are . . . absolute favorite. Can't seem to pace myself with these nuts. They're going down in waves.

LunaMoonCrafts: Am I detecting a sense of humor?

ChrisEcrafts: Am I actually reading words? Not just barking?

I laugh out loud, and my eyes float to my door. I wait a few seconds to see if Farrah is going to burst through. She doesn't. I need to keep it together.

LunaMoonCrafts: That was weird, wasn't it?

ChrisEcrafts: I mean, first time I've ever had a girl bark at me, especially with such rabid fangs.

LunaMoonCrafts: First time a guy pissed me off so much that I reverted to barking.

ChrisEcrafts: I need to keep that in mind the next time someone pisses me off.

LunaMoonCrafts: What I wouldn't give to see the posh and sophisticated Alec Baxter dig deep into the pit of his stomach and let out a yelp.

ChrisEcrafts: I wouldn't yelp—I'm not a goddamn Chihuahua. I'm a St. Bernard. A good Aaaroof with girth and bellow is the way I would bark.

I snort even louder.

LunaMoonCrafts: If you had a beard, I would consider the girth and bellow. But right now, the only thing I can possibly bump you up to is a greyhound.

ChrisEcrafts: I should be insulted, but I can kind of see it.

I should not be enjoying this conversation. I shouldn't even be partaking in it, to be honest, but I can't help myself. With the stress of the competition and the constant pressure to do my best for my brother and Declan, the realization that Alec is struggling even more than me, and actually cares about it . . . well, I've reached my breaking point.

I give in.

I allow myself to talk to someone who actually knows what I'm going through.

LunaMoonCrafts: Glad you've come to terms. How's the cake coming along?

ChrisEcrafts: I was just waiting for you to ask. Here's a pic.

I wait for it to download, and when it does, I snort so loud my nose stings.

"Oh my God," I say quietly, taking in the heap of "cake" that's crumbled and stacked together. At least my skills aren't as bad as Alec's. It's like a messy science-fair volcano. There's no rhyme or reason to it: icing is sporadically stroked all over, berries are sticking out on every end. And there are so many crumbs that I'm pretty sure he didn't grease the pans.

ChrisEcrafts: Nailed it, right?

LunaMoonCrafts: That is . . . something.

ChrisEcrafts: I've never baked a cake in my life and now I know why. That was unpleasant.

LunaMoonCrafts: Then you don't want to see mine.

ChrisEcrafts: Let me guess, perfectly symmetrical, smells like a dream? The complete opposite of the pile on my counter? I pulled mine out of the oven and cringed. It did not smell good. Think I put something in there I wasn't supposed to.

LunaMoonCrafts: It's nice that you tried. And if we're being honest, I screwed up my first batch of batter. It tasted horrid and I had no idea why.

ChrisEcrafts: Be still my heart, Luna Rossi is admitting imperfections.

LunaMoonCrafts: Gloat much?

ChrisEcrafts: Not really, actually. Nothing to gloat about, but I'm going to keep trying with this cake thing. I'm determined. Tomorrow I'm attempting practice cake number two. Any advice?

LunaMoonCrafts: Grease the pans before you put the batter in.

ChrisEcrafts: No wonder you have over five hundred thousand followers.

LunaMoonCrafts: How was round number two?

ChrisEcrafts: Have you ever had one of your cakes grow a goiter?

Sitting on my bed with a fresh glass of tea on my nightstand, I chuckle and shake my head. I spent the entire day catching up on my projects, eating the cake I made last night—relieved that it didn't taste like rat poison—and wondering when I was going to hear from Alec about his second attempt.

After I gave him some advice last night, he signed off, claiming he needed to dispose of the "evidence." I wished him luck and then went back to the kitchen, where I finished icing and putting my cake together, wondering how it was possible for Alec to screw up as badly as he had.

LunaMoonCrafts: Can't say that I have. I'm going to need a picture.

ChrisEcrafts: Steady yourself. It's a horror show.

The picture comes in, and I nearly fall off my bed in a fit of giggles. Thankfully Farrah is out on a date right now, so I can be as loud and alarming as I want.

Flat on the counter, with no plate underneath, is a lopsided cake. It has more structure than yesterday's, but it's on the verge of toppling over because with each tier, there is a massive "goiter," misshapen and bulbous, making the tops incredibly uneven.

ChrisEcrafts: It looks like it's about to morph into a creature and eat your face off, right? To be honest, *Leans in, whispers* I feel like it's the cake from yesterday reincarnated.

LunaMoonCrafts: I am scared for your life.

ChrisEcrafts: What I'm really wondering is how it put itself back together and climbed up the trash chute?

LunaMoonCrafts: I would be worried about it having a key to your apartment, and who else it handed a key to.

ChrisEcrafts: Shit, I didn't even think about that. I just shivered in my briefs.

LunaMoonCrafts: Time to change the locks.

ChrisEcrafts: I'm on the phone with a locksmith now.

LunaMoonCrafts: While you're on the phone, I'll let you know, it looks like you overmixed the batter.

ChrisEcrafts: You can overmix batter? Jesus. I didn't even know that was a thing.

LunaMoonCrafts: Baking is a science. There are many ways you can screw up.

ChrisEcrafts: I'm finding that out. Hell . . . I'm trying here, and all jokes aside, I really feel like I'm going to let Thad down again. It's a tough pill to swallow.

I feel for Alec, I really do. I couldn't imagine being in his shoes (or, more accurately, loafers)—having a rocky relationship with my brother already and then feeling like I'm constantly failing him. It tugs at my heart and makes me want to do something stupid.

Really stupid.

LunaMoonCrafts: I can show you if you want.

I press send and realize the mistake I've made.

Show him, as in, I would go to his place or he would come here. Wait, no, not here, most definitely not here. Farrah would lose her mind.

Hoping he's one of those people who says, "Oh no, I don't want to take up your time," I hold my breath, waiting for his answer.

ChrisEcrafts: You would seriously do that?

Shit.

Now what?

I bite my bottom lip. The longer I wait to answer, the more it will seem like I didn't mean it. And I guess I didn't mean it, but I don't want him to know I didn't mean it—then he'd just think I'm rude. And even though we've been rude to each other in the past, I feel like we've turned over a new leaf. I'll probably have to go through with the offer, even though it makes me sweaty and nervous, and, oh God, why did I get close enough to smell him the other day, and why does he smell like a man who just came out of a pool of pheromones?

Damn, I really need to stop rambling.

What it comes down to is this: I need to follow through on the offer my fingers tricked me into making, because it's the kind thing to do.

LunaMoonCrafts: I would. But you'd owe me.

ChrisEcrafts: I'll provide dinner. Whatever you want.

Crap. Dinner and baking. Feels like a date.

LunaMoonCrafts: I like tacos.

God, why did I type that? My fingers are reacting before I can even fully process what's going on.

ChrisEcrafts: Perfect, so do I. I'm assuming we live in the same neighborhood, which means you probably know about Stuff My Shell.

Ugh. That's my favorite tacos place.

LunaMoonCrafts: How do you know we live in the same neighborhood?

ChrisEcrafts: The diner. No one goes there unless they're in the neighborhood.

I forgot about the diner. Apparently he hasn't. Does he have the mind of an elephant? They have good memories, right? That phrase *elephants never forget . . .*

LunaMoonCrafts: You're an elephant.

*ChrisEcrafts: *Scratches head* Trying to figure out how that came out of the blue, but I'm afraid I'm not putting the puzzle pieces together. A little help, please.*

Look who's panicking now. Might as well be in the middle of the extract aisle, bumbling around with a stack of macadamia nut cans.

*LunaMoonCrafts: You know . . . elephants never forget? *cringes**

ChrisEcrafts: It's good to know I'm not the only one who can make a buffoon of themselves in this relationship.

Oh, God. Relationship. I know he means it in a friendly way, but my heart trips over the word, which doesn't help the teeny, tiny, positively miniscule crush I might be—or maybe not; could be indigestion—developing.

I'm hoping that tingle in my sternum isn't coming from his humor, his humility, his honesty. I'm chalking it up to the pad thai I had for lunch.

But then . . .

ChrisEcrafts: Granted, I'm the bigger buffoon, but at least you're showing signs of buffoonery and it's giving me life.

I'm smiling so hard.

Cheek-to-cheek smile.

The kind of smile observant people catch and say, "Oooo, what's making you all giddy?"

Answer: Alec Baxter, the last person I ever thought would make me smile. He's made me scowl, but smile? Color me surprised.

ChrisEcrafts: So . . . Tacos and baking? Tomorrow night at six? You in?

I don't think I even have a choice in the matter.

LunaMoonCrafts: I'm in. Send me your address. Get ready to work.

ChrisEcrafts: I wouldn't expect anything less.

CHAPTER THIRTEEN
ALEC

Fuck, I'm nervous.

Like really fucking nervous.

The type of nervous that rips through your entire body, making you jittery and cold but sweaty at the same time.

Luna Rossi is coming over to my place to teach me how to bake a cake. What are the odds of that happening?

Was I expecting her help?

No, not this kind of help. Maybe tidbits here and there, but not an actual tutorial. Nor was I expecting to invite her over for dinner.

But here I am, pacing the length of my spotless apartment, hand pushing through my hair as I wait for her to come over. I went in to work early this morning so I could get everything done before I took off to grab the tacos and head back to my apartment. I had a cleaning service come by to make sure every surface was spotless, especially the kitchen. I cleaned it myself, but there was still flour everywhere; apparently, a law degree is not useful in figuring out how to gradually add flour while mixing.

I changed out of my suit and into a pair of jeans—my after-work sweats seemed way too casual—and a short-sleeve black shirt. I debated putting shoes on until I realized it would be weird if I wore shoes in my own house, so I stuck with just socks, because jeans with no socks sends a mixed message. I've been told jeans with no socks is sexy; I don't want Luna coming into my apartment, seeing me in jeans with bare feet, and then thinking I have other ideas about the kind of cake we're going to make. If you know what I mean. *Wiggles eyebrows*

This is strictly a professional visit, even if I think Luna is gorgeous and she makes me laugh, and I could see myself cuddling with her on the couch . . . or even better, pulling her back to my bedroom and slowly stripping off her clothes before tasting every inch of her body.

Christ, I'm having fucking fantasies after years of swearing off any kind of relationship. Pull it together.

I clear my throat. *Business, Baxter. This is strictly business.*

Knock. Knock.

My head snaps up to the door. She's here.

Oh fuck, she's here.

I spin around in a panicked circle, for who knows what reason. *Answer the door, you raging moron.*

Right.

Be cool, be casual, don't say anything stupid.

With a deep breath, I open the door to reveal Luna standing on the other side, wearing a pair of black leggings that emphasize her petite frame and a red shirt—which is really her color. Her hair is pulled up into that signature bun she likes to wear, large black glasses frame her face, and her skin is practically glowing without any makeup. A canvas bag is slung over her shoulder. Her smile twitches ever so slightly, and I wonder if she's just as nervous as I am.

"Hey," I say.

"Hi." She gives me a curt wave. "You going to let me in?"

"Oh yeah, sure, sorry." I step aside and shut the door behind her.

She takes in my apartment, and there doesn't seem to be any praise or disapproval in her eyes. I feel the same way: neutral.

"Did you have an easy time finding the apartment?" I ask, stuffing my hands in my pockets.

"It's actually three blocks away from my place."

"That close." I nod, feeling so awkward it's painful. "Imagine that."

"Yeah," she says, avoiding all eye contact.

Silence coils between us, and I feel like it's about to eat me alive. This is it, how I go: painful silence with a girl I've come to be *sort of* fond of. And here I thought my impending doom was going to be one of my client's exes, angry because I won over the prized yacht he never used in the divorce proceedings.

Unsure of what to say, I let out the first thing that comes to mind. "This was easier when we were fighting. Want to fight about something?"

She chuckles, and it eases the tension in my chest. "I don't know, the night might still end in fisticuffs and a trip to the emergency room. And to be honest, I really don't feel like driving around in a cop car tonight."

"Are you implying that I would be the one headed to the emergency room?"

She holds up her fist. "Take a look at this. Total knuckle sandwich. I'd stuff it down your throat before you could even think to chew."

"Yikes, Luna." I hold up my hands. "That's a little aggressive."

"Got to be when you're in New York City. Not all of us can afford a car service to drive us around so we don't scuff our hideous loafers."

I chuckle and shake my head. "I'm a lot more down to earth than you think." I point down my hallway, toward my room. "And down there are all five pairs of my shoe collection. Please peruse them and see that I don't have just loafers."

"Only five? Hell, I have more shoes than you."

"You'd be surprised what you'd find if you stopped judging a book by its cover and actually flipped it open." I almost smile, remembering one of our first conversations.

She gives me a sly once-over. "Maybe I'll give it a flip tonight, but first, tacos. I'm starving. I usually eat at five on the dot."

"What are you, eighty?"

"Technically the elderly are known for eating at four."

"Well, I don't want you dying of starvation."

I direct her to the table, where I have a dozen tacos waiting to be consumed as well as some chips and salsa. As she sits down, I go to grab some glasses of water for us.

"I only have water. I hope that's okay. Drank all my beer the last couple of nights and didn't get a chance to restock."

"Water is gr—oh my God, you got the pineapple salsa."

"You like it?"

"It's my favorite." She dips a chip in it and pops the whole thing in her mouth. "Ugh, it's so good. Thank you."

"Of course. Just remember the salsa when you're elbow deep in flour with me."

I set the two water glasses down and start digging in. Luna does the same, taking three tacos and putting them on her plate along with some chips and salsa.

"So." She holds a taco up to her mouth. "Why are you being nice to me?"

I laugh out loud, thankful I haven't taken a bite of my taco just yet. "Just going to come in hot with the questions, huh?"

"I don't beat around the bush."

"So I've noticed." I take a bite, chew, and swallow. "Honestly, I never wanted to be mean to you in the first place. It just happened. I was in a shitty mood, and I took it out on you. I tried to bridge the gap, but you went all dog on me and made it impossible."

"A tip from Farrah."

"Does she often have to fight men off?"

"More than I'm sure she cares to admit. Glad the barking worked, though—helped me focus."

"Why? Was I distracting you?" I raise a brow at her, and her eyes widen.

"What, no, I mean . . . no. Not like *that* kind of distracting. Not the sexual kind. But you know, the competitive kind."

I smirk. "Why don't you act a little more horrified? Feels really good."

She laughs this time and leans back in her chair, studying me. "I'm a little nervous, okay? This all seems so weird and strange, so excuse me if I'm a little awkward."

I drum my fingers on the table, studying her in return. "I'm a little nervous as well."

"Really? The man who doesn't seem to show any sort of emotion? Nervous?"

"I am." I pick up my taco. "Not every day I get to be in the presence of DIY royalty."

She rolls her eyes and throws her napkin at me. "You are every weekend, and I'm not talking about me."

"Then who? Wait, are you talking about Mary DIY?"

"Uh yeah. She's the queen."

"She's fucking rude."

"What?" Luna asks, as if I've just insulted her. "Mary DIY is not rude. Well . . . I mean, she's—"

"Have you actually met her yet? Like, officially met her, talked to her when the cameras weren't rolling?"

"I mean, she's busy. . ."

"No one is that busy. Hate to say it, but the lady is self-absorbed."

"Yeah." She sighs. "I didn't want to believe it, but she is sort of rude."

"She is, and I'd be worried if I were her—I think there's going to be a new queen in town."

Luna points to her chest with a chip. "Are you talking about me?"

"Who else would I be talking about? Know-it-all Helen?"

"Well, she does seem to know how to tell everyone what to do but has no actual skills, which is rather impressive in itself."

"Not as impressive as the things you've been turning out week after week," I admit.

She twists her water glass as she looks up at me. "Are you giving me a compliment, Alec Baxter?"

"Yup. And I mean it. You're good, Luna. Really fucking good. Cohen is lucky to have you as a sister."

Growing serious as well, Luna says, "That means a lot to me. Thank you."

"I mean it."

"I know you do."

And then we stare at each other again, but this time we're not avoiding eye contact, we're not awkward. We're just observing one another, appreciating the understanding we've come to. Maybe we've gone from judging the book by its cover to starting a whole new chapter—one where we can be friends.

"Gah, no!" Luna shouts, stopping me from pouring baking powder into the cake batter. "Dry mixture—put it in this bowl." She hands me a bowl and directs me to dump the rest of the dry ingredients in. "We mix dry and wet separately."

"Technically, sugar is dry."

"Sugar doesn't count." She hands me a mixing spoon. "Carefully fold the ingredients together, and then we'll combine everything."

"Hmm, you left those instructions out when you sent me the recipe."

"Based on the profile I was sending them to, I assumed that would be common sense."

"Didn't even cross my mind."

She chuckles and leans against the counter while I finish up. "So you've really never made a cake before?"

"Nope." I shake my head. "Growing up, my parents didn't exactly spend weekends doing fun things with us like making cupcakes or throwing a baseball. We were on our own, which meant I had to learn whatever I could by myself and teach everything to Thad."

"Oh . . . I didn't know." She looks down at the ground. "You had a bad childhood?"

"From the outside looking in, we would have seemed perfect—Park Avenue apartment, fancy private schools, extravagant birthday parties, and even more extravagant presents. Our friends thought we were so lucky, but nothing went deeper than our possessions. We had nannies, but they were there just to make sure we stayed alive. There was no emotional connection because my parents wouldn't allow it." I shrug. "Thad and I only had each other."

"Wow." She faces me and puts her hand on my forearm. "I'm sorry, Alec. I had no idea."

"You don't have to apologize."

She bites her bottom lip. "What happened between you and Thad that put such a strain on your relationship? And feel free to ignore my question if it's too personal."

"Nah, it's probably good to talk about. I've been ignoring our issues since college."

Luna flips on the electric mixer—the one she was really impressed that I have. "I want to listen, but real quick, gradually add in the dry ingredients, but not too slowly because we don't want to overmix the batter."

I nod. "When we were young, I made sure Thad was always taken care of. I never wanted him to have to listen to our parents' constant fighting, so I was always sheltering him. I had to get creative because there was only so much two young kids could do." I shuffle the flour mixture in, staring down into the bowl as the wet ingredients mix with it, forming a batter. "When I graduated from high school, I went to Columbia. I stayed close to home in case Thad needed me, but just far enough away so I wouldn't have to deal with the pain every day. My parents divorced my freshman year, and I thought that it was going to be better for Thad, who was fourteen at the time. But the divorce took a toll on my mom. She lost pretty much everything. She and Thad had to move into a tiny apartment in Brooklyn, which was really hard on Thad. He lost most of his friends and his childhood home. My dad forgot we existed, except to send checks for my room and board and child support for Thad. And I became . . . numb. I was so relieved to be done with my toxic family and to leave my childhood behind that I just . . . left everything behind. I got a job for the summer, rented an apartment with a few guys, and lived my life."

"Oh no, Thad."

"Yeah. I left him to face the nightmare alone. But even at that . . . he didn't care. He still wanted to see me, hang out with me, talk to me. And I'd see him from time to time, but as we got older, those hangout sessions became even fewer and further between. I buried myself in work, and when I finally came up for air, Thad was grown up. He was engaged and going to have a baby, and I'd missed all of it. This competition was Thad's way of bringing us closer together, and I've done nothing but push him further and further away because I'm an asshole who can't seem to be comfortable with being uncomfortable."

Luna switches off the mixer, the batter all mixed in, and leans one hand against the counter, facing me.

When I don't look at her, she pokes me in the shoulder, drawing my eyes to hers.

"You're not an asshole. You can act like one, but you're not an asshole. If you were, you wouldn't be making your third cake of the week, trying to win this ridiculous wedding competition for your brother. Sometimes we need that little push we didn't think we needed. It's actually pretty cool of you to be doing this for Thad. I really think if you were an asshole, you never would have said yes in the first place."

I give her a soft smile. "Yeah, I guess."

The cake pans have already been buttered and dusted with flour, so Luna places the mixing bowl beside them and hands me a measuring cup. "Start dividing the batter; fill them a little past halfway so the cakes can rise but don't overflow."

"Okay." I start filling them. "He's mad at me. I can feel it. He usually texts me throughout the week, telling me what kind of challenge we're going to face, how this is going to be *our week*, and how he can't wait to see me on Saturday. He's even invited me over a few times to practice."

"Oh God." Luna brings her hand to her chest. "I think Thad just won a place in my heart."

"I think he's won a place in everyone's heart. He really is a great guy. A little over the top at times, but a truly wonderful soul." I shake my head. "No idea why he's been hanging on to me."

Luna stops my scoops with a hand to my forearm, and I meet her gaze. "You said you're the one who took care of Thad?"

I nod.

"Then that wonderful guy you talk about? He's a reflection of you, Alec. He is the way he is because of what you taught him, the love you showed him, despite what might have happened after high school."

Her earnest eyes, her warm hand, her kindness—it's all overwhelming and making me feel things I swore I'd never feel. My body desperately itches to pull her into a hug and thank her—for thinking the best of me when she could easily be thinking the worst.

But instead I just whisper, "Thank you, Luna."

Her eyes still intently on mine, she says, "I only speak the truth." Then she releases my hand and gets back to work. I've never met anyone who speaks about feelings so easily and openly—except maybe Thad, but he only ever talks in hysterics. Luna is different, in so many ways, and I can feel myself growing attached. Especially after our banter and jokes on Instagram. Luna is just fun to talk to, and I can't remember the last time I actually had fun.

"When the batter is poured, you want to . . . are you paying attention?"

"What? Yes." I blink a few times. "Yes, sorry. I'm paying attention."

She studies me for a few beats, her dark eyes a complete mystery I want to figure out. And those lips, plump, glossy—I wonder what they taste like? Just having the thought speeds up my pulse, making me very aware of how close we're standing. And if I was a braver man, I could pinch her chin and bring her mouth close to mine.

"Okay, because if you still need to talk, we can do that too."

I swallow hard and shake my head. "No. I'm good."

"Okay . . ."

She continues, but what she's saying goes in one ear and out the other, because just one thought circles through my head: *When did Luna Rossi become someone I desperately want?*

And when would be the appropriate time to go after what I want?

Luna: How did the cakes turn out?

I stare down at my phone and then back at the perfectly round and solid cakes on my cooling racks. After we put everything in the oven, Luna helped me clean up but then said she'd come over tomorrow to finish up. It was an abrupt end to our night. I'm not sure if it was because I'd creeped her out with my staring or if she really did have to go. Either way, when she asked for my number before she left, a sense of relief ran through me.

And the same relief filled my body when her text popped up on my phone just now.

I take a picture of the cakes and send it to her.

Alec: They look amazing. And they don't smell like rabbit turd.

Luna: LOL. Do you often smell rabbit turd?

Alec: Only in the spring.

Luna: I heard it's ripest then.

Alec: Something to do with wanting to help fertilize the spring flowers . . .

Luna: Are we really discussing rabbit poop?

Alec: I would like to say you started it, but we both know that's a lie.

Luna: Especially because if you scroll up a few messages we have evidence that you in fact started it.

Alec: Moving along . . . the cakes look amazing.

Luna: Once they've cooled, wrap them up like I told you to. And I'll be over tomorrow.

Alec: Does this mean I have to provide more tacos?

Luna: No, I'll bring over my famous goulash, then we'll eat some cake after decorating it.

There's that relief again. Maybe I didn't creep her out. Maybe she really did just have to go, and I've been overthinking all of this way too much.

Alec: Sounds good.

Luna: Same time?

Alec: Yup. And hey, Luna?

Luna: Yes . . .

Alec: I know I said it before, but I figured I would say it again: thank you. I'm not sure you'll understand how much your help means to me.

Luna: You're welcome, Alec.

CHAPTER FOURTEEN
LUNA

Alec: Thought I would try to impress you and make the icing before you got here. Big mistake.

I chuckle at his text and type him back as I walk to his apartment.

Luna: What happened?

Alec: You'll see.

Luna: Should I be scared?

Alec: Very.

Luna: Be there in five.

I put my phone in my purse, clutch the container of goulash closer to my chest, and pick up my pace. Not just because I want to see what happened, but also because I'm excited to see *him*.

Last night was . . . intimate. More intimate than I'd expected. I saw a new side of Alec, one that's incredibly endearing and sexy. Not many men can admit to their faults, but Alec did it with such ease that it made me realize the kind of man he really is. He might be hard as stone on the outside, but he's also kind and thoughtful and has a heart I never saw coming.

I meant what I said last night: that Thad is a reflection of him. There is no way he's not, especially with the hand Alec had in raising him. I can't even imagine what that must have been like, feeling the need to protect your sibling from your parents while missing out on your own childhood.

Cohen and I didn't grow up that way. Our family was a solid unit of four. We did everything together. My parents fought, sure, but never in front of us, and even when we knew they were fighting behind closed doors, we never doubted how much they loved each other.

Plus, Alec is . . . fun. He's different. He makes me smile and laugh. He's more down to earth than I would have expected. In other words, he's exactly my type.

I know I should be cautious with him, given our rocky start and the fact that we're competitors, but hell, I can't help but want to hang out with him again, especially after last night.

Sheesh, last night.

It was more than intimate. It was intense.

So intense that I felt like if I stayed any longer, I might have done something I probably shouldn't have, like leaning in for a kiss, caressing his pecs, running my hand down his stomach. Because good lord, did I think about it. I thought about it when we were pouring the batter into the cake pans, when my hand was on his muscular forearm. I thought about it when we were saying goodbye, as he gave me a curt wave and I smiled like a fool. I thought about it afterward, as I lay in bed texting him. Hell, I thought about it this morning when I woke up.

I wonder if his lips are as soft as they look.

I bet they are.

When I reach his apartment building, I tap in the code he gave me and head to the elevator. I was a little surprised that Alec lived off Amsterdam and Eighty-Second. The neighborhood doesn't scream bachelor pad. It's nice, but it's not posh by any means, and given the guy is a top-rated divorce attorney, I'd think he'd be at least closer to Central Park or maybe somewhere a little trendier. His apartment is definitely bigger than mine and he has nicer furniture, but there is nothing ostentatious about the way he's living. Very modest . . . normal. An apartment like the rest of us have—no personal brownstone or spacious loft, just a normal apartment.

Although, I realize as I step into the elevator, the man does have the KitchenAid mixer of my dreams, and I'm pretty sure he used it for the first time this week.

The elevator doors part, and I head to his apartment. I knock on the door, and it opens immediately.

It takes me a beat to realize what I'm staring at—and then I break out into a fit of giggles.

"Yup, laugh it up. Get it all out," Alec says, gripping the edge of the door, his handsome face the poster child of a Pinterest fail.

His face is covered in powdered sugar. His eyebrows are caked, his cheeks are washed in white, and it continues down his neck to his chest.

"Turn on the mixer too high?"

"Yup."

I laugh some more, shake my head, and step into his apartment. I grab him by the hand as he shuts the door behind me and lead him to the kitchen, where I wet a paper towel and start wiping away at his face. He just stands there, letting me take care of him. The paper towel rubs against the hard scruff covering his jaw, and I realize he hasn't shaved.

"Growing a beard?" I ask, finishing up.

"I have to if I want to be a Saint Bernard in your eyes. None of this greyhound shit."

"You can't be serious." I chuckle.

"So serious." He winks, then takes the paper towel from me and tosses it in the trash. "Thanks for soothing my distraught baking heart. I had all these hopes of proving something to you, but I just proved that I suck at this."

"Just a learning curve, that's all." I hold up the goulash. "Shall we?"

"Yeah, let me go change my shirt, give my face a good rinse, and I'll be right out. Think you can handle grabbing some bowls for us? I got some more drinks in the fridge this time."

"Sure. Should I just dig around in the cabinets?"

"Have at it," he says as he takes off toward his bedroom.

Have at it. Simple as that. Like we're longtime friends.

Okay.

I set the goulash down and turn toward his cabinets. Where would he put bowls?

I reach for a cabinet that I would consider a bowl cabinet, and I'm pleasantly surprised when I find them on my first try. Means he has a good sense for organization. I find spoons right off the bat as well and take everything to the table, along with a large serving spoon and napkins.

Drinks are next.

I open the fridge, and I'm surprised again to see that it's stocked full of Sprite, strawberry Bubly, and cans of my favorite blackberry-lime sparkling tea. Suspicious, because these are all my favorite drinks.

"Find what you need?" Alec asks as he walks back into the kitchen quicker than I anticipated. The sugar is out of his scruff, and he's wearing an olive-green shirt that makes his eyes stand out even more against his incredibly dark eyelashes.

Yup, he's handsome. Stupidly handsome. The kind of handsome that makes your hands clammy and your stomach flip in a million summersaults.

"Uh, hard to choose." I try to gather my wits about me. "This fridge seems to be carrying all my favorites."

He shrugs. "Saw you drinking them on set." He reaches past me, his cologne wrapping me up in his sweet and spicy scent.

"You got me my favorite drinks?"

"Yeah." He cracks open a Sprite. "Why not? You're doing me a huge favor—it's the least I can do. Plus, it's nice seeing that smile." He nods and then walks over to the table, where he starts scooping goulash into the bowls.

Umm . . . pardon me as I attempt to catch my breath.

He likes my smile? I shouldn't feel giddy over that, but I really freaking do. So giddy it's embarrassing.

Before I let out all the cold air in his fridge, I grab a Sprite as well and shut it, and then join him at the table.

"I've never had goulash before," he admits with a boyish grin. "Does that make me an uncultured swine?"

I snort and shake my head. "Just means you're not hanging out with the right people. Don't worry, I'll change that."

We both take a seat, and Alec dips a spoon in his pasta, blows on it, and takes a bite. I watch as his eyes light with interest and the corners of his mouth turn up. "Hell, this is good, Luna."

Pride surges through me, just from a little compliment. I didn't know how much I wanted to impress him until this very moment.

"I'm glad you like it," I say after eating my own spoonful.

"Not just like it, love it." He takes another bite and then asks, "Is this your own recipe or something that's been passed down? From generation to generation?"

"My mom taught me how to make it when I was seven."

"Seven?" He looks surprised.

"I was eager. It's a family favorite. Straight from my nonna's recipe book. Although, she would use homemade sauce. I cheat in that regard."

"Tell me more, Luna." His eyes command my attention and strip me bare as I feel myself wanting to tell him everything.

Clearing my throat, I say, "My mom would serve it every Sunday night. The smell floating from the kitchen into the living room, where Cohen and I would be playing a board game, became so familiar that I wanted to help create it. Technically the dish is supposed to have beef in it." I smile. "But when I became in charge of Sunday-night dinner, I gave it my own twist by adding buffalo as well. I think it adds a richer flavor."

"Bold." Alec smiles. "How did your parents take the change?"

"Dad was skeptical at first. He's not much for change when it comes to his meals, hence the Sunday-night goulash, but he gave it a shot."

"Let me guess—he loved it."

"Says it's the best he's ever had." I can't contain my smile. "It's not traditional goulash by any means, but it's the Rossi Way, and that's all that matters."

He holds a spoonful up to me. "Well, I like the Rossi Way. It's fucking delicious."

"Thank you." I can't help feeling flustered by his intense gaze and the way *fucking* rolled off his tongue so easily. He doesn't seem to swear much, but hearing it just now was incredibly sexy.

"I buy us tacos, and you bring over an amazing homemade pasta dish. I need to step up my game."

"Do you know how to cook?" I ask, realizing he probably didn't have anyone to teach him growing up.

"A little." He sighs and shakes his head. "This is going to sound really pathetic, especially after the story you just told me."

"I'm sure it's not."

"It is, trust me." He lifts a brow. "I lived off takeout until two years ago, when I hired a personal chef to actually show me the basics of cooking. We were never taught when we were young, so I knew nothing when it came to the kitchen . . . hence my baking fiascos. But I was sick of takeout, so I decided to learn a thing or two. I'm no master chef at all. I know the basics of an omelet, grilling, and roasting veggies. But that's the extent."

"Why would I think that's pathetic?"

"Because." He stirs his spoon and then scoops up some pasta. "You actually had someone teach you—someone who loves you. Your family is wonderfully connected. I'm sure if I'd paid the chef enough, he would have pretended to be my father, teaching me the ways of the kitchen, but it was just a stranger."

"That's not pathetic, and it's not your fault, Alec. At least you decided to learn and made it happen. That says more than just hiring the personal chef to do all the work."

"When I burn my chicken in the oven, I often think about how much easier it would be if I'd hired a chef." He chuckles and then takes another bite. When he swallows, he says, "Is it weird that I feel intimidated by you?"

"What? No, you don't."

He nods slowly and meets my gaze. "Hell yeah, I do. Very intimidated."

I nudge him with my foot under the table. "I'm not an intimidating person. I might have been a little brash out of the gate—"

"That's not it," he says. "It's your optimism, your knowledge, the way you effortlessly love your brother, and your thirst for life. It makes me want so much more than the life I'm living now." He chuckles and pushes his hand through his hair. "Christ, there's something about you that makes me get way too chatty."

"I like it," I say quietly. "I like flipping over the cover and seeing what's inside."

"About time," he says with a wink before scooping up the last of his goulash and emptying his bowl.

"You left the butter out," I say, surprised.

"I do read directions on occasion." He laughs and then nudges me with his shoulder, the playful gesture adding to my already-heightened senses.

That miniscule, tiny, itty-bitty crush I was talking about? Yeah, pretty sure it's grown over the last two days.

"You might read instructions, but you don't operate the machinery properly."

"Not quite." He chuckles. "But I'm a good student, so teach me your ways."

"Do you happen to have a hand mixer?"

"Uh, I have this." He points to the KitchenAid mixer. "It has other attachments."

I laugh. "I know. But I prefer a hand mixer when making frosting. I feel like you can get a better whip, and you have more control. Lucky for you, I brought mine just in case."

While I grab it from my purse, Alec slow claps for me. "Travels with own hand mixer. That's really impressive, Luna."

"If anything, I'm prepared. And I know for certain the set will have both, so when you're making the cake, be sure to use the stand mixer for the batter and the hand mixer for the frosting."

"I can do that."

I hold up the mixer. He goes to plug it in, but I stop him with my hand to his forearm. He looks at our connection for a brief moment before I say, "Always put the beaters on first, because if it's plugged in, and you put on the beaters and accidentally switch the mixer on at the same time, you're going to have some gnarly hands."

"Ouch. Okay, noted."

I attach the beaters in their respective spots and then plug in the mixer before handing it over to him. "We beat the butter first."

"Sounds so wrong. Beating the butter." He lowers his voice conspiratorially. "Hey, I'm going to go in the other room and beat the butter real quick—don't wait up."

I pause and tilt my head, blinking.

Blinking.

"Did you . . . did you, Mr. Top-Rated Attorney, just compare beating butter to jacking off?"

He switches on the hand mixer. "Matter of fact, I did. And guess what, both actions cream."

"Oh my God." I pretend to gag, and he laughs out loud. "I don't think I can ever look at you the same."

"Luna Rossi, are you a prude?"

"What? No."

"Seems like it, if you can't take a little masturbation joke."

"Dude," I deadpan, and his smile grows even wider. "We're making white frosting, which we're about to eat, and you're talking about masturbation. You don't see anything wrong with that?"

"Not really, no. But this conversation has led me to believe that maybe, just maybe, you're a little bit of a prude."

"I'm not a prude."

"Prove it," he says playfully.

"Prove it? What do you want me to do? Go 'beat the butter' in the other room while you're creaming the butter in here?" I say, using air quotes.

His head tilts back as he laughs. "I mean, I was looking for a little anecdote from your past, but if you want to go beat the butter, by all means, feel free. All I ask is you wash your hands after. You know, for sanitary purposes."

"And here I thought you were more dignified than most of the men I date . . ." Oh fuck. "I mean hang out with. Not date. I didn't mean to say 'date.' Just, you know . . ." I sigh and press my hand to the cupboard.

"I think beating the butter in your bedroom would be less humiliating than this right now."

He just smiles and turns off the mixer, the butter properly creamed. "What next, boss?"

"Soooo," I drag out, "you're just going to skip over that embarrassing remark?"

"I was planning on it, despite liking the way your cheeks are all flushed, but *you* seem to want to keep talking about it." He crosses his arms over his chest and props his hip against the counter. "By all means, let's dive deep into what you really meant."

"I'd rather not."

"That's what I thought." He reaches out and tips my chin up. "Now tell me what's next, so we can move past your awkward moment and get on to my awkward moment. I'm sure one will happen soon."

Sweet. That's what he is, a sweet, funny man.

And dangerous.

Dangerous because he's a lethal combination of everything I'd look for in a guy.

"Vanilla," I say out of nowhere. "We need to add the vanilla and whip that in too; then we gradually add the powdered sugar."

"Got it." He pours in the vanilla, and when we're ready, I slowly add in the powdered sugar while he mixes. Silence falls between us, and I know it's because I made that weird comment, something that just slipped, and made that Whitney Houston upper-lip sweat reappear with a vengeance.

And I know the silence isn't awkward for him, but it is for me, and I need to do pretty much anything to end it, so I blurt, "Elevator."

He switches off the hand mixer. "Did you just say elevator?"

"Yeah, I did." I swallow and nod for him to keep mixing. "I, uh . . . I once flashed a guy on the elevator. Someone I didn't know. Someone who kept staring at my boobs the whole way up, so I thought, Why not just give him the whole show, since he's trying to rip my shirt off with his eyes? When I neared my floor, I turned toward him, lifted my shirt, and then left, leaving him there, looking pretty shocked."

"Um." Alec's Adam's apple bobs in an intense swallow. "That's . . . wow, why would you tell me that story?"

"To prove I'm not a prude. I'm the exact opposite. I'm a . . . a sexual exhibitionist."

He smirks, just the right side of his mouth lifting up as his brow quirks. "A sexual exhibitionist, huh?"

"Yup, big time."

"Okay. So what else have you done to earn the title 'sexual exhibitionist'?"

"Too many stories to even choose from. We're talking so many stories I could fill a book, and I frankly don't want to bore you."

"Try me."

His challenging nod grates on my nerves, just like the first weekend we met each other, but instead of wanting to give him a good *pow-pow* to the pectoral, I want to pull his head in with both hands and run my tongue over his face.

Show him exactly what kind of sexual exhibitionist I am.

He continues to whip, patiently waiting as I think back to all the crazy and outlandish things I've done. The only thing that comes to mind is positively pathetic, but it flies out of my mouth before I can stop it.

"I was a Christmas tree for Halloween once. Yup, a Christmas tree. Homemade costume. Very eye catching."

"Naturally," he says.

"And being the clever minx that I am, I decorated myself with ornaments."

"Wouldn't expect anything less."

I peek into the bowl and place my hand on top of his, turning up the speed to really whip the frosting, but I keep my hand over his to help guide him as well. I study his reaction, and when I feel his body

170

shift closer to mine, I nearly jump out of my socks in excitement. He's so close, inches away from pressing against me. His breath tickles the loose strands of hair on the back of my neck, and beneath my palm, I can feel strength in his fingers, his commanding grip. What would those fingers feel like gripping my hips?

Is he good in bed?

Who am I kidding? Of course he's good in bed. He practically has SEX VIRTUOSO tattooed across his forehead.

"So, the ornaments."

"What? Oh." I laugh. "Sorry, yes, uh, the ornaments, sexual exhibitionist, sex-ebitionist." He laughs as well. I like that sound, a lot. Deep and intense, but also full of humor. "So, I had them hanging off me, and get this." I lean in a little more, trying to be sly. "I hung two ornaments right over my covered nipples, my very own Christmas melons." I wiggle my eyebrows, and he laughs so loud I can practically feel the vibration in his chest.

"Wow. You're such a freak."

"Right?"

"Positively a menace to society."

"That's exactly what I'm saying . . . sex-ebitionist."

"Wait!" Alec shouts, stopping my hand with his. "Let's . . . let's just stare at it for a few more minutes."

"It's been twenty minutes."

"I know, but I think it's the prettiest thing I've ever made."

I take in the two-tier cake—we kept it simple, with naked frosting and berries as decorations—and I smile. It's really nice. I let him do all the decorating, just helping him occasionally with angles, and I have to admit it: he did a really good job.

And can we admire the sense of pride running through this man right now? It's so freaking adorable.

He won't stop smiling.

He's taken a bunch of pictures of it.

And he keeps thanking me over and over again.

"You did an amazing job. Unless Team Hernandez comes in as cake ringers, I think you have a good shot with placing second."

"Second?" He shoots a look at me. "Why not first?"

"You're going up against me, the master." I wink.

"Yeah, someone who admitted to leaving a cake on the windowsill for the rats to eat."

"I was joking." I roll my eyes. *Sort of joking.* "But just because we're friends now, that doesn't mean I'm going to go easy on you."

"You're calling me your friend?"

"Yeah." I tilt my chin up. "Have a problem with that?"

"No, I like it." He nods toward the cake. "Think I could have a picture with my friend and the cake?" He holds up his phone.

"Of course."

"Here." He hands me the cake carefully. "You hold it." He puts his arm around me, his strong arm gripping me tightly as he squats down to my height and holds his phone up to us. "Smile," he singsongs as he takes a few pictures. When he stands, he checks them out. "Man, I have a great smile."

"Oh my God." I set down the cake before elbowing him in the side. He laughs.

"What? Looking for another compliment? You know I like your smile."

"Not looking for anything but a piece of cake. Can we cut into it now?"

"Fine, destroy my hard work."

"Destroying it is the best part—that means you get to eat it." I cut the cake and serve us up two large slices.

He nods toward the couch in the living room. "Let's sit and eat."

We both take a seat. I sit down first and he follows, keeping little distance between us as he turns toward me, curling one leg on the couch and resting the arm that's holding his plate along the back of the couch. He cuts into it with the side of his fork and scoops up his first bite. I do the same and hold my fork out to him.

"Congrats on a job well done, Alec. You're going to do great on Saturday."

"Thank you. And thank you for the help. You know this means a lot to me."

"I do."

Our eyes connect, something passing between the two of us . . . admiration maybe? But before I can truly analyze it, we both take a bite, breaking up the moment.

Subtle flavors of vanilla and berries hit my tongue. Soft and sweet, the cake is perfect. I truly think this might be the best I've ever had.

"Oh my God, Alec, this is so good."

He quickly takes another bite, his eyes wide in surprise. "Holy shit, did I make this?"

"You did."

He glances at me. "We did."

"You did the work; I directed."

"So I would win the Academy Award for best actor, and you would win for best director, if this cake were a movie?"

"And I'm pretty sure we would both be up on stage for best picture too." I take another bite, savoring how moist the cake is. I moan. "This is so moist."

"Beyond moist. The most moist in all the land," he says with a smile.

"If there was a picture in the dictionary for moist, this cake would be famous for setting the standards of moistness."

"If this cake hosted a party, they would call it the hostess with the moistest."

I snort so hard that I swear cake almost flies through my nose. I swallow quickly and catch a breath, but I can't contain my laughter. My hand falls to my chest. I try to gather myself, but it's impossible. Tears stream down my face.

"Hashtag . . . Hostess . . . with the Moistest," I choke out between fits of giggles.

Alec is laughing too, the sound much deeper and much more steady, as if he's laughing more at my laughter than at the actual joke.

"Oh shit." I wipe under my eyes and take a steadying breath. "That was a total dad joke."

"Easily," he says, his smile impossibly wide on his face. "Frankly, I'm a little shocked I even came up with such a lame pun and got a laugh for it."

"I think I'm going to make a shirt with that saying on it. Top line: 'Cake.' Bottom line: 'Hostess with the Moistest.'"

He laughs. "They would sell out in seconds."

"Like hotcakes."

He tips his fork at me. "Like moist cakes."

"I hate you." I laugh some more.

"You might have before, but you don't now."

I shake my head. "I really don't."

"Yeah?" His brows rise. "Does that mean you would consider me a good friend?"

"Maybe." I shrug.

"Well, well, well. How the tables have turned."

I nudge his leg with my foot. "Don't make a scene."

"Hey, Thad had to learn it somewhere."

"The secret comes out." I wink and take another bite. "So are you bringing this cake to the table on Saturday?"

"Yup. Which means you need to come up with something else."

"Excuse me?" My brows lift in surprise. "Uh, I was the one who shared this recipe with you. This is mine."

"Ah, yes, but the teacher never steals from the student. They teach and they move on."

"That . . ." I shake my head. "That doesn't make any sense."

"It did in my head." He sets his fork down and wipes his mouth with one of the napkins we brought over. "Please, Luna. I know Thad would love this cake, and it would mean a lot to him . . . a lot to me." He bats his ridiculously dark eyelashes at me. "Let me take the cake on this one?"

"Oh my God."

"Can't I have my cake and eat it too?"

"'Hostess with the Moistest' brought you next level; those last two just brought you down to basic."

"Ouch." He chuckles. "You know, when you want to sting, you sting hard."

I lick the frosting off my fork and catch his gaze on my tongue, his eyes glazing over ever so slightly. Just to torture him, I lick the fork one more time and then scoop up another bite. His eyes drop and he swallows hard, making me believe that maybe he wants to be more than just a *good friend*, that maybe I have an effect on him too.

Probably not as much as he has on me, though.

"Cohen taught me to never take crap from anybody." Quietly, I add, "If only he took his own advice growing up."

"Was he bullied?" Alec asks, growing serious.

I nod. "He was. But not because he was gay. He didn't come out until high school. But middle school, ugh . . . it was bad. He would come home and just sprint to his room, where I would hear him crying. He was different. He liked the simple things, like creating and building. He was never into sports, superheroes, or video games. He would spend hours upon hours just working on structures, perfecting some new design. Woodshop was his favorite class. He'd spend his lunches in there so he wouldn't have to worry about the kids. Until his favorite teacher moved because his wife got a new job, and the new woodshop teacher wouldn't let kids work on things during the lunch break."

"Leaving Cohen to deal with the other kids," Alec says, understanding.

"Yup. It was upsetting, to say the least, to see him go through such a difficult time. No friends, completely alone. He would read during recess and lunch, but they would pick on him because at the time, he was small—an easy target. It wasn't until his freshman year of high school that he really started to grow, but by then, the damage had been done. When he came out to me, he was terrified of what would happen to him if the kids at school found out, so he crawled even further inside himself. It's why he's so reserved now. But at least with Declan, he can truly love his life. I just wish he would indulge more in PDA. He doesn't hold Declan's hand in public, and he wouldn't dare kiss him. He always says he doesn't want to bother the people around him or make them uncomfortable, so he keeps his love to himself."

Alec's brow furrows. "How's that fair to him? Or Declan, for that matter?"

"It's not, but one of the reasons I wanted him to do this show was because I knew it would push him out of his comfort zone, make him lower his defenses a bit. He's still reserved in front of the camera, of course, but he's participating, and that's what truly matters."

"It does." Alec studies me for a second. "You're a good sister."

"Thank you. My family is my world. I don't know what I would do without them."

"I'm hoping I can be the same way," Alec says, looking off to the side.

I lean forward and press my hand to his thigh. "You're taking the steps toward that goal, and that's truly commendable. Plus, you're already an amazing brother. You just had to dust off the title a little."

He chuckles. "More like take a leaf blower to the dust, but I'm slowly starting to get there."

I set my plate down on the coffee table and curl into the couch, bringing my knees to my chest. "So, you think you'll be mean to me on Saturday?"

"Depends. Do you plan on barking?"

"Maybe." I smirk.

He chuckles. "I plan on at least saying hi."

"Yeah? Plan on asking for coffee?"

He shakes his head, his eyes playful. "I learned my lesson the first day. I prefer milk and sugar in my coffee, not a loogie."

"Smart man."

His eyes fall to the plate that's still in his hand, now lowered to his lap. "I'll be honest. I'm going to be nervous as hell."

"Why?"

He glances up at me. "The stakes have been raised. Now I might not only let down Thad and Naomi—I might let you down too."

"Stop." I nudge him again. "The only way you can disappoint me is if you beat me. Then I'll be very disappointed that I taught you my tricks."

He laughs, then sets his plate down on the coffee table and stretches his arms above his head. I take in the way his biceps flex next to his ears before glancing down to his waistline, where a light patch of taut skin peeks through. What does his skin taste like? How would it feel under my palms? And below his waistline? How would it feel to slip my fingers under his briefs and—?

"Luna?"

"What?" I snap my eyes up to his. He just smiles as my entire face flames with embarrassment. Oh good lord, he saw. He saw me ogling him. He saw my eyes transfixed on his crotch.

If only the ground would swallow me whole right about now.

"You okay?" he asks, bringing his arms back down. "You look a little . . . flushed."

"Fine. Just fine." I stand quickly from the couch. "Fine. I'm completely fine." I wave my hand over my face. "Just a little hot. You know how ovens can really heat up a space. But I'm fine. Don't worry about me. I just . . . sheesh, it's late; I think I should get going. I'm sure you want me to get going. I have no problem leaving. It's fine. I'm fine. We're all fine." I hurry around the couch, but in my attempt to flee, I trip over his rug and tumble to the ground, whacking against one of his living room chairs with an *oof*.

Why, God . . . why?

"Luna." I can feel Alec rush to me, but I quickly stand and push my hand over my forehead as I maneuver around the furniture, face flaming. "Hey, slow down. Are you okay?"

"Fine. I told you I was fine. Everything is fine. Just grabbing my hand mixer." I race to the kitchen and toss it in my bag, which I left on the counter, and then spin around . . . and slap into Alec's chest. He steadies me, his hands on my shoulders.

"Whoa, take it easy."

I don't even bother looking up. Instead, I step away from him, take his hand in mine, and give it a firm shake while I bow my head awkwardly. "Thank you. Good cake."

I move past him and over to my shoes as he says, "Not just good cake—moist cake."

I slip the shoe over my heel and place my foot on the ground, taking a deep breath. He's trying to lighten the mood, and I appreciate it, given the rather ungraceful exit I'm attempting to make.

"Very moist." Slipping on my other shoe, I lift my bag over my shoulder and wave at him. "See you Saturday."

"Hey." I freeze, and he walks up to me, his eyes never leaving mine. My breath catches in my throat as he comes to a halt less than a foot away. "Thank you for everything," he says before wrapping both his arms around my back and pulling me into his chest.

Instinctively my arms go around his waist and my cheek lands on his thick pecs. My nerves light up from the warmth he's spreading through me, from the way I feel so protected, appreciated . . . oddly fragile in his arms. I've experienced my fair share of hugs, but there's something in the way Alec is holding me, the way his body feels against mine, that has my mind whirling into new territory.

This is the type of hug you don't easily forget. The type of hug you go home and obsess over. The type of hug that keeps you up at night, wishing those arms were still wrapped around you, holding you as you drift off.

I sigh, and my eyes drift shut for the briefest of moments before I pull away and look up at him. I can't hold back the smile that stretches across my face.

"See you Saturday."

He steps back and pushes his hand through his hair as he smirks. "See you Saturday."

Chapter Fifteen
ALEC

"What's with the beard?" Thad asks as he comes up to me and takes a seat on one of the stools next to our designated workbench. He carefully rubs his finger over the dent he put in it a few weeks ago, when he slammed scissors into the top—a total diva moment that's been etched into my brain, especially the crazed look in his eyes.

I scratch my jaw. "Do you like it?"

"It's thick." Thad examines it for a second, but then I think he remembers he's supposed to be mad at me, because he quickly turns away and starts pulling papers out of Naomi's purse—which he carried into the studio for her because he's a confident man who doesn't give a shit about what people say.

"Hey." I poke him in the side, and he swats me away. The set is pretty quiet. Most of the contestants are still arriving and grabbing their morning sustenance, so I push him to talk with me. "Thad." He turns farther away from me. "Thaddeus." Still nothing. "Thaddeus Marlene Baxter."

He whips around, his eyes scorching with lightning as he leans in. "How dare you say my middle name in public."

"Well, don't fucking ignore me. I'm trying to talk to you."

"Take the hint, Alec. I don't want to talk to you."

"Well, that'll make it difficult to win this challenge."

"Why? It's not like you help anyway."

Okay, I deserved that one.

"About that, I'm sorry I've been unenthusiastic about this."

"That's stating it mildly." As he sifts through papers, I pull on his shoulder, forcing him to face me.

"Thad, I'm apologizing. It would be nice if you actually looked at me."

"Wow, what an apology."

Christ.

I drag my hand across my beard. "Listen, I don't want to fight with you. I want to do the exact opposite. I want to . . . to get to know you again. I want to be a part of your life, a real part, not just someone who drops in every few months."

Thad's scowl lessens as he leans against the workbench and folds his arms. "I would like that."

"So would I." I shove his shoulder. "I miss you, man."

"You do?"

"I do."

He nods. "Okay." I can still sense he's a little salty, and I can't say I blame him.

"And the challenge this week—I've got it."

His eyes narrow. "What do you mean, you've got it? I told you we're not paying off the judges. I refuse to win that way."

"I've been practicing."

Thad snorts, and the residue from his nose hits my hand.

Gross.

I wipe the back of my hand on his pants.

"I'm serious," I say.

"*Pfft* . . . you . . . Alec . . . you've been practicing?"

"I have."

"Okay." He rolls his eyes. "After I asked you multiple times to practice with me, you're saying you actually practiced?"

I pull my phone from my pocket and quickly locate the picture of me and the cake—minus Luna—and I shove it in his face.

"I've been practicing."

Thad gasps and pulls the phone closer. "You made that?"

"I did, you fuckhead. So when I say I've got this, I mean it."

"Holy shit," he whispers, staring at the picture. And then slowly, like Tom Hanks from *A League of Their Own*, he says, "We're going to win." He glances back at me, and then the phone. "We're going to fucking win." He spins around and presents his backside to me. "Pinch my ass cheeks. Make sure I'm not dreaming."

"Get out of here." I push him away and take my phone back, mainly so he can't scroll through the pictures and find out Luna was involved.

"I can't believe you practiced. Alec . . . dude." He opens his arms wide, and before I can sidestep him, he pulls me into a hug. "You care."

"I care about you," I say quietly, not wanting to make this a huge moment in front of the whole cast and crew. Luckily, we're the only contestants at the workbenches right now.

"You're going to make me fucking emotional, when I need my game face." He pushes me away and dabs under his eyes. "Okay, this means we don't have to make the chocolate cake I had planned. Thank God—I attempted the frosting last night, and the powdered sugar sprayed up my nose." I can understand that more than he knows. "Go get some coffee or something. Leave me be."

I shake my head and step away. "Don't fuck with my plans today. Got it?" I call over my shoulder. "None of this 'Thad surprise' shit. Follow my lead."

He holds his hands up in defense. "If you produce another cake like that, I'll do whatever you say."

He'd better.

I leave him to himself and head toward the coffee, where I spot Luciana and Amanda talking quietly to each other.

"Good morning, ladies."

"Hello," Luciana says, her tone curt.

"Good morning," Amanda replies, giving me a slow once-over before they both move away.

What the fuck was that about?

I mean, I know I haven't been the most welcoming person on set, but the slow once-over . . . and then it clicks. I glance down at my loafers and wonder if they'll be reporting back to Helen, the shoe snob. My guess is yes, because heaven forbid I wear the same shoes I wore during our first filming.

Seriously, what's wrong with them?

Not wasting any more thought on it, I make myself a cup of coffee.

"Hey." That sweet, now-familiar voice sends a shiver up my spine. I turn and find Luna smiling up at me. I have to repress the urge to lean down and kiss her. Her hair is tied up in a bun, and her lips are doused in red. I can't help but stare at them for a few seconds before I return her smile.

"Morning." I bring my cup of coffee to my lips and blow on it before taking a sip. I glance down at her shirt—and it takes everything in me not to spit out my coffee. I let out a bubbly laugh instead as coffee drips out of my mouth. She hands me a napkin, a knowing smile on her face. "You fucking made it," I say, dabbing at my chin.

Her smile grows even brighter. "I told you I would."

"'Cake: the hostess with the moistest.'" I chuckle in disbelief. This girl is so fucking adorable. "No one is going to get that."

"We do," she says with a shrug as she makes herself some green tea. I watch as she puts a teaspoon of honey in it and a squeeze of lemon. "Sometimes it's nice to be on the inside of an inside joke, don't you think?" She turns back toward me, and her face brightens my day.

"It is."

183

She nods to the side, and I follow her to a sectioned-off area near the cameras, away from the food and drinks, and lean against the wall. "I half expected a text from you last night, a picture of you and another cake, just to show how much you really practiced."

"Want to know a secret?"

"Always." She leans in, clutching her tea near her collarbone.

"I made more frosting last night. Made sure I really whipped it long enough."

"Yeah? What did you put it on?"

I hold out my hand. "My fingers; then I licked it off."

"Stop, you had icing fingers last night? Please tell me there was dinner involved."

"First of all, you used the term 'icing fingers' as if that's a normal thing, and of course I had dinner. I finished off the goulash you left behind."

She smiles softly at the mention of her meal, and I'm overcome with the urge to pull her close and kiss the corners of her mouth, to make that smile even brighter.

"'Icing fingers' is a very common term in baking."

"Is that so?" I raise a brow. "Should I look the term up right now to confirm?" I pull my phone out of my pocket, and she pushes it down.

"No. It's slang. Won't be on the interwebs."

"You know, using terms like 'interwebs' and being a pro knitter aren't making you look any younger."

Her eyes widen. "Are you calling me old?"

"I mean . . ." I shrug.

"Watch it, Baxter." She points her finger at me. "I could still use the same recipe as you and blow you out of the water."

I would love if she blew me . . . not out of the water, though.

"Why did your eyes just glaze over like that?"

"Huh? Like what?" *Jesus Christ, man.* "My eyes are not glazed over."

"Yes, they are. It's like they got a fresh coat of shellac."

"Well . . . you . . . uh . . ."

Think of something, man. Anything . . . just don't mention her blowing you.

She taps her foot and points at the imaginary watch on her wrist. "Waiting."

"Uh . . . you're, uh . . . your lipstick's nice."

Makes no sense, but compliments are always a win.

Her brow furrows. "You're acting strange."

Probably because in a matter of seconds, I've gone from just being attracted to you to being genuinely happy to see you. Because hearing you say hi to me this morning actually filled my lungs with air. Because I'm a hot-blooded man who's starting to have dirty thoughts about you. Because I really fucking like everything about you.

"Nerves," I answer, rocking back on my heels, one hand in my pocket as I take a sip of coffee.

Her face softens. "You'll do great. Just remember what we talked about. Don't overmix, and for the love of God, don't let Thad touch anything."

I laugh out loud. "Trust me, I already told him this morning he is not allowed to help. He can read the recipe to me, but that's about it."

"Then you'll be good." She winks, and I turn into a fucking puddle of mush inside. "I should find Cohen and Declan to go over our recipe. Good luck."

She starts to walk away when I say, "Hey, Luna?"

She glances over her shoulder.

"My shoes—you still hate them?"

She looks down and then back up at me. "Why does it matter?"

"Team Hernandez sneered at them. My ego was bruised."

She rolls her eyes. "Well, if you're looking for me to mend your ego, you're looking at the wrong person. Anyway, I'd have no chance of mending it when you're wearing those shoes." She smiles and takes off.

"What's wrong with my shoes?"

No answer.

Smiling to myself, I sip my coffee. I can feel it: it's going to be a good fucking day.

"One minute!" Mary calls out.

Sweat drips down my back, and my hands shake.

One more minute.

Steady hand, man. Steady hand.

I've refused to look around the room. I've refused to take in any of the hustle and bustle around us. Instead, for the past hour and fifty-nine minutes, I've focused on the cake and the cake alone.

Three tiers is way more of a challenge than the two-tiered cake I made with Luna, but she told me how to handle it, helped me figure out the recipe for the perfect amount, and told me about the stabilizers for the cake so the extra tier wouldn't flop over or sink in.

So far, so good.

My sponges—fancy word for cake—were firm but also felt bouncy, which meant good things inside. I made Thad check off each ingredient as I went so I didn't miss anything, and I had Naomi help me measure things out since my hands were so shaky.

The frosting came out amazing, and now we just have to finish decorating.

"Thirty seconds."

"I think I might pee myself—I seriously think I'm going to pee," Thad says, bouncing next to me. "Oh God, I am going to pee, it looks so good."

"Can you stop talking about pee around the cake? Jesus, Thad."

"I'm sorry. I'm just so excited."

I lay down my last blueberry and then step away.

"Shit, the mint." I've grabbed it from the workbench and am placing it next to the small pile of blueberries on top just as the timer goes off.

The whole crew applauds as we all step away from our cakes.

My hands fall to my knees as I stare up at my cake in disbelief.

It's perfectly golden brown with naked white frosting—just a light scrape of it along the edges, but coating the top of each layer. Berries adorn the top tier and cascade down along the sides. It's nothing of the chaotic mess that's been the wedding so far, but the bright colors of the berries, the rough edges, remind me of Thad in every way.

"Holy shit," I whisper. I did that. I fucking made that. Hands still on my knees, I glance to my right, where I see Luna looking at me, a giant smile of approval on her face.

Fuck.

I want to run up to her and give her a hug. I want to lift her up and spin her around, then set her on the workbench and press my mouth to hers. Thank her. Show her exactly what I'm feeling.

Gratefulness.

Happiness.

Pride.

I have some underlying feelings that I can't quite process at the moment—the type of feelings I never in a million years thought I would ever feel, let alone acknowledge—but seeing Naomi and Thad so happy together, the joy they share, being a part of a competition that celebrates what I demolish . . . it's all softened me. It's made me have second thoughts on my ideals of what kinds of relationships truly exist out there and the kind of impact they can have on your life.

I know whatever is going on between me and Luna . . . it's having one hell of an impact that I don't want to let go.

Thad claps me on the back. "You're amazing." I slip my arm around him and give him a hug. I catch the astounded look on Naomi's face, the tears welling in her eyes. I motion her in for a hug too, and we squeeze Thad between us.

We're acting like we just won the entire competition. But fuck, it feels like we won. After one unsatisfying challenge after another, actually succeeding at something feels good.

Diane calls cut and then says something about cleaning up before we move on to judging. The PAs make quick work of all our dirty utensils, which gives me a second to look at the other two cakes.

At the neighboring workstation, it looks like Luna has made a red velvet cake, which is surprising. I wasn't expecting that at all, because we practiced vanilla. I thought maybe she would change the frosting or the filling, but she changed all of it. I wonder if that was for my benefit, to help my cake stand out.

Secretly, I hope that it was.

I nod at her cake and smile at her, and she smiles back, dark eyes gleaming.

Then I glance over at Team Hernandez, and hope leaps in my chest. They're covered in flour, and Helen looks half-dead, draped over the workbench while PAs move around her.

Are we going to need a medic?

Neither Amanda nor Luciana looks too concerned about the wilting woman next to them, so I chalk it up to Helen's normal dramatic nonsense and focus on their cake.

Chocolate—at least I hope for their sake it's chocolate, and not burned—with minimal frosting, but it doesn't look purposeful like mine; it just looks like they ran out of time. There are no decorations to speak of, and one side of their cake has no frosting at all.

Just from the look of it, I think we easily secured second place.

"Dude, look at Helen," Thad says, standing next to me. "Do you think she needs oxygen after all that yapping?"

"She was yapping?" I ask. "I didn't hear her."

Naomi joins us. "You were so in the zone that I don't think you heard anything. Helen was being so loud I wanted to strangle her. No wonder their cake looks so bad."

Thad turns to me, and the excitement on his face makes me laugh. "Dude, I think we at least got second. I will scream like a lady if we don't."

"Which no one wants." I pat his shoulder and take a deep breath. "I think we got it, man. I think we got it."

I plop down on my couch, prop my feet up on the coffee table in front of me, and lean my head back. Tension leaves my body as I let out a giant exhale.

Fuck . . .

Knock. Knock.

I glance at the door, and then at the time on my phone. Nine o'clock. Who the hell is here?

Cautiously, I pad across the floor, my legs sore from being tense all fucking day. I look through the peephole and straight into a pair of eyes I'm starting to grow quite fond of.

I open the door. "Wasn't expecting you to come over."

She stares up at me, one hand on her hip, the other clutching a Tupperware. "Let me in this instant."

Chuckling, I push the door open, and Luna walks in under my arm. She slips off her shoes, goes to my kitchen, pulls two forks out of the drawer, and then walks to my couch and points at it. "Sit. Now."

Unable to contain my smile, I do as she says. She sits next to me and opens the container in her hand; inside are one slice each of our cakes.

"Care to explain why you're here?" I ask.

"Yes. I need to make sure you didn't pay off the judges today. Your cake looked amazing, but how could it possibly beat out my red velvet? Going into Saturday, I researched the judges and knew they all favored red velvet, so unless you paid them . . ."

I laugh so hard that my stomach hurts. "Luna Rossi, are you a sore loser?"

"I'm a gracious loser, and if I truly think your cake is better, I will shake your hand and be on my way."

"Is that so? You'd admit defeat?"

"If defeat is earned, then yes. But I'm telling you, my cake is unlike anything you've ever had. There's no way it should have placed second."

Yup, you heard her right—yours truly pulled out a first place. I can still hear Thad's screech of joy ringing through my ears. Team Rossi took second, and poor Team Hernandez sucked up third place. Helen had to be pumped full of fluids afterward. She claimed there should have been a redo, since she was incapable of helping the whole time, but according to production, she was quite alert during filming. Naomi and Thad were correct—the lady just would not stop talking.

But I've never in my life felt better about a win, especially when I glanced at Luna and she gave me a sly smile and a shake of her head. I expected a text tonight, not a visit. Though I can't say I mind.

"Only way to find out." I take the fork from her. "Whose should we try first?"

"Mine, of course," she says, holding the Tupperware between us. "Make sure you get a hefty bite of both cake and icing."

"I'm well aware of how to eat, Luna."

She smirks, a wicked glint in her eyes. "Can't be too sure." She digs her fork in and holds it up to mine. "Cheers." She clinks our forks together and then takes a bite. I watch as her lips work slowly over the fork, her eyes shutting for a second. Hell, I'll say her cake is better just from the show she's putting on while eating it.

Not wanting to get caught staring, I take a bite as well and . . . damn, this is good.

Cream cheese frosting and a subtle chocolate flavor to the sponge, with small chocolate chips inside the mix . . . it's really fucking good.

"Well?" she asks expectantly. "What do you think?"

Just to be an ass, I shrug. "Eh, it's okay."

"Bullshit." She pushes at my leg and laughs. "I saw your eyes roll to the back of your head. You want to marry this cake."

"Okay, let's not overexaggerate."

"Then tell the truth."

"Fine." I clear my throat. "It's really fucking good."

"I knew it." She clenches her fist and looks up at my ceiling. "I freaking knew it. I knew that it should have—"

"Before you start celebrating, you still have to try mine." She pauses—she knows I'm right. She cleans off her fork with a napkin. "Make sure you get an equal sponge-to-icing ratio," I say as the fork glides effortlessly through the sponge.

She rolls her eyes at that and waits for me to load up my fork. Then she holds up her fork, we clink them together, and we both take a bite. I already know what my cake tastes like because I had some on set, but the look on Luna's face as she discovers my little hidden secret is probably one of the most satisfying things I've ever seen.

Her eyes narrow. "You bastard," she whispers.

My head falls back, and I laugh so hard I almost choke on the cake in my mouth.

"How did you know?"

I take a second to swallow and then cough out my laugh. When I've gathered myself, I set my fork down. "I can research too, and I stumbled upon a little factoid last night that had me practicing icing fingers into the wee hours of this morning."

"Almond extract," she says, like it's some dastardly villain.

Like any good villain, I rub my hands together. "I just kept thinking, What if Luna comes in with the same cake? How can I elevate this? So I started researching cake flavors yesterday, when I should have been going over a deposition." She smiles. "I was knee deep in ganaches when I realized I should add a flavor I know Thad and Naomi adore, for that personal touch. Katherine Barber, the cake master, isn't always about flavor but about the story behind the end result. She gushed over Thad and Naomi sharing a liking for almond and how they would always try to find new almond-flavored pastries."

"And Katherine is also obsessed with an almond-and-vanilla flavor combo. Damn it," Luna says, slumping back into the couch, defeated.

"I researched several almond icing flavors, went home last night—after going over the deposition, of course—"

"Of course."

"And I started testing out different recipes. Like a freak, I cut some of the cake we made together, cut off the icing, and then started taste testing with the new frosting so I could have a feel for the flavor combinations. But the moment I found it, I knew. I was coming in hot with a winner."

"I can't believe you did that." She shoves at my leg, but I dodge her and grab her hand instead.

The surprise on her face doesn't deter me as I entwine our fingers and press our palms together. Her hand is tiny compared to mine, but so soft, except for her calloused fingertips, which graze the back of my hand.

"I did it for two reasons."

"And what were those reasons?" she asks, staring down at our hands.

I drag my thumb over hers very slowly and deliberately. "Well, I wanted to win for my brother, to start to mend that relationship."

"And did it?"

"It was a start," I answer, reveling in the fact that she hasn't pulled her hand away, that she actually seems to like it.

Sitting here, with our hands clasped, our bodies only a few inches apart, I feel like a teenager again. The excitement and vulnerability, the fear and possibility—they're all rushing back like a tidal wave, pulling me under and making me forget everything I thought I knew about relationships.

"And what was the other reason?" she asks.

I take a deep breath and look her dead in the eyes. "You."

Her breath catches in her throat as her eyes search mine. I want her to see it, the way I long for her, how she has me thinking in an entirely new way.

When she looks away, my heart sinks for a moment, but then the smallest of smiles tips up the corners of her mouth. My confession didn't scare her, not in the slightest. Coyly, she tilts her head to the side and asks, "Why me?"

This is it. An opening. I've been developing feelings for this girl, the kinds of feelings I haven't had in so long, maybe not ever. Luna is special—I knew that from day one, when I attempted to "apologize," and she wouldn't have it. She's so strong in her convictions, and so loving. Incredibly loving. When I opened up about Thad, she showed me more empathy than I've ever experienced before.

And this past week, we dropped our shields and swords and actually spoke to each other like human beings. There's so much I don't know about this girl, but I want to know it all.

"Why you?" My gaze falls to our connected hands. Heart thrumming, gut churning with nerves, I gather enough courage to tell her the truth. "Because I want to impress you, Luna, so when I ask you out on a date"—I look up—"there's no way you can say no."

Her smile softens and she leans toward me. "And you think getting first place in a cake challenge is going to do that?"

"It's one way."

"What's another?"

Christ, she's tempting me.

I want to kiss her, desperately.

I've thought about those lips. I've wondered what they taste like, how they'd feel sliding across my body. I've wondered if she has the same thoughts—and from the way she's leaning in toward me, and the way her eyes flutter open ever so softly, I'm going to guess she has.

I turn her hand over and trace a circle along her palm. "I think that a new pair of shoes might make me date material."

She laughs and leans her side against the couch, curling her legs behind her and inching even closer to me.

"New shoes very well might do the trick."

"I know that would do it for Helen. That old minx has her eye on me—I can feel it in my bones. She makes fun of me, but deep down, she wants a piece of this." I gesture toward my body.

"Is that right? You think Helen has a thing for you?"

"Easily." I reverse my circles on her palm. "The whole shoe thing is a total front. She's trying to make me think she doesn't like me, but really, she's wondering when she can have her way with me in the interview room."

"Wow, that's quite the fantasy you've drawn up. I'm not sure it's Helen who's got it bad. Maybe it's the other way around."

"I mean . . . when she sat on you during the first challenge, it really got my engines roaring. I like a woman who doesn't mind using her ass as a weapon."

She chuckles and shakes her head. "You're deranged. My life was at risk. She might be a slight woman, but she's tough. I felt her butt bones—they left bruises on my stomach."

"Look who's exaggerating now."

"Okay, maybe not bruises, but I definitely felt her butt bones, and it was weird. I don't think you should ever feel another person's butt bones."

"Could not agree more. I like a little meat on an ass."

"Oh?" Her brows rise. "A butt man?"

"Not really. I appreciate everything about a woman's body." I glance down at her mouth. "Especially the lips."

Her tongue peeks out and licks hers, and I have to look away so I don't conjure up any more dirty mental images.

Clearing my thoughts, I ask, "What about you? Do you have a favorite part on a guy . . . or girl?" I add, just to double-check. You can never be too sure.

She laughs. "My favorite attribute on a *guy* . . . hmm." She taps her chin. "I would have to say the penis."

"What?" I simultaneously laugh and choke on my saliva.

"The penis. You know." She nods at my crotch. "The man noodle guys carry between their legs."

"I know what a penis is," I say, coughing. "I just . . . wow, you just jumped right in there, didn't you?"

"What? Did you expect me to say the eyes? Because they're the windows to the soul?" She shakes her head. "No, I know what the good stuff is. It's all about the penis." She holds her hand up before I can respond. "And don't get all judgy on me—you can't tell me lips are your favorite because they're delicate tulip petals on a lady's mouth. You totally like lips for blow jobs."

"I mean . . ." I chuckle. "That's a nice benefit from lips, but you know, I enjoy making out too. I like the way a woman's mouth feels against my skin. I like my chest to be sucked on, kissed. My abs, my hips . . . my cock . . . but yeah, lips are cool."

"Just had to throw cock in there. I see what you're doing. Sure, a mouth is great, especially when it's between a pair of legs." Christ, this is a side of Luna I never would have expected. I have to wonder what kind of adventures she enjoys. "But a confident penis is key to me."

"A confident penis? Didn't know penises could have emotions."

"Oh, they for sure do. The sad ones are always wilted. The excited ones are always knocking on your door, looking to play . . ."

"Okay." I chuckle. "What's a confident penis like, then?"

"A confident penis doesn't have to be big or girthy. It could be on the smaller side, maybe a grower, maybe a little crooked. Maybe it has so much penis skin that it confuses people."

"Okay, the 'too much skin' has me gagging."

"You're gagging? Think of the lady blowing it." She waves her free hand. "That's beside the point. A confident penis is one that knows exactly what to do with what it's been blessed with."

"You're only concerned about the penis? What about all the other parts that go into sex, like foreplay?"

"Trust me." She snags my hand and turns it over on my knee, her turn to do the touching. "Every confident penis I've come across has a sex-educated body attached to it."

Every penis she's come across? How many has she been with? Not that it really matters, but still, the thought of her being with enough men to have a clear idea of the kind of penis she likes *is* daunting.

She slowly drags her fingertips over mine. "Did I freak you out?"

"No." I shake my head. "You just made me wonder if my penis is confident or not."

Her laugh echoes through my silent apartment. "I'm sure it's confident." She yawns and covers her mouth. "I should get back. Double set of interviews tomorrow. Not looking forward to it."

"Me neither."

She stands from the couch and stretches her hands over her head. Her shirt clings to her breasts as she moves side to side. From my vantage point, they look just big enough to fill my palm. Just perfect.

"You can keep the cake."

"Huh?" I ask, blinking up at her.

She smirks, and I wonder if she caught me staring. "The cake—keep it. I can't possibly have the reminder of my loss sitting on my kitchen counter."

I stand as well. "Wouldn't want the great and powerful Rossi to have to swallow her pride, now would we?"

"Never." She walks over to the entryway and slips her shoes on before slinging her bag over her shoulder and holding her hand out. "Congrats on your win. Well deserved."

Fuck, she's adorable.

Sexy adorable.

Tempting adorable.

Everything about her, from her hand in mine to the confident penis talk, has my mind swirling and my need for her growing as I step toward her. As my eyes fall on her lips, she quickly licks them, as if she's anticipating something more from me than a handshake.

It's a minor movement, but it gives me just enough courage to cross that line with her.

I close the distance between us and take her hand in mine, pulling her close so her other hand falls to my chest. From behind, I open the door to my apartment and then maneuver her so she's up against the doorjamb. Her chest rises and falls as she stares up at me, waiting.

"I'm not really into handshakes for congratulations."

"No?" she asks, her voice quavering slightly. "What are you into?"

I don't answer; instead, I bring my forefinger and thumb to her chin and tilt it toward me. I bring my mouth down to hers—then I pause, mere millimeters away, making sure this is what she wants and I'm not reading her wrong.

Her eyes search mine, and with a deep breath, she slides her hand up my chest to my jaw, closing the space between us and pressing her lips against mine.

The first touch is soft, timid. Our mouths are slightly open, exploring. Easy and supple, just what I thought our kiss would feel like, but then she moves her hand up to the back of my head, deepening our kiss and sending a spark of excitement all the way to the tips of my toes. She's making me feel goddamn weak in the knees.

I grip the doorjamb above her head to steady myself and then move my other hand to her hip, holding her in place as I savor the taste of her.

And fuck, does she taste sweet. Like cake and sweet cream and berries, even sweeter than the cake we just ate.

I step in closer, close enough to feel her leg slide between mine but still have a good angle on her mouth. Her free hand moves up my chest, passing over my nipple in just the right way and sending a bolt of lust straight to my cock.

I groan against her mouth.

She moans against mine.

Her grip tightens.

My fingers dig into her skin.

Her mouth opens wide.

My tongue slips in.

And we make out.

And it is amazing. Our tongues dance and collide as we reach for more and more, as if all our pent-up tension and arguments over the past few weeks have been nothing more than intense foreplay—foreplay we didn't even know was happening until just now.

The passion rolls and builds between us, climbing to a crescendo.

More.

I want so much fucking more.

But then her mouth leaves mine and her forehead falls to my chest. She takes a deep breath.

"Oh God, I kissed you."

"You did." I awkwardly chuckle, hoping to fuck she doesn't regret it. "Is that a bad thing?"

I hold my breath as she slowly looks up at me, her chin now on my chest. "No, just a scary thing."

"Scary?" I lift her chin up. "How's it scary?"

"So many reasons. You're . . . you're—" She bites her bottom lip and looks away.

"I'm what?"

She sighs and leans back against the doorjamb. "Alec, you're kind of out of my league."

Talk about a belly laugh—the fucking chortle that flies out of my mouth comes from the depths of my stomach.

"Luna, you've lost your damn mind."

"I'm serious." She pokes my stomach and gasps, then lifts the hem of my shirt to reveal my stomach. "Oh my God, this is exactly what I'm talking about." She pulls my shirt up higher, and I just stand there, enjoying every second of it. "Look at that! A freaking six-pack. I've never kissed a guy with a six-pack."

"Glad I could be your first." I wink.

She points at my face. "And your charm is entirely too much for me to handle. I hated you a week ago, and look at me now, standing half-in, half-out of your apartment, practically eating your face off. You charmed me. I don't know how you did it, but you did, and that's unnerving."

"Want me to be an ass again? I'm really good at it."

"And the joking—you're funny *and* hot. That combination shouldn't be allowed in one human." She holds out one hand. "You're either funny." She holds out the other hand. "Or you're hot." Then she claps her hands together. "But putting them together . . ." She shakes her head. "Nope, should be illegal."

"You're funny and hot." I grab her hips.

"And the compliments have got to stop, man." She presses her hands to my chest, as if to keep her distance, but it's all for show, because there's no pushing away. "They're lethal and they're undoing me."

"Is that so?" She nods. "Well, if that's the case, have I told you that I think you have the prettiest fucking eyes I've ever seen? I just want to get lost in them."

"Ahh, I see what you're doing."

"And your lips—they're the softest pair of lips I've ever had the privilege of kissing."

"Uh-huh, not going to work."

"And the look of concentration on your face when you're in the midst of creating something—it's sexy as shit."

Pressing her lips together, she looks up toward the ceiling and exhales heavily. "Nope, not going to happen. I will not break."

"And the love I see in your eyes when Cohen walks in the room, when you're interacting with him—that's why I was drawn to you in the first place. I wanted to know how it felt to have Luna Rossi look at me with complete adoration."

Her eyes widen.

Her mouth parts.

Her chest heaves ever so slightly.

The air stills around us, and then finally . . .

"Damn it, Alec." She stands on her toes and presses her lips against mine again, this time opening her mouth wide and sliding her tongue across mine. I groan and melt into her touch, running my hands up her back. Just as I start to get settled, she pulls away and pushes out of my grasp.

She grips the strap of the bag resting on her shoulder as she stands in the hallway of my apartment building, her eyes heady, full of lust as they focus on my mouth.

"This . . . we can't . . . we can't bring this on set."

I grip the side of the door and lean in. "You mean I can't pull you into a dark corner and run my tongue over your delectable lips?"

She shakes her head hard. "No, none of that."

"And when you walk by, you don't want me grabbing your hand, just so I can feel your palm against mine?"

"No." She sighs. "No hand-holding."

"And when I see you for the first time tomorrow, I can't tell you how pretty I think you are?"

"I mean . . . you can text me."

I chuckle, wanting to pull her in close again, but I keep my distance this time. "Will you text back?"

"Depends on if it's a good text or not."

"It will be a good text."

"I'll be the judge of that." She shrugs and starts to walk away.

"Go out with me tomorrow night?"

She stops. "Is that a command or an ask?"

I should have known better than to say it like that to Luna. "An ask. Tomorrow night, the diner."

She gives it some long thought. "Maybe."

She moves down the hall, and I call out, "How can I get a yes?"

She spins and walks backward for a second. "Depends on how good your texts are tomorrow."

"Are you challenging me, Luna Rossi?"

"I am. Hope you can handle it, Alec Baxter." She winks and then spins around, disappearing around the corner.

Damn.

I shut the door and lean against it, a huge smile on my face. I'm not one to get excited over a date, but hell if Luna Rossi hasn't captured me in her crafty, flirty world.

Chapter Sixteen
LUNA

"Are you going to tell me why you're just sitting there, staring at the wall?"

I blink a few times and look over at Farrah, who's ready for bed, her hair in braids so she'll achieve that beach look tomorrow and wearing a rose-and-cream-colored satin pajama set. The pajamas match her complexion, making her blonde hair stand out even more. Farrah is the only person I know who buys pajamas specifically because they're flattering.

On the other hand, I'm wearing a holey pair of sweats and an oversize T-shirt. When I got dressed for bed, I was in a haze, with one thought circling around in my head: *Oh my God, Alec kissed me.*

Going over to his apartment was an impulse.

Letting him hold my hand was indulgent.

Kissing him back was pure insanity.

It didn't feel real, not one second of it. From the moment I stood from the couch to his swiveling me against the doorjamb, it all felt like some sort of fantasy I conjured up in my head, something that would never in fact come true.

And yet, he kissed me.

No, he didn't just kiss me; he rocked every inch of my body with his lips.

It was one of those kisses that you never forget, one that makes you tingle from the top of your head to the tip of your toes. A kiss so grand, so intense, so beautifully unexpected that it alters your world, tilts your axis, sends you into a spiral of lust.

And I'm lusting.

Lusting hard.

It's ten thirty at night, I'm in my most horrendous nighttime garb, and I'm gripping the couch tightly, staring at the wall, forcing myself to stay put so I don't do something like fling my apartment door open and sprint the three blocks to Alec's apartment just for one more taste.

"Earth to Luna. Are you there?" Farrah snaps her fingers in front of my face.

Before I can even register what I'm saying, I mumble, "I kissed him."

"You kissed him?" Farrah asks, completely confused. "Who? Who did you kiss?" She sits down next to me and grips my shoulders so I'm forced to twist in my seat and face her. "Tell me, woman, who did you kiss?"

I swallow, my heart beating so rapidly that I'm truly afraid it might pop out of my chest.

"Alec," I whisper.

"Alec? Who's—?" Farrah's eyes widen. "Noooooooo," she groans. "You didn't."

"I did."

"How? What do you mean? You kissed him? Why? Did he force you?" She shakes my shoulders. "Did he drug you?"

I slowly shake my head. "He didn't. I willfully allowed him to kiss me."

"Like . . . a peck?"

"Tongue." I stare off over Farrah's shoulder. "So much tongue."

"Jesus Christ . . . tongue," she whispers, leaning against the arm of the couch. "How much tongue is so much tongue?"

"Minutes of tongue, and I felt his hard nipple."

Farrah sits up straight. "You felt his hard nipple? Did he feel *your* hard nipple?"

"No, I was the pervert. I was such a pervert. He was respectful, and I was trying to maul his beautiful face off. Oh, and the compliments." I fling myself back on the couch and stare up at the ceiling as I drape an arm over my forehead. "So many compliments." I sit up on my elbows, unable to get comfortable. "The kind of compliments that make your lady bits do a jig."

"Your pussy did a jig?"

I flutter two fingers at her. "As if it was one of the ten lords a leaping."

"Good Christ, what kind of compliments give you a ten-lords-a-leaping jig?"

"Lips, eyes . . . my love for Cohen."

"Oh damn." Farrah waves her hand in front of her face. "Oh . . . damn. Not the Cohen card."

I slowly nod. "He pulled the Cohen card."

Farrah looks off to the side and then slams her fist against the back of the couch. "That son of a bitch. How dare he. After all he did to you, he flips a switch in one day and then pulls the Cohen card? Oh hell—"

"It wasn't just one day."

Like out of a horror show, Farrah turns her head slowly, eyes wide, jaw clenched. "Excuse me? What do you mean, 'It wasn't just one day'?"

Oh God, I knew I should have told her earlier.

Sitting up, I twist my hands together, knowing I'm about to get a bunch of crap from my best friend. "Um, you know how I said I was at the library researching different ways to tailor a vest?"

Her nostrils flare. "Don't you dare tell me you weren't at the library. Don't you—"

"I was at his apartment." I cringe as she gasps so loudly I'm pretty sure our neighbors could hear her through the walls.

"You *lied* to me?" she whispers.

"Only because you hated him so much that I was nervous to tell you I was helping him."

"You were *helping* him?" Her voice rises now. "You were helping the guy who snapped his fingers and demanded coffee from you."

"Technically, he didn't snap," I say, a little frightened for my life.

"Irrelevant." Farrah shoots off the couch and starts pacing across our plush cream rug. "He was rude to you. He insulted you." She pauses and whips her head toward me. "He called you 'repugnant.'"

"Valid points. All very valid points, and trust me, I was a hater for a very long time . . . I mean, I barked at him for weeks."

"Yeah, until you let him lick your face," Farrah says, arms crossed over her chest.

"Farrah?" She doesn't look at me. "Farrah." I poke her with my toe. She barely lifts her eyes to me. "I like him."

Her anger deflates in seconds as she flops on the couch and sighs loudly. "Ugh, fine. Tell me what happened."

I recount everything, from how I saw him completely flattened after the bouquet challenge, to his fake profile, to the macadamia nuts, to his devastating confession.

"Ahh, I see. You're a sucker for a broken man."

"He was *so* broken," I say, my heart tripping up just thinking about it. "And his attempts at baking were so sad that I felt like I didn't have a choice."

"And then you told him all your secrets, and he got first place."

"Yeah . . . *that* I wasn't expecting." I smile, thinking about how proud he was. "But it was one challenge. I'm not worried."

"Does Cohen know?"

"Not yet. I plan on telling him soon, though. I, uh, kind of have a date with Alec tomorrow. I maybe want to see how that goes first and then tell Cohen."

"Think he'll be upset, since Alec is the competition and all?"

I shake my head. "Cohen isn't like that. He doesn't really see this as a competition—more of a way to create a wedding for him and Declan. He won't have a problem with it." At least I don't think he will. "If anything, he'll be concerned at first, since he knows I've been barking at Alec."

"Naturally." Farrah sighs again and shakes her head. "I can't believe you kissed him."

I slouch back on the couch with her. "I can't believe it either."

Farrah reaches for my hand and squeezes it while rolling her head to the side to look at me. "How was it?"

Staring up at the ceiling, I can't contain my smile. "The most magical and spectacular kiss I've ever experienced."

"Toe curling?"

"Nipple hardening."

"Oh . . . damn."

I nod. "Oh damn is right."

◆ ◆ ◆

"They're not poisoned, Helen," I hear Alec say as I make my way on set.

"How do I know that?"

"Because they're still sealed. See?" Alec lifts a can of macadamia nuts up to her and takes the lid off, revealing that they are in fact sealed.

Helen looks at the seal and then back up at him. "I don't like you, and I don't like you trying to give me your nuts. It's disgusting." She whacks the nuts out of his hand and walks away.

"Christ," I hear him mutter as I step into view. He bends down and picks up the can, and when he stands back up and spots me, a soft smile crosses his lips.

"Offering another lady your nuts already?" I whisper, shaking my head. "Should have known you were a player."

"Jealous?"

"Of Helen?" I glance over his shoulder. "Totally." I hold my phone up. "Expecting a text. See you around, Baxter."

The corner of his mouth lifts into a smirk, and before I can feel too tempted to kiss that corner, I walk over to my workspace, where Declan and Cohen are already getting ready for the day.

"I thought they were splitting these time slots up so we wouldn't all be here at the same time," Declan says. "Helen is driving me insane with her constant tongue-clicking."

Cohen leans in. "She is such a pill. Yesterday she asked me who the girl in our relationship was."

I'm in the middle of taking my bag off when my head snaps up. "She did not."

Noticing the instant anger that sprouts up out of me, Cohen places his hand on my shoulder. "Cool it, Luna."

"What did you say to her?"

"That I would check inside our underpants later and get back to her." My mouth falls open. "No, you didn't."

"He did." Declan nods. "And he checked last night—looks like we're both the guy. Wonder how that's going to work?"

I clamp my hands over my ears. "Please don't tell me about your bedroom antics. You know I don't want to know about my brother and his willy."

Declan laughs and leans into Cohen, who briefly kisses the top of his head before pulling away. A surge of pride shoots through me at that little public display of affection from my brother. It was small, and I'm sure Declan would have hoped for a longer embrace, but it was more than I've seen from Cohen in a long time. Maybe this competition *has* opened up my brother, given him more courage to truly be who he is. I hope so. Baby steps, but moving forward is all that matters.

I feel my phone buzz in my back pocket but leave it there. "Please tell me Helen turned white at your response."

Cohen chuckles to himself and grips the counter. "No, she said she would appreciate it if I followed up."

"Stop it." I laugh harder than expected. "And did you?"

He nods. "Went up to Helen this morning and told her that it was difficult research, especially having to stick one hand in my pants and another in Declan's at the same time, but it looks like we both have dicks."

"Oh Jesus." I clutch my cheeks. "Did she pass out?"

"She gave me a sneer and was about to let me have it, but I stopped her and asked if she'd ever asked her daughter who the man was in *her* relationship."

"Ohhh, good one."

"To which she replied: 'It's Luciana—she's the one who wears the strap-on.'"

Together, Declan and I throw our heads back and laugh. Cohen joins us, and it takes a few moments before we gain our composure, but when we do, I say, "How did you keep a straight face?"

"I didn't," Cohen says. He seems more loose and casual than ever, like he's actually comfortable in his skin. "I snorted and was about to tell her, 'If that's the case, looks like Declan and I are both the man and the woman in our relationship,' but she stomped away before I could reply."

"Oh shit." I hold my stomach. "Why wasn't that recorded for the show?"

"Imagine the ratings." Declan chuckles. "Talk about spicing up *The Wedding Game*. Not just about nuptials, but sexual education as well." In a deep announcer voice, Declan says, "This week on *The Wedding*

Game, we dive into sponges, buttercreams, and how the gays decide who is the male and who is the female in the relationship. Stay tuned as we discuss the complexity of strap-ons, hands in pants, and, of course, cake toppers."

"Helen would have an opinion about the strap-ons for sure," I say as my phone buzzes again.

"Helen has an opinion about everything," Cohen says as he stretches side to side. "I'm going to grab some fruit and coffee. Want anything?"

"I'll go with you," Declan says. "Daddy needs some tea."

"Can you not call yourself that, please?" I shiver. "Seriously, Declan."

"What?" He smirks. "Don't like knowing your brother calls me Daddy in the bed—"

Cohen pushes Declan to the side and looks me in the eyes. "I don't call him Daddy."

Feeling ill from thinking of my brother in this way, I say, "Thanks for clarifying that."

He winks and takes off as I call out, "Some of that sparkling Zest Tea for me, please."

When they're out of sight, I dig into my pocket and pull out my phone. Sure enough, there are two texts from Alec.

My entire body heats up with a giddy, schoolgirl excitement.

I open his messages and force my face to remain neutral.

Alec: Nice tits.

Alec: Great ass.

I snort so hard my nostrils sting.

That's his text message?

That's him waxing poetic?

That's his attempt to get me to go out with him tonight?

I look up and spot him, standing in the corner, leaning against one of the many set designs, arms folded and a smirk on his face as he stares back at me.

He thinks he's so smooth . . .

Luna: I was promised texts about how pretty you think I am.

He texts right back.

Alec: Nice tits and great ass are supreme compliments. The kind of compliments I don't hand out lightly. Now, pretty. I could say that to Naomi . . . or even Helen despite the weird way her hair is today. But I would never tell Naomi nice tits and great ass and I sure as fuck would never say that to Helen.

Luna: Oddly your logic works, but I was expecting more.

Alec: Are you high maintenance? Just tell me right now so I can prepare myself.

Luna: Slightly. I like romance . . . so if you want that date, romance me.

Alec: I knew nice tits and great ass weren't going to fly with you but I tried anyway.

Luna: Worth a shot. But try again.

Alec: *ahem* Luna, darling . . . when you walked onto the set today, my breath caught in my throat, because all I could think about was how you made it all the way in here without anyone telling you your fly is undone.

I gasp and fumble for the fly of my jeans, and . . . it's zipped. My phone buzzes.

Alec: Made you look.

Oh my God, I hate him. My eyes shoot up to where he's standing, laughing by himself.

And even though I want to throat-punch him, I can't help but chuckle as well.

Luna: Enjoy dinner by yourself tonight.

Alec: Ahh, come on, that was funny. The panic on your face was priceless.

Luna: You really think you're going to win me over by teasing me?

Alec: Not one of those girls?

Luna: No.

Alec: I beg to differ, given our initial interactions, but fine. Okay, here we go . . . Luna, I thought about our kiss all last night. I wanted to beg you to come back, to give me one more taste of your lips, but I knew if you did come back, you wouldn't be going home.

The tips of my ears flame as I try to shrink into my seat, as if that will keep people from noticing me.

Luna: Lies or truth?

Alec: All joking aside, that was the honest truth. I woke up this morning with the taste of your lips on my tongue. I couldn't get here quickly enough, just so I could catch sight of you, and maybe even pull you to the side, despite what we decided on last night.

Okay, maybe he's a little good at this.

Luna: And why didn't you? You had your chance.

Alec: Respect, Luna. Wanted to show you I keep my word.

I bite my bottom lip, thinking of all the guys who've let me down in the past. Nothing that's truly devastated me and kept me away from the dating scene, but little letdowns here and there that have stuck with me enough to know that when I date again, I want a guy I can trust. Someone I can rely on.

Alec seems like that kind of guy.

His kiss alone tells me he's different from any other guy I've been with.

And he's not just a *guy*. Alec is a man—that much became clear last night.

Luna: I like that.

Alec: Do you like it enough to go out with me tonight?

I glance up and catch him staring back at me. Holding back my smile, I type back.

Luna: What can I say? You had me at nice tits.

From across the set, I can hear him chuckle as he shakes his head.

Alec: You're brutal—you know that?

Luna: I have to make you work a little. Have fun in your interviews today.

Alec: You too. Try not to cry too much over your loss yesterday.

Luna: Trying to go to dinner alone again?

Alec: Nah, just trying to show you I'm not the uptight asshole you initially thought I was.

Luna: Don't worry, you proved yourself worthy this past week.

I set my phone down as Declan and Cohen return. Declan hands me my drink, and Cohen hands me a plate of pineapple and grapes. He knows me so well.

"What's with the smile?" Cohen asks. "Last time I saw you smile like that, you found waterproof decoupage."

"That was a special day, wasn't it?" I open my drink and take a sip, growing warm when I remember how Alec stocked his fridge.

"You made me a birdhouse, for my apartment in the city."

"Pigeons need love too." I wink and pop a grape in my mouth.

"Seriously," Declan says, nudging my shoulder. "What's with the good mood? I half expected you to show up today in a state of panic because we got second place yesterday. Speaking of, did you try Baxter's cake?" Declan leans in and whispers. "That was really good cake—like, I want him to make our wedding cake."

Cohen laughs and leans in as well. "Did you hear Helen complaining to the producers, saying she swears she saw him use a box cake?"

213

"She did not," I say with a roll of my eyes.

"She did. I understand her confusion. Team Baxter hasn't been able to pull it together the entire competition, and then all of a sudden, the guy pulls a cake that belongs in a bakery out of his ass. Suspicious."

"Maybe he just practiced," I say, realizing I probably shouldn't be defending Alec in front of Cohen and Declan—at least not until I see how tonight goes.

I could find out that Alec in fact is a really good first-time kisser but follows up with a sophomore slump of epic proportions, something like dead-fish lips.

But I think deep down I know that a case of dead-fish lips won't be the problem: me falling head over heels for him will be.

"Or he paid off the judges," I add, just because that sounds more like me.

"I don't know." Declan waves a piece of pineapple on a fork at me. "Helen could be on to something."

"Helen is on something all right. Just not quite sure it's legal."

Cohen nudges me with his foot. "Seriously, sis, why are you so happy?"

Crap, why doesn't he ever let anything go?

"Just excited to be here." I grip their forearms. "I love you guys."

They both stare at me for a few seconds and then at each other. As he spears another piece of pineapple, Declan says, "Your sister totally had sex last night."

"Declan, don't say that shit," Cohen says while I madly blush. "As far as I know, she doesn't know what a penis is."

"That's a lie and you know it." I point at Cohen. "I know what a penis is because you forced me to look at sex positions for gay men."

"*What?*" Declan says. Cohen groans and buries his head in his hands.

"Wow, Luna, it's been, what, ten years? You're going to bring that up now?"

"I panicked." I laugh and turn to Declan. "In our defense, we were drunk and Cohen wanted to become an expert, so we spent some time on the internet researching illustrations. There was no brother-sister porn watching going on, just to clear the air on that. Strictly illustrations."

"Yeah, that makes it better," Declan says on a laugh.

Picking up a grape, I ask Cohen, "Should I expect a lecture later tonight?"

"I think you know what time."

I nod. "I'll be sure to let the call go to voice mail."

Alec: Running late. Thad decided to tell his entire life story and relationship with cake. Meet me in half an hour?

Luna: Running late too. But not because of Thad, because I decided to curl my hair to have dinner in a diner and it's taking longer than expected.

Alec: You getting all gussied up for me?

Luna: No. I have a date with someone else after you. You're just the appetizer. Main course is with Frederick later.

Alec: Going to make something clear: no man named Frederick will ever be the main course. He's a palate cleanser at best.

Luna: Are you saying you're main course material?

Alec: And dessert. See you in a bit.

CHAPTER SEVENTEEN
ALEC

I lean against the wall of Dining Hall, my hands stuffed in my pockets, my eyes scanning the calm streets, waiting for Luna to show up. I love this neighborhood. It's quiet—pretty much the opposite of Midtown—like its own little borough, tucked away, where you can find solace in this mad, crazy city.

And to think, in this few-block radius, I've been so close to Luna and never noticed her—it feels odd.

I glance at the time on my phone. She's one minute late. Technically, we're both half an hour late. But now she's thirty-one minutes late, and that makes me fucking nervous she might stand me up.

I've been stood up before, back in college, when I thought it was cool to grow a mustache. I was a punk back then and didn't really care. I took off, called my buddies, and went drinking.

Now, if she stands me up, my night will turn into me sitting on my couch, staring at a wall, with a patty melt from the diner in a takeout container on my lap—I'd be too goddamn mad to eat in the diner.

Mad and upset.

Probably more upset than mad, because hell, Luna has done something I was not expecting. She's made me want to give a relationship a try.

Yeah, a *relationship*.

I've had a few, but nothing that made me really want to buckle down and make things work, to put everything on the line and give love a shot.

Luna is different. She's seen me at a low, and instead of walking away, she pushed past our original animosity and helped me.

She looked past our differences and got to know me on a different level.

She flipped open that cover, and now that my book is open, I can't seem to close it, no matter how much my scared heart wants to.

"Hey."

I look up from my shoes to find Luna, smiling and dressed in a cute red romper. Her hair cascades in waves over her shoulders, and her lips match her outfit perfectly.

Hell, she looks good.

"Hey, you." I internally wince at the relief in my voice.

She must notice, because she says, "Sorry I'm a little late. On the way out, the strap on the sandals I was wearing snapped and I had to change, which then made me rethink my outfit decision, but I thought to hell with it if my shoes don't coordinate perfectly."

I take her hand in mine and entwine our fingers. "You look stunning, Luna."

She smiles before pressing her hand to my forest-green button-up shirt. "You look pretty good yourself."

"Just pretty good?" I tease. "I pressed this shirt myself."

"Well, look at you, all domesticated. Can bake cakes and press shirts."

"Not just any cake. Wedding cakes. There were tiers involved. Tiers and layers."

"How long are you going to talk about the cake?"

I wish she would close the space a little bit more so I could kiss her, but I have no idea what's appropriate and what's not at this point. I'll settle with hand-holding.

"I'm going to hold on to that win for a very long time."

She sighs and bumps her shoulder against mine. "Are we going to get something to eat? I'm starving."

I open the door to the diner and let her in. I follow close behind, her hand still in mine. Fay is carrying a tray of sodas when she spots us. "Take a seat anywhere." Her eyes fall on our hands, and she stops, tilting her head to the side. "Why did I have a feeling I would see you two in here together at some point?"

Before we can answer, she walks away, toward the loud table in the corner. I nod toward the opposite corner, where it's quiet and secluded. Luna agrees, and we walk over to a small two-person booth next to the window and slide in on either side.

"I don't normally sit on this side," Luna says, looking around.

"Neither do I. I feel kind of weird about it, actually." I look around as well. "I don't feel like I'm in the same place at all."

"Are you going to need to sit on the other side?" she asks.

I shake my head. "Nah, I'm good. This can be our side."

"Confident enough to claim a side of the diner we frequent as *our* side?"

I nod. "Yup." I pick up the menu and peruse it, even though I know exactly what I'm going to get.

"What makes you so confident?" She folds her arms over her chest.

"You're the one who felt up my nipple last night."

She purses her lips and raises a brow. "It was an accidental nip graze."

"Oh yeah, okay, sure." I wink at her and set the menu down. "Accidental. Got you. Just like it was an accident that your tongue got lost in my mouth."

"Why are you so difficult?"

I wince. "Coming on too strong?"

She holds up her fingers, then brings her index finger and thumb together. "Just a little."

"Fair enough. Maybe we should start over, switch gears." I clear my throat. "Hey, you." I give her a slow once-over. "You look so goddamn beautiful."

She looks down and smiles. "You know, people have told me I'm beautiful before: Declan and Cohen are constantly telling me; past boyfriends have thrown out the compliment as well." She looks up at me through her lashes. "But you're the first person who actually makes me feel like what you're saying is true. And I'm not fishing for compliments—just trying to tell you that I believe what you're saying, and that's new."

"If we're being honest—" I push my silverware to the side, needing something to play with—"I wasn't really in the market to meet someone, but there's something about your personality, the way you didn't hesitate to help me, that hit me hard, made me crush on you. Big time. I mean, I thought you were beautiful the first time we met, but your general disdain threw me off."

"And the barking."

I laugh. "The barking for sure was different."

"It was new for me too."

"Yeah? Would have guessed you'd been doing that for years now, with the kind of volume you got on some of those woofs."

She fluffs her hair. "Why, thank you. I might have practiced in the mirror a few times before I came to set. I never like to go into anything unprepared."

"So the barking was just for me?" She nods. I clutch my chest. "I'm honored."

Fay stops at our table and pulls a pen from behind her ear. "Do I even need to write it down?" She waves the pen between us. "Two patty melts, one Sprite, one Coke. Crispy fries."

"Uh, yeah," Luna and I say in unison.

Fay sighs. "I should have hooked you two up months ago." She takes off toward the kitchen.

Fay might be a little rough around the edges, but no diner is complete without a curmudgeon of an employee—Fay fits the bill and gives the diner plenty of character.

"Patty melt, huh?" I ask, leaning back in the booth. "She's right. She should have hooked us up months ago."

"You think you would have asked me out?"

"Easily."

"Even in my hungover state, wearing pajama pants, my breath reeking of last night's booze?"

I chuckle. "The booze breath might have deterred me for a second, but the minute I looked into your eyes, it wouldn't have mattered."

"Such a charmer," she deadpans as Fay drops off our drinks without a word and leaves.

We both take a sip, leaving the straws to the side. "So," I ask as we set our drinks back down, "when did you know you wanted to make things for a living?"

"High school."

"Really?" I say, surprised. "I thought you were going to say something like when you were four years old."

"When I was in grade school, I wanted to be a veterinarian. I would play vet with my stuffed animals—line them up for the day and see them one at a time, fixing all their ailments. Our family dog, Ralph—he was a yellow Lab—would sit by my side and act as my nurse."

"Shit, that's adorable. I can picture it."

"My mom has so many pictures of me tending to my stuffed animals, but then . . . Ralph got sick."

"Oh hell." I scratch the side of my jaw. "I don't foresee this going well."

"It didn't." She sighs. "I tried everything I could to make him better, but no amount of kisses could have scared the cancer away. A few months later we had to put him down."

"I'm sorry."

"I was devastated, to say the least. I couldn't fix him, and that really upset me. After Ralph passed, I stopped playing veterinarian. It wasn't the same without him by my side, and that's when I really started to get into watercolors. I would spend hours painting portraits of Ralph."

"Christ, Luna, you're hurting my heart over here." I wish this table wasn't between us, or there was enough room for me to slip into her side of the booth and hold her. "How many portraits did you end up with?"

"Thirty. Big and small. I hung them up all over the house, but mostly in my room. 'An Ode to Ralph' is what I called my first showing."

"Showing?" My brow furrows.

"Yup. I made some signage and flyers, handed them out, cleaned the house, made some lemonade and almond drop cookies, and invited people in for a viewing party. Sold one piece of art that day, to a lady down the street. It was an abstract piece of Ralph, but she said it touched her soul."

"And you didn't know then?"

She shakes her head. "No, but I knew there was something inside me that liked being praised for the work I did. I dabbled in a lot of crafts after that. Mom and Dad didn't care how much money they spent at different craft stores—they were just happy I was busy and not getting into trouble."

"You have good parents," I say, wondering how it would feel to have parents that involved in my life.

"They kept me busy, all right, and when I hit high school, my mom found a flyer at the local deli for a craft fair. I'd made so many things at that point that she thought I should try selling them. Maybe make some of the money back we spent on crafts."

"Makes sense. How did you do?"

"Well, my setup was awful. I have a picture of it back at my parents' house. It was in a small indoor gym a town over from ours. I was so proud, but there was no rhyme or reason to it. Nothing was priced. I really was just so excited to be there."

"I bet you did awesome, though, right?"

She leans forward on the table. "It was a slow day. I mean . . . slow. People would walk by, say how cute my stuff was, but they never actually bought anything. Until this one lady came by. Mrs. Rose Waters."

"Rose Waters?"

She chuckles. "Yup. Her daughter just had a baby, and she was looking for a homemade gift. I had an afghan made out of rainbow yarn. It was originally supposed to be for Cohen, but boy did I get the dimensions wrong. The yarn caught Mrs. Waters's eyes, though, and she said something that vibrant and beautifully made could only bring joy to someone, so she bought it. I asked for fifteen dollars, but she gave me fifty and told me not to undersell myself." Luna smiles. "A few months later, I got an email from her—she took one of my business cards that I *wrote* on—and she sent me a picture of her new granddaughter wrapped in the blanket. It meant so much to me, seeing how something I made could have an impact on another person's life. And that's when I knew."

"You were meant to create."

"Exactly. And my parents were really supportive. They took me all around the Northeast so I could sell at different craft fairs. But . . ." She smiles and takes a sip of her drink. "When my senior year rolled around and they asked what I planned on doing for college, they were definitely surprised."

"They weren't on board with crafting for a living?"

She shakes her head. "Not even a little. Mind you, they're pretty easygoing—they're world travelers now that their children are grown. They'll just make it back from Australia in time for the wedding. But they were *not* happy about me not going to college."

"I don't think most parents are happy about that kind of decision. My parents would never have let it happen, even though neither of them was involved enough in my life to have any say."

Luna gives me a soft smile. "Given the lack of involvement, I'd say you turned out pretty great."

Heat creeps up my cheeks, and I think it's the first time I've actually blushed in front of a girl. I'm not a blusher. Never have been. I'm the guy who dishes out the compliments, who makes girls blush. But as my face heats up, I realize I truly do care what Luna thinks about me.

I clear my throat. "So what happened? Did you compromise?"

She shakes her head. "No. I stuck to my guns and told them going to college would be a waste of their money and my time. I knew what I wanted to do."

"Bold."

"Tell me about it. I can remember the exact conversation. It was during a family meeting."

"You had family meetings?"

"Oh yeah." She chuckles softly. "We're one of *those* families where the parents declare a family meeting and all members are required to attend, no matter what—and you could tell immediately from the tone of voice what kind of meeting you were going into—good or bad. This was a bad one." She leans forward and presses her hand on mine. "They had a PowerPoint presentation, which meant business."

"Oh shit, a PowerPoint?" I laugh. "That's serious."

"Clicker and all. It was very serious in the Rossi household. Both my parents were teachers, so it's sort of weird that Cohen is marrying a teacher, but we won't dive into that psychological nightmare." We both laugh. "They were very up on their presentation skills. They went through all the pros and cons, obviously preparing a fair statement, but the cons were easily outweighed by the pros of going to college. There were pictures and everything." She rolls her eyes. "It was ridiculous, to say the least. And it was during that meeting that I stepped up to their computer and surprised them with my own presentation."

"And it was badass, wasn't it?"

"Yup. After the initial college conversation, I'd called Cohen up. He was already working construction at that point—another noncollege child. I was our parents' last hope, hence their desperation. But what Cohen told me will always stick with me. He said I have to follow my passion. If creating and crafting was my passion, then I needed to show Mom and Dad how it could support me—not just financially but mentally and emotionally as well. They needed to know I was going to be okay."

"And that's what you did with your presentation."

"Exactly. Cohen was on the phone, of course, because all members were present, and I can still hear his small chuckle at our parents' surprise. I laid it all out for them. I showed them my finances, my bank account, my website, my tutorials. How I was going to tackle the world of crafts, how I could get sponsorships that would not only offer me supplies but actually pay me to recommend products I like. I told them about this whole new world of social media business and that I was going to be a part of it."

"Were they impressed?"

"My dad sighed, leaned back in a chair, and gave me a slow clap."

"Really?" I laugh. "That must have been satisfying."

"More than you can imagine. Of course my mom shushed and told him they needed to talk, but when they walked away, my dad winked at me and gave me a thumbs-up. Took a few more weeks, but they caved. They came back and said they would give me a year to make something of myself, and if I couldn't comfortably live on my own after a year, I had to go to college." She shakes her head in disbelief. "I've never worked so hard in my entire life. Every night I was making something, videoing, creating content. I was relentless, but I was determined to prove something to them."

"And you did."

She smiles brightly. "I did."

Fay comes up to our table and sets down our plates without a word. And like the good waitress she is, she plops down some ketchup and leaves.

Luna and I reach for it at the same time, but I let her win, and I watch as she carefully squeezes the ketchup into a puddle on the side of her plate. When she hands it to me, I squirt it over my fries—she gasps out loud and brings her hand to her chest.

"No, tell me it's not so. You . . . you put the ketchup directly on your fries?"

Not even apologetic, I say, "Yup." Then I snag a fry and put it in my mouth. "Perfect."

"I don't know." She leans back. "I don't think I can stay on this date, not with someone who uses ketchup like that. Let me guess," she whispers. "You put the toilet paper on like a mullet, not a beard."

"Mullets do have more fun."

"Check!" Luna shouts. "We need a check!"

"What made you want to be a lawyer?" Luna asks. She's calmed down since the ketchup and toilet paper fiasco, but it wasn't an easy feat. I had to put a puddle of ketchup on the side of my plate to make her feel comfortable and promise to try putting the toilet paper on like a beard . . . at least once. I promised I would take a picture of my toilet paper roll when I got back to my apartment.

It was shaky there for a bit, but I think we're back on track.

"My mom," I say honestly. "You know, seeking justice that she didn't get with my dad. Well, not necessarily for my mom, because she wasn't exactly a ray of sunshine in my life. She's the queen of unhealthy coping mechanisms, and we're definitely not close. I guess it's more that I'm seeking justice for families. Which, ninety-nine point nine percent of the time, is the wife, since she's the one taking the kids." I shrug. "If I wasn't so bitter in college, I think I would be doing something different with my life."

"Like what?" She plops a fry in her mouth. Our plates are practically empty, with just a few scraps left.

"Well, after yesterday, probably bake cakes."

She rolls her eyes and gives me a "be serious" look. "It was a good cake. Move on, Baxter."

"Oh, you'd like that, wouldn't you? Want to forget the painful loss you suffered yesterday?"

She holds her hand up again. "Check!"

"Knock it off," I say, reaching over the table and pulling her arm down. "You're going to bruise my ego."

"Ahh, poor Alec." She chuckles. "Seriously, what would you be if you weren't a lawyer right now?"

I lean back in the booth and drape one arm over the back of the seat. "I don't know. Something that helps people, because I enjoy that part of my job. I only represent women who are getting screwed over by their husbands. It's satisfying when the men leave the conference room with purple faces because they're so angry, but I know there's more to life than giving people like my dad their comeuppance. Not super healthy, you know? And I'm really not into the whole money thing."

"I noticed," she says, giving me a shy look. "Knowing you were a lawyer, I half expected a giant penthouse, but you live quite modestly, considering."

"I don't need things—I just need a happy life."

"And are you happy?"

I scratch the back of my head and look out the window. "I think I can get there. Before *The Wedding Game*, I could tell you honestly that I wasn't. I barely spent any time outside of my office, and when I did, it wasn't for anything that added value to my life. I pretty much ignored Thad, and I can't tell you the last time I saw my mom, or my dad. I've spent a lot of time keeping my distance and avoiding all contact with them. I was just breathing, getting through my daily work, but not living." I glance at her. "I may not be on speaking terms with my parents, but for the first time in a while, I actually feel like there's more to my life, like maybe I could be happy."

As I look into Luna's deep eyes, something unexplainable switches inside me, as if the dark cloud that's been hovering over my head parts and finally makes way for some sunshine. Seeing Thad with Naomi, even Cohen and Declan, has shown me what a relationship really is about. Protecting each other, loving each other, being there when you need someone the most. It isn't all doom and gloom, especially when you find the right person.

"Yeah?" she asks.

"Yeah . . . and of course it has nothing to do with you," I joke, and she picks up her napkin, wads it, and throws it at me. I don't even flinch as it hits me between the eyes.

"Ugh, you're annoying."

"And yet you're still here."

"Destructive behavior. Always going after the wrong guys."

"What kind of guys?" I ask, curious for a glimpse of her dating history.

"All kinds." She sighs. "I went through an artsy phase. I was all about guys whose life mission was judging other people's artwork and feeling superior. That was until I'd show them my work, and they'd inevitably tell me I was selling out or not a true artist because I wasn't starving, something along those lines."

That makes me snort. "You don't have to be a struggling artist to be an artist. What idiots. You can make money and create."

"Yeah, that's what Cohen said too, so I moved on from the artsy guys and found the athletes."

"Oh yeah? Should I be concerned that you're grouping men together?"

She just shrugs. "Testing the waters—don't act like you didn't do it in college."

"Fair." I wave my hand. "Continue."

"So I went to the jocks, and can we just say . . . yum? Ugh, the arms on these guys; none of them had abs like you, but their di—"

"Okay, details not needed. Just tell me why it didn't work out with them."

She chuckles and gives me a playful eye roll. "Kidding. I dated one jock for a year, but then he was drafted and moved to California. So that ended things. Uh, do you know Nyatt Sampson?"

Is she kidding? "Nyatt Sampson? As in three-time football MVP and champion? The quarterback sweeping the nation? Whose *ESPN* cover photo is of him holding a football in front of his crotch?"

"Oh, so you have heard of him."

"Every single human in the country has heard of him. You dated Nyatt Sampson? For a year? And broke up because he was moving across the country—even though you can do your job anywhere? You realize he's already rumored to be inducted into the Hall of Fame, right?"

"Yeah, yeah, yeah, all that's fine, but it didn't matter to me."

"Was he an ass to you?"

"What?" She shakes her head. "No. He was amazing, actually. First guy I loved. We're still on good terms, and even talk now and then, but there was one thing I couldn't take to California—Cohen. I couldn't leave him," she says softly. "He was going through such a hard time when I was dating Nyatt. He wasn't with Declan yet, and he was really struggling with his sexuality and being comfortable with who he was, especially since he was working in such a hypermasculine field. I knew that if I left, it wouldn't be healthy for Cohen, so I stayed in New York."

"Wow." I let out a long breath. "You're . . . fuck, Luna, you're one hell of a person."

"I have my moments." She shrugs and looks toward the door. "Want to get out of here? The grease is starting to really seep into my pores."

"Yeah, sure," I say, feeling like I might have said something wrong. She really is one hell of a person, and I hope I didn't startle her by stating that. Maybe too much too soon? I throw some money down on the table—it will easily cover the bill and leave Fay a nice tip—and stand from the booth. I hold my hand out to her, and she takes it with ease.

When we're out of the diner, she tugs on my hand. "Want to just . . . walk?"

"I'd like that." I'm still nervous as we take a left out of the diner and slowly walk down a brownstone-lined street toward the riverfront, the green of the trees along the sidewalk richly illuminated above the streetlights. This is New York City to me, holding the hand of a beautiful girl, walking along the old concrete, and soaking in the stillness of the summer air. Our little slice of the Upper West Side is tranquil, and the street is close to deserted, so our voices aren't drowned out by traffic.

"Did I say something wrong back there?"

"What? No, of course not. It's just . . . you're different from any other guy I've dated. Nyatt was great, but he was a bit immature, which he admitted to me after we broke up. He wasn't ready for a serious relationship, wasn't ready to commit to being there for someone else. And a few guys after him turned out to be the same way—always the boy, never the man."

"I see."

"But you." She squeezes my hand. "You admit when you're wrong, you admit to having faults, and you're willing to change, to grow."

"Are you saying *I'm* a man, Luna?"

"I am. A man who can bake one hell of a cake."

I pause and tug on her hand so she stops with me, and then spin her into my chest, where her hand falls for balance. Her hair whips across her face, and a few strands stick to her lips. I reach up and remove them, letting my hand stray for a few seconds. We pause beside an old redbrick church that's under construction, the scaffolding giving us shelter from the lights around us.

"When you admit things like that, it makes me want to kiss you . . . kiss you really fucking hard."

Her eyes light up, her body leans into mine, and a wicked smile plays across her lips. "Then do it."

Three tempting words—three words that have my body humming.

What I wouldn't give for another taste, another chance to hear the softest moan rumble up Luna's throat as my mouth presses against hers. I reach out, tilting her chin up with my index finger.

Lick my lips.

Stare down at her, letting her know my intentions.

I catch her chest rising and falling rapidly, the quick swipe of her tongue along her lips, the intake of breath as I close a few more inches between us.

I want it . . . bad.

But so does she.

And because she wants it so bad, I say, with an evil grin, "I'll wait."

She gasps, mouth falling open, eyes widening.

She nudges my shoulder playfully. I laugh, continuing down the sidewalk, while she tails me, pouting.

"What do you mean you've never had pineapple?" Luna asks, her eyes nearly popping out of their sockets. We're sitting on a bench along the Hudson River Greenway a block from Luna's building, gelato in hand, the moon hanging over us like a lamp, providing just enough light so I can see the tiniest difference between her irises and her pupils.

"Just never have. Yellow fruit freaks me out."

"What does that even mean? Have you had bananas?"

"Yeah, bananas are more like a cream color when they're out of their peel. But pineapple . . ." I shake my head. "What manufacturer is pumping that thing with yellow dye?"

"Uhhh . . . Mother Nature," Luna says in an affronted tone. "Please tell me this is all a joke."

"Nope. Sorry."

"I can't even with you right now. It's such a simple fruit."

"A fruit that used to be a luxury. Even my parents grew up thinking it was an exotic privilege."

"Hence why you should have taken advantage your whole life. My God, Alec, the years you've wasted not knowing what pineapple tastes like. Why do I feel like I'm going to be showing up at your apartment with a pineapple tomorrow?"

"As if it's a hardship." I wiggle my eyebrows.

"It is when I'm seeing a guy who's never had pineapple before."

"Seeing a guy?" I ask, loving her little slipup. "So does that mean there will be a second date?"

"Ugh, stop it—you know this is going well, despite the whole pineapple thing. Of course there will be a second date."

"How about making our second date tomorrow morning, or we can just make this date last until tomorrow morning. I have a comfortable bed—want to test it out?"

I lean toward her, but she palms my face, pushing me away. "You're cute for even thinking that's an option."

"It's not?"

"No." She puts a spoonful of gelato in her mouth. "It's not. Farrah would probably murder me. She's still a little salty that I didn't tell her about you right away, and she's not exactly your number one fan yet. If I spent the night—*man*, would she be mad."

"I see. So, I have to win over the best friend?"

"Oh, for sure. She keeps texting and asking me when I'm coming home. Asking me if she needs to prepare to kick you in the crotch."

"She's a violent one."

"Only when she needs to be."

After I finish off my gelato, I stand and hold my hand out. "How about we go solve the problem with Farrah right now?"

"Like, go to my apartment?"

"Yup." I take her hand in mine and help her up. "Show me the way."

She shoots me a suspicious glance. "I don't know if you're ready for her."

"Not sure I'll ever be. But better to get it over now, because I'm not going to let her prolong the inevitable."

"And what's the inevitable?"

"A friendly sleepover—of course, one that involves wearing matching pajamas and watching *Grease*."

"Uh-huh." She chuckles and leads the way to her apartment.

Chapter Eighteen
LUNA

"Oh hell no," Farrah says when we walk into the apartment, hand in hand. "Over my dead, Froot Loops–powered body will you be fornicating with that man, in this apartment, when I'm only a few feet away. Not going to happen. Not when he called you . . . 'repugnant.'"

She is *ripe* today. This might be harder than I anticipated.

"We're not here to fornicate, Farrah." I shut the door behind us.

"Uh-huh, well, feeling his weenie up in your bedroom isn't acceptable either."

Alec chuckles, and I elbow him in the stomach. He's not helping. "There will be no touching of body parts. We're here so you can get to know Alec."

Farrah crosses her arms over her chest, lips curled in a sneer. "Get to know him? What's there to know? You kissed my best friend, and now she thinks you're a good guy."

"Technically," Alec says, holding up a finger, "I kissed her *after* she changed her mind about me."

"Fighting with her is not going to help your case," I say from the side of my mouth.

"She's right—fighting with me will not help your case, but it will sure help my rage." She pretends to roll up her nonexistent sleeves and thrusts her fists into the air. "All right, let's duke it out." She bounces around the living room in her bare feet, jabbing at the air.

"Okay," Alec says, taking his shoes off and putting up his fists as well, approaching without any caution.

"Whoa, hold on," I say, but Farrah holds up her hand.

"Stay out of this, you repugnant swan."

"Hey." My brow furrows.

"I said 'swan,'" she says just as she's smacked in the stomach with a throw pillow. She stands up straight. Blinks. "You did not just chuck a pillow at me."

"Stop stalling," Alec says, grinning. I blink, hardly believing that he's facing off against my best friend, proving that he's not only in this, but that he's also one hell of a good time as well.

"Why, I oughta . . . ," Farrah says in an old-timey New York accent, jabbing her fists toward him but not making contact.

He jabs back, feet away, but she ducks anyway.

And just like that, they take part in the weirdest—and only—air fistfight I've ever seen.

"Take that." Farrah throws a punch, and Alec whips his head back, his hair flopping to the side. He pretends to check his nose for blood and then sets his sights on the enemy again.

"A little blood never hurt anyone," he says, bouncing his fists up and down.

There is no blood.

None.

There's no contact, for fuck's sake.

But the punching sound effects coming from both parties are entertaining, to say the least.

Pow. Zap. Swap. Kapow.

I feel like I'm watching an old episode of *Batman*.

"*Ga-zoonga!*" Farrah shouts as she roundhouse kicks thin air.

"*Ha-cha . . . cha, cha, cha,*" Alec says as he rapidly uppercuts nothing.

"Look out, Baxter, this train has a one-way ticket with your name on it." Farrah pulls the imaginary whistle near her head. "*Woo . . . wooooo.*" She charges toward him while his back is turned to her. She leaps on top of him, landing in the piggyback position.

Unsure of really what to do, I stand there, staring . . . and wondering how far this is going to go.

Alec twirls her around in circles as she clings to his shoulders. "Ride it, bitch, ride it!" Farrah calls out, swinging a nonexistent lasso above her head.

What in the ever-living hell is happening?

Alec stops, twists one way and then the other and then the other, and then he tosses Farrah onto the couch. "Is that all you've got?"

"Hell no, son!" Farrah stands. Both of their chests are heaving from the exertion, but she cocks her arm back and yells *"Ka-blammy!"* while flinging her fist toward Alec. He reacts by twisting in a full three-sixty, head cocked to the side, and then landing on the ground. "Ah ha! Knocked that motherfucker to the ground. TKO, baby, TKO." Farrah hops up and down, celebrating . . . well, I don't even know what she's celebrating.

After a few "raise the roofs" from Farrah, she turns to me and grins. "He's awesome—let's keep him."

Jesus . . . Christ.

"You don't have to use the ice pack anymore for your fake injury."

Alec chuckles and lowers the ice pack that he's had on his eye for the last twenty minutes. "Made her feel special, so that's all that matters."

We're standing in the hall outside my apartment. Inside, Farrah is tucked in nice and tight, very pleased with how her evening ended.

I grab hold of Alec's pants pocket and pull him close. "Pretty sure you're her new best friend now, and you're going to be expected to fake fight whenever you come over."

"I mean, better than real fighting, and she's pretty cool. I can see why you guys are best friends."

"You know." I tug on his pocket. "You're so different from what I expected."

"Yeah? How so?" he asks, tucking a piece of hair behind my ear, his hand lingering on the nape of my neck.

"I guess I didn't expect you to loosen up. I wouldn't have predicted in a million years that I'd see you fake fighting with my best friend and purposefully taking the imaginary knockout like a champ."

He shrugs and steps a little closer so I really have to look up to meet his gaze. "I'm a lot more fun than you make me out to be, especially when I'm really feeling the girl I'm with."

"Feeling me, huh?"

"A whole fucking lot." He moves his hand from the nape of my neck up to my jaw and runs his thumb over my bottom lip. "I like you, Luna. I want to see you again, date you, get to know you even better."

"I'd like that."

"Good." He leans down so our foreheads are touching. "I don't want to mess this up, what we have going on here."

"Then don't." I smile, wanting him to close the last few inches of distance between our lips.

"I'm going to do everything I can not to, which brings me to this . . ."

I lean back, searching his eyes. "This? Uh oh, am I not going to like what you say next?"

"Maybe not, but I'm not sure how to navigate this relationship and the show without this request."

"Oh . . . kay," I say slowly. "What is it?"

His thumb drags over my cheek, and he sighs. "Thad is a bit of a drama queen."

"I've noticed." I chuckle.

"And I feel like if he found out I was seeing you, he'd lose his damn mind, especially since you're the competition. And I'm really trying to make things right with him, you know?"

"Let me guess: you want to keep this relationship between us."

"Yeah." He winces. "I know that's asking a lot."

"It is." I take a step away. "I don't keep secrets from Cohen. We're open and honest about everything."

"Cohen is also emotionally stable. Thad can fly off the deep end at any point. Please, it's just a few weeks. We can be low key about it, and then after the weddings, we'll let them know. When the dust has settled."

"I don't know." I look off to the side, pulling my lower lip under my teeth.

"I understand if you can't," he says. "Your trust with Cohen means a lot to the both of you. So maybe we just . . . I don't know. Put this on hold for now, until the show is over."

"On hold?" I ask, the thought of pressing pause making me panicky inside. I don't want to press pause with Alec, not after this past week, not after that kiss, not after watching him pretty much wrestle with my best friend to prove that he's a good guy and will do just about anything for me.

"It wouldn't be that long, and I guess it would give you time to really think about being with me. You know, decide if it's something you want."

"Yeah," I say with a defeated sigh.

He reaches out and tips my chin so my eyes meet his. "It's okay, Luna. It really is. I don't want to pressure you into anything you're not comfortable with." He leans in and presses a very light kiss against my lips before stepping away and slipping his hands in his pockets. "Centerpieces this week." He gives me a crooked smile. "Good luck—I know my team's gonna need it." He lifts his hand and waves and then takes off down the hall, leaving me to wonder what I've just agreed to.

This was not how I was planning this evening to end—not in the slightest. I was hoping for a grand kiss, one that would rival our first. I was hoping he would press me up against the wall again before making plans for the second date we keep talking about. I was hoping he'd even ask to just snuggle for a little bit—from the look of his arms, I know he would be a good snuggler.

But instead, I got a whisper of a kiss and a gentle "break" before we've even started going out?

How the hell did that happen?

And why am I feeling incredibly sad about it, like "stick my face in a carton of neapolitan ice cream" sad about it? Why does it feel like he's just walked away with a piece of my heart?

I roll onto my side, the darkness of my room making me feel more depressed than before.

Because Farrah went straight to bed, I didn't want to bother her with what happened out in the hallway, and eating ice cream by myself just felt too *Bridget Jones's Diary* to me. I don't think I'm at that point yet.

Instead I got ready for bed, flopped onto the mattress, and stared up at the ceiling, recounting everything he said. I mean . . . would it be that terrible if we kept quiet for a couple more weeks? We have two more weeks of challenges and then the weddings. Friday, Saturday, and Sunday, all back to back.

So, three weeks—would that really do any harm?

If I confirm the suspicions of Cohen and Declan, then there's a good chance Declan might let it slip at some point, especially while we're filming, which would be the worst-case scenario. I love Declan, but he's been known to have a bit of a loose tongue.

And I really do like Alec . . .

Irritated, I pick up my phone, type out a text, and impulsively hit *send.*

Luna: Are you up?

Immediately the dots start dancing on my screen. Glad to know he's not sleeping either.

Alec: Can't seem to fall asleep.

Luna: Can I ask you something?

Alec: Ask me anything.

Luna: If you didn't walk away, how would our night have ended?

I unplug my phone and roll onto my back, my pulse picking up as I wait for his response. It feels like forever before he answers.

Alec: I would have cradled your beautiful face in my hands, thanked you for a great evening, and then I would have slowly backed you up against the wall of your apartment building and claimed your lips, making sure they remembered exactly who made them light up the night before.

I groan, squeezing my eyes shut with disappointment.

Alec: Would you have kissed me back?

Is he serious?

Luna: I would have.

Alec: It would have been hard for me to leave.

Luna: It would have been hard for me to let go.

Alec: And yet . . . you did.

Luna: Alec.

Alec: I know . . . I know. Okay, I'm going to try to get some sleep. See you on Saturday, Luna Moon.

Luna: Alec?

Alec: Hmm?

Luna: Can I come over tomorrow?

Alec: You know I'll be desperate to see you. Come over whenever you want.

Luna: Okay.

Alec: Okay.

CHAPTER NINETEEN
ALEC

I stare at the phone, my nerves shot.

I've been at a standstill for the last ten minutes, my finger hovering over the call button.

Just fucking do it.

I massage my brow as I press call, and with each ring, the need to throw up grows stronger and stronger until . . .

"Hello?"

Fuck, this was a mistake, a giant mistake. What the hell was I thinking?

"Hello?" That voice, raspy and full of unwanted memories. It rolls my stomach, twists and turns it, and not in a good way.

I should hang up. Just lower the phone and press the end button . . .

"Hello? Alec?"

Fuck.

Clearing my throat, I hold the phone closer to my ear and say, "Hey, Mom."

"Alec," she says, her voice neutral. "You're calling."

This won't be an awkward phone call at all.

"Yeah." I nod, even though she can't see me.

"Are Thad and Naomi okay?"

"They're okay."

And that's it. No, *Are you okay? How's life? Haven't talked to you in a while.* Then again, I'm the one who called her and can't seem to find any words.

Since talking with Luna last night, I've had an overwhelming urge to reach out to my mom. If I truly want to be happy, I need to patch up the holes in my life, one of which is my relationship with my mother. I thought calling her was the first step, but if calling her is this difficult, how is it going to feel when I actually have to see her in person?

"Well, if everything is okay . . ."

Shit. Say something before she hangs up.

"Uh, would you want to maybe see me . . . on Saturday?" I swallow hard. "Thad told you about the show, right?"

"Yes," she says, sounding confused. I don't blame her. I can't honestly say when we last talked, let alone saw each other in person. "It's very nice that you're helping him. He told me you made a wonderful cake."

Of course he did.

"It was a good challenge," I say, sounding like a robot. "Uh, so we're allowed to invite a guest if we want, for the next episode. Thought it would be fun to surprise Thad."

"Oh yes, he would enjoy that. I haven't seen him or Naomi in quite some time . . . or you, for that matter."

"I know." I sigh, picturing her disapproving gaze. "I'm, uh . . . I'm sorry. I kind of got caught up in other things."

"You don't need to explain yourself, Alec."

But I do. Maybe not over the phone, though.

Moving past the elephant in the room, I ask, "So, do you think you can make it on Saturday? I can text you all the information."

"Yes, I don't have anything going on. I can be there."

"Okay, cool. Thanks . . . Mom."

"Of course. Anything for Thad."

Yup. Anything for Thad.

I squeeze my eyes shut as guilt washes over me. Guilt for staying away for so long, for not thinking my family was important enough to keep in my life, for wasting so much time that could have been spent with them.

She sniffs. "Well, okay then," she says, voice shaky. "I'll see you Saturday, Alec."

"See you Saturday," I reply and then hang up. I toss my phone on the couch, run both hands through my hair, and let out a sigh of relief. The easy part is done—now to worry about Saturday and how I'm going to explain to my mom why I've been absent all these years and why I want to change that, be a part of everyone's lives now.

I've had sporadic visits with her since college, which dwindled as time went on and eventually turned into only holidays, and then not even that. I honestly can't remember the last time I saw her, and I certainly can't remember the last time she was sober and not abusing prescription drugs. And when she's in those manic moods, lost to pills and vodka, she says mean, spiteful things.

Things like, *You're just like your father.*

Your heart is just as black as his.

You never cared about me or your brother.

You know, the good stuff that really cuts to a son's heart.

My parents' relationship was tumultuous. Dad was addicted to making money, to investing and spending hours upon hours on Wall Street, wining and dining the next biggest client. When he would finally come home, if he decided to come home that night, Mom would get on his case about never paying attention to her—mind you, never said anything about the kids—and then they would lose it. Throwing things, calling each other names. It was in those moments that I would take Thad away, cover his ears, and protect him from the storm of hate brewing through our house.

Dad would leave for the night to do God knows what, never once caring that he had two sons, and Mom would draw herself a bath and drown herself in alcohol and pills until she was numb, leaving me with Thad.

The shitty part of it all: I felt bad for my mom, even though she couldn't get it together and be there for Thad and me. I still feel for her, but I also have so much resentment toward her. She could have left sooner, she could have taken care of us, she could have loved us . . . but she chose not to.

Scrubbing my hands over my face, I stand from the couch. I head to the bathroom and switch on the shower. Not sure when Luna is going to come over, or if she's going to come over at all, but at least I can be ready if she does, and I need to wash away the nerves from that conversation.

Once again, I find myself staring down at my phone, but for an entirely different reason. It's nine o'clock, and there's no sign of Luna.

No texts.

No calls.

No knock on my door.

I've thought of texting her at least a dozen times, asking if she was coming over, but I didn't want to pressure her. I already knew my ask last night was a big one—keeping things quiet for the sake of Thad and our growing relationship. I'd like to think he would be mature about everything, but knowing him, he would think I was in cahoots with Luna and jeopardizing his chances at winning and providing a new life for his family.

I flip through the channels on my TV mindlessly, wondering why I even pay for cable in the first place.

Frustrated, I turn the TV off before tossing the remote to the side with my phone and leaning back into the couch. Maybe I should just go to bed. Or read a book. Do a word search. Plan for Saturday's challenge, despite knowing nothing about centerpieces; at least it would get my mind off—

Knock. Knock.

I fly off the couch before I can even register what's happening, practically salivating like one of Pavlov's dogs. I peek through the peephole, and standing on the other side is a very nervous-looking Luna.

I whip the door open, and without a word, she ducks under my arm to enter. Like every other time she's been to my apartment, she slips off her shoes and then walks over to the couch, where she takes a seat.

Fuck. This is even more nerve racking than talking to my mom on the phone.

I have a feeling I'm not going to like what she has to say.

With a defeated sigh, I shut the door and take a seat across from her. She's resting her chin on her fist and staring off toward my kitchen, a crease in her brow.

I want to ask her what's wrong, if there is anything I can do to make it better, but my tongue freezes. For what has to be the first time in my life, I don't have anything to say. Instead, we both sit there. I stare at her; she stares at the kitchen.

Silent.

After what feels like hours, she asks, "What do you have planned for this weekend?"

Okay, wasn't expecting that. But from the defensive way she's holding herself, I'm going to guess she doesn't want to talk about what she's really here for . . . *Are we going to call it quits?*

I clear my throat and shift on the couch. "Uh, you mean . . . for the centerpieces?"

"Yeah. What were you planning on making?"

I scratch my jaw. "Wasn't really thinking about that. Probably some feather thing."

"You should probably go into it with a plan. You want to be prepared, Alec. That's how this works: you prepare yourself for every challenge. If you truly want a chance at winning, you should start drawing up images or at least googling centerpieces with feathers. I saw a blog the other day about dipping feathers in glitter to give them a little bit of that boho look, and I know Vicki and Amanda are doing that, but it wouldn't hurt to bounce some of their ideas off to Thad. Although he might freak out if—"

"Hey." I rest my hand on her thigh. "What's going on?"

"Nothing, I just thought you should be prepared—that's all. What are you even planning on doing Saturday? Just showing up? Are you bringing anyone to the taping? We don't have anyone to bring, but I didn't know if—"

"Slow down. You're rambling."

"I'm nervous. Okay." She presses her hand to her forehead. "I'm nervous, and I almost didn't come tonight, but I hated the thought of not seeing you, so . . . tell me something. Tell me anything about Saturday. Take my mind off all the emotions whirring through my head."

She's freaking out a bit. I can see it in the wildness of her eyes, how they're darting all over the room. She needs a distraction, and I have the perfect one for her.

"My mom is coming to the show . . . and I invited her."

Luna's eyes focus on me for the first time since she walked into my apartment. "You invited your mom to the taping? You?"

I nod. "Tonight. I called her."

She softens, her shoulders relaxing as she carefully takes my hand in hers. "You called her? Alec, that's . . . wow, that's amazing."

"You, uh . . . you inspired me to reach out, to be better."

"Alec . . ."

"I'm serious." I grip the back of my neck as I keep my eyes trained on hers. "I see what you have with Cohen, how strong your bond is. And the stories you told about your childhood, about your parents . . . I know I can never have what you have, but I can at least try to repair things with my family. God forbid something ever happens to us—I don't want to look back and regret never even trying."

"That's . . . that's amazing, Alec."

"It's a step in the right direction."

"It is." She smiles, which causes me to lean into her and squeeze her hand.

"Why are you here, Luna?"

She traces her finger along my palm. "I don't want to put a pause on things." She exhales sharply. "I want to see where this goes."

"Yeah?" I'm half-terrified that if I get too excited she might change her mind. Her body is humming with energy—excitement or anxiety, I can't tell, but I can feel it, see it in her eyes.

She nods. "Yeah. I talked to Farrah about it, and she pointed out that a few weeks isn't that big of a deal. And I agree. I can keep this between us for now. I want you to have a real relationship with Thad, but it's going to take some big steps to get there, so I understand why you don't want to tell him about us. And frankly"—she smiles wickedly—"that kiss last night left me more frustrated than anything."

I catch my breath at her little smile.

"Wanted more, huh?"

"So much more."

"Then get over here," I say, tugging on her hand and guiding her onto my lap so she's straddling me, her thin leggings rubbing against my flimsy shorts.

She sits directly on my cock and wiggles, pulling a chuckle from the back of her throat. Her lips land on mine as my hands find her hips. Her lips part and her kisses settle into a deep, sensual rhythm. She's addicting, how her mouth moves along mine, making me dizzy with lust.

I need more.

My body hums for more.

My hands grip her tightly, begging for more.

Her tongue swipes against my lips and then dives into my open mouth, teasing me, tempting me. Her hips move along mine, and my cock quickly turns rock solid within a few glides. When she feels me harden beneath her, she smiles against my mouth and pulls away, but I pull her close and trail wet, hot kisses along her jaw, down her neck and then back up, my beard scraping along her skin, my tongue pulling sweet, tiny moans from the back of her throat.

While my mouth works to her earlobe, I glide my hands under her shirt and up her back until I reach the clasp of her bra. I want to undo it, free her, feel her, but then think better of it and slide my hands back down her ribs. Too much, too soon. *Don't scare her away.*

To my surprise, she protests with a groan and brings her hands to her back, unhooking her bra herself. She does some magic to slip it out of her shirt and then brings her hands to my chest again, gripping my shirt. *Holy shit.* Completely unexpected, but there's no way in hell I'm turning her away.

"Touch me," she says as I nibble the spot right below her earlobe.

"I am."

"Under my shirt."

"I am," I repeat, unable to control my smile.

She grinds her hips into mine. "Touch my tits, Alec."

Well . . . damn.

Chuckling, I reach one of my hands to the front of her torso but don't quite touch her, not yet. Instead, I keep my hand just below her breast and then press my lips against her mouth before plunging my tongue inside. She groans and moves her hips against mine continuously, up and down, up and down, rubbing my cock in such a way that my spine tingles, my limbs start to go numb. The friction between us is fucking magic, turning me on and overtaking my body. There is no doubt in my mind she could get me off like this in minutes.

"Shit, Luna," I say, pulling away for a breath. "You're going to make me come in my shorts if you keep doing that."

"Good." She reaches for the hem of my shirt and pulls it up and over my head. She tosses it to the side and leans back to take in my bare chest. "Jesus," she mutters, her hands gliding down my torso, down to my abs, and playing dangerously with each divot. "Thank the good lord for abs and pecs."

I chuckle, and that only makes her sigh more.

"When you laugh, your abs contract and your pecs shake. It's really hot."

"Stare all you want, Luna Moon," I say, bringing my spare hand behind her neck so I can pull her lips closer. When our mouths connect, something unhinges inside of her because her hands float up my chest to my pecs, where she grips them hard, and she moves her lips slowly, methodically. The combination spreads warmth through my body as sweat gathers along my back.

My hand itches to move up, to touch her, to ravish her body, but I also know I don't want to take this all the way. Not yet. But hell, getting off as she dry humps my lap seems like a good second option.

Savoring her, I move my mouth back down her jaw to her neck as I run my hand up and over her breast and cup it, my thumb rubbing over the nub of her hardened nipple.

"Oh God," she moans, her head falling back, her hips grinding even harder. "Alec . . . I could come just like this . . . God, I could come so hard."

"So do it," I say, licking the column of her neck. "Get off. Make us both come."

She swivels her hips, and I bite down on her neck. She yelps, startled. "Shit," I breathe out. "Sorry."

"Do it again," she whispers as she grinds her hips, over and over again until I feel dizzy, unable to comprehend the thick pulse that's pounding through my veins, breaking down my walls, and turning me into a puddle of need.

I bite down on her neck again and then kiss, bite, and kiss. I repeat the process until her head is falling to the side and her hand grips the back of my thighs.

In a haze, I scan her body, one hand still up her shirt, and take in her pert nipple pressing against the fabric of her shirt, her neck, her delicate collarbone. I want to run my tongue along it, back up her neck, to her mouth. Her sweet fucking mouth.

I need control. I remove my hand, grip her lower back, and then scoot off the couch, guiding us both to the floor. I lay her down carefully, and her legs fall to either side of my hips. I help her spread them wider and then grip her hands and bring them above her head, pinning them with one of my hands and lowering my mouth to hers. We devour each other, hungry and desperate for more. With each pass of her tongue over mine and every nibble of her teeth on my bottom lip, I crave more. I lower my hips and position my covered cock over her before driving my hips down, across her clit.

"Alec, yes!" she calls out.

I pull back just enough to catch a glimpse of the lust smoldering in her eyes, which turn heady as I stroke up her center.

A breath escapes her.

Her legs fall open even wider.

Her hands tighten on mine.

Greedy for more, I glide my hand up her shirt again and find her breast. I keep her covered and feel instead, stroking my thumb over her peaked nipple. From what I can feel, it's small, tight, and so sexy. With every pass, my balls tighten farther and farther.

"Hell," I grit out, feeling an orgasm stirring.

"Just like that, right there," she says, breathless, her lips finding mine again, the electricity of her touch lighting up every nerve in my body.

I grind down on her.

She grinds up.

I groan against her mouth.

She moans along my tongue.

My hand tightens around hers.

Her fingers dig into the back of my hand.

I pull my mouth away.

Her forehead presses into my shoulder.

My hips fly.

Her moan radiates through my body.

"Yes, oh fuck . . . yes, Alec!" she yells, her body tensing and then falling apart beneath me, right there on my living room rug.

"Mother . . . fucker," I mumble as my spine straightens, my balls tighten, and my cock surges with my orgasm, spilling into my shorts. My legs shake with every spurt. Breathless and shaking, I ride out both of our orgasms until there's nothing left. "Fuck," I say, depleted as I let go of her hands and press my weight into my forearms, still straddling her.

I touch my forehead to hers as we both try to catch our breath. What we just did reignited a passion inside me I hadn't realized was dead. A dam has broken within me, and there's only one person to thank for it.

"Luna Moon," I say with a slight shake of my head. "What are you doing to me, girl?"

She chuckles and brings her hands to the back of my neck. "What am I doing to you? What are you doing to *me*? I don't dry hump guys in their living room . . . not anymore, at least." She laughs. "That was some old-school stuff right there."

"You started it." I run my nose along her jaw and kiss the spot beneath her ear.

She sighs. "I didn't have a choice—you pulled me onto your lap. Was I just going to let you be hard underneath me?"

"You could have, and that would have been fine." I raise my head so she sees how serious I am.

She reaches up and cups my cheek. "I didn't want to. I wanted you to embarrassingly come in your athletic shorts."

A chuckle pops out of me. "Trust me, Luna Moon, there was nothing embarrassing about it. I would do that over and over again, if it meant having a little piece of you."

Her eyes soften, a smile plays at her lips, and I see it—the attraction, the yearning she has for me. I created that look with my words. Me. The guy who could barely stand the idea of a relationship. And yet, here I am, happily letting Luna lasso a rope around me and claim me as hers.

"You like me," I tease.

She rolls her eyes and tries to push me off her, but I hold her tight, keeping us planted where we are.

"You really like me. You're crushing hard, aren't you?"

"Get over yourself." She laughs, still pushing at my chest.

"Luna and Alec sitting in a tree . . ."

"Oh my God." She laughs again. "You're obnoxious. Thank you for reminding me."

"You like it," I say, grabbing her hands and pinning them above her again. I move my mouth over hers, and she immediately kisses me back. Her lips are just as eager as mine. "Stay the night," I say, in between kisses. "Just to let me hold you."

"Farrah is expecting me back."

"Text her. She likes me."

Luna smiles against my mouth. "She does, but I should get going." She presses a few more kisses across my mouth. "You have work, and I have some planning to do and a lot of projects to catch up on."

"Then see me tomorrow. Come over."

"That I can do." I release her hands and sit back on my heels. She glances down at my crotch and laughs. "Might want to go take care of that."

"At least I'm not the one who has to walk back to my apartment with arousal in my leggings."

"Don't call it arousal. Good God, what are you, fifty?" She stands, grabs her bra, and smooths down her shirt. "It's a quick walk." Leaning down, she places a soft kiss on my lips and grips my jaw. "You and me, right? No one else?"

It's her way of checking on what this is between us, making sure I plan on being exclusive, and I really like how upfront she is about it—it shows she cares as much as I do.

"No one else," I answer, my eyes on hers.

"Good." She gives me one more kiss and then takes off toward my door, where she slips her shoes on and grabs her bag. "See you tomorrow, Chris E."

"Tomorrow . . . Luna Moon."

Chapter Twenty
ALEC

"Don't make fun of me."

"I would never," Luna says with a cheeky smile.

"I'm not kidding, you can't laugh."

"Please, Alec."

I sigh and show her my drawing of my centerpiece—she snorts and quickly covers her mouth.

"I told you not to fucking laugh."

"I didn't. I, uh . . . had a bug fly up my nose."

"There are no bugs in my apartment," I deadpan, giving her a serious look.

"Microscopic. You can't see them because you're a man, and men have terrible eyesight."

"Says who?"

She waves her hand vaguely. "All the professionals."

"What professionals?" My eyes narrow.

"You know." Her smile widens. "The researching kind." She snorts again.

I toss my paper to the side and lean back on the couch. "You're really fucking nice, you know?"

"Don't be like that," she says, climbing onto my lap, just where I want her.

Worked like a charm.

I place my hands on her legs and smooth them up to her waist, but she stops them, her eyes narrowing. "Oh no you don't. Nice try, mister, but none of that tonight."

"What?"

She removes my hands from her body and sets them on my stomach. "We've been doing that all week. You have to make a centerpiece in two days, and instead of making out with me, you need to focus on what you're going to present to the judges on Saturday."

"But your tits help me think. Your nipples are like magical idea devices. Let me suck on one—I'm sure an idea will sprout in seconds."

"Yeah, well, you sucked on them last night and nothing came up."

"Oh, something came, all right."

She rolls her eyes and gets off my lap, leaving me half-hard and wanting her. "Where are you going?"

"You need to come up with some ideas. I was hoping your drawing would be magical enough that we could spend the rest of the evening with our hands down each other's pants, but it looks like we're going to have to actually practice." She picks up a heavy canvas bag she brought with her and carries it over to the couch. She sets it down and unzips it, revealing an array of tools and craft accoutrements—everything we need to make a centerpiece.

"Uh, you know, I'm feeling a little worn out from work. I think we should just do the hands down the pants thing. That seems more relaxing."

She gives me a "get real" look and starts unloading the bag.

"I'm serious." I fake a yawn and stretch my arms over my head. "You know, maybe we should just go back to my bed."

"If you're so tired, then how would you be able to perform?"

I wiggle my fingers at her—the same fingers that made her come twice yesterday. "These aren't tired."

She pushes my fingers away. "Why are you such a dignified lawyer in your real life but an immature frat boy when it comes to sex?"

"I didn't hear you complaining yesterday, or Tuesday."

"Settle down." She smiles to herself, but I catch it.

"Ha, admit it, you like that I'm an immature idiot."

"I would never admit to liking that." She stops unloading for a moment, holding a glue gun and a jar of glitter. "I will admit to you having a great mouth with an equally nice set of fingers."

"And you as well." I wink.

Her face reddens, and I know what she's thinking about: how she pulled my pants down yesterday and not only gave me the best hand job of my life but also ended it with her mouth on my cock, ruining me for every other woman out there. The way she sucked and pulled . . . fuck.

"I'm getting hard," I say.

"Seriously, Alec?"

"What?" I shrug. "You're hot, you give good head, and you're smart—all turn-ons for me."

"Gives good head—think I should put that on my résumé?"

"Uh . . . no."

She laughs and unpacks more of her bag. "We're focusing on the centerpieces. I told you I would help you think of some good ideas, and that's what we're going to do. You want to help Thad . . . right?" She lifts a brow.

"You're an evil wench, you know that?" I scrub my hand over my face as she chuckles. Sitting up, I survey the different items Luna's brought over—ribbons, twigs, a glue gun, and feathers, lots of feathers. "Aren't centerpieces made of giant flowers and shit like that?"

"Yes, but don't you remember your theme—Flamingo Dancer? You have to incorporate that somehow. And last I recall, there were no flowers involved, since you didn't choose any, which means you need to get creative with feathers."

"Oh, I know how I can get creative with feathers." I flash her a wicked grin.

"I'm going home." She stands, but before she can even move an inch, I pull her back down on the couch, laughing the whole time while pressing kisses along her neck.

And she lets me.

◆ ◆ ◆

"Don't fucking move—do you understand?"

Wearing nothing but her bra, Luna is sprawled over my bed, hands gripping the black bed frame above her head, her legs spread and her chest heaving.

In just my boxer briefs, I circle her before grabbing a white feather from the nightstand and kneeling on the bed. Centerpieces were forgotten the minute I started running this feather up and down her arm, and then her neck, and back down again. When a moan escaped her mouth, I knew exactly what was going to happen next.

"Alec, please."

I ignore her and draw light circles around her belly button with the feather, loving the way her stomach contracts with each pass. I don't have to reach between her legs to know she's wet. I can tell, just from the way she's wiggling under my touch and the impatient look in her eyes.

I'm going to have some fun.

I brush the feather down her waistline, to her pubic bone, where I swish it back and forth until I'm barely grazing it over her slit. She sucks in a sharp breath and spreads her legs farther. I bring the feather back up to her stomach and graze the front clasp of her bra. Leaning forward, I unhook it, letting the sides fall and exposing her perfect tits.

I bring the feather up between her breasts and then circle one nipple, which peaks quickly. I move to the other nipple, giving it the same treatment, passing back and forth, watching as her breath catches in her chest, as she swallows hard and wiggles beneath me, her hands itching to move.

"Are you throbbing?" I ask, bringing the feather back down to her center.

"Yes," she gasps.

"Do you want my mouth on your clit?"

"Yes." She nods. "Badly."

I run the feather back up her body, around her nipples, between her cleavage, and then around again, creating a figure eight with my motion. Her chest lifts from the bed, her breasts begging to be touched, her eyes glassy with lust.

It's almost painful how hard I am. If I were any less of a man, I would have her let go of the headboard and feel my cock, drag her hand over it, work me to relieve my aching, pulsing length.

But I'm not that kind of man. I move the feather back down one more time, teasing her with whisper-like passes over the juncture between her thighs, turning her legs into quivering messes.

Just as she lets out a long moan, I position myself between her legs and test her slit with my finger.

So fucking wet.

I part her with two fingers and then dip my head between her thighs and press my tongue against her clit. She hisses in response.

Very lightly, I move my tongue up and down, lightly, just enough so she can feel it without pushing her over the edge.

Just a tease.

"Fuck," she moans. "Alec . . . please."

Loving that she's always saying my name . . . rather than God's, I begin to flick my tongue up and down.

"Yes, just like that. Oh Alec . . . oh, right there."

I move my hands up her thighs to her breasts and pinch both of her nipples at the same time. Something unintelligible flies out of her mouth as her hips buck up against me. I let her ride my tongue as she builds and builds and builds . . .

"Alec, yes, you're so good. You're so good."

Fuck, that makes me even harder. My cock grinds against the mattress as I swivel my tongue, savoring every last bit of her arousal until . . .

"Oh fuck." She bucks against me and then screams out my name, her orgasm ripping through her faster and harder than ever before. "That . . . oh, Alec." Her head falls to the side as she catches her breath.

After a few seconds, her beautiful eyes open and a lazy smile spreads across her face. "Take off your briefs," she says. "I want you to straddle my face so I can suck you off."

Holy fuck, I very well might love this woman.

"What are you thinking about?"

"Huh?" Luna looks up at me as she twirls a feather between her fingers. "Nothing."

"Liar."

She glances down at the feather and then back up at me. "Is this the one we used last night?"

"Nah, I saved that in my nightstand. You know, just in case you ever want to run it up and down my dick again."

Her breath catches in her throat as her cheeks redden once again. I'm starting to notice a trend here. She's a dirty girl, but talking about it brings out her innocent side.

Last night, after I made her come, I was about to follow her orders and straddle her face when she pushed me back on the mattress and instead teased me with the feather—and Christ, I came just from that.

It was slightly embarrassing, coming so hard from just a feather, but if I had the option, I'd do it all over again.

"We can do that again, you know . . ."

"No." Her eyes snap up to mine. "Tomorrow is a big day. We are not going to be distracted." She points to the half-finished centerpiece on my coffee table. "Focus, Alec."

"Fine." I sigh and pick up a twig I dipped in gold paint. "At least talk to me about something so I'm not constantly thinking about sex every time my fingers run over one of these godforsaken feathers."

She chuckles. "Hope you don't get hard on camera tomorrow when you're fondling these."

"Hell, I didn't even think about that. Women have it so easy—they don't show any signs of being aroused."

"Women have it easy? Did you really just say that?"

I pause, considering my words. "I would like you to strike that from the record."

"Consider it expunged."

"Thank you, Madam Counselor." I tip my head in her direction, and she rolls her eyes.

"You can be really corny sometimes, you realize that?"

"Yup, but I know you like it, because every time I'm corny, you grace me with that perfect smile of yours."

"And there's the charm." I wink in response and turn back to the centerpiece. I start messing around with a mass of fresh feathers as she asks, "So . . . are you nervous about tomorrow?"

"Not really. I mean, I feel like this is the best I can do, given the resources and theme."

"No." Luna sets down her feather. "About seeing your mom."

"Oh." I set down the feathers I was working with as well and lean back on the couch. Luna scoots in closer and puts a reassuring hand on my thigh. "I'm not really nervous—more concerned about what I'm going to say, how I'm going to react. I have a lot of pent-up anger toward my mom. I've been stewing over things for years that I never talked to her about. I don't want it all to come flooding back tomorrow, you know?"

"I understand. Maybe if you talk about it with me, you can get it off your chest so you can have a nice day tomorrow, before you ease into solving those issues with your mom."

"Maybe." I sigh. "But I really don't feel like talking about it. Opening that can of worms right now would make it hard to shut tomorrow."

"Yeah." She looks off to the side. "Then tell me something else, something to help get your mind off it all. What's your favorite meat?"

"What?" I laugh. "That's what you're going to ask me? What's my favorite meat?"

"I panicked. I didn't want you to get mad at me for asking about your mom, and all I could come up with was meat."

"It's going to take a whole lot more to make me mad at you, especially after what you did with that feather last night." She smirks devilishly. "But if you really want to know my favorite meat, I'm going to have to go with steak."

"Steak, very popular choice. The filet?"

"T-bone."

She scrunches her nose. "Really? You like all that excess fat and stuff?"

"Chew it right up."

"Blah," she says, gagging. "Oh God, maybe . . . maybe we don't talk about this."

"And leave me hanging about what your favorite meat is? That's not fair."

"Well, it's not T-bone."

"I think we established that. So what is it?"

"Uhh . . . I really like chicken."

"*Ehhh*, wrong answer," I say, impersonating a buzzer. "You should have said, 'Alec, your penis is my favorite meat.'"

"Oh my God." She pushes away from me as I laugh. "What the hell is wrong with you? You graduated from Columbia, for crying out loud. Show some class."

I rest my hands behind my head and kick my legs up on the coffee table. "Sorry, Luna Moon, I have none."

"Clearly."

◆　◆　◆

"Are you sweating?" Thad asks.

"What? No." I scan the set, looking for someone I haven't seen in years.

"It looks like you're sweating. I see beads of sweat." Thad leans forward, and I swat him away.

"I'm not fucking sweating."

"Whoa, whoa, whoa, no need to drop the f-bomb. We're in a family-friendly environment."

I press my fingers to my forehead, wishing Luna had spent the night last night—at least then I would have been able to wake up with her in my arms, have her say some reassuring things to me, and maybe feel her up a little bit before we had to leave. But no, she went back to her place . . . again.

I'm tense—I know that. And I'm *not* sweating—just tense. I want the initial surprise of my mom being here to be over. I want to hug, move past the awkwardness, and then maybe go out later for dinner or something, start that healing process.

"Hey, did you see the drawings Team Hernandez has?" Naomi whispers, hurrying over to our workbench. "They have some kind of stick triangle thing with flowers . . . and a feather."

"What?" Thad exclaims. "We are owning the feathers in this competition. Have they not seen our vision board? The damn thing is covered in feathers. I can't believe they're ripping us off."

"It's just a feather, Thad," I say, realizing it's the wrong thing to add to the conversation the moment it comes out of my mouth.

"Just a feather? *Just* a feather?" he says a little louder. "That's where it starts—next thing you know, they're trying to pull off some boho-chic bullshit wedding with a Miami-at-night vibe. I will not stand for it." He slams a fist on the workbench.

"That can't happen, because the venues are all set," I remind him. "Next week is decor, and I'm sure they're going to stick with their lace crap."

"If they use feathers, I will scream. I will scream right here on set."

Jesus Christ. The last thing we need is more screaming.

"Don't scream, for the love of God." From my back pocket, I pull out a piece of paper and unfold it, showing my drawing of what I was thinking for the centerpiece. Simple vases spray-painted pink to go with the theme, with large feathers cascading from the top. "I was thinking of things this week and came up with this. It's different, but it could work."

Thad holds up the paper, examines it with what he calls "his good eye," and then sets the paper down. "That is hideous."

"What?" I ask, surprised that he would think that. "It's not hideous. It's classic."

"And this is not a classic wedding. This is a creative one. We want flamboyant." Dramatically, he raises his fist in the air.

"But you're not gay."

Thad scoffs. "Wow, that's very stereotypical of you, Alec. You don't have to be gay to be flamboyant, and you don't have to be flamboyantly gay. Look at Declan and Cohen—I never would have guessed they were gay."

"I didn't mean it like that." I pull on the back of my neck. "Hell, I don't know what I mean. I'm just . . ." I glance around—nothing. I don't see her. "When do we start?"

"In five minutes," Naomi says, giving me a confused look. "Is everything okay?"

I glance at my watch. She should be here by now. "Uh, I just need to make a quick phone call. Give me a second."

I step off the set and find a mostly secluded corner before I pull out my phone and dial my mom's number for the second time this week. It rings and rings and rings.

Then finally: "Hello?"

"Mom?" I ask. Why does her voice sound so distant?

"Alec?"

"Uh yeah, where are you?"

I hear rustling against the phone. "Home."

I feel the blood drain from my face. "What do you mean you're home? I thought you were coming to the studio today."

"Well, something came up. I can't come."

"What? Why can't you make it?" I ask, anger starting to take the place of embarrassment, anguish.

"Rough night."

Rough night . . . what does a "rough night" mean, exactly? Back when I was in high school, I found a bunch of prescription medications in my mom's drawer. I asked her once what they were for, and she brushed me off, telling me they were old. But I knew better, especially when Thad told me after I left that he kept seeing Mom take pills and he didn't know what for. So I can only imagine what this rough night might have entailed.

"You told me you'd be here today, so why would you have a rough night if you knew you were supposed to be somewhere the next morning . . . early?"

"Spare me the lecture, Alec."

"I'm not lecturing you, Mom. I'm trying to understand what could be more important than coming to see your two children." I press my fingers to my brow, attempting to comprehend what would push her to fall back to her coping habits. What triggered her?

"You wouldn't understand." It's that response that pushes me over the edge, those words. When I was young, after Thad was asleep and Dad was gone, I would go to my mom's room and try to comfort her, try to talk to her, but with those three words, she'd turn away and shut me out of her life.

"You're right, I don't understand." I angrily thread my hand through my hair. "I don't understand how you could commit, and then not even show up. Did you think it was going to be okay to just be a no-show? Do you realize how hard it was for me to make that call this week, to reach out to you, to try to mend what we've lost?"

"I can tell you're getting upset. Maybe we should just try another day when you've calmed down."

"When I'm—" I breathe out a heavy breath. "Yeah, let's try another day." I hang up before she can reply and stuff my phone in my pocket. "Unbelievable," I mutter, combing my fingers through my hair as I pace back and forth.

"One minute!" a PA calls out.

Great.

Taking a deep breath, I try to ease the tension in my shoulders, break up the tightness in my throat, and will back the angry tears that threaten to fall.

I thought she was going to show up. I thought this was going to be a chance for me to clear things up, but once again she's let me down. I don't matter enough to her to try. Never have.

Probably never will.

When I get back to our workstation, Thad gives me a once-over. "Uh, your face is red."

"Can you stop fucking observing me?" I yell. The whole cast and crew swivels around to stare. I can feel Luna's eyes on me. I can sense her questioning, but I don't turn around to face her. I can't, not when I'm this upset.

"Dude, settle down. Everyone is looking."

"Great, let them fucking stare." I snatch my drawing from the workbench and crumple it up. "Let's just get this over with."

Thad sighs next to me. "And for a second there, I thought you'd turned over a new leaf. Same old Alec."

Before I can reply, Diane calls out "Quiet on set!" and points to Mary, standing in front of the table of mystery supplies.

Just fucking great.

CHAPTER
TWENTY-ONE
LUNA

"That wasn't a fun day," Cohen says, sighing as he opens the door to O'Leary's, his favorite Irish pub, in the Village. Declan follows behind me, and the hostess leads us to a round booth in the back, which gives us enough room to spread out.

"Brutal," Declan says, picking up the menu. "And the tension was high, wasn't it?"

"It was," Cohen says while I stare down at my phone, willing it to beep with a text, with anything.

I sensed it the minute I glanced over at Alec. Something was wrong. His shoulders were kissing his ears, his brow was creased, and he was snapping, truly snapping, at Thad. They usually bicker like a pair of old hens, but there was anger in his voice this time, the type of anger I can only attribute to his mother not showing up.

Trust me, I was looking all over the place, waiting for her to come to set, to hug her boys, to tell them how proud she was of them working together. High hopes, I know. But when Alec disappeared and came back right before we started filming, absolutely livid, I knew she wasn't coming. And it probably wasn't for a good reason either.

"You were distracted," Cohen says, nudging my foot under the table.

"Was I?" I ask, sweat breaking out on my back. "I thought I was all there. I mean, it was pretty impossible to beat what Team Hernandez put together—those teepee sticks with flowers were adorable."

Yup, Team Hernandez took first, we took second, and, unfortunately, Team Baxter took a very brutal last place with their dilapidated centerpieces and constant arguing. The tension was really high between all of them. When we were done filming, Alec and Thad exchanged a few more terse words, and then Alec took off, his face flaming with anger. I sent him a text, asking if he was okay, but I haven't heard anything back yet—hence all my surreptitious checking.

"I don't care that we got second place," Cohen says, "but it just seems like something's worrying you. You keep checking your phone and chewing on the corner of your mouth."

Crap, crap, crap.

"Just lots of work and stuff." I hate that I just told my brother a lie, but after today, I'm so glad Alec and I are keeping things under wraps. If I told Cohen, he'd keep it quiet, but he would tell Declan, and I can't be completely sure Declan wouldn't let the truth slip by accident. And after seeing Thad and Alec today, I'm guessing that relationship is on the rocks again. The news that Alec and I are together would probably destroy it completely.

And that makes me sad.

Declan sets his menu down. "Next week is the last week—decorations and final picks. Then it's all over. We'll get to enjoy a great wedding, and then get back to normal life."

"And win," I add.

Declan shrugs. "Honestly, I don't care if we win or not."

Cohen's brow furrows. "Don't you want to live in Manhattan?"

Declan smiles and cups Cohen's cheek. Cohen stiffens, but only for a second before he relaxes into Declan's touch. "I like our life, Cohen. I don't need more than what we have."

"Oh God," I say, hand to heart. "That's so—"

"Give us a moment," Cohen says.

"Oh sure, yup."

I love the way they speak to each other, with so much care and devotion. I marvel at the way Declan can so easily put Cohen at ease, the way my brother visibly relaxes with Declan, and I realize . . . I want that.

I want someone who makes me feel both protected and needed, someone who makes me feel loved, and makes me feel . . . the way Declan and Cohen clearly make each other feel.

I've come to a point in my life where I don't mind being single. I'm not desperate and boy crazy, but I've noticed a shift. I've established myself as a creator—some of the judges have started following me on Instagram, mentioning how much they love my work. Even without the recognition, I would be content with where I am in my career, but something's missing. I can feel it like a hole inside me, but from the minute Alec kissed me, that hole started to fill.

And ever since that kiss, the hole continues to fill, bit by bit. I've never felt this way with another man. As I stare down at the tabletop, I realize something: Alec is a forever type of guy. Not a stepping-stone, not a free trial, not a one-night stand—he's the real deal.

And he's hurting right now.

Which means . . .

"You know, I'm not feeling too great, actually." Another lie—well, half lie. I do feel sick to my stomach from not knowing how Alec is. "I think I'm going to head back to my place, if that's okay."

"Oh sure," Declan says. "Do you want us to walk you to the train?"

"No." I shake my head. "You guys enjoy your dinner."

I stand from the booth; Cohen does the same and pulls me into a hug. "Are you sure everything's okay?" he whispers.

I squeeze my eyes shut and take a deep breath. "Yup, everything's okay."

I step back from my brother's barrel of a chest and give Declan a quick hug as he stands up from the booth as well.

"Text us," Declan says, squeezing my hand briefly.

"I will." I give them a quick wave, shoulder my bag, and then leave the restaurant, heading straight toward the subway—and Alec's apartment.

The hall leading to Alec's apartment is dreary, matching the overall feeling of the day. It's dark, almost spooky in a way, as if, if I turned around, I would see a guy standing behind me with a hood over his head holding a shank.

Open up. Open up.

I twist my hands in front of me, waiting for the door to unlock, waiting to stare into Alec's brilliantly green eyes. But he doesn't open up, and I really start to worry.

I knock a little harder this time. "Alec, are you in there?"

I hear something crash on the floor and then a man's voice, muttering something unintelligible.

"Alec, it's Luna. Please open up."

Footsteps fall across his floor, and the lock slides open. The door opens a few inches, but no one greets me from the other side. Instead, I just hear retreating footsteps. Cautiously, I push open the door. On the other side of the living room, Alec is taking a seat on the couch and burying his head in his hands. Across from him on the coffee table are an empty tumbler and a half-empty bottle of Jack Daniel's. I'm hoping that isn't a new bottle.

I step into the apartment, take my shoes off, and set my bag down. Not sure what I'm getting into, I approach Alec, who's in a pair of sweatpants and a plain white T-shirt. His hair is standing on end, and his entire body looks painfully tense.

I sit down beside him and place my hand on his thigh. His hand lands on top of mine, and he tangles our fingers together.

Gently, I rub my thumb over the back of his hand. "Alec, what's going on?"

He turns to face me just enough so I can see his bloodshot, tear-soaked eyes. The look on his face is enough to break me. I cup his cheek and lean in closer.

"Alec," I whisper, just as a tear falls down his cheek. I wipe it away, unsure of what to really do. But I don't want to press him, so I hold his hand, and I wait.

I wait as his head slumps forward.

I wait as he reaches for the tumbler and bottle again—and downs two fingers in one fell swoop.

I wait as he leans back into the couch and presses his fingers into his brow.

Unable to handle the wait any longer, I turn toward him and straddle his lap, resting my hands on his chest. His hands fall to my legs, and he blows out a long breath.

"She doesn't love me," he finally says, another tear rolling down his cheek. "Fuck . . ." He covers his eyes with his arm. "Why doesn't she love me?"

From what I saw today, I'm going to guess "she" is his mom. And the question just about shatters me. I can't imagine a life where my mom—either of my parents, for that matter—doesn't love me, doesn't want to see me, doesn't want to try to have a relationship with me.

And how do I even respond to his question? He's in such a fragile state that saying the wrong thing might make this even worse.

So, I try to be a sounding board for him instead.

"She didn't come today." It's a statement, not a question, but Alec still shakes his head.

"No. 'Rough night,' she said." The tang of whiskey wafts from his tongue. "Rough fucking night. When she knew she was supposed to come to set today." He pinches the bridge of his nose, his chest rising and falling more rapidly, the tension in his body mounting. "She fucking *knew* she was supposed to show up. Does she know how fucking hard it was to make that call? To suck up all the pain I carry around to reach out to her?"

I rub his chest in response.

"Same old story with her," he continues. "Thad looks past it, but I've seen her drawer of pills, I've seen the 'medicated cocktails' that began when she and my dad started fighting. I know exactly how she spends her nights: with pills and vodka." He moves his hand over his brow. "And here I am, acting just like her, turning to a bottle when things get tough. Fuck . . ." He shifts me off his lap and stands, picking up the bottle of Jack and striding to the kitchen. From the couch, I watch him chuck the bottle into the sink. I jump as the glass cracks and liquor splashes all over the kitchen.

He lurches away and leans against the dining room wall before sinking down to the floor and hunching forward. He sobs into his hands, his pain so heavy, so potent, that I can practically feel every tear that falls from his eyes.

My heart breaking, I give him the one thing I know he needs right now . . . some love. Standing from the couch, I walk over to him and take his hand in mine. When he looks up at me, I nod for him to stand, and I help him up.

Hand in hand, I walk him back to his bedroom, where I don't even bother with the lights. Instead, I pull the blankets back on the bed. Then I turn toward him and lift his shirt up and over his head. He stands there, letting me take over as I push down his sweats as well. He steps out of them and leaves them on the floor. I make quick work of my pants, too, and go to his dresser, rummaging around until I find one of his shirts and exchange it for the one I'm wearing.

Feeling comfortable, I maneuver us both into bed so he's lying flat on his back and I'm curled into his side, propped up so I can look down at his handsome face. Cupping his cheek, his new beard rough under my palm, I swipe away his tears before placing a gentle kiss on his lips. I linger for a few seconds, waiting for him to kiss me back, and when he does, my heart speeds up in my chest.

There is nothing sexual about our kiss, no tongue, no neediness.

It's pure, comforting connection with another human.

I pull away, still cupping his face. "You're important to me, Alec. You matter to me. I cannot speak for your mother, but I truly feel excitement at the prospect of seeing you, let alone getting a call or text from you. I know that doesn't matter as much, but I wanted you to know I care . . . about you."

"It means more than I think you know," he says, eyes heavy.

"And you believe me?"

He nods. "I do."

"Good." I press my mouth against his again, and even though he's kissing me back with sweet intensity, making me want more, I don't take it any further. I don't want our first time together to be when he's distraught.

So I slowly pull away and lie down, clinging to him and resting my head on his shoulder. His arm wraps around my waist, and he holds me tightly. And like that, as the sadness and frustration of the day hangs above us, we fall asleep.

◆ ◆ ◆

Bzzz.

Bzzzzz.

Bzzzzz.

What's that noise?

Alec shifts beside me, his arm still wrapped around my waist.

"Ahh, fuck," he mumbles, his voice sounding like sandpaper dragged along wood. "My head."

"What is that?" I ask, pressing my palm to my eye.

"A phone?" he asks. I've heard morning-man voice before, all gravelly and hot, but I must admit: Alec wins the prize for the sexiest, that's for sure.

"What time is it?" I ask, lifting my stiff body from Alec's.

"Uh . . ." He twists toward his nightstand. "Eight fifty-two."

"Eight fifty—oh my God, Alec, we have eight minutes to get to set." I spring out of bed. "We're going to be late, both of us."

"Shit," he mumbles, sitting up, very slowly. "Fuck, my head is pounding."

I grab my clothes, grateful we have to wear the same thing two days in a row for filming purposes, not grateful that I didn't get to wash my clothes. I pull up my leggings and snap them on my waist, then throw my shirt on. I run to his bathroom, not even bothering to go pee, and undo my hair before throwing it up into a fresh bun.

Behind me, I can hear Alec moving, still slowly, but moving at least.

"Using your toothpaste!" I call out, spreading some on my finger and working it around my mouth. Not very effective, but it's the best I can do.

"Mouthwash is under the sink," he calls out as I hear him open and close the dryer in his bedroom closet. "At least I had the decency to wash my clothes."

"Shut up!" I call out, running to my bag and then back to the bathroom. I bring my makeup on set for touch-ups, and I couldn't be more grateful for that decision as I touch up yesterday's face. Good lord, I'm going to need a facial scrub after this.

Lazily, Alec walks into the bathroom, shirtless, with jeans hanging low on his hips and a sexy-as-sin look in his eyes.

I pause, touching up my eyeliner. "How is it fair that you look like *that* hungover, while I didn't drink an ounce and somehow look like the bride of Chucky?"

He gives me a quick scan and scratches his chest. "I think you look hot."

"Your eyes are still blurry from sleep."

He turns the faucet on and dips his entire head in the sink, getting his face and hair wet. I watch in fascination as he takes a bar of soap, lathers up, and rinses everything out.

"What the hell was that?" I ask as he dries off and sets his towel to the side.

"Sink shower." He picks up his toothbrush and squeezes toothpaste on it. "All-in-one soap bar—works like a charm." He leans against the counter, his abs contracting as he brushes his teeth.

Irritated that it's so easy for men, I finish up my makeup and pack everything up. I glance at my phone. Nine o'clock. We are officially late.

"Crap. We are so late. I'm, uh . . . I'm going to go, so at least we don't show up at the same time. See you there."

"Hey." Alec spits out his toothpaste and rinses, snagging my hand at the same time. He pulls me back and wraps his arm around my waist. After wiping his mouth on his arm, he leans down and places a gentle kiss on my lips. "Thank you."

"Oh . . . no big deal," I say, trying to be as casual as possible.

"It is a big deal to me." He smooths his hand up my back, to my neck. "I can't remember the last time anyone comforted me like that. Thank you, Luna Moon."

I lift up on my toes and kiss him, letting myself get lost in his lips for a moment. "I care about you. Don't forget that."

"Never will," he says, letting me go. "I'll pace my time out. Be safe getting there."

I nod and take off, thinking up all the excuses for why I'm late, and the only thing I can come up with is . . . comforting my broken boyfriend.

Not sure that's going to fly. Must do more thinking on the way.

◆ ◆ ◆

"Luna, can I speak to you for a second?" Marco Vitally, beloved judge and the paper genius, says.

What's he doing here? Judges don't come in on Sundays. Mary DIY is the only one who has to come in on Sundays, and then she's mostly in her dressing room. We still haven't actually met, which is such a disappointment—I really looked up to her. It's always disappointing when you meet your idol and she turns out to be awful, despite having fantastic taste in macramé.

Gathering myself after the whirlwind that today has been, I plaster on a smile. "Of course." Cohen and Declan both shoot me a quizzical look before I follow Marco over to the table where the judges watch the challenges.

"Take a seat," he says. He takes a seat as well, but he leaves one chair between us before turning toward me.

"Different view from here," I say. "Must be fun to watch us run around like mad people."

He chuckles. "It's pretty comical from this vantage point. Especially when Helen gets on one of her rants—priceless."

I laugh along with him. "I'm sure watching Helen sit on me the first week was a high point."

"That will go down in history as one of my favorite moments."

"One of my most humiliating moments, but I can laugh at it now."

"Good to hear." He clears his throat. "But . . . what I did want to talk about was invitation week."

"Oh yeah. I wish I'd had more time to work on the design for Declan and Cohen, but I'm happy with what we could do in the amount of time we had."

"It was really impressive, actually."

"Oh, really?" I ask, feeling hopeful butterflies float up in my stomach.

"Yes. I wanted to see what else you design, so I checked out your social media, and you really are the jack of all trades."

"I'm a little crazy, so it's hard to choose a lane sometimes. I just really love creating."

He nods. "And that's what I saw: the love you put into everything you do. I went back to my team and showed them your designs and your work." *Oh God, don't cry, don't cry. He showed my stuff to his team . . . don't freaking cry.* "Everyone was gushing over your creative eye and color combinations. We would love to collaborate with you on a new line of wedding invitations."

Oh Jesus lord. DO. NOT. CRY.

"Wow, that's . . ." My eyes well up. Shit. "That's . . ." I wave my hand in front of my face, and Marco chuckles softly.

"It's okay, Luna, you can cry."

Tears roll down my cheeks, and I immediately apologize. "I'm so sorry. I don't mean to be emotional, but this show has been challenging, and I think it's all hitting me at once . . . you want to collaborate?"

"We do. We want to put a fresh spin on our designs, create a line that's a little flashier and more modern, edgier. I know you're working on a rustic wedding for your brother, but the designs in your shop are exactly what we're looking for when it comes to catering to a modern bride. We want our invitations to speak to brides who aren't looking for something traditional."

"I love the idea, and I'm not just saying that because you want to collaborate with me. I would totally be one of those brides. Bright colors, a graphic feel, but still playful . . ."

"Precisely." Marco smiles brightly. "Would you like to come down to the offices after the weddings? We can walk through everything, and you can meet the team. I don't want to take up your time right now, but once we wrap up, we would really like to sit down and see what we can come up with together."

"I would be truly honored," I say. "This is a dream, Marco—you have no idea."

"Well, we're very excited about you."

"Would it be okay if I drew up some ideas in the meantime? I don't want to get too ahead of myself, but my mind is already racing."

"Then let your mind race. Design to your heart's content. Bring in what you have, and we can go over it."

"Fantastic." We both stand, and Marco holds out his hand, which I take.

"I'm going to have my team email you some contracts and such so we can get right to work after the show. Does that work?"

"Send away." *I know someone who can look at them for me . . .*

"All right, have a good week." He winks. "Rooting for Team Rossi."

"Thank you, Marco." I head back to Cohen and Declan, ready to explode with excitement, when something out of the corner of my eye catches my attention.

Alec is leaning against a wall, his head in his hand and his shoulders slumped. I hesitate for a second—my first instinct is to go over and comfort him. But then I realize where I am.

In public.

"Luna, what was that about?"

"Huh?" I say, looking away from Alec and toward Cohen and Declan, still at our workbench, waiting impatiently for me to say something. "Oh." I smile again, but this time it feels a little forced. "Marco wants to collaborate with me on some wedding invitations."

"Seriously?" Cohen asks, his face lighting up. "Holy shit, Luna, that's amazing!"

He picks me up in a giant hug and spins me around. I meet Alec's questioning eyes from over Cohen's shoulder, but Thad calls him into the green room, and he disappears.

"That's so great," Declan says, taking his turn to hug me once Cohen sets me down. "I knew this show would be good for you. I just knew it."

"I didn't apply—"

"We know, we know," Declan says with an eye roll, "but you being discovered is a huge bonus."

Cohen pulls me into a hug again. "This is amazing. You have to call Mom and Dad tonight and tell them."

"I will," I say, calculating in my head when to call them if they're currently in Australia. "Hey, when are Mom and Dad getting back?"

"Talked to them last night. They're headed home the Monday before the wedding, and they said they have lots of Vegemite for us."

"Oh . . . wonderful." I laugh and let out a long sigh, pressing my hand to my stomach. "Wow, okay, I was not expecting that."

"Neither was I," Cohen says. "But I'm not surprised either. You're amazing, sis."

"You're pretty amazing yourself."

Chapter Twenty-Two

ALEC

"Next week is our last week before the weddings. Please be on time," Diane says, looking directly at me. As if I've never been on time. One fucking day. One fucking day I'm late, and now I'm the person who gets scolded. I wasn't even *that* late. Just twenty minutes late, but I received quite the look from Helen, who had to do her interview first this go-around in my absence—heaven forbid—and the cold shoulder from Thad.

Just add it to the shit-filled twenty-four hours I'm having.

The only good thing about all of this . . . the girl who's packing up her bag and avoiding all eye contact with me. I got her text last night, but I didn't want to drag her into the dark hole I was headed down, and I sure as shit didn't want her to see the emotions I was holding at bay. And yet, I should have known she was going to show up at my door—because that's the kind of girl she is. Loving, caring, a fixer.

Seeing her walk into my apartment cracked me open. I tried to avoid my emotions, wash them away with a bottle of whiskey, but it didn't work. Instead, I broke down in front of her. When she could have turned away, she didn't. She held my hand; she listened to me. And then she did the best thing she could have done for me in that moment. She stayed.

She held me.

She made me feel worthy of someone's love.

And even though this morning was stressful, she still took the time to comfort me one last time before she took off.

Within the last twenty-four hours, I've realized two things: my mom still doesn't care about me—never has, probably never will—and Luna Rossi is cementing herself in my heart, which I was never expecting. Not because I didn't think Luna was a forever kind of girl, but because I didn't think I was the kind of guy who could let someone into his heart in the first place. I wasn't sure I was capable of the kind of feelings I have for Luna—nor did I think I wanted those feelings.

As the set begins to empty out, I want to call out to her, take her hand, and let everyone know that this is my girl.

My fucking girl.

My fucking girl, who looked really excited just now, and I couldn't even ask her why.

"Hear that?" Thad mutters beside me. "Be on time."

Yeah, Thad has been a bitch this entire day, putting on a smile for the camera but undercutting me every chance he gets when the red light isn't on. It's been . . . fun. *Insert sarcastic thumbs-up here*

"Safe travels, everyone. We will see you next week. Hope no one is getting cold feet," Diane says before taking off, Marco and Mary DIY already gone.

"Let's get out of here," Thad says to Naomi, turning toward the exit, but she stops him with a hand to his arm.

"Hold on a second." She holds my gaze. "Alec, is everything okay?"

"He's clearly hungover, Naomi." Thad gestures to me as I sit on one of our workbench stools. "I can smell the booze on him, under all the aftershave he thinks is covering it up. He doesn't care about this, so why should we care about him?"

"He's trying, Thad."

"Is he?" Thad shoots back, but he stares at me while he says it. "One week he cared. One week he made it seem like he'd really changed, but now it just seems like he's taking after our dad, brushing me off and drinking too much."

"Thad," Naomi chastises.

"It's fine." I stand from the stool and move away from them, hand in my hair. "Maybe you're right, Thad—maybe I was following in Dad's footsteps, but I know one thing: he never would have shown up to this . . . and neither would Mom. I'd think about what someone might be going through before making yourself the victim." I nod at Naomi. "See you next week."

As I turn and walk away, I hear Naomi mutter to Thad to go after me, but no footsteps follow me, and that's fine. Right now, I just want to go back to my apartment and try to figure out what the hell I'm going to do to make this all better.

Luna: Farrah wants you to come over. She says she has a right hook she wants to test out on you.

Alec: As appealing as that sounds, it's better if I stay here. Alone. Not in the best mood.

Luna: Want me to come over?

Alec: I would give anything right now to have your body on top of mine and my hands up your shirt, but it wouldn't be for the right reasons. Plus, you should probably give Farrah some attention if she's gearing up a right hook. Might need some Luna Moon love.

Luna: Farrah has enjoyed the alone time. Don't tell her I told you this, but she mentioned being able to masturbate in peace.

Alec: LOL. Okay, I just spit water down my shirt.

Luna: Oh no, you're going to have to take off your shirt now. What a shame.

Alec: You're not even here to enjoy the show.

Luna: No, but you can send me a picture . . . *prayer hands*

Alec: [picture] My girl asks, my girl gets.

Luna: *sigh* You even got your nipples in the shot. I really like your nipples. Not too small and not too big, the perfect size for a man.

Alec: Thank you?

Luna: Ha ha. You're welcome. But seriously, I can come over, we can talk . . .

Alec: How did I know you were going to say that?

Luna: Bottling it up is not going to help, Alec.

Alec: I know, Luna Moon. Just give me a little bit of time, okay? Everything is so raw right now, shit is floating up from the past,

Thad is . . . hell, he's being Thad but on a whole new level. I just need a second to breathe.

Luna: I understand. But I'm here for you if you need me.

Alec: I know. Want to go out tomorrow? Someplace nice?

Luna: Are you asking me out on a date?

Alec: I am.

Luna: I might be interested.

Alec: You better be. I really want to take you out.

Luna: Well, if you REALLY want to take me out, then I guess I don't have a choice. What time?

Alec: Seven. I'll pick you up. Farrah can show me her right hook, and then we can head out.

Luna: I just told Farrah that and she immediately stood up and started jabbing the air. I'm going to take that as a yes.

Alec: Perfect. Hey, I meant to ask, what was all the excitement about today on set?

Luna: Tell you about it tomorrow.

Alec: Okay. Have a good night, Luna Moon.

Luna: You too.

Note to self: drinking heavily is no longer in my repertoire. Two days after my night of Jack Daniel's, and I'm still feeling like utter shit. I know some of the blame has to go on my family baggage, but 90 percent of the blame goes on the whiskey—because holy fuck, my body is feeling it.

My muscles ache.

My head still hurts.

And if I sniff just right, I can still smell the booze clinging to my body, despite the many showers I've taken.

Taking a deep breath, I gulp some more water down and try to focus on the private investigator report spread out on my desk.

Concentrate, Baxter.

The words swim together, *T*s looking like *L*s and *M*s looking like *W*s. *Wow, this is worse than I thought.*

I lean back in my chair as my office phone rings.

"Hello?"

"Alec, I have Naomi here to see you?" our receptionist, Anita, says. "Do you have time to meet with her?"

"Yeah, sure," I say, surprised. "Send her back."

I stand from my desk and take another sip of water. I consider putting my suit jacket back on, but she's about to be my sister-in-law, so there's no need for formality. Instead, I push my sleeves up farther and am grabbing a water from my minifridge for her just as she knocks on the door and steps inside.

"Hey, Naomi," I say, feeling a little awkward, given how we ended things yesterday. "How are you?"

"Good." She shuts the door behind her. "I'm sorry about stopping by uninvited, but I figured this would be the best way to talk to you . . . without Thad."

I nod and offer her a seat along with the water I pulled from the fridge. She sits down and sighs, leaning back, her hand to her rounded belly. "Do you happen to have anything to eat? I forgot a snack, and this baby is sucking me dry."

I chuckle and head toward the cabinets next to my minifridge. "How about some trail mix?"

"Is there chocolate in it?"

"What's trail mix without chocolate?" I say, grabbing a bag for each of us.

"A boring healthy snack."

"Exactly."

She tears open her package and tips it directly into her mouth.

"I might need another one," she says after chewing and swallowing. "But let's see how this first one goes."

"I have plenty." I chuckle as I take a seat on the chair across from her.

"What a hostess."

With the moistest . . . I inwardly laugh.

"Not to be rude, Naomi, but why are you here?"

"Yes, let's get down to business." She takes a sip of water and then crosses one leg over the other. "What happened on Saturday? You were off. And then you showed up late on Sunday—that's not like you."

"Just—"

"And don't lie to me. We might not know each other as well as I wish we did, but I'd at least hope you wouldn't lie to me."

Man, she's a tough one. I can't imagine what living with her must be like. Thad probably can't get away with anything.

I have two options here: I can lie through my teeth and let her believe it was some work thing, or I can be open with Naomi and hope this helps me get a bit closer to Thad. Option one is easier, but option two might settle some of the rattling that seems to be going on in my hollow chest.

I sigh and lean my forearms on my knees. "You know how we were allowed to invite people to set on Saturday?"

"Yeah, Helen brought her uninterested husband with the hairy ears. I can see why she's such a pill."

"Is that who that was?"

Naomi nods. "Oh yeah, Barry, I believe his name is. I had the distinct pleasure of being introduced to him while I was trying to run to the bathroom before we started filming. But that's not what we should be talking about. Did you invite someone?"

"I did." I clasp my hands together. "I invited my mom."

Naomi slowly sits up. "You invited Meredith?"

I nod. "Yeah. I, uh . . . I called her earlier in the week. To say she was surprised to hear from me is an understatement. I told her I would like it if she came to filming, and that I wanted us to start working toward rebuilding our relationship. It was a huge step for me."

"Wow, Alec. I had no idea."

"I didn't say anything to Thad because I didn't want to get his hopes up. He's already stressed, and I know how much pressure he's under to keep our family from falling apart. I wanted it to be more of a surprise than anything." I rub the back of my neck. "But she didn't show. Right before we started filming, I stepped aside to call her and see what was going on."

"And?" Naomi asks, setting her trail mix on my desk.

"She said she'd had a rough night." I shake my head. "Same fucking story. I thought that since I was reaching out this time, maybe she could pull it together for us, but apparently not. I was . . . hell, I was so mad that I shut down."

"Which made Thad think you just stopped caring," Naomi finishes for me.

"Exactly."

"I knew something was wrong. You really seemed like you were changing, like you wanted to make things better with Thad."

"I still do," I say. "I don't want to give up, but climbing out of the hole I'm stuck in seems next to impossible."

"It's not impossible." Naomi smiles. "Because you have me."

"Are you saying you're going to help me?" I ask, taken aback.

"Of course. What kind of future sister-in-law would I be if I didn't help you?"

"Not the good kind." I chuckle.

"Exactly." She grows serious again. "I don't know your mom that well, but I do know she's . . . self-centered." Naomi winces. "Sorry if that's rude."

"Not rude—accurate."

"I've gotten to know her, and it's been difficult, to say the least. She's canceled on us so many times—she's just not shown up. She's even asked Thad to get a prescription for her under his name."

"Jesus," I mutter, shaking my head.

"Thad sees the kind of person she is, but he's still holding on to her despite their toxic relationship. She's always taking, taking, taking, but I think he holds on because he doesn't really have anybody else."

My stomach sinks, heavy with guilt. I'm the reason our mom is his only option. He's a family man, always has been, and he's reaching for whatever small piece of family he can.

"I want to help you repair your relationship with Thad—at the very least, it might help him distance himself from your mom. You've been MIA, but I at least can see love in your eyes when you're around him—can't say the same about Meredith. You care about Thad. You wouldn't be helping with the wedding otherwise."

"I do care about him." I meet Naomi's gaze. "I care about him a lot."

"Then let's find a way to make things better, okay?" I nod and stand. She does as well, and I pull her into a hug—the first hug we've ever shared.

"Thank you, Naomi, for reaching out. I really fucking needed this."

"I could tell." She rubs my back and then pulls away, holding me by the shoulders. "I'm not sure your mom will ever change, for either you or Thad, but I'm joining this family soon, and I'll be damned if you and Thad don't have a relationship. And hey, if you need a little motherly hug or kick in the ass, I'm your girl. Okay?"

"Can I call you Mom?"

She laughs and steps away, grabbing our packets of trail mix as she goes. "If you want Thad to freak out, sure." She pauses. "You know, please do. I would love to see his reaction."

"I'm on it." I wink and stick my hands in my pockets.

She stops at my office door. "You know, Alec, you're a good man. Maybe a bit lost, but a good man. I can see where Thad gets it." With a wave of her hand, she reaches into her purse and pulls out a small square piece of paper and hands it to me. "For the uncle-to-be."

I stare down at the black-and-white photo of what looks like a little lima bean.

"Is this . . . ?"

Naomi nods. "The baby, yes. Thad wanted to give it to you on Saturday but refused after your argument. Thought it might lift your spirits."

"It does," I say, my throat growing tight. "This means a lot to me—thank you."

She smiles kindly. "See you Saturday, Alec."

My throat grows tighter. I regret a lot of my decisions, but I'll always be proud of the moments when I could protect Thad and give him the childhood I never had. I know it had an impact on him, and it's probably the only reason he still wants to have a relationship. I'm glad Naomi can see that good side of me: the kind, caring brother I used to be.

I give her a small wave. "See you Saturday, Naomi."

The door clicks shut, and I head back to my office chair, where I stick the picture right under my computer screen so I can stare at it.

A good man.

If someone asked me if I thought I was a good man, I'm not sure I'd say yes.

I help people get divorced for a living. I had my reasons for that choice, but the more I let myself think of my mom, the more I realize I've spent all these years helping these other women so they wouldn't end up like her, so they wouldn't hurt and neglect their children like she did. I thought I was seeking justice, but I think I was trying to change my mom—projecting my childhood issues on my clients.

Jesus Christ, that's beyond fucked.

That doesn't make me a good man. It makes me a perfect candidate for therapy.

I round my desk, pick up my phone, and dial Lucas.

"What's up, man?"

"I need a therapist."

He doesn't laugh. "I have just the person for you."

CHAPTER TWENTY-THREE
LUNA

Farrah: Running late. Don't leave for dinner until I show him my right hook. No more than forty-five minutes. Sorry.

I set my phone down just as a knock sounds at the door. I stand from the couch and go to answer it.

I've been mentally preparing myself all day for this date. Alec hasn't been texting, and even though he said he'd be okay, I didn't believe it. He suffered a big blow this weekend, and I can't imagine him being able to work through it all on his own. I desperately wanted to go over to his place and hold him, let him know I was there for him if he needed anything, but I respected his wishes. And it was painful.

It was also painful not hearing from him.

The only text I got today was right before he left his apartment, letting me know he was on his way. So going into tonight, I really have no idea what to expect. Is he in a good mood? Has he spent too much time thinking? Is he standing outside my apartment door, ready to break things off with me?

That's the fear swirling through my head like a storm ready to break. I'm afraid our relationship is going to be too much for Alec. Maybe it would be best for him if he took a break and figured out his life. I'd step aside, if that were the case, and let him rebuild his family—despite how devastating it would be. Whether I like it or not, Alec has dug himself under my skin. He's all I think about. Even when I'm crafting, my thoughts drift to Alec and the way he so carefully touches me, how he can make me laugh without even trying. After Marco offered me the collaboration, the first person I wanted to tell was Alec, despite my brother standing only a few feet away. I wanted to see the pride on Alec's face, the excitement—that smile.

With a trembling hand, I steel myself and open the door.

A second later, a pair of strong arms scoops me back into my apartment, spins me around, shuts the door, and presses me against it. Then a pair of lips is pressing against mine.

Firm, demanding lips.

Hungry, devouring lips.

The only lips I want.

His mouth is the first thing I register, followed by his hands on my lower back, then the rough scruff of his beard. A sweet groan floats up from the back of his throat.

Hot.

Needy.

Relief washes over me.

My hands fall to the back of his neck, where I grip him tightly, beyond relieved that *this* is the kind of greeting I'm getting—and not the other one I was dreading.

"Where's Farrah?" he asks, resting his forehead against mine.

"Late."

"Really?"

I nod. "At least forty-five minutes."

He lifts me up by the ass, and I wrap my legs around his waist. "Where's your bedroom?"

"Down the hall. Door on the right."

He takes off, and I giggle as he practically sprints down the hallway. Skidding to a halt, he kicks the door open, strides inside, and slams it shut before tossing me on the bed. From behind his head, he tears his shirt off and tosses it to the ground, revealing his perfectly defined chest and magnificent abs. The view will never get old.

Never ever.

"Shirt off." He nods.

I do what he says, revealing my moss-green bra.

"Pants too."

I chuckle and get rid of those as well.

"Matching set—I like it," he says, crawling over the bed and pressing a kiss on my lips. But then he pauses and leans back a few inches. "What's wrong?"

"Nothing's wrong."

"Not buying it. There's worry in your eyes."

"I'm just . . ." His warm body is hovering over me, and the last thing I want is to distract from where the evening is headed, but Alec needs the truth. "After not hearing from you and all the drama that went down this past weekend, I thought you might have to—I don't know—ask for time apart to figure things out."

"What?" His brow creases. "Where would you get that idea? You're the only reason I'm surviving this whirlwind."

"I know it was crazy, but it was just a thought. I didn't hear from you all day—"

"Luna." He brings his palm to my cheek. "Not on purpose." He kisses the inside of my wrist. "I was catching up on work so I could come tonight. Plus, Naomi stopped by the office."

"She did?"

He nods. "She did. She wanted to check up on me. I told her about my mom not showing up to set. She was surprised I even invited her in the first place, but I told her I wanted to repair things. And we eventually came to the conclusion that the relationship with my mom might never change, but the one with Thad can. And she's going to help me make sure that happens."

"Oh, Alec, that's . . . that's great."

He studies me. "You're saying that, but how come it's not accompanied by one of your amazing smiles?"

"Ugh, I'm sorry. I'm being stupid."

"Let me guess, you wanted to help fix my relationship with my mom, right? And you're feeling a little sad that you're not the one who could help."

"What? Why do you say that?"

"Because, Luna Moon, you're a fixer." He turns my palm over and kisses that as well. "It's in your nature."

"I just like to help."

"And I love that about you," he says, the *L* word falling so easily from his tongue. I know he didn't say he *loves me*, but still, hearing the word on his lips sends a thrill through me.

"Are you doing better?"

"Much better now that I'm here." He lowers himself down, and our bare stomachs press together as he sighs, resting his forehead on mine. "I didn't realize how much I needed to see you until just now. It's been a shit few days."

"I know." I swallow back my exciting news—now is not the time. "But I'm glad you're here now."

"So am I." He presses a light kiss across my lips. "I don't think I ever said thank you."

"For what?"

"For everything." His lips fall to my jaw and travel up to the sensitive spot near my ear. I grasp his shoulders and twist beneath him as his mouth whispers across my skin. "For coming to my place the other night, for holding me, making me feel like I matter." He props himself up on his elbows. "For being mine."

I smooth my hand over his beard, my eyes not leaving his. "You don't have to thank me, Alec. I want you in my life. I was devastated at the thought of you ending things today. It's weird to think that this all started with an irritated demand for coffee, but I'm glad it did, because it led to us, and I truly believe you're the first man to actually capture my soul in his hands."

"Hell . . ." He exhales heavily. "I feel the same damn way, Luna. The same fucking way."

"Like . . . you can't stop thinking about me?"

"It's constant."

"Like . . . you want to tell me everything and anything all at the same time?"

"I feel tongue tied when I'm near you—I'm just so excited to have a conversation."

"Like . . . ," I start, my heart hammering. "So excited that if you're not inside me soon, your skin might very well disintegrate into nothing?"

"Desperate, Luna. So fucking desperate for that."

My stomach bottoms out, and I realize this is it: the moment I've been craving for a while now.

Letting him know where my head is at, I spread my legs wide and wrap them around his waist, pressing my center to him. His head falls against my shoulder, and he lets out a shaky breath.

"Are you sure?" he whispers.

I nod. "Beyond sure. And ready. I want you, Alec. Need you."

In response, he reaches behind me and unhooks my bra. Using just his fingertips, he drags the fabric down my shoulder, his fingers running over my skin.

He lifts up my arm so he can remove my bra completely, and instead of bringing his lips back to my mouth, he moves down my body, to my breasts, his beard scraping along my hardened nipples, which he sucks into his warm, wet mouth.

"Yes," I whisper, my hand falling to his hair.

Unapologetically, I move my hips against him, searching for any way to release the pressure coiling between my legs.

While his mouth works one of my breasts, his hand moves down to my thong. He runs his fingers along the waistband, taking in the fabric, almost as if he's memorizing the feel against his fingertips. And when I think he's going to continue to torture me, his touch so close to where I want him, he drags my thong down my legs, and I help him kick it to the side. He sits up and stares down at me while my heart pounds away in my chest.

"So hot," he says before grabbing both of my breasts, squeezing them together, and bringing his mouth to them.

He kisses.

He licks.

He sucks.

And good God, he pinches.

"Oh fuck, Alec." He groans against me and repeats the process, playing with my breasts until I feel myself unhinging. I need him to push forward, to take me completely, but he doesn't.

He pinches.

And pinches.

And pinches until the throbbing between my legs reaches such a crescendo that if he does it one more time I will come.

"Alec, please. I need you."

He licks my nipple, soothing the pleasurable pain before dragging his tongue down the center of my stomach, to my pubic bone. Then he pauses and reaches down to his pants. He pushes them off, along with his briefs, freeing his beautifully hard cock.

God, he has an amazing dick. Like the lord himself spent a great deal of time carving it out, making it perfect.

"I'm so goddamn hard," he croaks—before pressing his mouth between my legs. I sit up on my elbows, my mouth falling open as his tongue runs along my clit. His hips move, grinding his cock into the mattress, probably trying to ease some of the pressure that's built up inside him as well.

"Stop," I breathe out.

He pauses, looking concerned. "Everything okay?"

"I love your mouth on me, but I want your cock, Alec. I don't want you grinding against anything but me. Right now."

He chuckles and gently pushes me back down onto my back. "You don't make the calls, Luna Moon. I do." And then he puts his mouth back on my pussy and flicks his tongue along my clit—and before I can argue, my muscles melt. I feel nothing but the solid beat of my heart and the quiver at my center.

"That's it, Luna, let go," he says, pausing for a moment before diving right back between my thighs.

"Oh . . . right there. Right . . . fuck!" I scream. White-hot pleasure rips through me, shooting stars behind my eyes. My body lifts off the mattress, and I'm almost in disbelief as his mouth continues to work me over and over again.

"Alec, oh fuck, Alec," I call out, and he grunts something as he pulls away.

Just as I begin to come down from the euphoria of his mouth, I hear a condom wrapper being ripped open and feel his hands spreading my legs far apart. I reach out and take his length in my hand, helping guide it to where I want him to be. He smiles lustfully down at me while the tip of his cock plays at my entrance. The look of tortured pleasure that passes over his features as he slowly enters me is by far the sexiest thing I've ever seen.

"Mother . . . fucker," he breathes out heavily. "Shit, Luna, you feel so good. So fucking good."

"So full," I whisper.

He stills.

I breathe heavily.

His control is slipping by the second.

But he still manages to take it slow, placing his hand on my stomach to hold my pelvis still as he works in and out of me. The pace is agonizing, but in the best way possible.

"So good," he mumbles. He lowers himself down and kisses me, parting my mouth with his tongue and diving deep. I gasp into his mouth as he continues moving in and out, seeming to drag out every pleasure point I have.

Sweat slicks our bodies.

And he makes it impossible not to moan after three long . . . slow strokes.

"Christ, Alec, I need you to move faster. Harder."

"But . . . it's . . . so . . . good," he grits out.

I'm in a state of sexual purgatory, with no relief in sight if he keeps this up, so I do something I know will tip him over the edge.

I squeeze myself around him just as he thrusts inside me.

"Holy . . . oh fuck, Luna." He stops, breathing heavily. "Don't do that."

He pushes in again, and I squeeze.

"God dammit." I do it again and again until he roars, pins my hands over my head, and loses all control. Just what I need.

He fucks me.

He wanted slow, he wanted to draw it out, but not anymore.

He gives me what I want.

Hard. Sloppy. Uncoordinated.

And oh so delicious.

"Yes, yes . . . ," I moan as I feel the orgasm mounting, ready to spill over. "I'm there, Alec, I'm there."

He groans against my shoulder, bites down, and then unleashes a flurry of pumps so hard that he pushes us up the bed. When my head hits the headboard, he lets go of my hands, presses his against the board, and continues to pound into me.

Above me, his muscles ripple and sweat drips down his chest. His body is so beautiful moving in and out of me, and that's my undoing.

Bliss tears through me as my legs spasm and my mouth falls open, though no noise escapes me as I am submerged beneath waves of pleasure.

"Oh . . . shit," Alec says. "I'm coming." He stills above me, his groan one of the most provocative things I've ever heard.

A roar so delicious that it keeps my orgasm spasming, my body tingling and seeking more as his hips slowly move against mine.

"Fuck, Luna," he murmurs, pressing his face against my neck, his breath hot on my skin. "You just about killed me."

I chuckle. "Pretty sure it was the other way around." I cradle his face and bring his lips to mine, letting them take over as we ride out the postorgasm bliss, our bodies connected, our breaths evening out.

He lifts up slightly, his smile crooked and lazy. "You've ruined me, you realize that? Absolutely ruined me."

I nudge him onto his back and lay my head on his chest. "Can I be honest with you?"

"Always."

I nibble on my bottom lip, nervous, but knowing it needs to be said. "You're, uh . . . you're starting to . . ." I roll my lip under my teeth. "I'm liking you a lot . . . a lot."

He smiles softly. "I'm liking you a lot too, Luna Moon."

"Scary-like? Or serious-like?"

"Very serious-like," he answers, his voice husky and beautifully lazy. If Farrah weren't due back soon, I would stay like this all night.

"Yeah?"

He nods. "My feelings are strong, Luna, and getting stronger every second I'm with you."

My toes curl just from that little sentence, just from knowing that he's in the same boat as me, and we're not off course.

"Me too."

"Good." He rubs his hands over my back. "Should we go rinse off?"

"Probably." But I don't move. Instead, I drag my finger over his chest. "Are you okay? You know, with your mom and everything? You were really upset on Saturday, and I don't think that just goes away in a few days."

"It doesn't." He sighs, rubbing my back. "The pain is there, the realization that she'll never be the mom I want her to be, but I also know there are other people in my life who care about me. Who cherish their time with me . . ."

I lean in and press a kiss to his lips. "I do."

"I know." He kisses my forehead. "And I'm grateful for you. I'm grateful for Naomi wanting to help me, and I'm grateful I've been able to see past all my baggage and realize how much I miss my brother."

"And you can lean on me—you don't have to shut me out."

His fingers drag up my back, then over my shoulders and back down, sending chills along my skin and making me yearn for him again.

"I know that, but I also don't want to be another project you can fix."

"Hey!" I snap, insulted. "That's not why—"

"I didn't mean that to hurt you; I meant it so you can understand that I don't want to be something you make better. I want to be the man you deserve. The strong, put-together man. Not the crumbling guy who can't seem to hold it together, who reverts to drinking his problems away."

"I don't see you that way, Alec."

"Well, I see myself that way, and you deserve more than that man. It's why I didn't want you to come over on Sunday. You already saw me at my worst—you didn't need the sequel."

I pause, letting his words sink in and trying to calm the irritation building inside me. I take a calming breath. "The point of being with someone *is* to see them at their worst. A relationship isn't surface level: it's deep and multifaceted, it has ups and downs, and we need to experience them together. You don't have to be this macho man who's always strong and protecting me, Alec. I like seeing your vulnerable side. It's what made me fall—" I catch myself and swallow hard. "It's what drew me to you in the first place. That flash of vulnerability showed me that there's a real person under this handsome exterior. A person I want to know."

He lets out a heavy sigh, his hand dragging over his face. "Fuck, why do you always make sense?"

I laugh and lean down to kiss his jaw. "Because even though you're older, I'm wiser. Never forget that."

"I don't think you would let me." He sits up on the bed, dragging me with him so I'm sitting directly on his lap, his cock against my entrance.

God, that feels good. I shift and groan at the pressure on my clit.

"Hey, Horny Henrietta, slow down for a second."

"You're the one with the erection."

"Because your wet pussy is gliding along it." He chuckles and stills my hips. "We will get to that in a second. Shower sex—you, me, and some nice hot water." That sounds divine. "Look at me, Luna." I meet his eyes. "Feelings are new for me. I blocked them for so long that I've forgotten it's okay to show them. I swore off relationships a long time ago, so take it easy on me while I navigate my way through this relationship. Because I'm falling—" He stops, and then winks.

"You're falling?" I ask, looping my arms around his neck.

"Hard and fast, Luna Moon."

I press our noses together before kissing him. "Me too."

◆ ◆ ◆

"I still don't think she accidentally hit me," Alec says, rubbing his arm as we peruse our menus at one of the nicest restaurants I think a boyfriend has ever taken me to. It's not posh by any means, but it's romantic, with dim lighting, earthy plants, and plush velvet seating. We took the subway down to Hell's Kitchen for the dinner, but now that we're here, it was well worth it—not that the travel was painful, but after what we just did, I felt pressed to stay home, in bed.

"I'd like to say it was an accident, but I saw the look in my best friend's eye—it was a warning hit."

"I thought I won Farrah over the last time I saw her."

"Oh, you did." I nod, setting my menu down. "She just likes to keep you in check—that's all."

He rubs his arm like a baby. "Can she do it verbally next time?"

"It was *not* that hard."

"Easy for you to say. You weren't the one who was punched."

"She has bird bones. There's no way her fist did that much damage." I roll my eyes.

"Maybe I'm trying to show you more of my sensitive side so you'll nurse me back to health after this. I heard tits have amazing healing powers. Can I suck on yours after this?"

I try to hold back the laugh, but it's impossible. "You're really awful, you know that? Night and day with you."

"Keeps you on your toes." He winks and reaches across the table, taking my hand in his. "Plus, I wouldn't mind round three tonight."

"For an old man like you? Impressive."

He leans forward and points a finger at me, laughter in his eyes. "I am thirty-fucking-two—I'm in the prime of my virile life."

"Is that what the men's magazines are telling you?" I smirk.

"Look who's the jokester now, and ripping at my age. Okay, I see you, Luna Rossi. I see you."

I roll my eyes. "What are you getting?"

"Depends on what's for dessert. If it's a quick peck to the cheek and a pat to my ass to send me on my way, then the mac and cheese, because at least I can be bloated and happy."

"Charming."

"But," he continues, "if I'm looking at naked time with my girl, then I'll go with the Cobb salad so my muscles pop when I'm thrusting inside of her. So . . . what do you think I should get?"

"The mac and cheese. Definitely the mac and cheese."

"Damn, Luna." He laughs and reaches across the table, taking my hand just as our waitress walks up to our table.

Ready to order, I turn. "Hello, I would like—"

My words fade away as I make eye contact—not with our waitress, but with the one and only Mary DIY. Fear niggles at the back of my neck as I realize I'm sitting across from Alec, holding his hand, in a romantic restaurant.

This doesn't look like friends hanging out, or enemies making a truce. It looks like so much more.

"Wow," Mary says. "How nice to see you two when the cameras aren't rolling."

Alec's eyes narrow, and I'm pretty sure I know exactly what he's thinking.

How does she even know who we are, if she's never actually introduced herself?

But like the pleasant person I am, I say, "Mary, hi, how are you?"

"Great. I saw you two walk in and thought, 'Hey, I know them.' I just had to come say hi."

"Just had to, huh?" Alec says, his voice clipped, making me break out in an instant sweat. I kick him under the table, but he doesn't seem to care.

"Why, of course." Mary smiles, knuckles white on her clutch. "Thought I'd say congratulations." She stares down at our hands for a brief second, and I tear my hand away, as if Alec has just burned it. I shoot him a quick look; by his furrowed brow, he's connecting the dots as well. If she says something to Thad, we're both screwed.

"Congratulations on what?" I ask, my voice shaky.

"On the deal with Marco, of course."

"Deal?" Alec asks from across the table.

Crap, I never got a chance to tell him.

"Oh, she didn't tell you? Well, I guess she wouldn't, since you're competitors after all." Mary smiles again, but there's an agenda behind those veneers—I'm just trying to figure out what it is. "Marco is collaborating with *Luna* on his new modern bride line."

Alec blinks a few times, staring at me. I can see the question on his face . . . *Why didn't you tell me?*

"Isn't that just a dream come true?" Mary continues, her sweet voice not matching her cold eyes. "A real Cinderella story."

"I would hardly call it a Cinderella story," Alec retorts. "Luna isn't going from rags to riches. She's established herself in the industry, and you'd have recognized that if you didn't keep your head buried in your own—"

"Thank you, Mary," I say, cutting Alec off before he can finish what I'm sure would have been a flavorful insult. "I'm very excited."

Still clutching her bag, Mary stares Alec down for a few beats before sticking her chin in the air and turning toward me.

"Yes, well, you should be. I was speaking with Marco the other day about the line, and what he has is incredible. I'm still a little shocked he passed on my idea, but then again, he wanted to make it a *charitable* collaboration."

What. A. Bitch.

I realized she was a self-involved diva after only a few episodes, but she's reached a new low.

Still, I'm professional, and I'm never one to burn bridges, so I plaster on a smile. "I consider myself very lucky." Then, to get her out of here, I dismiss her. "See you Saturday, Mary."

"Mm-hmm." She gives me a slow once-over and then turns to Alec. "See you . . . Saturday."

And as abruptly as she appeared, she retreats, meeting some man at the door and disappearing into the city night.

"I can't believe—"

"That's what you were celebrating on Sunday, wasn't it?" Alec asks, sadness and anger colliding in his voice. "Hugging Cohen—that's what it was, wasn't it?" I nod. He leans back in his chair. "Why didn't you tell me, Luna?"

"You weren't in a very good place—"

"That's bullshit. Just because it wasn't the best moment of my life doesn't mean you have to hide your accomplishments. You should have told me. That's kind of big news, and if it was mine, I'd want to tell you no matter what."

"I wanted to, Alec. You were the first person I wanted to tell, but I . . . I don't know, it just didn't feel right. I planned on telling you tonight. Once we ordered, I was going to tell you everything."

His tongue presses against his teeth as he taps his fingers on the table.

"Okay, so tell me, then."

"I'm not going to tell you when you're angry."

"I'm not angry," he snaps.

"Uh, I beg to differ."

He shifts in his chair, looking out to the door. "I mean . . . why did you just let her walk all over you? She was being a bitch on purpose because you clearly beat her out for whatever this collaboration is. And you didn't stick up for yourself."

"Because what's the point, Alec? It's not like anything I would have said was going to change her—it just would have pissed her off, and if you didn't notice, she saw we were holding hands. She doesn't seem like the kind of person who's just going to let that go, especially if I provoke her. It was best that I let her insult roll off me. The last thing we need is her telling Diane about us. I prefer Mary ignoring my very existence."

He licks his lips, clearly not convinced. Sighing, I stand from my chair and round the table, where I sit on his lap. His arm automatically wraps around me.

I sift my fingers through his dark hair. "I'm sorry I didn't tell you. I was trying to be sensitive. I'll make sure to never consider your feelings again." He snorts, and I can feel him relax beneath me.

"I just want to be the guy you celebrate with."

"I want that too," I say, leaning in and pressing a kiss on his mouth, not even caring that we're in a full restaurant. "Trust me, you were the first person I wanted to run to, but given the circumstances, I held back. Don't worry, next time something big happens and you're going through something emotional, I'll be sure to kick you in the balls and tell you my amazing news."

"That's all I ask." He smiles, and I'm relieved that he's okay, that we're okay.

"Did we just have our first fight?" I ask.

He shakes his head. "More of a quarrel."

"Oh . . . so then no makeup sex."

His brows shoot up to his hairline. "Actually, that was a fight. Huge fight. Giant. I'm . . . wow, I can't believe we survived that. We should really have the makeup sex—all the makeup sex."

I roll my eyes and am going back to my chair just as the waitress appears at our table.

She introduces herself, rattles off the specials, and then turns toward me. "I'll take the salmon with asparagus and rice." I hand her my menu.

Alec hands her his menu as well and says, "I'll take the Cobb salad." He winks at me with such a goofy grin that I can't hold back a chuckle.

When she leaves, I pick up my water glass. "You're truly hoping for a three-peat, aren't you?"

"A boy's got to dream."

"Keep dreaming."

"I will." He takes my hand. "Now tell me all about this collaboration . . ."

CHAPTER TWENTY-FOUR

ALEC

"What are you doing here?" Thad asks as he opens the door to his apartment. I hold back a wince at the fake powdered cheese caked in the corner of his mouth.

And this man is about to be a father . . .

"Came to see Naomi," I say, striding past him and straight into his apartment, where Naomi's sitting on the couch, a giant bowl of Doritos on her lap.

"Hey, Alec, want some Doritos?"

"Would love some, thank you." I take a seat next to her, which, judging by the warm cushion, is where Thad was sitting. I pick up a cheesy chip and pop it in my mouth.

"Uh . . . what the hell is going on here?" Thad asks, shutting the door and moving in front of us, blocking the TV, which is playing reruns of *The Big Bang Theory*.

"We're trying to eat chips and listen to Sheldon be a little bitch," I say, motioning to the screen behind him. "You realize your torso isn't a window, right?"

Thad picks up the remote and turns the TV off before leaning over to his pregnant fiancée and grabbing the bowl of Doritos like a true savage.

"Knock it off." He motions between the two of us with a cheese-covered finger. "This is not a thing—you two have never been a thing—and I specifically told you on Sunday that I was writing him off . . . *Naomi*," Thad says. "So what the hell is going on?"

"He told you that?" I ask her.

"He says a lot of things that I don't pay attention to. Like that he was going to start waxing." She leans into me. "Think he's gotten rid of that jungle on his chest?"

"I said I was doing it for the wedding night. I'm not about to let the hairs grow in partially and poke you in the eye while you're playing with my nipples."

"Nipples?" I raise a brow at Naomi.

"Loves nipple play, that one." She shrugs and jabs a thumb at Thad, who looks like he's about to blow a gasket.

"Don't do that. Don't talk about me as if I'm not in the room."

"Didn't think we were doing that," I say. "She pointed at you, so we know you're in the room."

Thad gasps, fists clenched at his side. "I am going to scream in about three seconds if you two don't tell me what's going on."

I stifle a laugh. "I thought we could go over tomorrow's challenge and our final picks." I reach into my back pocket and pull out some of the ideas Luna helped me come up with this past week . . . while we were naked in bed.

That woman just about wore me out, and I'm grateful for every second of it.

Thad eyes the packet of paper and slowly takes a seat on the coffee table. He snatches it out of my hand and sets the chips down beside him.

He scans the first page, brow furrowed. "These are decorations?"

"Yeah, statement piece for the ceremony."

Thad studies the idea I put together with Luna: strands of feathers, strung up and cascading behind the bride and the groom. His lips quirk to the side, and then he looks up at me. "Where did you come up with this?"

I shrug. "Just thought of it."

"Uh-huh." He looks at the paper again. "This doesn't look like something you could draw."

Shit. Maybe because I didn't draw it.

"Took me a long time."

"Uh-huh," he repeats, and then he turns to the next page, where Luna drew out a feather garland that was hard to understand, but once she got the supplies and showed me what to do, I understood it. Thad lifts an eyebrow. "This looks complicated."

"It's not. I practiced."

"You *practiced*?"

"Yeah, went to the craft store, and Lu—" Oh shit. "Luu-oopy drunk." I try to make the save, but Thad's eyes narrow. "Just loopy drunk, I came up with the idea. Should try it. Craft stores and buzzed— you come up with great ideas."

"Why are you being weird?"

"I'm not being weird. Am I being weird?" I ask Naomi.

"A little weird. Kind of jittery."

"Yes." Thad snaps his fingers. "Jittery. That's the exact word I was looking for. You're acting jittery."

"Just, uh, nervous to hear what you think. I worked hard on this."

Thad studies me a few beats longer, his eyes like laser beams trying to cut me in half. "What's your game?"

"Maybe he's just trying to be helpful," Naomi says.

Thad holds up the papers. "This is helpful. And I appreciate it." With two fingers, he points from his eyes to mine. "But I have my eyes on you, Alec."

"Okay . . . ," I say.

"Your eyes are shifty, and I don't like shifty eyes."

"Maybe because you're being weird and making me feel uncomfortable."

"I'm always like this. You should know that by now."

Valid point.

"Are you staying for dinner?" Naomi asks, and I send her a silent *Thank you* for breaking up the weird staredown.

"Would love to," I say, thinking of Luna, who's having dinner at Cohen and Declan's right now and prepping for tomorrow. I told her I was going to do the same, and she told me I was cute. I prefer sexy but settled for cute. She also gave me some encouraging words and reminded me that breaking Thad was probably going to be difficult, but not to give up.

She could not have been more right.

"Wonderful. I'll order some pizza. Thad, why don't you go wash your face? You have Dorito cheese dust caked all over your mouth."

"And you let me intimidate my brother like this? Christ, Naomi." Thad stomps off toward the bathroom.

I chuckle and pull out my phone as Naomi orders pizza.

There's a text from Luna.

Luna: How's it going over there?

Alec: Just as you'd expect.

Luna: Thad giving you the side eye?

Alec: Heavily. And he called me out for having shifty eyes and being jittery.

Luna: Are you acting weird?

311

Alec: A little.

Luna: Relax, Alec. Just be yourself.

Alec: It's encouragement like that, that makes me . . . fall.

Luna: It's admissions like that ^^^ that make me . . . fall.

Alec: Can't wait for this to be over so I can kiss you in front of everyone—let them know how much you mean to me.

Luna: Can't wait for this all to be over so I can knit a pair of handcuffs to gently bind your hands to your headboard.

Alec: LOL. Something to look forward to.

"Helen is ripe today," Thad says from the corner of his mouth, his hand on my shoulder. "Look at her—I think I see fangs poking out of her mouth."

"She's not happy about the Twitter trolls," Naomi says.

The first episode of the show came out on Wednesday. There is a much-needed delay between filming and airing; the show is constantly moving from state to state, providing viewers new contestants, but pre-filming gives the crew and judges a break. Luna and I watched the first episode together on Wednesday, and I laughed so hard tears were rolling down my face. The editing they did of Helen sitting on Luna was the most priceless thing I had ever seen. Thank God I recorded it at my place too, because it has been endless entertainment. Not to mention the people at work keep sending me memes from the first episode, making my week that much better.

"What? They're talking about us on Twitter already? In that Facebook group?" Thad asks. "What did they say?"

"It's not important," Naomi says, giving me a look.

Things Thad doesn't need to know—how much America thinks the judges were high when they picked our theme to win the first week—which they unanimously claimed to be vastly original. To say viewers weren't nice about it on social media is an understatement.

"It is important. Who's in the lead? Who's the front runner?"

Naomi glances at me, and I just shrug. She sighs and says, "Based on the comments . . . Team Rossi."

"Bastards," Thad whispers as he whips his head to look over at Luna, Cohen, and Declan, who are bent over their workbench, strategizing. "Good news, though—America really despises Helen."

"Join the club, America." Thad places both hands on the workbench. "Our true competition is Team Rossi, and we need to make sure we're on point today. Naomi, really play up the pregnancy to the cameras. America loves pregnant women."

"Do they?" I ask.

"They would be heathens if they didn't." Thad points to Naomi's substantial bump. "This woman is sharing her body with another living being. She's letting it suck the life from her. See these dark circles?" Thad motions to Naomi's eyes. "No concealer can cover them up, and they weren't there before. And you should see her nipples. Never in my life have I seen—*oof*." Thad bends forward, holding his stomach.

"Don't talk about my nipples," Naomi says as Thad, still bent over, draws a large circle with his finger and mouths, "Huge."

"Mary, we're ready!" Diane calls out as Mary walks on set.

Her heels clack across the concrete floor, and as she passes our workbench, she pauses and reaches over, caressing my arm. "It was great seeing you on Monday, Alec." She winks. "Looking forward to what you create today." With that, she takes off toward her spot. I quickly glance over at Luna, who looks ready to kill.

"What the hell was that?" Thad asks. "Did you go out with her?"

"What? No." I shake my head. "She saw me with Lu—" Fuck. "Lucas," I say to recover. "We were having dinner and ran into her. No idea why she's touching me."

"She probably thinks you're cute. If you do her in her dressing room, think she could sway the votes for us to win?"

"I don't think my penis is that powerful," I deadpan.

"Mine is," Thad says with pride. "Got this one pregnant, and you should see the armor she wears as underwear."

"You realize I can murder you in your sleep, right?" Naomi asks.

"Quiet on set," Diane says and then points to Mary.

Plastering on that fake smile, Mary goes into her spiel, reading off the intro they have on cue cards in front of the camera.

Today we have an hour to create the rest of our decorations, and then we're going to have half an hour to utilize the rest of our budget on anything we want to upgrade. So we get to go through all the aspects of the wedding and decide if we want to add more to our food and beverage plans, change out the bouquets or the decorations, or tweak the attire. We will have time—not much, but we'll make it work. We've already decided to use the extra $1,000 we've saved up for the bouquet and boutonnieres. Swapping out our horrendous creations was an easy choice to make.

"Are you ready, contestants?" Mary asks, clasping her hands together.

We all nod and get in position before a white curtain screening off the supplies we'll use for our final decorations. Once something is taken, that's it—there are no replacements, just like in *Chopped* when there's only one ice cream machine. You have to be the fastest, or you're screwed.

But I think we're ready.

"On your mark, get set, create!" The curtain drops, and I have a moment of uncertainty as I take in all the different ribbons, strings, paper, florals, and mounds of tulle. *Focus, Baxter.* Helen, surprisingly, is the first to the table and starts grabbing every spare feather and spool of string she can get her hands on.

"She's stealing all the feathers!" Thad shouts and then charges toward Helen, blocking her and trying to gather the remaining feathers.

"Get off me, you monster!" Helen shouts.

"Don't hit him!" Luciana calls out.

"Ouch. Did you see that?" Thad screams. "She hit me."

"It was a tap."

"Luna, wood triangles?" Cohen asks, holding up a package.

"No," she says, digging around. I know she's mentally flipping through all the sketches and supply lists she's made this week.

"Careful of my wife, careful!" Thad calls out.

Naomi holds her belly and shouts, "I'm so pregnant! I'm so pregnant!"

Christ.

"Stop staring and find the string!" Thad shouts at me.

"That's what I'm looking for," I say, scanning the table, even though Thad was right—I was staring.

I spot the burlap ribbon I know Luna was hoping would be there, and without even thinking about it, I pick it up and shout, "Hey, Luna—here." I toss her the ribbon, and she catches it, a stunned look on her face. Icy realization washes over me, but I have no time to recover.

Oh shit.

I glance over at Thad, whose mouth is hanging open in shock, his eyes burning with anger.

"One minute!" Mary calls out.

Ignoring him, I scour the table for the rest of our supplies, but it feels like nothing is left, so I instead just start picking up different sheets of cardstock I think we could work with, knowing we need at least something to use for decorations. We could cut out feathers, or something like that.

I'm just reaching for a scrap of bright-pink paper when Mary calls out for us to put our hands up and go back to our workbenches.

We make it back, and Diane yells, "Cut! Clean up. Five minutes, and we are getting started again."

Thad whips around to me. "What the fuck was that?"

"All of the stuff was taken—I just grabbed what I thought could work."

"I'm not talking about the things you grabbed," Thad says, seething. "I'm talking about you handing shit off to Team Rossi, as if you know exactly what they need."

My stomach drops. How on earth do I talk myself out of this one? There's no valid explanation. Can I claim I was confused?

Mind control?

That could work. Luna has been working on mind control and is perfecting it on me. It's a stretch, but if I play it right, I think I can convince Thad—

"That was so sweet of you to help your girlfriend back there," Mary says, coming up to the workbench and talking loudly enough for the entire set to hear. "She looked so frazzled searching for that ribbon. She's lucky she has you." Mary pats my shoulder and walks away.

Fuck.

Fuck. Fuck. Fuck.

"Girlfriend?" Thad asks, in seeming disbelief.

"You guys are dating?" Helen asks.

"What?" I hear Cohen quietly ask. I turn toward Team Rossi's workbench. Luna meets my gaze, her eyes wide and her lip trembling.

Jesus Christ, what do we do?

"I should have seen it," Helen continues, and if I didn't have just feathers and fabric on my workbench, I'd seriously consider throwing something at her. "I saw the way he was looking at her." Then she gasps. "Wait a second, does that mean these two teams have been working

together, colluding against Team Hernandez? Is that allowed? Diane!"
she shouts. "Diane, we need to have a conversation."

"Luna, what's going on?" Cohen says. Tears begin to well in Luna's
eyes.

Fucking hell. I take a step toward her, but Thad pulls on my shoulder, forcing me to face him.

"Tell me she's lying. Right now, Alec. Tell me Mary is lying."

"Alec?" Naomi looks up at me, confusion pinching her brow.

Fuck.

What the hell do I do? I don't think lying at this point is going to
get me anywhere—probably only make the situation worse.

I drag my hand over the back of my neck. "Yeah, we're dating."

"You've got to be—" Thad sucks in a sharp breath while pressing a
finger against my chest. "You asshole. You fucking asshole."

"Thad, it's not what—"

"Not what I think it is?" he finishes, his voice growing louder and
louder. "Because from the looks of it, you're dating the competition,
and—" As if everything starts clicking in his head, his eyes dart back
and forth, and he pulls away from me. "Holy shit, has she been giving
you advice?" Thad glares over at Luna. "Have you been giving him
advice? Telling him what to do so you can sabotage us?"

"Don't," I say, gripping the front of Thad's shirt and pulling him
back to me. "Do not fucking talk to her like that."

Thad pushes my hand away. "Those drawings, those weren't yours.
They were *hers.*" Thad points, his anger growing. "And how funny that
everything we needed was miraculously taken, and we ended up with
shit." Thad waves at the pile of junk on our workbench. "She set you
up, and you fell for it."

"She did not set me up."

"You're so desperate for any kind of female attention, because Mom
never liked you, that you fell for her scheme."

"Watch it," I say slowly, deliberately.

"Thad, maybe we should talk about this somewhere else," Naomi says calmly.

But Thad has truly lost it. Planting his hands on his hips, he nods toward Cohen and Declan. "Did you know about this?"

I glance at Cohen, who's standing ramrod straight, anger rolling off him in waves.

Fuck.

"He didn't," I say, facing Team Rossi. "Cohen, please, this is on me. I asked her not to tell you. She wanted to, but I wanted to keep it a secret until the end of the show. This isn't her fault."

His jaw works to the side. "This is her fault. Because my sister knows better than to keep secrets, especially about something this important."

"Cohen . . ." Luna reaches for him, but he turns and walks off the set. Luna chases after him. Declan glances at me, giving me the most profound look of disappointment I have ever experienced before walking away as well.

Spinning toward Thad, I say, "Why the fuck did you do that? Make those accusations?"

"I didn't do that." Thad points at me. "You did that." He shakes his head. "I thought you were going to change. I thought you were actually going to try to be a part of my life, but that's not the case. I should have known. Ever since you left for college, it's always been about you. What you want."

"Thad, I spent my entire fucking childhood taking care of you. I had the right to focus on me for a goddamn second!" I yell, feeling my control slip.

"But you didn't have to forget about me," he says, his voice low now, any traces of hysteria vanishing from his eyes as he gives me a slow once-over. "You used to be my hero, but now you're just like Dad— another selfish man who's left me disappointed."

"I'm *not* Dad," I say through clenched teeth, pushing Thad in the shoulder. "Don't you dare compare me to him."

Thad pushes me back. Naomi gasps and hurries to stand in front of Thad, her back to his chest. "Why did you have to make this competition about you?" Thad asks.

"What are you talking about? This has been about you the entire time."

"This was *supposed* to be about creating a wedding for me and Naomi, but it became about you, about the two of us holding your hand through the whole process, encouraging you to keep helping, giving you all the credit for the cake, making sure you're not too depressed or angry during the challenges. We're walking on eggshells around you just so I can have my brother around. And then this . . ." Thad shakes his head in disappointment. "I'll make it easy on you. After this, don't even fucking worry about talking to me, because we're done."

With that, Thad walks away.

"Naomi, I didn't—"

"Don't, Alec, not right now." She takes off after Thad, leaving me with a million questions in my head, but the one that keeps playing on repeat . . . *Did I really make this about me?*

CHAPTER TWENTY-FIVE
LUNA

"Cohen, wait!" I call, my heart nearly pounding out of my chest as I trail after my brother. "Please, let me explain."

He stops, hands on his hips, head tilted down. "Why, Luna? What does it even matter anymore? You're dating. Cat is out of the bag."

I hurry around him so I can see his face. Off in the distance, I spot Declan, still on set and standing to the side, looking ready to step in if he's needed.

"I know, but at least let me tell you how it happened."

"I don't care how it happened. I just care about why you didn't tell me."

"I wanted to, I really did, but Alec—"

"Alec doesn't control this," Cohen says, motioning between us. "He doesn't control our relationship—you shouldn't have given him that opportunity."

"It's not like that," I say, my throat growing tight. "He was going through a rough time, and Thad is an emotional basket case."

"Thad has the right to own his feelings," Cohen shoots back. "That still does not explain why you wouldn't tell me."

"Because then you would have told Declan, and Declan could have—"

"Respected your wishes and not said anything to Thad?" Cohen looks to the side and lets out a sharp breath. "You really think if you told us something so important, we would say something?" He shakes his head. "I thought we were closer than that, Luna."

He starts to walk away, but I block him and press my hand to his chest. "Don't say that, Cohen. You're my best friend."

He runs his tongue over his teeth and looks straight ahead. "Does Farrah know?"

My stomach churns, nausea rolling up the back of my throat.

"Did she know about the application to get on this show?"

"Cohen."

His head drops, and he focuses his eyes on mine. Pain, disappointment, and anger are all there, written like a novel across his face.

"If I were your best friend, Luna, you wouldn't have gone behind my back about the application—and you wouldn't have hidden this relationship from me. You would have trusted me to keep this quiet, for Thad's sake, but you didn't even give me that option. It's like you can't seem to give me any options."

"What are you talking about?" I ask. *Where is all this coming from?*

"I'm talking about this godforsaken show, and all the decorations, the cake, the wedding attire. Every challenge consists of you telling us what to do, what we'll win. You've been like this our entire life. 'This is when you need to tell Mom and Dad you're gay. This is how you should do it. This is how you should live your life with Declan—show more love, kiss him in public. Make red velvet cake because the judges like it, not because we do.' You're not giving me a goddamn choice in anything, and I'm sick of it."

"Cohen, that's not . . ." A sob escapes me. "I'm not trying to take away your choices—I just want to help."

"You're not helping—you're making it worse. You're not letting me authentically live my life. You're trying to make me live the life you think I need, because that's your personality—you're a fixer, you're always meddling, trying to make sure things are perfect, and you don't care about what anyone else wants." My chest heaves as more tears run down my cheeks. "And this is just one more example of you taking control of my feelings, my chances at being the brother I want to be." He wipes his hand over his mouth and then drops it at his side. "You didn't even give me a goddamn chance."

"I'm sorry," I blurt as he turns away. "Please, Cohen, listen to me."

But he just walks away, past Declan, who snags his hand for a few brief seconds and lets go. Declan's eyes meet mine before he turns and goes after Cohen.

Unsure of what to do, I lean against the wall and slide down to the floor. Cradling my head in my hands, I let all the sorrow that's been building up wash over me in an instant.

Devastation.

Regret.

Embarrassment.

There's a reason for every single tear that hits my pants, soaking into the fabric and reminding me exactly of what got me here.

"Luna." I feel his hand on my back before he squats down next to me. "Luna, I'm so—"

"Not here," I say, wiping my eyes before I face Alec. With a deep breath, I stand back up. "Not here."

That's when I see the pure anguish in his face, and even though my heart lurches in my chest at the thought of him taking another step back in his pursuit to make things right with Thad, I'm in my own personal hell too, and for the first time, I'm not going to try to fix someone else's problems . . . especially not when I have enough of my own.

"When?" he asks, swallowing hard, his hand reaching out to me. I refuse to take it.

"I don't know, but not here," I repeat before striding past him, our shoulders skimming, his fingers gliding along my hand.

Not sure what to do, I go back to the workbenches, where Team Hernandez is sitting on their stools, waiting for everyone to return. I wipe at my eyes, trying to get my emotions in check. We still have the rest of the show to film, and I'm sure, as they say in the business . . . the show must go on.

I grab my water and take a sip, reaching within the depths of my soul to pull it together, just as Helen catches my eye, her expression smug. "You really should have told your brother."

I slam my water on the workbench and yell, "Shut up, Helen!" before walking off again.

You can imagine how the rest of the day went.

Tensions were high. Cohen barely spoke one word to me, and when he did, his words were sharp. I felt his resentment of every decoration I'd crafted and every upgraded choice I suggested in our final picks.

Team Baxter didn't seem to fare very well at all, creating some kind of garland that ended up looking like an octopus tentacle. Needless to say, they came in last. Thad blamed Alec, claiming his brother was in cahoots with me and had destroyed his chances at winning this entire competition. I don't think I've ever seen Alec look so low, not even when his mom didn't show up to set.

Team Hernandez strung together a feather decoration like the one I told Alec to do, which of course didn't go over well either. Thad claimed sabotage, which insulted Helen for God knows what reason, and Diane, the poor director, had to talk everyone off the ledge after it was all said and done. We stayed late to complete interviews, since Diane wanted to give everyone a break before the weddings next weekend. And honestly, I think she was just at her wits' end. She'd been the one to corral *everyone*, have makeup run past the faces of everyone involved in what she's calling "the meltdown," and then try to get through the rest of filming. I know she's probably at some bar right now, hating her life.

When she called it a night, Cohen took off immediately. I tried chasing after him, but Declan stopped me, telling me to give him some time. Thad stormed off as well, with Naomi trailing behind, and Helen caught Diane by the wrist, insisting she wanted to revisit the possibility of corruption just one more time, given that two people were dating from opposite teams, which created an "unfair advantage."

Helen needs to get a life.

I didn't want to stick around and stir up any more trouble, so with a heavy heart, I went back to my apartment, where I broke open a new package of fudge-striped cookies. I didn't even bother decorating my fingers with them—just shoved them in my mouth as quickly as I could.

I've sent at least ten texts to Cohen, all of which have gone unanswered, and my heart breaks a little more with every second that goes by without a response.

The moment Alec tossed me the burlap ribbon, the exact ribbon I'd told him about this past week, hoping it would be there, I knew we were in trouble. It was only a matter of time before we were figured out; I just didn't realize things were going to explode as violently as they did. Nor was I expecting Cohen to completely tear me apart, in front of everyone. I stuff some more cookies in my mouth, my sadness replaced by a surge of anger. Sure, I ultimately decided to hide this from Cohen, but I can't help but place blame squarely on Alec. *He's* the one who wanted to keep secrets.

Knock. Knock.

I look at my apartment door. *Speak of the devil.* I know exactly who's on the other side—I'm just surprised it's taken him this long.

I heave myself off the couch and go to the door. As I open it, I keep my body firmly in the doorway, not granting any access.

"Luna," Alec says, his face looking like it's aged at least five years. "Can I come in?"

I shake my head. "I don't think that's a good idea."

"We need to talk," he says a little more sternly. "And I'm not about to talk in your hallway."

Ugh. He's right. I spin on my heel and head toward the sofa, leaving him to deal with the door. I hear the soft click as he shuts it while I dig for another cookie, my stash already starting to run low.

Alec takes a seat next to me. "I'm sorry, Luna."

"Yeah, so am I."

"What are you sorry for?" he asks, confusion in his voice.

"Sorry for getting involved in all of this. I shouldn't have."

"Involved in . . . what?"

"The show . . ." I swallow hard. "You."

He sighs heavily. "Luna, I know today was tough, but—"

"Today wasn't tough, Alec," I say, finally facing him. "Today ranks up there as one of the *worst* days of my life. My brother pretty much told me I've been controlling his life since he came out to me. Controlling." Tears well in my eyes. "I wasn't trying to control him. I just wanted to . . . help him."

"And you were."

I shake my head. "No, I was stifling him." Taking a deep breath, I continue. "Cohen means everything to me. Everything." I let out a sob. "He's my best friend, my rock, the one person who knows me inside and out. Without him, I'm nothing, and you . . . you made me lie to him."

"We didn't lie, we just . . . didn't tell anyone what was going on."

"It's the same thing." I wipe my nose with the back of my long sleeve, not even caring at this point. "Lying by omission is just as bad."

"Things are raw right now, but Cohen loves you. It will blow over."

"You have no right to say that. You weren't there—you didn't see the look in Cohen's eyes. He's not just upset . . . he's disappointed. He's disappointed in me." I press my hand to my head and sink back into the couch. Alec reaches out, but I push him away. "No, I can't, Alec. I just . . . can't."

"Can't what?" he asks shakily. "Can't right now, or can't ever?"

My lip trembles. I press my knuckles to my chin and look out my living room window, pain rippling through me every time my mind flashes to Cohen, his harsh words and retreating back.

It's all too much.

Cohen's hurt.

The show's a mess.

I've been stifling my brother . . .

This relationship.

Alec's problems.

I can't handle it all.

"Ever," I whisper.

From the corner of my eye, I see Alec straighten. "I told you we could press pause," he says. "I gave you the option to wait it out until after the show."

Slowly, I turn to look at him, eyes narrowed. "Are you really blaming this on me right now?"

"You're fucking blaming this on me, Luna." Alec stands. "I told you I could wait, and you were the one who chose to lie, to keep it a secret."

"Because I wanted you!" I shout, bewildered that he would even bring this up. "I wanted you more than anything. You asked me to keep it a secret. I'm sorry that I was so infatuated with you that I thought it could work, that even if I had to lie, I could at least be with the man I was falling for."

He sighs. "I'm sorry, I'm just—fuck, this is such a mess."

"Because of you," I say, springing up from the couch and pacing the room. "If you just had the balls to talk to your brother, this wouldn't have been a problem. But you have such a shitty relationship with him that you just had to drag me down and make my relationship with Cohen just as shitty."

"Wow." Alec blinks. "So you think everything that happened with Cohen is my fault?"

"You certainly didn't help!" I shout. I know I'm being irrational, that the words coming out of my mouth are spiteful and untrue, but there is so much anger and pain building up inside of me that I just can't stop them. "We could have avoided this whole shitstorm if you hadn't asked me to lie."

"I gave you a goddamn choice!" he yells, spreading his arms. "I gave you a choice, and you chose me."

"I chose wrong," I say before I can stop myself.

He rears back, stunned.

And I realize what I said, what it means for us . . . for him. I wait with bated breath to see how he reacts.

I stare into his eyes as they grow darker and darker.

He presses his lips together, nods, and then walks past me toward the door. My heart sinks. He turns the handle but then pauses and glances back at me. "For what it's worth, I thought I chose correctly, because I chose you." And then he's gone, letting the door click quietly shut behind him.

I crumple to the couch and bury my head in my hands, sorrow sweeping over me faster than I can blink the tears away.

I lost Cohen today, and I just pushed away the man I love, the man who's worked his way into my life faster and deeper than anyone ever has.

And even though I want to point the finger at everyone else, I know that if I want to peg the blame on anyone, I should go look in a mirror.

Luna: Cohen, I'm so sorry. Please, will you answer my calls?

Luna: Please don't be mad at me. I can't take this.

Luna: Cohen, this is breaking me.

Luna: Please, Cohen, you're getting married on Friday. Four days. I don't want to taint this happy moment.

Luna: I love you and I'm sorry. Please just call me, text me, visit me, anything. Please let me show you how sorry I am.

I sent the last text ten minutes ago, and still nothing. I even tried texting Declan, but given the lack of response, it seems like Cohen has shut down all communication with me. And that hurts, more than I can even describe.

We've never not talked; we've never fought like we did on set. I've done some pretty stupid things that have affected Cohen, but nothing of this magnitude, nothing that made him so mad he surpassed the vein popping in his forehead and went straight to disappointment . . .

and unbridled anger. Anger so deep, so palpable, that I could feel it steamrolling over me as he walked away.

I wipe away a tear and take deep breaths as I try to comprehend the magnitude of this fight, of his distance and silence. I hate to admit it, but I'm not sure this is something I can fix my way out of. I think this is a situation where I might just have to let Cohen take the lead, and that's entirely new territory for me. Taking the back seat, waiting, hoping . . . praying that he will come back to me and accept my apology.

Chapter Twenty-Six
ALEC

"Hey, man, how was your week—whoa, what the hell happened to you?" Lucas asks as I stumble into his office and shut the door behind me.

I'm currently dressed in what some people might call sweatpants and a holey shirt, but I call them my breakup gear. For my first-ever breakup. Heather-gray sweatpants with elastic around the ankles, a Columbia shirt with holes in the armpits, holes so large you could apply deodorant through them. In a concession to professionalism, I'm wearing dress shoes—without socks—and have a tie wrapped around my neck haphazardly.

Honestly, I thought the tie was a nice touch.

I slouch in the chair and rest my hands on my stomach. "My life is shit. Absolute shit."

The creak of Lucas leaning back in his chair fills his questioning silence as he studies me, probably trying to decide where to even begin.

I don't give him a chance to guess.

"Luna broke things off."

"Yeah, I could have guessed that."

"Mary DIY—your bitch with a glue gun—spilled the beans about our relationship. Thad freaked out, just like I thought he would. Cohen was insulted. Luna cried. Helen threw a hissy fit."

"The overbearing mom?"

I nod. "Thought it was an unfair disadvantage that we were dating, said we were ganging up on them. Diane lectured us. Cohen walked off set without Luna. Luna walked off set without me. And Thad won't return any of my calls or texts."

"Jesus Christ . . ." Lucas falls silent for over a minute, scratches his jaw, and then asks, "Did they happen to catch that all on camera?"

"Are you fucking kidding me right now?"

"I'm sorry, I'm sorry." He waves his hand and clears his throat. "Did Luna end your relationship while you were on set? Maybe it was a heat-of-the-moment kind of thing."

I shake my head. "No, I wanted to talk to her then and there, but I could tell it wasn't a good idea—she was way too upset to talk, and I didn't want to do any more damage, so I went home, took a shower, and changed before heading over to her place, hoping she'd cooled down a little so we could figure out how we could make this all better."

"She wasn't cooled?"

"No." I glance down at my hands. "It was like all the life had been sucked out of her. I've never seen her with an actual frown on her face, but she had one. She was sad, dude. Really fucking sad." I press my lips together and look up at the ceiling. "And I had a hand in it all. Fuck." I breathe out. "What the fuck is wrong with me?"

"An inhospitable environment growing up, no example of what a loving relationship looks like, saw alcohol and prescription medications used as a coping mechanism, had to grow up faster than a kid should . . . shall I go on?"

"No," I deadpan. "Your honest approach is positively refreshing." I press both my palms to my eyes. "I really need to go to therapy."

"That would be step number one to getting healthy. Just like I said the last time you were looking for a therapist."

"And what would step number two be?"

"Fix things with Thad, because unless you two are okay, you're never going to be able to patch things up with Luna."

I fiddle with my tie. "Fix things with Thad . . . easier said than done. In case you were wondering, he fucking hates me."

"Looks like you have to make a grand gesture, then."

"To Luna?"

Lucas shakes his head. "To your brother."

The door opens, and I can feel my entire body stiffen as I gaze into a pair of eyes that perfectly match my own.

I had my first therapy session yesterday—Lucas's therapist, Margaret, was able to fit me in that day because I paid her overtime. Diving into my childhood wasn't fun, but it at least granted me a little relief. And I mean a *little*, because I probably have about two years' worth of heavy sessions in front of me. This is not an overnight cure, but it's a step in the right direction.

I told her about my current predicament, and that I need to patch things up with my brother, with no idea of how to make that happen. Given that I'm on a short timeline, his wedding being on Sunday, I need to act quickly. Not knowing me just yet but doing the best she could, Margaret said it seemed like Thad was holding on to the past, so maybe I should show him what the future of our relationship could look like.

I smiled, nodded, and walked out of the office, texting Lucas that Margaret was "really helpful."

Enter sarcastic tone

But the more I've thought about it, the more I've realized Margaret might be right. I need to show Thad what our future could be if we manage to move on from this.

It's why I'm here, staring at the person who's broken my heart more times than I can count.

"What are you doing here?"

"That's a great way to greet your son," I say. My mom clearly wasn't expecting company; in lieu of her usual slacks-and-sweater set, a robe is cinched tightly around her waist, and her hair is pulled back into her night turban, which keeps her hair silky—at least that's the explanation she gave me years ago.

Not waiting for an invitation, I let myself in, maneuvering past her and keeping my hands in my pockets.

"Where do you keep all of our childhood pictures?"

She shuts the door and crosses her arms over her chest, looking me up and down—I'm sure taking in everything she hasn't seen in a while. "You look just like your father."

It's a dig, one I was expecting.

"Where are the pictures?"

She leans against the wall and gives me a withering look. "Thad called and told me what happened. Sleeping with the competition? Something your father would have done."

I bite the inside of my cheek.

"Pictures, Mom. Where are they?"

"I heard about Walter Reed's divorce from Florence. She told me you didn't push for the yacht. Losing your touch?"

I take a deep breath and count to five in my head, trying to replicate the coping techniques Margaret taught me yesterday.

"Am I going to have to tear your place apart to find them? Because I will."

"Why are you here? To patch things up? Now that your brother has decided to give up on you?"

"I've been trying to patch up that relationship for the last two months, but thanks to you, I have no idea how to have a healthy relationship—with anyone. But that ends now. I know I can't repair whatever happened with us. I'm not even sure I want to, but there's hope for Thad."

Her eyes narrow and her shoulders stiffen. I'm contemplating the possibility of actually tearing the place apart when she says, "Under the TV, in the living room."

Before she can say anything else, I stride into the living room and go straight to the cabinets. I pull them open and find exactly what I'm looking for: "The Thad and Alec Album" our nanny made for me when I graduated high school. I left it with Thad, knowing he would need it more. I tuck it under my arm and head back to the entryway. My mom is still standing there, blocking the door, her arms hugging her torso.

"You always reminded me of him," she says, quietly. "The spitting image of your father. The only thing you got from me were my eyes. But everything else is from him . . . his charm, his intelligence, his wit. It was hard to be around you, to see you and not treat you like you're the one who hurt me."

I let out a sharp breath through my nose. "That doesn't give you the right—"

"It's not an excuse. It's just a fact—one I'm not proud of, but one you should know." She looks up at me. "I'm not claiming I was a great mom; probably never will be. But you gave me moments, moments to be better, like when you would come into my room and try to cheer me up. But I never took them. I didn't think I could—I didn't think I deserved them. And now, well . . . I'm too bitter, and I don't think that will ever change. And you might be right: we might never have a relationship. There's too much bad blood, but Thad . . ." She pats her heart. "Thad needs you, Alec. He always has, and despite what he might have said this past weekend, he always will. If I did anything right in this life, it was making sure you two were never split up. I wasn't nurturing or supportive, but I always knew you two belonged together. Fix this, and keep it that way."

My chest tightens as acceptance brims in my heart. Acceptance of what could have been but never will, acceptance of my mom's admission, and acceptance that this is what my relationship will be with her. I give her a curt nod.

Her honesty moves me more than I ever thought possible, so when I find myself leaning forward and giving her a hug, I surprise myself more than I surprise her.

It's brief.

It's uncomfortable.

It's not something I could see myself doing again.

But it was needed.

When I pull away, I say, "See you at the wedding."

She nods. As I leave her apartment, I glance behind me and see the smallest glint of a tear in the corner of her eye.

It's not the beginning of anything, not the start of a much-needed mending, and it's not the love I want, the love I've needed my entire life. But it's something I can build off in my pursuit to mend things with Thad, and to start living a healthier mental life.

"Motherfucking tape," I growl out as I shake my hand, desperately trying to relieve my finger of the double-sided tape that won't fucking give up. Unable to shake it, I pick up my water glass, press it down on the loose piece of tape, and free my finger. "Finally."

I exhale and lean back in my chair, inspecting the book in front of me.

In my head, this was going to be so much better than it actually is. It looks like a second grader put it together, not a man in his thirties who's been tying his shoes for over twenty-five years.

I might have been "crafting" for the past two months, but it's obvious it hasn't rubbed off on me—too bad I've run out of other options.

If Luna were here, I know this would have been better. She'd have helped me with my vision, guided me, encouraged me, just like everything else in my life.

Picking up my phone, I flip it over so I can see the screen. Nothing.

No messages.

No calls.

Silence.

Not hearing from her has to be the most wretched and gut-wrenching thing I've ever experienced, because all I can think about is whether she truly meant what she said in her apartment.

That she chose wrong.

That she regrets everything we shared.

And that realization steals my breath, leaving me with depleted lungs and a goddamn broken heart.

I swing my legs off the bed and push my hands through my hair, trying to shake off the empty feeling that's taking up more space in my heart with each day that goes by that I don't hear from Luna. I think she's truly done with me.

But I need to set my heartbreak aside and focus on another relationship.

Thad and Naomi's wedding is in four days, and it's been four days since the big blowup. Thad should have had enough time to at least calm down, which is important. When it comes to my brother, reasoning is out of the question when he's hysterical. But today is the day, whether I'm ready or not. It's time to face the music.

◆ ◆ ◆

I rock back on my heels, clutching Thad's present to my side as I wait for him to answer the door. I sent a text to Naomi earlier, asking her if

I could come over. I explained to her that I'm trying, and that I want to patch things up before the wedding. Her response was brief, but she said she'd make sure Thad was home. Now I'm wondering if she set me up, since no one is answering the door.

I'm shifting from side to side, ready to knock again, when the door finally cracks open. Half of Thad's face appears—his eyes immediately narrow.

"What do you want?"

"To talk."

"I'm good." He goes to shut the door, but I palm the wood and push forward. I've always been stronger than Thad—I'm glad that hasn't changed as I push my way into the apartment and shut the door behind me. "You can't just come in here—"

I thrust the ribbon-wrapped box toward him. "I made you something."

He stares at the box but doesn't take it. "What do you mean you *made* me something?"

"I mean exactly what I said. I made you something."

"Why?"

Okay, this is going to be much harder than I thought.

I sigh. "Because, Thad, I love you. I care about you. And I hate that I hurt you. I want to show you that despite what you might think, I really want to be a part of your life." I hold out the box again. He takes it this time but doesn't say anything; he just unties the ribbon and lifts the lid.

I chew on the inside of my lip as he reveals the small scrapbook I put together. It's full of pictures of our past: the two of us as kids and teenagers, running around and getting into trouble, giving each other bunny ears and grinning at the camera. As he flips through the pages, his face remains expressionless, stoic, as if someone slipped him a Xanax before I came over.

I clear my throat. "I, uh . . . I split the book up into three parts. The past, the present, and the future. I wanted to remind you of what we shared as kids." He continues to flip through the pictures, faster than I expected. "Show you the present, the few pictures we've taken recently." He flips again. "And then the future. Those pages are empty, because, uh, I want to fill them with what I hope will be memories of me, you, Naomi, and your child."

He snaps the album closed and tucks it under his arm. I want to tell him I worked really fucking hard on it, even if it looks like I paid a child to make it. I want to force him to listen to me, really listen, and understand everything I'm trying so hard to communicate.

But from his blank expression, I have a feeling this is not going to go in my favor.

"Why her?" he asks. "Out of all the women in New York, why her?"

Yup, I was right. This is not going to go the way I planned.

But I want to make good with him, so I follow his lead. "She understood me, saw me, really saw who I was."

"Well, at least someone does," Thad replies, nodding toward the door. "You can show yourself out."

"Thad," I beg. "Can we talk, at least? I'm trying here—you have to meet me halfway."

"I don't *have* to do anything, Alec." He tosses the book on an end table. "Do you even realize how embarrassing that was, you helping someone else from the other team? You know how important this competition is to me. How important it is for me to find a bigger place, a better place to raise my child. But you've been treating it like a joke the entire time."

"That's not true," I shoot back. "If I thought it was a joke, I never would have worked as hard as I did the past few weeks. I wouldn't have put in practice time at home, gone to craft stores, baked cakes. Dude, I've been trying."

"You've been helping the competition."

"She's been helping me!" I yell, and then pull on my hair. "Fuck, I don't want to yell at you. I want to make things better." I point at the scrapbook. "I wanted to show you where we started, how much fun we had when we were young, even though we were going through some heavy shit. I wanted to show you that, yeah, we've grown apart, but it's my fault and I regret that so fucking much. And I wanted to show you where I want to be with you, where I want our relationship to stand. I want to be your best friend, the guy you lean on when you don't think you can do this parenting thing. I want to be there for you, every step of the way. But I can't do that if you don't give me a chance."

Thad nods and looks toward his bedroom, where Naomi probably is, letting us hash this out on our own. He slowly lets out a breath. "I gave you your chance, Alec. Many times. You ignored it."

"That's not fucking true. I took this chance. This *Wedding Game* chance. I might have been unenthusiastic to start, but I picked it up. I helped—I wanted to be there to help you. Don't you see that?"

"How did she help you?"

"Jesus Christ, is that what's really bothering you? That I started dating Luna?"

"She's the competition."

"She's more than a goddamn competitor. She's a person. A person who—" I catch myself and remind myself that this person wants nothing to do with me. "What do you want? For me to never see her again?"

"Yes," Thad says, but I see his answer even surprises him.

"Done, fine. I won't see her again. Not like she wants to fucking see me anyway. But even if she did, if that was the only way to get you to understand how serious I am about mending things with you, then fine. I won't—" My breath catches in my throat. "I won't see her again."

"Thad," Naomi says, appearing in the bedroom doorframe. "I know Saturday was a tough pill to swallow. It was confusing for me too." She gives me a sympathetic look. "But Alec has been trying, and you need to recognize that."

"He's been sleeping with the enemy," Thad says, motioning toward me. "He's seen me on the weekends, but that's it. If he wanted to practice, he should have practiced with me, not her. How many times did I invite him over? Begged him to spend a little bit more time with me, with us, with the idea of putting together an amazing wedding?"

And there it is, the part of this entire argument that I've been missing. Thad wanted more than just time on set. He wanted me to help him. He wanted to bond.

Fuck. How could I have been so blind?

"Shit, Thad." I take a step forward. "I didn't even think. Hell . . . I'm sorry. I was so focused on trying to be better for you that I didn't think about being better *with* you."

Thad takes a deep breath. "I would have liked to try baking with you. Doing invitations—hell, anything at this point. I miss hanging out with you, Alec. The show was a chance to see you, but it was stressful, and I never got a second to just . . . enjoy you. And I don't know, hearing that you did all this stuff with someone else, someone who's trying to win the penthouse for *their* family . . . it fucking stings. She might know her shit and have better skills, but what would it have been like if we'd worked together to create something?" He shrugs. "We could have won."

"We could still win," I say. Thad shakes his head.

"I've been trolling all the comments on social. Team Rossi is the clear winner. No one likes Helen. People think our wedding is a joke." Thad lets out an exhausted breath and sits on his couch. "It doesn't fucking matter at this point. It's over this weekend, and then we can move on."

"Move on in what way?" I ask.

"I really don't know." Thad stands again, leaving the scrapbook on the table. "But this weekend hurt, and if I'm hurt, I can't imagine what Cohen must be feeling."

He heads toward the bedroom, and I call out, "Thad, where do we stand?"

He pauses but doesn't look at me. "I'll see you on Friday, for the Rossi wedding."

"What does that mean? Are we working on us?"

He pauses at the bedroom door. "It's going to take a bit. You might not see it this way, but I felt betrayed. You chose her over me, and that fucking hurts, man."

"I'm choosing you now," I say, my voice growing hoarse. "It's over with her. Over."

"Choosing me now . . . after she ended things." He nods and walks into the bedroom.

Fuck.

Naomi shuts the door behind him, and as I press my hand to my forehead, ready to fucking lose it, she murmurs, "I'll talk to him. It will be okay, Alec."

I bend over, hands on my knees as the simple act of filling my lungs with air becomes increasingly difficult.

"This shouldn't be this hard," I say as Naomi rubs my back.

"Just breathe, in and out, Alec."

I press my fingers to my eyes, my emotions spilling over in a matter of seconds.

"I want everything to be normal, and no one seems to want to forgive me. I know I fucked up, I know I hurt Thad, but I'm . . . fuck, I'm here now, begging for forgiveness." Tears roll down my face. "I'm trying, Naomi."

"I know, shhh," she says, still rubbing my back. "I see your effort. But is Thad the only reason you're upset?"

"What? Of course."

"You didn't get truly upset until you started talking about Luna," Naomi says, helping me straighten up. "Do you . . . do you love her?"

"Does it matter?" I ask. "Thad clearly doesn't want me to be with her."

"If you didn't like me, Thad wouldn't give two shits. He'd still marry me. So Thad doesn't get to dictate who you want to be with. What I want to know is if you love her."

My teeth roll over my bottom lip. Quietly, I say, "Yes, I do." My heart twists at the truth in my words.

Naomi gives me a curt nod. "Then why don't you let me work on Thad? He'll come around. You know him—he puts on a front, but you know the minute you leave, he's going to be buried in that album, crying his eyes out and asking me to order him a calzone to heal his wounds." I snort. I can picture the entire thing. "So that means you need to work on Luna, because if you're not happy in here"—she taps my heart—"then how are you going to be able to give one hundred and ten percent to Thad when he needs you? You know he'll demand it."

"He will." I chuckle, already starting to feel lighter. "I just don't know how to get to her, how to make things better."

"What matters the most to her?" Naomi raises a brow at me.

"Cohen," I answer, not even having to think about it.

"Exactly. Which means you need to help repair that relationship. And the rest will fall into place."

"You think?" I ask as hope blossoms in the pit of my stomach.

"I do. Now get out of here so I can watch Thad cry like a baby."

I laugh and nod, pulling her into a hug. "Thank you, Naomi. I'm really excited you're going to be my sister."

She pulls back and smiles. "Glad you're going to be my brother. Now get out of here."

I'm not going to say how I got this address, but I will say it was not entirely kosher. But, you do what you've got to do sometimes to make things right.

It's closing in on an inappropriate time to be visiting people when I knock on my second door of the night. Taking a deep breath, I step back from the door, clutching the bakery box I brought like it's a shield.

I hear footsteps and the press of a hand against the door. There's a pause, and then the door is unlocked and opened. Declan stands on the other side in a pair of striped pajama pants and a plain red shirt. His glasses are perched on his nose, but his normally styled hair is comfortably disheveled.

He folds his arms over his chest. "This should be good."

"Can I please talk to you and Cohen?"

"Who is it?" I hear Cohen call from within the apartment. Declan pushes the door fully open, revealing not only me but also the fact that Cohen and Declan are wearing matching pajamas.

"What are you doing here?"

I motion to their clothes. "I thought that was just a lesbian thing."

"Did you want to come in?" Declan asks.

"Yes, sorry." I clear my throat. "Can I please talk to you two?" I hold up the box of muffins. "I brought the muffins Luna once told me you guys like—which, by the way, it's surprising you two like muffins, you know, given you're gay and all . . ." They narrow their eyes. *Wrong thing to say.* "I, uh, make really inappropriate and terrible comments when I'm uncomfortable and nervous."

Cohen sighs. "Come in, but you've got five minutes."

"Yeah, sure," I say quickly, stepping inside their modest apartment and glancing around. The space is bigger than Thad and Naomi's and definitely better decorated. Very minimalistic, with high ceilings, exposed brick on the wall that features a pair of black-framed windows, and sleek furniture that almost looks untouched.

Declan takes the muffins from me and sets them to the side before standing shoulder to shoulder with Cohen. Both of them have their arms crossed, both visions in red—and both pretty intimidating, despite the tiny elephants that decorate the stripes on their pants.

"You going to talk, or stare at our pants the whole time?" Cohen asks. "Clock is ticking."

Jesus, very intimidating.

"Yeah, sorry. I, uh . . . I came to apologize to you. Luna won't speak to me, so I have no idea if you've made up or not—"

"Haven't talked to her since Saturday."

Oh shit. My heart immediately sinks for Luna and what she must be going through, what she must be feeling. Declan and Cohen are getting married in two days, and they're not talking to Luna? She must be losing her mind.

"Has she reached out?"

"Is that any of your business?" Cohen asks.

"No, it's not." I stare at their parquet floor for a second, trying to find my words. "I'll just get straight to the point. I never should have asked her to lie to both of you—well, not lie, but at least keep our relationship hidden." I dig my hands in my pockets, still trying to get used to this whole confessional thing. "I had a shit childhood, which led to me freezing out Thad. *The Wedding Game* was a chance for me to repair that relationship. I had no intention of falling in love with your sister, but it happened, and I was terrified that—"

"Wait." Cohen waves his hand. "In *love*? You're in love with Luna?"

I nod. "I am. Desperately." And hearing it out loud for the second time brings a whole new wave of regret and sorrow crashing over me. I knew I loved her; I could feel it deep in my bones, and when we told each other we were "falling," I meant it . . . so fucking hard. But admitting right now, to her brother . . . fuck. It hurts.

Declan mumbles something I can't quite make out as Cohen exhales loudly. "You're not just sleeping together. You're in love?"

"Well, I am. She's not." I shake my head. "She made that quite clear the other day after everything went down. But that doesn't matter." I take a deep breath. "What matters is your relationship with her. I'm sure there's a lot more that I don't know about, a lot more that's gone into your fight with her, but I wanted to let you know the circumstances. I asked her to keep quiet—it's on me. I know she made the ultimate decision, but I didn't make it easy on her. She wanted to tell you."

"She said that," Cohen says, his stern look relaxing.

"She loves you, man. The way she looks at you, it reminds me of the way Thad used to look at me when we were young. Like I could never do anything wrong. I was a hero in his eyes. There's no doubt you're a hero in hers, and if it weren't for me and my ignorant request, this wouldn't have happened. If you're going to be mad at anyone, please be mad at me, not her. She's worked so hard to make sure you have your moment with Declan, to celebrate the love you've always deserved to celebrate. Trust me—these major life moments need to be cherished with the ones you love. I've spent most of my big moments with no one. It's lonely, and it leaves everything feeling smaller, sadder. This argument is not worth it. Not even close to worth it." I take a step back as their silence hangs between us. "I should go. Good luck on Friday. I hope it all turns out the way you want it to."

I give them a curt wave and am headed out the door when Cohen calls out my name. I look over my shoulder. "She hasn't talked to you at all?" he asks.

"No, man. She's done with me. Pretty sure she needs you now more than ever." With that, I take off, feeling like maybe, just maybe, I've helped.

At least that's what I hope.

Chapter
Twenty-Seven
Luna

"I'm approaching slowly. The broom is in my hands again. Three feet away. Two . . . lowering the broomstick, annnnnd . . . a gentle poke," Farrah's voice whispers as the broom handle nudges me in the side. "Poke, poke, poke."

"You don't have to say 'poke' while you poke," I say, voice muffled as I lie flat on the couch, my face buried in a throw pillow. "I can feel it."

"Wasn't sure." She continues to poke. "You've been lying like that for the past half hour, and before that, you were sitting with your legs spread and your hand down your pants. What do I do with that?"

"Nothing. You do nothing."

"What happened to you going to see your brother?"

"I texted him. Told him I was coming over. He said don't bother." Repeating the words out loud makes my throat grow tight as tears build in my eyes. "He doesn't want me to be his sister anymore."

"Jesus, you're dramatic. Of course he wants you to be his sister, he's just . . . God, he's being bitchy."

That makes me snort all kinds of snot right out of my nose. I lurch from the couch and beg for a tissue, snot draining onto my lip.

"Good Christ," Farrah says in horror as she reaches for a tissue and hands it to me.

I laugh, then cry, then laugh as I wipe my nose.

"He's acting like he's never fucked up. Uh, I beg to differ. He's the reason Gregory Thompson broke up with you—remember that? He let the cat out of the bag about your first period and scared poor little Gregory away. Granted, if Gregory couldn't take a little period story, he shouldn't have been hanging out with a girl, but still, Cohen did that. And you were very upset."

"This is different."

"In what way? You didn't tell him about a relationship. Big deal. Do you tell him when you masturbate? Should he know your orgasm schedule? Does he need to know when you get waxed?"

"Why do all of your examples have to deal with my vagina?"

She opens her mouth to respond and then quickly shuts it. "Huh. Good question." She shrugs. "Either way, I think you need to realize he's not perfect, you're not entirely in the wrong, and instead of moping around here, you should be a couple of blocks away, making up with your Chris Evans look-alike. I miss him."

Yeah . . . I miss him too.

Badly.

More than I thought I would. Not that I didn't think I was going to miss him, but his abrupt absence hurts on an almost physical level. Every time I want to text him or run over to his place, I remember I can't, and the reality of how terribly I've messed everything up hits me all over again.

More tears stream down my face, and Farrah pokes me with the broom again. "See, right there—you still care about him."

"I more than care about him, Farrah." My lip trembles, and I feel my heart shatter in my chest as I whisper, "I love him."

"I *knew* it!" Farrah shouts, slamming the broom on the ground with both hands. She twists and punches the air a few times. "I freaking knew it. You don't get this depressed over your brother. You're yearning for your—"

Knock. Knock.

Farrah and I both crane our necks toward the entryway and then back at each other.

"If that's Chris Evans," Farrah hisses, "you are making up with him, and I don't want to hear another word about it. Do you understand me? I will get my sparring partner back." She springs over the couch and opens the door. Her shoulders slouch and she groans. "I'll have you know, you're the reason Gregory broke up with her, sooo you better get your shit together, mister."

"Good to see you too, Farrah," Cohen's voice rings into the apartment.

The sound makes my stomach do a somersault, and a flood of emotion hits me at once.

Nerves.

Excitement.

Relief.

"Are you here to make up with your sister?" Farrah asks, playing keeper of the door.

"None of your business, Farrah."

"Ohhh, no you don't." I see her poke her finger, probably hitting his chest. "Do you even know the number of times I've had to poke her with a broom this week? Because of you? Too many to count. Unless you're here to tell her everything's okay, you can leave, and I'm taking my wedding gift back, because there is no way in hell you'll get a three-hundred-dollar espresso machine from me. And yes, I may have stolen it from work because we have ten extra in storage, but you still won't get it."

Cohen exhales loudly. "I'm here to make amends."

"Did you hear that?" Farrah shouts. "He's here to make amends."

"Let him in, Farrah."

She steps aside and Cohen walks in, Declan following closely behind, but when he spots me, he stops abruptly, his eyes widening.

I smooth down my hair, which I know is fluffed out on the side, and straighten my shirt. "I, uh . . . I haven't had time to take a shower lately."

"More like she's been trying to sniff the essence out of the couch for the last few days." Farrah imitates me, collapsing on the couch and stuffing her face into it. "She's vile. I suggest keeping a two-foot radius at all times. I have plastic gloves if you need to touch her."

"You can leave now, Farrah," I say.

"No way," she says. She takes a seat at the kitchen counter and picks up a water glass. "This is going to be some good stuff. I've dealt with you for the past week—the least you can do is give me a front-row seat to Cohen eating crow."

"When did you get so annoying?" Cohen asks.

"Always have been." Farrah winks and gestures toward the living room. "Go on, tell her you were being bitchy."

Ignoring her, Cohen comes closer and sits on the couch across from me. Hope springs in my chest at just the sight of him.

"Hey," he says.

"Hi."

"Bor-ing!" Farrah shouts, cupping her mouth.

"Want to go for a walk?" Declan asks Farrah, taking her hand and pulling her off her stool.

"No, I don't," she insists as Declan strong-arms her toward the door. "Unhand me. Luna, help, help! He has me in his grasp."

I ignore her as Declan escorts Farrah out of the apartment. Once the door shuts, Cohen relaxes and reaches out to take my hand.

Before he can say anything, a stream of words rushes out of my mouth.

"I'm so sorry, Cohen. I should have told you about Alec and me. I never should have kept it a secret, and I'm sorry about *The Wedding Game* and making you feel like I control your life—that's not my intention at all. I'm just protective. I saw what happened to you in school, and I don't ever want to see that again, so I might be controlling at times, but it's just because I want you to be happy and to never get hurt. I want you to be able to live your life freely and openly, and I want all the best things for you, like a penthouse in Manhattan and a family and kids, and I want to be an aunt and I want people to—"

"Luna, slow down." Cohen squeezes my hand. "I know, okay? I know."

"You know what? I said a lot."

"I know all of it. I know you're sorry. I understand why you didn't say anything, and I came here to apologize to you. I was . . . hell." He exhales. "I was wound up from the challenge, nervous about the wedding being televised, frustrated that I was relying on you too much to create this moment in my head that I wasn't even sure I'd wanted in the first place." He squeezes his eyes shut, and then pops them open. "I put blame on you that never should have been there in the first place. You've been nothing but a loving sister to me. Supportive in every way, loving Declan like another brother." He cups my hand with both of his. "I'm sorry, Luna. I overreacted and never should have said the things I said to you. I didn't mean them."

"Really?" I ask, tears streaming down my face. "Because I can make it up to you. I can step away, give you your space, retract my opinion on everything. I want you to be happy, and if that means I need to take a step back, then I will."

"I don't want you to take a step back. I want you in my life like you've always been, especially if Declan and I decide to have children." He takes a deep breath and pulls me into one of his all-encompassing, life-affirming hugs. When he releases me, he leans back and lets his breath out.

"Come on," I say, nudging him. "I'm not that bad."

"You are." He laughs and nods to the bathroom. "Go take a shower. Mom and Dad want to have dinner with us in half an hour. I told them we'd meet at that Italian place down the block."

"Seriously?"

He nods. "Hurry up, Luna. Or I'm leaving without you."

Feeling a little lighter, I pop off the couch and rush to the bathroom, where I block out the hurt and pain of losing Alec and focus on the relief coursing through me that things are going to be okay with Cohen.

"To our beautiful children, the television stars," my mom says, holding up her glass of champagne.

"And to our daughter, for not swearing on national television while an old lady named Helen sat on her," my dad, ever the jokester, adds as we all clink our glasses together.

"I take it you watched the first episode," I say after taking a sip and setting my flute down. I'm sitting between Declan and Cohen because I needed to feel both of their love after our long week.

"Oh, we popped popcorn and everything," Mom says. She looks more beautiful than ever—her skin is glowing, and she can't seem to stop smiling. Australia treated them well. "That Helen—I can see why you refer to her as a 'pill' in all those emails. What a wretched woman."

"She's even more wretched in person," Declan adds.

My dad pats Declan on the back. "Well, at least you guys held it together. I can't wait to see how everything is pulled together on Friday."

"I'm also thrilled about the tea ceremony tomorrow Declan's parents put together. Moreen and I have been emailing back and forth about the details," Mom says with a soft smile.

"Yes, Jonah has been emailing me as well," Dad says. "Lovely people, but mainly, I can't wait to finally see you two get married. About damn time one of my kids finds the love of their life and settles down."

I keep my face neutral as Alec's face flashes through my mind. I wonder what he's doing right now, if he's made up with Thad—or even with his mom. Is he sitting at home, alone, with no one to talk to? My eyes start to tear just thinking about him being alone, and the pain he must be facing.

"Well, I might not be the only one of your kids in love . . . ," Cohen says with a smirk.

I could kill him.

"What?" my mom gushes. "Luna, are you seeing someone?"

"No," I say just as Cohen says, "Yes."

"Cohen," I whisper under my breath, but that doesn't stop him.

"Met him on the show."

"Cohen, stop."

"He's really handsome," Declan adds. I whip around, ready to chastise him, when my mom coos and claps her hands.

"Is he a PA? Maybe a set designer? Oh, honey"—she turns to my dad—"wouldn't it just be a dream if it was that Alec from the other team? We said he'd be perfect for Luna. Granted, he's competition, but oh so dreamy."

My mouth nearly hits the table. *Say what?*

Cohen laughs out loud while Declan clutches his heart.

"What?" My mom looks between us. "Is it Alec? Please tell me it's Alec."

"Oh, that's great." Cohen wipes under his eye. "Mom and Dad even picked him out for you."

"Is it Alec?" my dad asks now, looking positively giddy.

What is happening right now?

"I mean," he continues, "just from the one episode, we could see there's some pain hidden behind those green eyes, and who better to help him than our little Luna bear?"

"Well . . . is it him?" my mom asks, so hopeful.

Sighing, I move my silverware to the side to keep my hands busy. "It *was* him."

"Was?" My mom looks from one to the other among us. "What happened?"

"There's been a minor setback, but things will get back on track this weekend—don't worry, Mom," Cohen says.

"No, don't listen to him. I, uh . . . I broke up with him."

"Because you're an idiot," Declan says.

"Hey."

"He's right," Cohen replies. "You're an idiot, but I was the cause of your idiocy. So it's excused."

"Are we missing something?" Dad asks, looking thoroughly confused, his flute of champagne half-raised to his mouth.

"Nothing you should be concerned about," Cohen says with such confidence that I actually want to puke.

"Don't do anything stupid," I say. "I know I've intervened a lot in your life, but stay out of this, Cohen. I said something to him that I can never take back."

"What did you say?" Mom asks, leaning forward, as if she's watching a soap opera unfold.

"Not something we need to talk about. Hey, let's talk about how Helen is probably getting ready to make that cake, huh. Wouldn't I love to be a fly on the wall for that."

"Do you love him?" Cohen asks.

Everyone turns to stare at me.

"Doesn't matter."

"What?" Dad asks. "Of course it matters. The number of times I messed up with your mom is embarrassing, but because I loved her, I begged and begged for forgiveness—and she gave it. So it very well does matter."

"It does," Mom chimes in. "So . . . do you love him?"

"Do you?" Declan nudges me.

I glance around the table as their expectant eyes stare me down. Emotion climbs up my throat, and tears well up in my eyes. Before I can stop them, they fall over and onto my cheeks as I nod.

Cohen wraps his hand around my shoulder and brings me into his chest.

"It's okay, Luna girl. We will fix this, I promise."

He makes it seem so simple. Maybe I would believe him if Alec were texting me, or had come to my apartment, but at this point, I don't think there's any chance of bridging the gap I've put between us, of making him know he wasn't the wrong choice.

I haven't been able to see clearly for the last half hour as my brother and his love finally have their moment.

The cameras swirling around us, the guests sitting in attendance, the decorations—none of it matters as I hold my breath, waiting for Cohen to say his vows.

After a long "planning" session with my family on how to get me back with Alec, I kissed everyone good night and went back to my apartment. I held my phone close to my chest, wondering if I should text Alec like everyone suggested. But every time I started to type something out, my nerves took over, and I erased it quickly.

The tea ceremony was . . . God it was intimate and beautiful, a moment where Cohen and Declan were able to show appreciation to their parents for their support. I bawled like a baby.

And then, after I returned home, a heavy heart weighing on me, I attempted and failed to text Alec for the fifth time. Cohen texted, asking if I'd reached out to him yet. When I told him I couldn't get up the nerve, Cohen called and proceeded to tell me that Alec showed up at their apartment and apologized for everything that had happened.

I cried myself to sleep last night, my heart breaking at the thought of Alec visiting my brother and trying to heal the rift I never should have blamed him for.

And then this morning, after Farrah helped me get rid of my puffy eyes, Declan and Cohen cornered me, asking what I planned on doing when I saw Alec today, because we would run into each other. It's part of *The Wedding Game*—we all have to attend each other's weddings, and it's why they're all on one weekend. Back to back to back.

My answer to them . . . *I don't know.*

And as I'm standing here, beside my brother, at the fake altar we built with Cohen's chuppah and decorated with our baby's breath and fern garlands—unable to stand in a circle like I originally planned, now fully on display up front—I can't bring myself to look out into the crowd. I'm terrified I'll make eye contact with Alec—I still don't know what I'm going to do when I see him.

Do I give him a hug?

Apologize?

Duck away and hide for the rest of the night?

Cohen clears his throat, bringing my attention back to the wedding. He pulls his vows from his jacket pocket—the wedding attire turned out beautifully—and carefully unfolds them. I know this moment is huge for him—not only is he expressing his feelings, but he's doing it in public.

He takes a deep breath and looks up at Declan. "Love is a state of being in my family. When I was growing up, my parents spent countless hours every day showing my sister and me what true love looked like. It was an emotion I always felt, but an emotion I wasn't sure I was ever going to let out." He takes a deep breath. "Coming out to my parents, to my sister, that was never the issue, because like I said, they loved me unconditionally. But when it came to the outside world, to everyone else, that's where the problem was. As time went on, I started to feel more and more empty, and I believed that the beautiful love my parents have would never be something I could experience . . . until you." Tears run down my cheeks, and I don't even bother to wipe them away.

"You showed me that I am lovable, that I could spend countless hours sitting with you on the couch and feel happier than I ever have before. You showed me it's okay to love one another—not just behind closed doors, but out in the world too. You helped me build a home and a future, one I never thought I'd have. You changed my entire life with one little smile, and I promise you, till the day I die, I will make your life as meaningful and full of love as you make mine. I love you."

Oh sweet Jesus. I let out a breath and stare up at the ceiling, trying to keep my makeup from melting off before I have to walk back down the aisle.

I'm so distracted with keeping my eyeliner in place that I miss what the reverend says, and before I know it, Declan is cupping Cohen's cheeks and they're kissing so passionately that I feel my face heat up. Our friends and family cheer, and I let out a hoot myself. When Declan finally lets go, the reverend introduces them as husband and husband, and they're walking down the aisle, hand in hand. I follow behind, wiping at my eyes and trying to hold it together.

When we get to the end of the aisle, we step off to the side, and I wrap my arms around both of them.

"I'm so happy for you guys." I playfully push Cohen's shoulder. "Thanks for making me cry like an idiot."

"Anytime." He smiles and kisses the top of my head. "Now get in line."

"Get in line?" I ask. "What are you talking about?"

"Last-minute change." He smiles even wider. "We decided to have a receiving line."

I'm going to kill them . . . dead . . . on their wedding day.

CHAPTER TWENTY-EIGHT
ALEC

Fuck, she looks beautiful.

The moment she walked down the aisle, it felt like a bowling ball had knocked all the wind out of my body. From her beautiful green dress, to her silky long hair swept into a low bun, to the minimal makeup highlighting her gorgeous eyes, she stole my breath.

I couldn't take my eyes off her the entire ceremony. And as she cried happy tears for her brother, relief filled my body—if everything is right with them, then this terrible week just got a silver lining.

Sure, Thad isn't entirely happy with me, and Luna and I are still broken up, but all that matters is that she and Cohen have reconciled—I'd never forgive myself for wrecking their relationship.

When I arrived at the Shed this morning, I met up with Thad and Naomi, hoping things might have improved. Thad gave me a curt nod and stalked away, while Naomi shot me a sympathetic look. They probably shared a calzone when I left, but beyond that, no progress seems to have been made.

I didn't even push it. I didn't want to make a scene with Thad. I just followed them inside, hands in my pockets, my heart heavy.

I've never really had people mad at me like this before. It's uncomfortable, knowing that someone is dreading running into you. Contractually we are supposed to show up to every ceremony, but our contracts don't say anything about staying for the receptions. The crowd is full of smiles and love for the couple, and I would truly just bring everyone down. I think I'm going to do us all a favor and take off. I witnessed a beautiful ceremony, but the food and dancing will just make things incredibly awkward. Once this crowd clears up, I'm taking off.

"That was so beautiful," Naomi says. "Cohen's vows just about killed me."

Yeah, me too.

"It was really nice," Thad says, sounding uncharacteristically reserved. "What's happening right now?" He cranes his head over the rest of the guests. "Why is it taking forever to leave this room?"

"Receiving line," Naomi says.

"What?" I ask, my heart rate picking up.

"Looks like the whole wedding party," Naomi says, a small smirk forming on her face.

Fuck.

I scan the perfectly decorated room; Luna's vision has truly come to life, with all the twigs she scrounged, the garland she painstakingly made, the artfully arranged bouquets of burlap flowers, and the well-placed tree stumps. But it isn't just beautiful; it's touches of Cohen and Declan. It's the little grooms on top of the chocolate cake that speak so heavily of who they are. The pictures of them as a couple placed strategically throughout the venue, and Cohen's carpentry displayed so artistically on the table through candleholders. It's the perfect combination of everything I've heard Luna talk about. I wish I could tell her how beautiful it is, how much I can feel the love permeating the space.

Instead, I scour it for any other exit, but there are none, making me want to report the venue to the fire department—shouldn't there be an emergency exit?

An emergency exit made for moments like this, when a man has fucked up so badly he needs to flee the scene?

Naomi must sense my panic because she places her hand on my arm and whispers, "It will be okay, Alec."

I glance at Thad. He's watching Naomi and me with narrowed eyes. I half expect him to freak out about us having a "thing" behind his back.

But he doesn't say anything. Instead, he steps in front of us as we funnel into a line.

And in a matter of seconds, I can see the top of Luna's head, right next to Cohen.

With every step we take, drawing closer, my dread ratchets up to entirely new levels, until finally we reach Declan. Thad is the first to congratulate him, with a hug and a pat to the back. Given Thad's bitterness toward the whole *Wedding Game*, I can't quite believe how calm he is. I know he said we didn't have a chance at winning, and I really think he's taking that to heart. Instead of bashing the wedding, pointing out what he doesn't like and how he thinks ours is better, he's just soaking in the moment.

And it's somehow more terrifying than the hysterical brother who cried and screamed his way through the competition.

Naomi is next.

"Congrats, Declan. That was so beautiful. I'm really happy for you guys."

"Thank you," he says and then turns toward me.

I swallow hard and plaster on a smile. "Congratulations, Declan." I hold my hand out to him and he squeezes it, a little too firmly. A warning sign, maybe, of a protective brother-in-law.

"Thank you." He leans in. Very quietly he says, "Don't hurt her."

I don't have a chance to respond because I'm ushered to Cohen, who literally makes my balls crawl up into my taint with the look he gives me.

I hold my hand out again and swallow hard. "Congratulations, Cohen. Your vows were beautiful."

He takes my hand, another firm grasp distracting me, for just a moment, from how close Luna is—so close that if I move a few inches, she would be directly in front of me.

"Thank you," he says, leaning in just like Declan did. He whispers, "Be good to her."

When he pulls away, he pats me on the back and nudges me right in front of Luna.

Slowly, she looks up at me, her eyes watery, her smile fake. I know what a real smile from this girl looks like, and this is not it.

Immediately, tension starts to build between us as we stare at each other in silence.

I hate this. I hate standing in front of this girl—my girl—and not being able to sweep her into my arms. I hate the uncertainty between us. I hate that I can't reach out, cup her jaw, and feel her lean into my palm right before I bend down to kiss her. I hate that I can't hug her, congratulate her, hold her hand, and walk her into the reception, basking in the knowledge that she's all mine.

"Uh, congratulations," I finally say. "The ceremony was great."

Lame.

It's so fucking lame.

Tell her how beautiful she is. How she took your breath away the moment you saw her. Tell her you couldn't take your eyes off her the entire ceremony. Tell her you're pathetically sorry and would do anything to make things right again.

But I can't seem to move my lips, so I stand there, stiff, unsure of what to do next.

Gripping her bouquet, she gives me a curt nod. "Yeah, thanks . . . it was lovely."

Okay . . . uh, this is probably going down as one of the worst moments of my life.

It's as if I'm trapped in my own body. My heart is begging my brain to say something, do something, to let her know how much I love her, but my brain is on lockdown, not letting out any of the feelings my heart is throwing at it.

I give her a nod and take a step back. "Okay, well, have a good one." And then I leave, feeling so sick to my stomach that I stride past Naomi and Thad, who are waiting for me, and straight out the door of the Shed, onto the cobblestoned streets of SoHo. I press my hand into my hair and look around. A Postmates deliveryman on a bike with food in his basket is screaming by me, sending me back against the old brick building, just as I hear the door open.

"Alec," Naomi says behind me, her hand resting on my back. "Are you okay?"

I shake my head. "No. I can't . . . fuck, I don't know how to act around her. I can't be here right now. I don't want to make it weird for her, not on her brother's day."

"Are you going to leave?"

"Yeah." I look to the side. "I am. Can you tell the producers I wasn't feeling well or some bullshit like that?"

"What about tomorrow?"

"What's going on?" Thad asks, coming outside as well.

"I'm, uh . . . I'm going to head home. Not feeling well."

"Oh." Thad's brow creases. "Okay."

Naomi gives me a look that begs me to stay, but I really can't. I don't want to make things uncomfortable for Luna.

"I'll see you guys tomorrow. Just need some rest."

"Drink water," Thad says, actually sounding concerned.

"Yeah, sure." I give them a parting wave and then take off down the block, flagging a taxi to get me the hell out of here.

Alec: Do you have Xanax?

Lucas: I take it the wedding didn't go well today.

Alec: Wedding was fine, the encounter in the receiving line I had with Luna was fucking awful.

Lucas: Oh damn, a receiving line? There's no way of getting around that. What did you say to her?

Alec: Some stupid shit about the wedding being nice. I really wanted to tell her how gorgeous she looked. I mean, fuck, dude, she looked so goddamn beautiful it hurt to even look at her.

Lucas: I like seeing you lovesick. It proves you're not the robot after all.

Alec: How are you in any way being helpful right now?

Lucas: Oh, you wanted me to be helpful? Sorry, didn't quite get that cue from you. How did the rest of the night go?

Alec: Not sure, I left after the ceremony.

Lucas: Ahh, chickened out. Nice.

Alec: I didn't chicken out. It was obvious from the tension between us that she didn't want me there. You should have seen the fake smile she gave me. She practically begged me to leave with her eyes.

Lucas: Ouch. And you have two more days to be around her. That should be fun.

Alec: Seriously, why am I even texting you?

Lucas: Beats the hell out of me.

Alec: So no Xanax?

Lucas: No, but my suggestion is to talk to her, and not in a reception line. But that's a novel idea—you'd never go for it. Instead you take the hard ass route of avoidance. Maybe one day you'll grow a pair . . . *sigh* one day.

Alec: I'm saving this text. Hopefully you'll go through the same torture someday, and I can throw this back in your face.

Lucas: Try all you want, but I'm a smart motherfucker when it comes to relationships.

Alec: Says the single guy.

Lucas: I'm picky. I'm not about to jump into a relationship to jump into one. You have to use your head, man. And you're being a dipshit right now. You love her right? Then go after her. Stop hiding.

Alec: Why did I envision you clapping at me when I read that?

Lucas: Mentally I was. Come on, man. Go get her.

Alec: Easier said than done.

"Can we just talk about the elephant in the room?" Naomi says as she, Thad, and I stand at a cocktail table by ourselves, each with drink in hand—two beers and one iced tea.

The ceremony is over, Luciana and Amanda are wives, and they looked gorgeous together. Their vows were very heartfelt and touching, and their friend, who was the minister, did a fantastic job. The room was full of love for them.

"What elephant?" I ask, even though I could list two right off the top of my head: Thad's coldness toward me and my inability to stop staring at Luna, who's across the room with Declan and Cohen, wearing a cute black dress that flairs out at her hips and holding a glass of wine.

Naomi leans in and whispers, "Helen's hair."

Thad and I snort at the same time.

"I didn't know a woman's hair could go that high," I admit, spotting Helen's head easily against the crowd. It's as if someone took a beehive, wrapped her hair around it, and then shellacked it in place with hairpins and hairspray. Atrocious.

"It terrified me when I saw her at first," Thad adds.

"I heard your gasp," Naomi says, chuckling. "I think the entire wedding gasped the minute the doors opened, revealing her hairdo. I wonder if she's hiding something under there."

"Yes," I say, snapping my fingers at Naomi. "She's hiding something. What could it be?"

Naomi taps her chin. "A camera? Maybe she's going undercover for *The Wedding Game*, trying to get some dirt for them. If she starts asking us questions about the show, be on guard."

"Good point."

"Could be vodka, since they went cheap on the bar selection," Thad says, eyeing his Bud Light. "Not even an IPA. I thought this was a wedding for lesbians. Aren't they supposed to love IPAs?"

"Not all lesbians wear tool belts and drink IPAs," Naomi says, rolling her eyes. "You should know that after spending two months with them."

"But come on . . . Bud Light?" Thad says just as Cohen and Declan step up to our table.

Oh fuck. My back stiffens, and I glance around for Luna. But I don't see her.

"What are you talking about over here?" Declan asks, so casual.

"What Helen is hiding in her hair," Naomi answers before sipping on her iced tea.

Cohen and Declan both look toward Helen and chuckle. "Probably a microphone. I can imagine her trying to serenade Luciana and Amanda later," Cohen says.

"Or an emergency kit," Declan adds. "You know how serious she is about everything going right."

"Did you check out the cake?" Naomi asks, pointing with her iced tea.

We all turn toward the dilapidated cake—a lopsided three-tiered monstrosity with frosting that seems to be melting off by the minute.

Declan chuckles. "I was talking with a PA earlier who was there while they filmed making the cake. He said Helen was a rabid beast in the kitchen and wound up making everything worse."

"Shocking," Thad says with a snort and then glances at Declan and Cohen again. "Where's your sister?"

"Seems like she must have come down with the same thing Alec had yesterday. Went home early."

I wince. "Sorry about that."

"Yeah, what did they say was going around, again?" Cohen asks Declan, who rubs the side of his jaw, really thinking about it.

"What was it? Ah—" He snaps his fingers. "Wasn't it a case of being lovesick?"

"I think that's what it was, right, Alec?" Cohen asks, his eyes boring into mine.

"Lovesick?" Thad scoffs. "Alec isn't lovesick."

I chew on my bottom lip and take a sip of my beer, trying to avoid eye contact with everyone at the cocktail table.

"Alec isn't lovesick," Thad repeats. "That's over, right? It's been over."

"Thad," Naomi murmurs, gripping his arm. "Maybe we should go take a walk and have a conversation." She takes his hand and they walk off, leaving me with Cohen and Declan.

I clear my throat. "Nice wedding, huh? Think it has a chance at winning?"

"What are you doing about my sister?" Cohen asks.

Well, he just gets straight to the point, doesn't he?

"Uh, what do you mean?"

"You know exactly what I mean. Are you going to make a move?"

I glance between the two men, their faces completely serious. I think about what they said: that Luna has the same "illness" as me.

Luna lovesick?

Yeah, pretty sure that's one of the most inaccurate statements ever made. I saw the look in her eyes yesterday, the shield she put up. I heard the dismissal in her voice.

I set my beer down on the table and shake my head. "No, I'm not. Not sure what she said to you, but she made it abundantly clear that getting involved was a mistake, and her radio silence leads me to believe that wasn't just a passionate, in-the-moment kind of statement." I shift, trying to hide the hurt in my eyes, the devastation in the set of my shoulders.

"I see," Cohen says, so calmly that it almost freaks me out. "So you have no intention of trying to win my sister's heart?"

"Uh . . . I mean, I kind of got the impression that she didn't even want me near her. I'm all for following my heart, but I also know a lost cause when I see one."

"And following your heart would be what?"

I pull on the back of my neck, trying not to let my annoyance get the best of me. "With all due respect, I don't think this is any of your business. She doesn't want anything to do with me, and I'm going to respect that."

Cohen nods. "Well, has anything changed since you came to our apartment? Do you still love her?"

I chuckle as I look to the side. "Let me ask you something, Cohen. Would the love you have for Declan just automatically disappear within a week?"

"It wouldn't."

"Then there you go." I give them a salute. "See you around, boys."

I take off before they can say anything. I consider leaving the wedding completely, entirely too grumpy and "lovesick" to be there, but I know that wouldn't go over well with the producers—I can't handle any more disapproval from Diane—especially since Luna already left. So,

I find the appetizer buffet, fill up a plate, and hunker down in a dark corner, where I eat away my feelings.

With a deep breath, I open the door to the groom's suite of the old warehouse in Meatpacking, and I'm greeted with wall-to-wall brick, masculine furniture, and a poker table surrounded by leather-upholstered chairs. Thad hasn't arrived yet, but according to his itinerary, he'll be here any moment.

I woke up this morning with a horrible headache. It had nothing to do with alcohol and everything to do with the stress and anxiety clawing at me all night. Things are still weird with Thad, which is going to make the next few hours—where we get ready, just the two of us—beyond uncomfortable. Today is technically the last day I'll see Luna, and that added a whole new layer of agony to last night.

But I can't focus on that. I need to be here for Thad.

I set the box of stuff I brought with me on the table and start taking everything out.

A six-pack of Thad's favorite IPA.

Some wings from his favorite bar, where we used to go when I was in college.

A plastic crown, because lord knows he'll want to wear it and feel like a king.

A deck of cards, in case he wants to pass the time like we used to.

And the cuff links from my college graduation.

I set the box to the side just as the door opens. Thad's suit hook is hanging from his finger, the garment bag draped over his shoulder. His hair isn't styled yet, nor has he shaved, but that's because I have someone coming in to do all of that for us.

"Hey," I say, hands on my hips, hoping my little setup doesn't look too lame.

He hooks his suit onto a hanger on the wall and then studies the table. "What's all this?"

"Uh, you know, just some things to help you relax before the big ceremony. I know how you can get nervous, especially in front of a bunch of people." He doesn't say anything, so I start pointing out what everything is, as if he can't see it already. "Got your favorite indie, some wings from that place you love. Uh, the crown is to make you feel special, and the cards are to pass the time." I scratch the back of my neck, feeling like an idiot. "And these." I pick up the cuff links and swallow hard. "These are Grandpa's cuff links, the ones I wore for college graduation. Thought they might be special to you, if you wanted to wear them."

Thad takes the black velvet box from me. It creaks as he opens it up. He picks up a cuff link and brings it closer to examine the intricate B design. "You brought these for me?"

"Yeah. I know the bride is supposed to have something borrowed, but I thought it might be nice for you to have something as well."

Thad examines the cuff link a little bit longer before putting it back in its box, not saying a word. He sets the box down and just stands there, quietly, showing a side I'm not used to. I've only seen him this reserved a few other times—the first was when our parents told us they were getting divorced. The second was when I told him I was leaving for college, and then the third time was on the day I left.

"Thad." He looks up. Tears well in his eyes, and before I can ask him what's wrong, he steps forward and wraps his arms around me with such force that I stumble backward.

Once I regain my balance, I wrap my arms around him as well and give him the kind of hug I haven't given him since we were kids.

"Fuck," he mutters, holding me tight. "I just wanted you to care about me. About my life."

"I do, Thad," I say, fucking grateful he's actually talking to me. "I know it might not have seemed like it, but I care. I care so fucking much."

"I see it." His voice is clogged with emotion. "I feel it." He pulls away and wipes at his eyes. "And that photo album. You motherfucker. You made me sob in Naomi's arms."

I laugh so loudly that the sound is almost foreign. I was not expecting that kind of relief to come out of me, but it feels good. "I knew it would. I was going for the high emotional factor."

"Which I knew you were doing, but that didn't mean you were sorry—it just meant you were trying to make me cry."

I roll my eyes. "Dude, I went to Mom's place to get those pictures. I stayed up late scrapbooking that shit. I cared."

Thad shakes his head and holds up the cuff links. "No, *this* means you care. This was thoughtful, this is something a dad would give me, and what my big brother, Alec, the one who raised me, would give me."

Hell. My throat grows tight.

"I love you, Thad," I say, and his eyes start to water again. "I want to be a part of your life, and I'm sorry it's taken me this long to realize it."

"I love you too." He pulls me into a hug again, and we pat it out a few more times before breaking apart and cracking open a beer for each of us.

We each take a seat and open up the wings.

"So just like that, we're good?" I ask, feeling slightly uneasy.

"Yup." He bites into a wing.

"So if I brought you the cuff links earlier, you would have forgiven me sooner?"

"Yup."

"So I scrapbooked for nothing?"

"Hell no, that's my coffee-table book now."

"Great." I roll my eyes and take a sip of beer, letting it mix with the spicy hot sauce on my tongue.

"Maybe it's that easy with Luna—ever think about giving her cuff links?" I raise a brow at him, and he softens. "Naomi has been relentless about you and Luna. Dude . . . you love her?"

"Why don't we focus on you getting married, and save my issues for another day."

Thad pops the crown onto his head. "Okay, but don't think I'm going to drop this. If you love her, then we have to get her back . . . even if she's going to win the entire competition for her brother."

"You never know—we still have a chance."

Thad scoffs. "We can pretty much pull anything off, but those hot-pink bow ties and cummerbunds are going to do us in."

"Hell . . . I forgot about those."

CHAPTER TWENTY-NINE
LUNA

"Flashy."

"Slightly gaudy."

"Interesting . . ."

"Garish."

"Why do I think the flamingos work?"

Declan and Cohen stare at the reception space with open mouths.

Flamingo Dancer somehow works . . .

Feathers are scattered everywhere. It looks like they repurposed feather boas into garlands, there are added ruffles on the back of every chair—a detail I apparently missed on their vision board—and giant disco balls hang from the ceiling . . . where did they get those?

And oddly enough, it feels loving, spot on, and so Thad and Naomi. It might not be my style, or anyone's for that matter, but it's them, and that's what the competition is really about. About the couples.

"Why do I feel like this wedding is more suited for gay men?" Declan asks, nodding toward a feather centerpiece that's crowding our small cocktail table.

"Because it is," Cohen says just as a waiter comes up with a tray of coconut shrimp. We each take a piece and bite into it. Surprisingly, it's really good.

"How did they keep this all under budget?" Declan asks.

"Didn't use real flowers," I say, scanning the room, unsure of what to look at next. "I think it's the uplighting that's getting me."

"I think that's it too," Declan says with a nod. "Lime-green and pink—really interesting choices for colors. It's making us all look sickly."

"Yeah, that's a good way to describe it."

"Ceremony was great," Declan says, pressing his hand to his heart. "Thad breaking down was so endearing. The guy might be a little much, but you can tell he truly adores Naomi."

"He does," Cohen says and then nudges my shoulder with his. "Doesn't hurt that his best man was total eye candy up there, even if he was wearing a hot-pink cummerbund."

"Yeah, I might have stared a few times," Declan says. "That beard is totally working for him—brings the whole Chris Evans thing to life. Don't you think, Luna?"

I hate them both.

I'm already on the verge of a mental breakdown after seeing Alec and not being able to do anything about it. I don't need these two knuckleheads recapping how handsome Alec looked standing next to Thad. The pride on his face as he watched his brother get married was beautiful. And the handshake they shared afterward, which was followed by a giant hug . . . I teared up, knowing they'd worked things out.

And I guess that's all that really matters: Thad and Alec having a relationship. I know how much that means to Alec. It might have come at a cost, but family is worth everything.

"Are you not going to comment on how handsome Alec looked?" Declan asks.

"Why should I? You two are gushing enough for me."

"Oh, she's spicy today," Cohen says, laughing.

"When is she not spicy?" Declan asks between sips of his strawberry margarita, one of the wedding's two signature cocktails. Team Baxter chose to go with two signature liquor drinks and then fountain drinks, a cheaper option, but not as cheap as Team Hernandez's, who served absolute piss for drinks—Declan's words, not mine.

"Does this mean you're not going to go up and talk to him?"

"No way in hell," I say, wishing I had another one of those coconut shrimps. I glance around the room, searching for a waiter, but finding anyone feels next to impossible with all the dramatic lighting. *A little overboard, maybe.*

"Interesting," Cohen says, using the exact tone of voice he knows drives me nuts—elusive, but with a hidden meaning behind it.

I bite. "What?"

"Oh . . . nothing."

"Stop it." I practically stomp my foot. "If you want to say something, then just say it."

"I don't know if I should. What do you think, Declan?"

He shrugs. "I'm not sure she's stable enough to hear it."

"Hear what?" I look between the two men, loving them and hating them at the same time.

"Well, we happened to have a conversation with Alec after you left yesterday."

"You *what?*" I ask as fear creeps up my spine. "You didn't say anything about me, did you?"

"What kind of brother would I be if I did that? Nah, I just asked if he still loved you."

I gulp.

My breath comes out in short, quick bursts.

My pulse picks up, the *thump thump* of it almost blocking out all the noise around me.

"What, uh . . . what did he say?" I ask casually; at least I think it was casual, until Declan and Cohen both laugh out loud.

"I don't think she deserves to know," Cohen says.

"Oh look, her face is turning red . . . or is that the lights?"

"Enough!" I shout, startling both of them. "Just tell me what he said."

Cohen smiles widely. "He still loves you." My heart literally skips a beat—I feel it leap in my chest. "But he thinks you want nothing to do with him, so he's not making a move. He shut the door on the opportunity and claims he doesn't want to bother you."

"Oh God," I whisper, looking out toward the crowd.

"They're taking pictures," Declan says, "but they should be announced back into the room soon."

"He . . . he loves me?"

"Didn't know that?"

I shake my head, tears welling in my eyes for what feels like the hundredth time this week.

He loves me. I never expected him to feel that way about me, especially after everything I said to him. Even still, I need to hear it from him.

Not from my brother.

Not from Declan.

I need to hear those words straight from Alec's mouth.

"Ladies and gentlemen, can we clear the dance floor?" the DJ says into the microphone as Hall & Oates' "You Make My Dreams Come True" starts playing. "We're ready to get this party started, but first, I want to introduce the best man and the matron of honor. Put your hands together and please welcome Sarah Wilson and Alec Baxter."

The doors leading outside open, and Alec walks in with Sarah on his arm. They do a cute shimmy together. I can't help but feel a surge of jealousy as they laugh at each other, but the minute they part, Sarah goes straight to her husband's arms, while Alec awkwardly stands next to them, clapping with the rest of the crowd.

"They don't need much of a bridal party because they have all the love in this room," the DJ says, "so moving on to the main event, let's welcome the bride and groom, Mr. and Mrs. Thaddeus Baxter."

The room hollers with excitement as Thad and Naomi come charging through the doors, Naomi on Thad's back, whipping him in the butt with her bouquet as they gallop onto the dance floor.

All three of us, along with everyone else, laugh, and then the music dies down into a slow song.

"Can't Help Falling in Love"—the acoustic version—starts playing, and the room quiets down. The uplighting turns to all pink, and feathers fall from the ceiling, filling the air with so much romance that I actually think they have a shot at winning this entire competition.

Hands clasped to my chest, I watch as Thad places his hand on Naomi's lower back and guides her back and forth to the slow, melodic beat of the beautiful song, whispering things in her ear that make her laugh. Being in the presence of so much love makes you do weird things, like looking for the man of your dreams, who's standing across the room, hands in his pockets, looking straight at you.

My heart hammers in my chest.

My mouth becomes completely dry.

But my eyes never leave his.

I couldn't look away even if I wanted to.

"The bride and groom would like to call all couples onto the dance floor to join them," the DJ says into the microphone.

I feel Cohen's hand on my back as he brings his mouth to my ear. "Go ask him to dance."

"I can't—"

"You can. He loves you. Look at him. He's so desperate. Put the poor man out of his misery and make the first move."

"What if he rejects me?"

"Trust me, he won't." He gives me a little shove forward before taking Declan's hand. Together, they walk out on the floor, hand in hand, and join the crowd, dancing together.

I freeze in place for a few beats, watching as Alec stands there, all alone. He looks as handsome as ever, but with a sadness etched in his eyes.

And before I can stop myself, I pick up my long black skirt and shuffle along the dance floor. Couples part for me, stepping aside as I get closer and closer to Alec. His breath catches in his throat, and he licks his lips. When I reach him, I hold my hand out, hoping he doesn't see that it's visibly shaking. "May I have this dance?"

He looks down at my extended hand, and then back up at me.

Nerves build and swirl inside me as I wait for his answer.

One beat.

Two.

Three.

And then, without saying a word, he takes my hand, intertwining our fingers and guiding me out to the dance floor. He spins me before bringing me in close.

Really close.

His hand spans my lower back as my hand falls to his chest and glides up to the back of his neck, just as our eyes connect.

His eyes read like a picture book, showing every emotion within him.

Relief.

Excitement.

Love . . .

I hope he can see the same within me, because I'm about to burst— just from having him this close again, his eyes searching mine, his lips wet and waiting.

He sighs. And he tips his forehead against mine, like so many times before. "I love you."

My lip trembles, those three words cutting me hard and deep all at once, and I can't contain the sigh of happiness that pops out of me.

"I love you, Alec . . . so much."

"Hell," he says, nuzzling his head against mine. "Jesus, I needed to hear that. Badly." He lifts his head up just enough so I can look him in the eyes. "I'm so fucking sorry, Luna. For asking you to lie to Cohen, for—"

I stop him with my fingers to his lips and then bring them back to the nape of his neck. "I know. But you need to know something. When I said I chose wrong, I didn't mean it. I was angry and upset and I lashed out at you. You didn't deserve that, and I'm sorry." I grip him even tighter. "Coming to your apartment to help you bake a cake was the best choice I ever made, because it opened my heart to a confusing, beautiful, knucklehead of a man. I love you, with everything in me, and I hope you can find it in your heart to forgive me."

"Luna Moon, you don't need to ask for my forgiveness, because you have it. I just want to know if I can take you home tonight. Make you mine again."

"I never stopped being yours," I say, standing on my toes and pressing my mouth to his.

He hums against my lips and then parts his mouth, closing the space between us and delivering one of the most sensual and loving kisses I've ever experienced.

He pulls away, and from the corner of my eye, I spot Thad and Naomi, and Declan and Cohen, still dancing, but smiling ear to ear as they watch us make up.

"Are you back together?" Naomi asks, raising her voice over the music.

Alec brings his mouth to the back of my hand and kisses it. "We're back together."

They all cheer, and Alec picks me up and swings me around. Setting me back on my feet, he cups my cheeks and lights me up all over again.

I sigh into his hold and relish the knowledge that *The Wedding Game* wasn't just a challenge to create the best ceremony and reception. It was a challenge for my heart, opening it up to someone else and filling it with love.

At least I know one couple who won this season on *The Wedding Game*, and we didn't need a wedding to prove it.

EPILOGUE
ALEC

"Have I told you I really like this dress on you?" I murmur into Luna's ear, my arm wrapped around her waist.

"About three separate times," she says with a chuckle, moving her head to the side so I can kiss her neck. "But I'll never turn down a compliment from you."

"Are you flirting with me?" My lips press against the spot right below her ear, and she turns in my arms so she's facing me.

"Always. I'm always flirting with you."

I smile widely and gaze into her eyes, feeling like a goddamn king right about now. "Are you really going to move in with me?" I still can't quite believe she said yes to my proposition last night.

"How could I not? You built me a craft room." Yeah, I may have set up my second bedroom as a craft room for her. In my mind, we won't stay in the apartment longer than a few years. I have plans for a family with this girl, and we're going to need a bigger place for that, but what we have for now will work. "I still can't believe you did that. I don't think I've ever humped someone as hard as I humped you last night."

I laugh out loud, pulling the attention from everyone around us. I cup her cheek and quietly say, "The humping was very much appreciated, and feel free to do it whenever you want."

"I will." She rises up on her toes and kisses me lightly before spinning around in my arms. Just then Diane walks on set, which is a cube of a room, decorated with flowers and sectioned off in threes. Behind each team is a small replica of their wedding, pulled together by PAs. Just seeing them all together makes me laugh, especially with our incredibly flamboyant feathered theme against the two more neutral ones.

She spots us and, with her fingers, motions for us to break up. "Team Rossi, Team Baxter, get in your respective spots."

After Thad and Naomi's wedding, Diane asked if *The Wedding Game* could do some web content about our relationship, since it developed on the show. We of course said yes, because it would be great exposure for Luna—and it has been. Not only has her partnership with Marco been going better than she ever imagined—launch date next year—but collaboration requests from other wedding companies have begun to pour in, and she's been offered a DIY column in the top bridal magazine, aptly called *Brides*. She's been busy, and I couldn't be prouder. I told her that at the rate she's going, she could be my sugar mama and I could sit back, quit the divorce train, and just enjoy my girl's riches . . .

She said I would get too bored, which is true, but she *has* incorporated me into her YouTube channel. I have my own series, *Crafting with Alec*. It's cute shit. Watch me fuck up a lot while Luna patiently teaches me how to do things. On the rare occasion I do something right, I feel extraordinarily accomplished. I'm not ready to quit my job just yet, but Luna said her "hot boyfriend" has nearly doubled her followers.

I do look like Chris Evans, after all.

"This is the big moment. Please refrain from swearing if you don't win," Diane says, holding up a large envelope. "Graceful losers all around. Helen, Thad, I'm looking at you two."

"Why did you single us out?" Thad exclaims, panicking. "Does that mean Team Rossi won?" I grip his shoulder, trying to ease his anxiety.

Thad and Naomi found out they're having a girl, and Thad has been going crazy, overbuying things for his little girl—not ideal for their tiny apartment. There's an archway of baby things in their entryway that you have to walk under in order to get to their living room.

"No," Diane says in a clipped tone. "I'm saying stay calm and respectful. That's all. We don't need any hysterics. We only have one chance to capture a true reaction to the winner, so keep it together."

She hands the envelope off to Mary, who has been keeping her distance. Rightfully so. Rumor around set is this is her last season, and they're looking for someone to take her place.

Guess who wants to apply for the job? Luna, right? Nope . . . Thad. He's caught the crafting bug and thinks he would be an energetic and fun host. At least that's what a lot of the forums are saying online.

I mean, I can see it, actually.

"Places!" Diane calls out. "Remember, until I say cut, you need smiles on your faces, and then you're allowed to wallow. We will run through some quick interviews, and then you're free."

I stand next to Thad, my hand still on his shoulder as his body vibrates with excitement. A campaign on Instagram has started that's centered around Thad, earning him a cultlike following that loves him in all his dramatic glory. So by the time the final episode aired, Thad was actually hopeful that his popularity could mean a win—though Team Rossi easily had the best wedding. As for Team Hernandez, well . . . they had Helen.

I glance over at Luna, who is standing between Cohen and Declan. Last night I asked her how they were feeling about everything, and she said they had a second option if they didn't win the penthouse, which they were a little more excited about: an old brownstone they want to renovate in Brooklyn. People are calling it a money pit, but they see the potential.

Diane counts down and then points at Mary, who erases her scowl and turns on a smile for the camera. "America has voted, and the winner of *The Wedding Game* is . . ."

She has to count to five before she reads the card—Diane's orders. And it's annoying. I hate when reality shows do that. Just fucking say it already.

Mary unfolds the envelope, smiles, and then looks straight at the camera.

Thad tenses.

Naomi sucks in a sharp breath of air.

And I feel my butt cheeks squeeze together in anticipation.

"Team Hernandez."

"What in the ever—!" Thad shouts. I slap my hand over his mouth, and he continues to mutter obscenities against my palm.

Luciana and Amanda cheer while Helen swoons against their workbench. We watch them celebrate as Mary walks over to them, envelope in hand. She looks at the camera again and says, "Until next wedding season, keep crafting and falling in love."

Diane yells, "Cut!" and I release Thad's mouth.

"Way to keep it together, man," I say.

"I want to see those results," he seethes. "There's no way America liked Helen more than me. You should have heard the things they were saying about her beehive hairdo."

"Settle down," Naomi says, tugging on his arm. "It's okay, Thad."

"It's not. Have you seen our baby archway? Christ."

Team Rossi comes over to us, and I give them a sympathetic smile. "You truly had the prettiest wedding."

Cohen and Declan nod but don't look upset at all—their new project is going to be more fun for them to tackle . . . more them.

"She's a monster. She paid people off. There's no way she won."

Luciana and Amanda come up to us as well, hand in hand. "Sorry you guys didn't win," Amanda says. "I know how much this meant to you."

"Dammit," Thad says under his breath. Then he turns to Amanda. "How you grew inside that beast of a woman, I have no idea."

"*Thad*," Naomi reprimands, but Amanda just laughs.

"I ask myself that question every day."

"Luciana, Amanda, interview room!" Diane calls out. "Helen, you too."

Helen pops up from the workbench as if she never felt faint in the first place. She brushes off her dress as she walks by our little gathering, flashing us an evil grin. "Never underestimate the lesbians—they always find a way to be on top." And with that she walks away.

"Lesbians," Thad whispers, clenching his fist.

I wrap my arm around him and give him a squeeze. "I'm sorry, dude. I really thought we were going to win. It felt like we had a good chance."

"People loved the flamingos. Where were all the flamingo voters?"

"I voted for you," Cohen says.

"Me too," Declan announces.

Luna raises her hand. "So did I. Your wedding was the most magical to me." I pull her against me and kiss the top of her head. It was the most magical to me too, because that's when I got my girl back.

"Oh wow." Thad waves his hand in front of his eyes. "That . . . that means a lot to me."

"And hey," I say, "I know you really wanted the new place, but you did get more than a wedding out of the competition. You got a family."

Thad looks around our little circle and smiles.

Every Sunday, without fail, we all get together and have brunch. The host changes, but everyone's there, my family and Luna's family, forming one big ball of love. We had a small gender-reveal party, Thad has already claimed Cohen and Declan as "guncles" (gay uncles), and he's grateful for the number of people who are willing to babysit, even Luna and Cohen's parents—who are the parents I've always wanted but have never had. Luckily for me, they told me to call them Mom and Dad, and fuck . . . I do.

"I have the best family," Thad says, clutching his chest.

We all hug, and when we pull away, Luna says, "And now that I'm moving in with Alec, my apartment is going to be available. Farrah is moving into a studio to live her single life, and I'm good friends with our landlords, so they'll rent to whoever I suggest as a replacement. It's a two-bedroom with plenty of space, and it's only a few blocks from me and Alec—and it's rent controlled."

"Bless my nips, rent controlled?" Thad screams and claps, then lifts his fist to the air, pausing as if he's frozen. Beside him, Naomi's eyes begin to fill with tears, and from her reaction alone I feel my heart swell inside my chest.

Luna frowns. "Thad, are you—?"

He unfreezes himself and looks at the both of us, tears now in his eyes. "Seriously? I could live close to my brother and have room for my baby girl?"

"As long as you stop buying things," I say, just before Thad nearly tackles me to the ground with a hug.

If you told me a few months ago that I would be in love, have a solid relationship with my brother, be expecting a niece, and count myself as part of an actual family, I would have said you were crazy.

But here I am, a family, a partner, and a niece, all blessing my life with love . . . love I didn't think I wanted, but love I desperately needed.

Acknowledgments

I've always wanted to write a wedding-centered book, so when I sat down with one of my agents, Aimee Ashcraft, and came up with this idea on the spot, I was immediately excited about the prospect.

You might not know this about me, but I used to be a crafter. I would craft when I wasn't working and then take my fine artistic work to craft fairs and sell it. My medium was decoupage, and I was freaking good at it. There are people out there in this world who have my homemade signs from ten years ago. Luckily, I was able to take that crafting bug and apply it to my very own DIY wedding. My wife and I were trying to put on a pretty but cost-effective wedding, so relating to *The Wedding Game* characters was very easy. Funnily enough, we had a vintage carnival theme, and I found a weird clown figurine at the Thrifty store for under a dollar. Yes, I bought it. Yes, I spray-painted it hot pink. And yes, I displayed it on our dessert table with wood crates and burlap. *The Wedding Game* characters might not have wanted that clown, but I sure did.

To Kimberly Brower and Aimee Ashcraft, my agents, thank you for having confidence in my storytelling and for your passion for new ideas. You've truly made a huge difference in my life and in my career.

A huge thank-you to Lauren Plude for acquiring my ideas so I can write more wonderful stories for the Montlake team. Even though your "crafting" falls to stickering by numbers, your friendship and confidence have been unprecedented. Thank you.

Lindsey Faber, thank you for making the editing process an absolute breeze!

To the bloggers and readers, I don't even know how to express my deepest love for you. You take a chance on my books every time I release one of them, which is something I could never show enough gratitude for. Thank you for being the best fans a girl could ask for. You make this job so much fun!

I would be remiss not to mention my best friend in all of this. Thank you, Jenny, for handling everything behind the scenes, encouraging me, and being excited whenever I tell you about a new idea. Number one fan for life!

And lastly, thank you to my wife, Steph, for being my backbone, the girl behind the girl, and the best mother/wife a lady could ask for. Without your taking care of our children and supporting me in so many ways, I would never be able to do what I do. You are the reason I've been able to accomplish my dreams. Thank you.

ABOUT THE AUTHOR

Photo © 2019 Milana Schaffer

USA Today bestselling author, wife, adoptive mother, and peanut butter lover Meghan Quinn pens romantic comedies and contemporary romance. Quinn brings readers the perfect combination of heart, humor, and heat in every book.